Blood Sea Tales
Book Three

The Pirate's Bane

Chris A. Jackson

Published July 2019 by Jaxbooks Publishing

Cover design by Fiona Jayde
Images for interior from Pixabay have been altered for use

ISBN 978-1- 939837-25-7 (paperback)
ISBN 978-1- 939837-26-4 (ePub)
ISBN 978-1- 939837-27-1 (Mobi)

jaxbooks.com

Acknowledgements
As always, thanks to my wife, Anne, for her
help, patience, and passion for the sea.

Thanks to Stephen Martiniere for the inspiration of the sail
designs for the dragonship, from his "Skinner" painting.
See it here: https://www.martiniere.com/book-covers

A special thanks to those who have enjoyed and reviewed
the first two volumes in this series.
You inspire me.

This novel is dedicated to my dear friend,
Joseph Hinton Rogers III,
May 4, 1974 -
June 12, 2019
May your inspiration live on in all the lives you've touched.

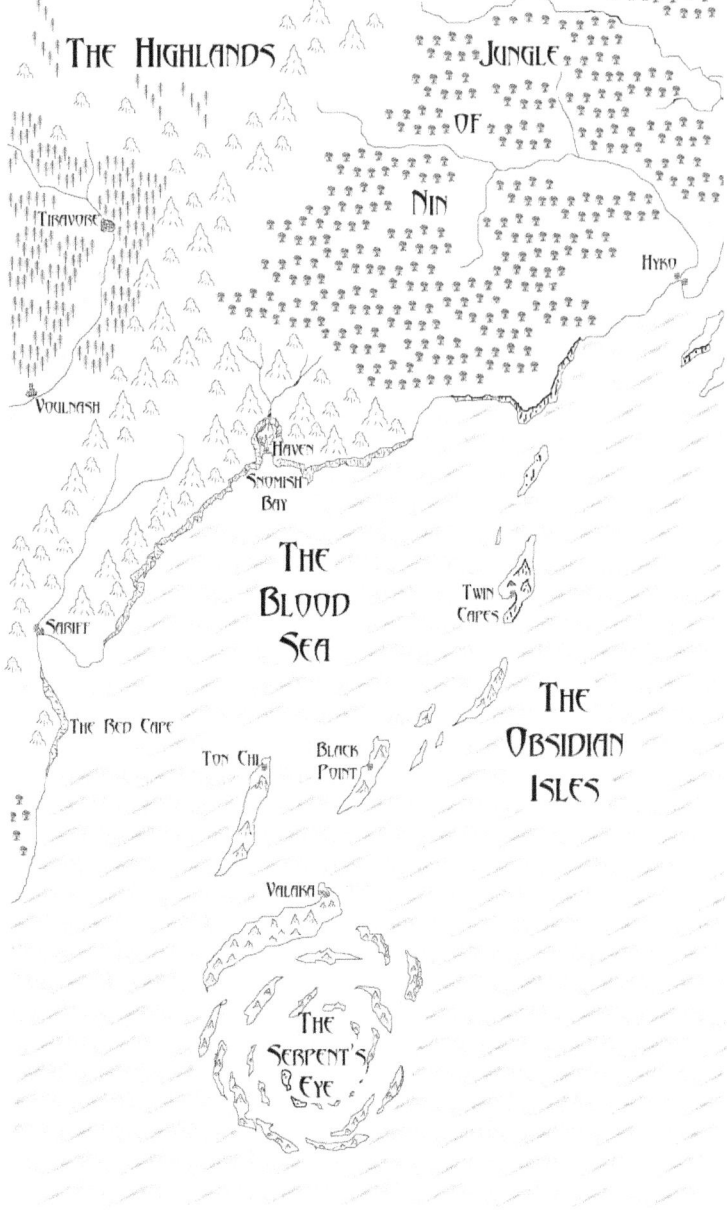

THE HIGHLANDS

JUNGLE

OF

NIN

TIRAVORE

HYKO

VOULNASH

HAVEN

SNOMISH
BAY

SARIFF

THE
BLOOD
SEA

TWIN
CAPES

THE RED CAPE

THE
OBSIDIAN
ISLES

TON CHI

BLACK
POINT

VALAKA

THE
SERPENT'S
EYE

Chapter One
The Wounded Dragon

The ability to reason effectively while in pain is invaluable.
The Lessons of Quen Lau Ush

From the journal of Jhavika Keshmir –
Until the day Kevril Longbright took my scourge, my hand, and Preel from me, I put people into one of two categories: assets or obstacles. I have had people murdered for thwarting me, yes, but I never truly hated them. Not until Kevril did I truly hate, and now that hatred has consumed me. I rue the day I first considered him an asset.

I woke from a fitful nightmare—Kevril slashing a cutlass through my wrist, then holding my scourge by its thongs, my severed hand dangling from the haft. Pain lanced across my cheek as I raised a hand to wipe my eyes, and I discovered the nightmare to be real. In place of my right hand gleamed the steel head of a boarding pike, the hook needle-sharp, the broad blade razor-edged. I stared at it for a befuddled moment before memories returned.

1

*My scourge stolen, my person maimed, Preel kidnapped from my home…
Damn you, Kevril!*

The party at Balshi's estate was supposed to have been my victory, my triumph. Kevril had turned it into a defeat, forcing me to play my final hand before I was ready. Though my wrath had torn through Haven like wildfire, not all had gone as I'd wished. Getashi Temuso was dead and his estate dispersed among his retainers, out of my reach. He'd obviously planned ahead for his own death. The surviving council members would no doubt oppose me at every turn, given that I'd tried to kill them all. Not that it mattered. In the end, I controlled seven houses, and therefore, the Council of Lords. I was effectively Queen of Haven.

So why am I on a ship, chasing that damned pirate, my kingdom thirty miles behind me?

The answer to that question was easy: I was going to catch Kevril and get back what he stole from me.

I shoved myself up from the chart table upon which I'd fallen asleep, twisting my neck to relieve the crick from sleeping slumped over. The dim light of dawn illuminated the great cabin of a galleon in muted hues of burnished pewter. The deck moved beneath me, the horizon canted to starboard outside the sweeping stern gallery windows. I'd commandeered Fa-Chen's flagship, *Tiger Lily*, for my own, and claimed several others, assigning my slaves as commanders, and the soldiers of several houses as additional crew. The chart before me showed seven tracks across Snomish Bay, the deployment of my armada.

Someone knocked at the door to the cabin, a muted voice calling tentatively, "Your ladyship?"

"Yes!" I wiped my face with my left hand and it came away bloody. I'd scratched myself with my boarding pike hand.

A young man wearing a merchant officer's uniform entered, two of my personal guards flanking him. The epaulets marked him as captain, though he was too young to have earned them. He had, however, ascended the chain of command upon the demise of more senior officers.

It had been a busy night.

The captain froze as the grim figure beside the door, my new komei bodyguard, drew a katana and held it before my visitor's throat. The officer swallowed and saluted stiffly, "*Golden Harlot* signals, sail sighted to the southeast. Captain Tan believes it to be the *Scourge*."

"Excellent, Captain Niland! Te-shan, stand down." My komei sheathed his katana in one smooth motion and bowed, my loyal slave. At Balshi's ball, he'd slaughtered his mistress, Lady Hatsu, at my command, and now served only to protect me from harm. With Captain Vakna's death, Te-shan was the most formidable warrior in my service, and he never left my side.

"The time?" I surged to my feet and reached for my cutlass, ignoring my aching back and neck. At least the stump of my wrist wasn't hurting any longer. Yin had treated my arm with a series of injections that permanently numbed the nerves from my elbow down. My alchemist had then brewed a potion to force the flesh to heal, and heal it had, even as my armorer drove screws into the bones, affixing the pike head permanently in place. I just had to remember not to scratch with it.

"Three bells in the morning watch, your ladyship." He saluted again as I lurched past him, Te-shan at my heels.

From the motion of the ship, we were beating into a head sea. My legs were long used to stone beneath my feet, and I staggered a bit before finding my balance. I hadn't been at sea for more than five years, but the previous decades were coming back quickly.

"Three bells." The light through the windows was pre-dawn then, and I'd barely slept an hour, but the sighting was welcome news. Even though we'd left Haven only three hours behind *Scourge*, I'd been afraid we'd lost Kevril. "And how far is *Scourge*?"

"About six miles, your ladyship. Visible from the quarterdeck." He hurried to follow, my guards at his heels.

People scrambled out of my way. Most of *Tiger Lily*'s merchant crew remained aboard, but an additional one hundred fifty of my soldiers precluded any thought of mutiny. Unfortunately, my people weren't sailors. Most were looking a little green around the gills, and some had been emptying their guts since we left Haven. On deck, a humid monsoon-season breeze laden with sea spray slapped me awake. I mounted the steps to the quarterdeck, cursing my lack of a

3

hat and resisting the urge to brush my hair from my eyes. Being one handed was taking some getting used to. I'd tie it back later.

"Spyglass," I barked, scanning the horizon and holding out my hand. Even in the dim light, I barely needed one to assess the disposition of my armada.

My seven ships lay in an arc of sea twenty miles wide, from east-northeast to southwest, exactly where I'd deployed them. I'd had no idea where Kevril would run to, and had distributed my forces to cover the widest swath possible, two on a port tack, and the rest to starboard. *Tiger Lily* sailed in the center of that arc, three ships to our north, and three south.

The farthest north, the beamy junk *Summer Violet*, sailed under the command of my guard captain, Yorish, no sailor, but not a fool either. The farthest south, another junk, *Jasmine*, I'd given to my nokitu captain, Busashi. Also to the north were the galleons *Hyacinth* and *Peony*—what pernicious god possessed Fa-Chen to name all of his ships after flowers, I didn't even want to know—commanded by my slaves Brilla Balshi and Ursula Roque, the crews also largely intact and kept from mutiny by their own substantial guard contingents. Directly to my south, *Bluebonnet* sailed under Tambris Matesh, yet another loyal slave, unable to betray me as Kevril had.

Only Captain Tan, commanding *Golden Harlot,* south and well east of *Bluebonnet*, wasn't one of my slaves. She had ranged ahead, her ship smaller but faster than the other merchantmen. Her ship, at least, I hadn't needed to commandeer. When I'd arrived at the waterfront with three other council members, their armies, and the forces of three more houses along with my own, Tan had few options but to follow my orders. With seven houses, I controlled Haven's Council of Lords, and she answered to the Council. With the corroboration of the three other lords, she'd swallowed the tale I'd concocted, that Kevril Longbright and his crew of pirates had attacked the ball at Lord Balshi's estate, killing Teris Balshi, Fa-Chen, Getashi Temuso, Lady Hatsu, and Blinth Tinworthy. Their heirs—save for Temuso, who had none—had given me control over their forces to avenge their fallen lords. In reality, I'd had their heirs abducted by my well-placed spies and held in my keep under the sword, forcing them to sign their houses over to my control.

The other five council members were cowering in their keeps, formidable in their own rights, but impotent to impede my wrath. I'd left enough loyal slaves in my keep to defend it and hold my hostages safe. I'd deal with the others when I returned victorious. Of that victory, I was certain. With seven ships chasing him, there was nowhere Kevril could run that I wouldn't find him.

Awkwardly adjusting the spyglass one-handed, I focused on *Scourge*, barely hull up, flying reefed courses, topsails, and a full array of trisails, a spire of white at this angle, visible from fifteen miles. She was beating hard into the steep seas, close-hauled. Suspicion rose up like sour vomit from my gut. This wasn't her best point of sail, and she wasn't carrying all the canvas she could in these conditions. I called a chart of the Blood Sea to mind, gauging his course and possible destinations. He was headed somewhere between Black Point and Twin Capes. The former would have been on a better tack in this wind, while the latter lay too far upwind to reach without tacking. That probably meant he intended to tack, but I had no way to be sure. This could all be an elaborate ruse. Was Kevril leading me on, luring me into a trap? Had he already recruited an armada of pirates? He'd threatened as much only days ago, vowing to blockade and starve Haven into submission if I didn't allow him to see Preel. Well, I wouldn't give him the chance to summon any allies.

"Signal all ships to converge on the target, Captain. Deploy fast cutters to those out of visual signaling range. Captain Tan is to maintain visual contact with *Scourge* at all costs, but not to engage without support." *Golden Harlot* sported a crew of only fifty fighting sailors, no match for Kevril's hundred. "Bend every sail she'll bear and trim smartly. I'm to be notified immediately if *Scourge* changes course."

"Yes, your ladyship!" Niland saluted again.

I handed back the spyglass and started for the stairs as the young captain began barking orders. I paused to watch the sailors work, to feel the movement of the ship, gauge her performance. It had been years, but a part of me missed this delicate balance of wind and water, cordage and canvas. *Tiger Lily* wasn't a corsair, but she was a fine ship and sailed well. When we settled on our new course, however, I found several deficiencies.

I rounded on my young captain and pointed at him with my pike hand. "What part of 'trim smartly' didn't you understand, Captain?"

"Your ladyship?" He gaped at me, wide eyes fixed upon the deadly implement capping my right wrist. Well might he fear it; I'd ended his captain's life with it.

"Your bosun either needs a lesson or is intentionally slowing our progress! The forestaysail is luffing, topsail braces are all ahoo, and the spanker gaff is lagging to leeward. I understand you're only a *merchantman*, Captain, but if you don't trim your sails properly, you'll be joining your former captain at the foretop! Do you understand me?"

"Yes, your ladyship!" Niland glanced aloft and swallowed hard. *Tiger Lily*'s former captain and two senior lieutenants swung by their necks from the foretopsail yard, grim reminders of what it meant to refuse me. "I'll see to it immediately."

"Do that, Niland, or I will command this ship myself." Whirling away, I glared up to watch the sailors work. Sails were trimmed, and the log was run again. We'd gained half a knot. Good enough.

With another scan of the horizon, I noted the disposition of my armada. Those within flag signal had already changed course to converge upon the fleeing *Scourge*, hounds on the hunt. But Kevril was a wily fox indeed, and I didn't believe for a minute that he was doing his best to evade me. Perhaps he had thought he'd be over the horizon before we even left Haven, but I couldn't shake the feeling that I was being led astray.

"Where are you going, Captain Longbright?" I muttered into the teeth of the wind. "You had to know I'd come after you. Where are you taking my scourge and my truthsayer?"

As I stalked for the great cabin, another worry niggled at my sleep-deprived mind. "Preel..." My guards shied away as I wrenched open the door. Te-shan closed it quietly behind us and took station beside the door, a silent statue.

A tray of food and a blackbrew service sat upon the leeward sideboard. The former captain's steward, an islander whose name I hadn't bothered to learn, bowed and hurried out, clearly and rightfully terrified of me. I ignored the food, but poured a cup of blackbrew, cursing the loss of my hand as I spilled it. I paced and sipped the scalding brew, willing it to clear my sleep-deprived thoughts. Twelve hours ago, I'd had Haven by the balls, wielding my scourge and truthsayer with impunity. Now, only one of the three was mine. The loss of the scourge felt like a piece of my soul had been ripped away, but the loss of my truthsayer, my *friend*, twisted the knife in a way I hadn't expected.

Preel... What was Kevril doing to her? What was he telling her? How would her subtle conditioning hold up under his interrogation?

Unlike most of my slaves, I'd endeavored to keep Preel ignorant of her enchantment, my manipulation of her subtle. With her truthsayer talent involuntary, the only other thing I'd needed from her was honest companionship. That I'd received, and in it I'd discovered one thing my life had been lacking: a friend. Yes, I'd commanded her to believe me, but that was only to set her mind against Kevril and accept the reality of her situation. Now, he would be telling her that everything I'd said was a lie, professing his love, promising her freedom. She would continue to believe what I'd told her—the magic of the scourge would see to that—but her memories of the months she'd spent with Kevril remained intact. That conflict—love against hate, trust against betrayal, freedom against slavery—would assault her mind. I'd seen the results of such mental conflict before in other slaves, recalled the vacant look in Brilla Balshi's face after I'd commanded her to take pleasure watching Nala and Binsh eviscerate each other. She was still obedient, still cognizant, but something in her mind had snapped. If Preel ended up like that...

Then I recalled Preel's last meeting with Kevril—the dagger he'd tossed down at her feet and wondering what it might mean—and I stopped cold, the cup of blackbrew trembling in my grasp.

Would he kill her? Would Kevril Longbright murder the dove that laid diamond eggs out of love, to keep her from becoming my slave?

No, I resolved. *No, he loves her too much. I won't let that happen.* I downed my blackbrew and returned to refill my cup, my vengeful thoughts congealing into fantasies of cold revenge.

"No, Kevril. Preel is mine. She loves me, and when I find you, I'm going to eviscerate you with this very same dagger." I reached down to pull the ruby-hilted blade from my boot, the same one he'd tried to murder me with, and reconsidered. "Or perhaps I'll hand it to the woman you love and command *her* to do it!"

Yes, I thought, admiring the blood-red gem in the pommel of the dagger. *Yes, that will be a sweet revenge indeed.*

Chapter Two
A Bird in Hand

A caged bird may beat itself to death against the bars of its prison.
The Lessons of Quen Lau Ush

From the journal of Preel Longbright –
Does a god-cursed soul pray for deliverance from torment? Should I? Could my situation truly be worse if I incurred the wrath of some petulant deity? I think not. At this point, I expect no pity from any quarter. It is curious that I found it unbidden.

A knock at the cabin door woke me from a sleep of utter exhaustion. For a moment, I thought the last few weeks had been a nightmare, that I had never been stolen away by Jhavika, that I was happy, free, in love. The golden manacles on my wrists, the chain run through an eyebolt on the bulkhead, revealed the truth.

The door opened, and Miko stepped in. "Sorry to wake you, but I've got to get the carpenters to work." She didn't even look at me as she waved in four burly sailors. They carried tools and armloads of iron bars. My cage.

9

I sat up and rubbed the sleep from my eyes to better glare, but my defiance was pointless. They went to work without paying me any attention whatsoever, fitting the bars over the stern gallery windows, drilling holes into the planks and sinking three-inch screws into the hardwood. As if I might rip out a lesser barrier with my bare hands.

"Once they're done, you'll be free to walk around the cabin. The manacles stay on, but at least you'll be able to move about." Miko strode to Kevril's cabinet and started stuffing his things into a burlap sack.

"Thank you *so* much."

Miko ignored my sarcasm as she delved every drawer and cupboard. "The captain's assigned Hemp to care for you, but I have to warn you not to speak to him about Jhavika. She lashed him with the scourge and ordered him to spy on you and Kevril. That's how Jhavika knew we'd be at the Folly."

I snorted in disbelief. "And Kevril didn't murder him?"

Miko looked at me then. "Of course not. It wasn't Hemp's fault. Just don't talk to him about it. Jhavika commanded him to cut his own throat if anyone pressed him for information, and, as guilty as he feels for betraying you, he might cut deeper this time."

Cut deeper... I thought as Miko finished filling her bag and left the cabin. I remembered what Bert had told me. Hemp had cut his own throat, but circumvented the intent of Jhavika's command with only a shallow slice. Hemp would never knowingly have betrayed Kevril, but he obviously had. The compulsion of the scourge could not be denied. He, like me, was Jhavika's slave.

The conflict within me rose again, memories clashing against emotions, love and hate as immiscible as oil and water. I had loved Kevril, but now hated him for manipulating me and maiming Jhavika. I had hated Jhavika, plotted carefully to manipulate her, even to murder her if I had the chance, but I now loved her as I had loved my dear sisters. I couldn't help it; the compulsion of the scourge could not be denied.

But might there be a way I could circumvent those commands as Hemp had? I tried to remember all the things Jhavika had told me to do: *Believe me, don't try to hurt yourself, love me like a sister.* Those three were all I could remember clearly. They had been enough. I'd hated her and then loved her, as I had loved my parents, then hated them for selling me into slavery. I'd come to grips with that duality long ago. I couldn't blame my father for what he'd done. What use does a goatherd have for a truthsayer when the money the lord paid for me allowed him to better support his family and feed his other children, his *useful* children. I had wondered at the time how many goats I'd been worth.

Could I justify Jhavika's actions similarly? Could I somehow deny what she'd commanded me to believe, that Kevril had never loved me, that he had manipulated me, seduced me? To attempt that, I needed to understand Jhavika's motives. Why had she enslaved me with the scourge but kept me ignorant of the fact? Why enslave me at all?

I didn't like the answers that loomed like unknown shapes from fog. Just like Kevril, Jhavika wanted me to accept my slavery, to be fooled into thinking I was happy, free, that I loved her like a sister. She needed that devotion, that companionship. I'd seen that longing in her firsthand, even used it to manipulate her, but that was before I knew the scourge had tasted my flesh. Kevril hadn't used magic, but seduction. Why he'd done so was obvious; he'd wanted a truthsayer in his bed, just like several of my previous masters had. They wanted to feel powerful by possessing something valuable and violating it at their will. Kevril had tricked me into wanting him, asking for his love, begging even. If it had been a lie, did that render my love for him false? Did magic render my love for Jhavika equally false?

The conflicts clashed within me even louder than the discordant clatter of wood and iron from the workers. I closed my eyes and pressed my palms to my ears, willing myself to feel nothing. *Please, Gods of Light and Darkness, turn me to stone. Make me inert, incapable of feeling, of thought, of love and hate.* I didn't expect any intervention from the deities, god-cursed as I was.

Nevertheless, it arrived.

"Good mornin', Lady Preel."

I blinked my eyes open and stared at Hemp. He stood beside the bed holding a tray laden with covered bowls, plates, pitchers, and pots, his homely face set in a pleasing smile. I hadn't heard him come in over the din of the carpenters.

"Breakfast!" He put the tray down on the foot of the bed and retrieved a folding lap desk from a cabinet. "Bert didn't know what you wanted, so she put together a bit of everything. We're ripe with stores, so there's plenty of fresh stuff. A bit of a trouncy ride today, so it's just as well you'll be eatin' in bed. Less to slide about, you know."

I found his prattling oddly comforting, but disturbing as well. He'd always been kind to me, solicitous, proud of his care of us. *Us... Kevril and me.* I swallowed hard, my memories a lump in my throat. "You don't have to do this, Hemp."

"Do so." He placed the desk over my lap. "Captain's orders. Besides, it gives me somethin' to do other than sit and darn socks, and this cabin's a right shambles, it is. That worthless scrub Whinn ain't got no notion of clean, and ain't never even *heard* the word tidy by the look of things. I'll get it all squared away as soon as these yahoos are done. I'll be sweepin' up wood shavin's for a month, I will." He piled the lap desk with plates and bowls: bacon, eggs, fresh fruit, porridge, and toast with a pot of tartberry jam. Enough for three. My stomach growled at the heavenly aromas. Hemp filled a cup with blackbrew and lightened it with fresh goat milk exactly to my preference.

So many memories of Hemp's tender loving care... Had that been a lie, too? Had Kevril ordered Hemp to be so solicitous to trick me into loving him? I looked at the food, the perfect placement of the plates, cups, and utensils, the beaming smile on Hemp's narrow face, and regretted my doubt. Then I spied the healing cut across his throat.

"I don't..." All of this was my fault; the curse of a truthsayer. The tale of the dove that laid diamond eggs held true; everyone who came into contact with me suffered. Some, like Captain Nightspinner, had earned his fate. Others—Hemp, Miko, Bert, Nala, Binsh—suffered merely through their association with me. "I don't deserve this, Hemp."

"Of course, you do!" He poured fresh orange juice into a glass, undaunted. "And from the yowlin' of that tummy of yours, you need it. Now, tuck in. If I take one bite of this back to Bert, she'll carve my arse into ham hocks."

It wasn't true, of course, but an on-going excuse Hemp plied to encourage Kevril to eat. *Kevril...* It all came back to him. Why would he order Hemp to take such good care of me? Another manipulation? I knew he didn't love me, had never loved me, had only seduced me, but after his lies and motives were laid bare, after what I'd said to him, after kicking him in the teeth rather than suffer his touch, why would he maintain the illusion?

It didn't make sense.

"Why?" I felt like crying, like screaming, throwing the tray across the cabin, but that would only serve to punish Hemp, just like I'd punished Nala and Binsh with my petulance. I waved a hand at the tray, at the whole cabin. "Why all this? Why not lock me in the brig? Why not have me flogged for striking the captain? Why would he assign you to care for me, Hemp? What's he trying to prove?"

"Prove?" He looked bewildered. "Nothin', Lady Preel. He just thought you'd like a familiar face, and that it'd give me somethin' to keep me busy. Now, you tuck in." Hemp turned away and started bustling about the cabin, muttering about mold and wood shavings, damp and lint, bloodstains and clutter.

That, too, I found both comforting and disconcerting. *Truth or lies? Love or more manipulation?*

My stomach growled again. Though I had no appetite, my stomach obviously did. I pushed the manacles up my wrists so they wouldn't knock any dishes off of the lap desk, and ate mechanically, but Bert's flavors were impossible to ignore. I was overfull and the plates were empty before I realized it. The carpenters finished their work and left, my cage complete.

Hemp came over, fishing the golden key to my manacles from a pocket. "Now you can wander about the cabin to your heart's content."

I held out my bound hands. "Tell the captain that these aren't really necessary. Jhavika told me not to try to hurt myself again."

"Oh?" He looked startled at my mention of Jhavika, then doubtful. "I'll tell him, then, but orders is orders until he gives me the okay." He worked the key in my right manacle, pulled the chain through the eyebolt, and reached for my wrist again.

"You don't trust me."

"I do, but it ain't my decision, Lady Preel." He clicked the manacle closed. "There you are. And don't you worry none. There's two guards at your door watch and watch. If you need somethin' and old Hemp's not about, just give 'em the word, and they'll fetch me."

13

"I'd like to change clothes." I raised both wrists, shook my arms so that the chain rattled.

"Oh, right you are." He quickly transferred my right manacle to my left wrist. "There you go; I guess it don't matter that they're both on one side. Yer clothes is right where you left 'em. If you need somethin' cleaned, just say."

"Thank you, Hemp."

"My pleasure, Lady Preel." He beamed and started for the door, but then stopped and looked back at me, his face pensive. "If you want to talk, or... Well, we only got one thing in common, and we best not go there."

One thing in common—we're both slaves to the scourge. "I don't need to talk about it, Hemp. We both know what it's like." There was another person aboard who knew as well, but I wasn't about to talk to Kevril.

"Aye, that we do." He nodded and left.

I got up and explored the familiar space. I found only two things changed: the newly installed bars on the windows, and Kevril's missing belongings. The cabin seemed too large, too empty, too quiet. Everything in it reminded me of him: the books, the chart table, the bed... I stared out the stern windows for a time, and glimpsed distant sails when we crested a wave. I wondered what ship it was, if Jhavika was chasing us, and what she would do if she caught *Scourge*. I knew the answer; her wrath would be terrible. She would slaughter everyone aboard: Boxley, Miko, Kivan, Bert, all the crew I knew. And Kevril, of course. She would make an example of Kevril. But that I would never see, for I had little doubt that *Scourge*'s captain would put a knife in my heart before he let me be taken again.

I'd asked him to.

I'd loved him then.

I hated him now.

Memories and emotions clashed once again. This cabin, the bed, the quarter gallery, even the stern gallery windowsill, all the places Kevril and I had made love taunted me like jeering faces. All lies. All manipulation. Or the truth, and I'd been commanded by Jhavika to believe it false. I closed my eyes against my memories, but tears spilled from beneath my lids.

"Dear Gods of Light and Darkness, change me to stone. Dear Jhavika, why didn't you command me not to feel anything ever again? Kevril, why didn't you kill me as you promised?"

I whirled away from the windows and strode to the liquor cabinet. Choosing a bottle at random, I slopped a hefty portion into a snifter. The spiced rum burned my throat, but I welcomed the oblivion it promised.

Chapter Three
Second Guesses

No battle plan survives first engagement with the enemy.
The Lessons of Quen Lau Ush

From the diary of Kevril Longbright –
Part of being in command is being confident in one's own judgment. Another part is utilizing the expertise of all those under your command. The third part is, when confidence fails, not showing it. Lately, I find myself adrift and reaching for any straw of hope. Whatever happened to the cocksure pirate I once was?

I raised my spyglass and gauged the approaching squall line. The wind kicked up ripples in advance of the driving rain, at least an additional twenty knots in the initial gust. Fighting the urge to call for shortened sail, I turned and focused on our nearest pursuer, *Golden Harlot*. She was hull down, but just barely. *Perfect.*

Captain Tan was smart enough to know she was no match for us, and was keeping her distance. A wise woman. The next nearest ships, two galleons I couldn't name, were nothing but intermittent flecks of white. We'd lengthened our lead over the last two days. In fact, we'd lengthened it too much.

It was time for something to go wrong for us.

"Are you ready, Mister Rauley?"

"Aye, sir. Ready." He didn't sound happy.

"Cheer up! It's not every day I give you permission to break something!" I'd banished all of my other officers below decks. If this stunt killed someone, it would ride on my shoulders alone.

"Aye, sir, but it's also me who gets to fix it, so..." He squinted at the coming squall and cringed.

"Think of it as job security." I glanced aloft. "Just tell me it's not going to be worse than we planned."

"No guarantees, sir." My sailing master looked aloft and wrinkled his nose. "Don't know why we can't just let her luff up or spill some wind to slow down."

"Because Captain Tan is no fool, and she knows we're not either. We've got to string them along and wait until we have a real destination before we lose them." In fact, we could have evaded Tan two days ago, but if we had, Jhavika would have sent her armada far and wide. Asking Preel where we needed to go to destroy the scourge could take us anywhere, and keeping Jhavika's ships all in one strung-out line gave us an advantage. If they were dispersed, we might blunder into one or two of them when we finally set course for our destination. Hopefully, we'd get that destination this evening and lose Jhavika's fleet in the dark.

With my luck, it'll be Haven.

"Here it comes!" Wix bellowed from forward, glaring so hard into the coming squall that I wondered if he might be trying to scare it away.

"All hands, hold fast!" We were already battened down, so I took my own advice, grasping the windward mizzen shrouds from a safe vantage. All hell was about to break loose.

The leading gust hit us like a charging bull, the wind shifting thirty degrees onto our beam. *Scourge* staggered like a drunk, heeling so hard her leeward rail plunged beneath the sea. A line parted forward—not part of my planned mayhem—and a jib tore itself to pieces. *Sauce for the goose*, I thought.

"She's rounding up!" the helmsman bellowed.

"Slack sheets on the courses!" My sore feet slid on the canted deck, but my grip held. We had a hundred yards before the rain hid us from *Golden Harlot,* and our ruse wasn't finished. "Rauley! Now!"

"Aye, sir!" He pulled on a line that ran up the mizzen mast. It led to a pelican hook he'd installed on the topmast quadratic stay. The hook popped open, simulating a parted stay for our audience. The rest was physics.

The mizzen topmast trestletrees disintegrated, sending twenty feet of spar, yards of canvas, and a quarter mile of cordage flying off to windward. More lines parted. A heavy block plummeted to the quarterdeck, felling one of the helmsmen, but Rauley was there to take his place. The spanker boom sagged, the sail ripping from luff to leech.

Scourge rounded up into the wind, her sails flagging, her deck leveling. I trusted Rauley not to allow us to cross through the eye of the wind, and hurried to the fallen sailor. A topsail tore apart a few seconds before the downpour enveloped us.

"Sheet in headsails!" Rauley bellowed, and Wix echoed the command. "Reef courses and topsails! Cut away that wreckage!"

Boarding axes thumped, severing the lines that trailed to our lost topmast. I knelt beside the fallen man and didn't recognize his face at first, thin and pox-scarred. Then I recalled—one of the newcomers. I struggled to place a name to the blood-streaked features. *Wayne or Wyann?* The falling block had been a glancing blow, but had cut his scalp to the bone. Though his chest rose and fell, he remained senseless. His blood flowed freely out the scuppers in the deluge.

Scourge heeled back to starboard, and Rauley continued to bellow orders to cut down the shredded canvas and trim sails. We had plenty of spare canvas, cordage, and spars; it was the toll in blood that we couldn't replace.

"WIX!" I bellowed over the din. I held the man's head in my hands to keep it from lolling with the pitch and roll of the ship. If his neck was injured, one unwarranted twist could kill him.

"Here, sir!" Wix thumped up behind me. "What the hell happed to Wybly?"

Wybly, I thought. I wouldn't forget again. "Fallen block. Help me get him below. I'll hold his head."

"Aye, sir." Wix lifted the scrawny man with little effort, and I gently cradled his head. "Bloody lubbers don't have the sense to duck!"

I didn't comment. The eleven newcomers, my erstwhile escort through the streets of Haven, were not sailors in any respect. They'd only been aboard a few days, but good food, clean clothes, and dry hammocks had convinced them I meant to keep my word to them. They'd saved my life getting me through Haven, after all.

White bone showed through Wybly's streaming head wound, but no gray matter, which was good. We descended the steps crabwise to the middeck, and a sailor opened the sterncastle door for us. I recognized Spike, the former leader of my band of vagabonds.

"He gonna live, sir?"

"I don't know. We'll do all we can for him." We edged through the door, and Spike closed it to the deluge. The quiet inside seemed surreal. "Bert!"

"Aye?" Her florid face emerged from the galley door, and her eyes widened at the sight of us. "In the wardroom! I'll be there in two shakes. Any others?"

"I don't think so, not this bad, but probably a few bumps and bruises." We crabbed down the passage to the wardroom door. Inside, Boxley and Quiff were already clearing the table of plates and cups, long accustomed to our use of their space for surgery. "Where's Kivan?"

"Sleepin' sir. She had the last watch." Quiff squinted at the bloody sailor. "One of the lubbers?"

"Yes. Wybly. He was at the helm and caught a fallen block." We lay him on the table, but I kept a good grip on his head.

"I'm needed on deck, sir," Wix said with a knuckle to his forehead, ignoring the blood on his hands. "Whole fookin' mess of shite to clean up."

"Go. Boxley and Quiff can help Bert."

"I'll see if she needs a hand, sir." Boxley saluted and ducked out.

Quiff muttered an oath about lubbers as he recovered a towel from a cabinet to staunch the flow of blood. Bert came in with her satchel, and Boxley followed with a pot of evil-smelling stuff in hand.

"Just the head wound?" my cook asked, plucking a razor from her bag.

"I don't know about his neck," I said. "Looks like a glancing blow, but..."

Bert muttered and examined the wound, shaving off the surrounding hair with deft efficiency and probing the bloody gash with her fingers. She then felt the back of his neck and muttered some more.

"Don't feel anything broke, but only time'll tell. His skull ain't split open, so we'll sew him up and hope for the best." She nodded to Quiff and Boxley. "Hold him down. Captain, you just keep a good grip on his head. If he wakes up and jerks, it'd be bad."

We did as we were ordered. In these matters, I had no problems deferring to Bert's expertise. She'd saved many lives aboard *Scourge*, mine included.

Thankfully, Wybly didn't stir while she stitched up the deep wound. When we were done, she instructed Quiff to get some crew to help sew him securely into his hammock with his head braced and a mate to watch over him. I followed her to the galley and washed the blood from my hands. If Wybly survived, I'd call our ruse well purchased. If he didn't, morale among the newcomers would suffer. They were a ragged lot, but close knit.

Back on deck, we'd broken through the squall into clear air and one of the freakish calms that often follow such torrential downpours. The sails flapped lazily, and we were barely making headway. I found Miko on the quarterdeck overseeing the repairs, and espied Rauley and Wix aloft. Topmen were knotting and splicing in the calm, shaking out reefs and setting all aright. Behind us, the squall loomed dark, blocking our pursuers' view.

On the quarterdeck, Miko greeted me with a salute. "I thought you said a *little* mayhem, sir?"

"Miko! I thought I told you to stay below."

"For the blow, yes, but that's past, sir." She made a face. "I heard we had an injury."

"Wybly took a block to the head. He's alive, but still unconscious. We'll see." I looked aloft at the carefully orchestrated chaos. "Rauley knows I don't want to get all of this squared away too quickly. We have to wait until Tan sees the mess."

"Aye, sir. In this calm, she'll catch up quickly. We should have the new topmast being hauled aloft and the new spanker bent by then."

"Good." I borrowed the spyglass from her and scanned the horizon, finding no sails to windward. The squall line blocked everything to leeward. "Very good. We'll have a destination this evening, and lose them in the dark, but I want them well in view at sunset."

"About that, sir, are you sure asking where we can go to destroy the scourge is the best question?" Miko looked dubious. "What about how, or who could best help us destroy it? Maybe we could learn who made the thing. Might save time in the long run."

"I'm not *sure* of anything, Miko, but pointing us in the right direction seems the best first step to me." I considered, then shrugged, beset by new doubts on my course of action. "We should probably ask Preel. She's better at such things than either of us."

"Aye, sir, she is, but she's also not in her right mind."

"She agreed to help us destroy the scourge, Miko. She's not insane."

She looked at me sidelong. "How's your jaw?"

I fingered my bruised face. "Tender, but that doesn't mean she's crazy. We don't know what Jhavika commanded her to believe, but hating my guts is certainly on the list."

"Well, *I* could ask her if she's willing to discuss potential questions, if you like. She might not kick me upside the head, at least."

Preel would certainly be more receptive to an overture from Miko than me. I nodded. "Please."

"Aye, sir." She saluted and hurried off.

I watched the crew at work and scanned the thick squall behind us. The wind began to fill in, and we started making some speed. Just as the new mizzen topmast began to rise from the hold, our lookout called out.

"Sail astern. She's *Golden Harlot!* Hull up!"

I looked over my shoulder and raised my spyglass. *Golden Harlot* charged from the depths of the squall under reefed sails, her rig intact, and barely three miles distant.

I suppressed a grin. "Just in time for the show, Captain Tan."

Rauley called down from the mizzen, "Haul aloft! Smartly now!" The new topmast trestletrees were ready.

"Trim smartly forward, there!" I ordered. "Helmsman, bear off a point."

The show of trimming and altering course would add as much to the ruse as a hasty replacement of our lost topmast. I looked back with my spyglass again and spotted a reflection of the sun on something shiny. Likely, Tan was watching us with her own spyglass, gauging our condition. I just hoped she believed this had all been an accident. I watched her crew shake out the reefs in their sails as we started to pull away.

Miko returned, looking grim. "She'll talk to us, but only about which question to ask."

"Well, that's good." Her mien didn't match the news, however. "Something wrong?"

"She's been drinking, sir. I don't know how much, but enough to slur her words."

"Damn." That wasn't like Preel. She didn't much care for drinking, uneasy with the loss of control. Then I thought about what she was going through, and couldn't really blame her.

"Do you want me to have Hemp take all the alcohol out of the cabin?"

"No. As long as she's not endangering her health, I see no real problem with letting her kill the pain." In truth, I thought it might keep her sane. "We'll talk to her this evening, and she can sleep through the night."

"Aye, sir." Miko looked aft at *Golden Harlot*, shading her eyes against the glare of the afternoon sun. "Can we lose them?"

"I think so, but it depends a great deal on luck. So far, ours has been holding."

"Aye, sir."

Aloft, hammers pounded in the fittings that secured the new topmast, and the stays were tuned. Finally, Rauley called down that all was ready, and we unfurled our new mizzen topsail. Behind us, *Golden Harlot* tried to keep pace.

"So, pray for luck, Miko."

"And the right answer from Preel."

"Yes, that, too." I'd been praying for Preel constantly for weeks, but now I added a new prayer to the list. *Just hold it together, love. Just remember us, and hold fast.*

Chapter Four
Dire Answers

Be careful what you ask for. You may get it.
The Lessons of Quen Lau Ush

From the diary of Kevril Longbright –
Why do we hurt the ones we love? Philosophers have been asking this question for eons and no one has yet levied a meaningful answer. I knew Preel didn't want to see me, didn't want me in the same room. I knew it would cause her anguish. And yet, I longed to inhale her fragrance, to hear her voice, to watch the pulse at her throat. Gods help me, but for once, my need superseded hers.

Miko and I entered the great cabin together. Hemp had done his job; the place was spit and polish, though the bars on the windows didn't do much for the decor. In the inky darkness beyond those windows, I caught a glimpse of *Golden Harlot*'s lights some miles behind. Night had fallen; it was time to make our move.

Preel sat on the bunk in a robe over nightclothes, her back propped against the headboard. A glass of wine sat in the bedside cubby, well within reach. She didn't look at me, her eyes fixed on the foot of the bed.

"Thank you for agreeing to talk this over, Preel. I know this wasn't part of our bargain."

She didn't answer, but reached for her glass, quaffing a third of its volume. Her trembling hand rippled the wine as she put the glass back in the cubby. Her dark eyes shone glassy in the lamplight. So many nights I'd stared into those dark pools, reveling in their reflected passion, longing, and love. Now they only radiated cold hatred.

An old Toki curse came to my mind. *May all the Gods of Light and Darkness damn you to the hell of your choosing, Jhavika.*

"So, we want your opinion about what question to ask." I took a seat at the chart table, Miko sitting opposite. Hemp brought us drinks, but I waved mine away; I wasn't in the mood. "It was my thinking to ask for the nearest destination we could sail to destroy the scourge. This gives us a direction to sail, at least. We can narrow down the details later."

"What makes you think the destruction of the scourge is dependent on a place?" Preel asked, still not looking at us. I could hear the alcohol in her words, but she didn't seem overly inebriated.

"Nothing really. I'm willing to listen to any suggestions you may have."

"I can't suggest anything without information." She took up her wine again and drank down half before putting the glass back. Still, her eyes remained fixed on her feet. "Have you already tried to destroy it?"

"Yes, but hacking at it with a boarding axe and throwing it into a coal fire accomplished nothing. It's not even scratched." I touched the coil of dragonhide at my hip. I hated the thing, but wasn't about to let it out of my sight. "Alternatively, we could ask who knows how to destroy it, or by what means it can be destroyed."

She shook her head, her unbound hair rippling over her shoulders. "The latter probably won't work at all, which you well know." She glanced at me then, a flicker of accusation in her eyes. "As to the former, a name won't gain you a destination. You'd be sailing aimlessly for four more days before you could get one, and I imagine those sails I've seen following us aren't friendly."

"No, they're not friendly. Seven ships are chasing us, but we can lose them if we have a destination. Sailing aimlessly, we're likely to blunder right into them."

She looked away, and I could see the turmoil in her. *Jhavika... She's thinking of Jhavika.* I wondered if Preel would betray our location to our pursuers if given the chance.

"You could ask where to find someone who knows how to destroy the scourge, but there's no guarantee that such a person exists. The thing could be ancient, its secrets forgotten."

"You don't think its creator might still be alive? Wizards live a long time."

"The creator is dead."

"How can you be sure?"

Preel took her wine and emptied the glass. "Because *Jhavika's* its master. Only the death of the previous master can give the scourge a new one." Hemp offered to refill her glass, but she shook her head. "The tale of the dove that laid diamond eggs holds true."

"Of course." I shared a glance with Miko. I seemed to be doing all the talking, and it wasn't getting us anywhere.

"I think where to go is still the best question," Miko said. "That way, if it's a person, a thing, or some magical widget we have to use, we're at least headed in the right direction."

"Preel? Your thoughts?"

She shrugged. "The answer may be not what you want to hear, like someplace halfway around the world. Also, if there's only one place, and it's not someplace you can sail to, you probably won't get an answer. If you omit that requirement, I can think of nothing better."

"If it requires overland travel, we'll just have to deal with it. I'd like to ask your permission to employ your truthsayer talent." I'd promised her never to use her talent without her permission, and I meant to hold to that promise.

Muscles bunched at Preel's jaw, and I knew she was clenching her teeth. "I'll consent, if *Miko* asks it."

"I..." The spurn seemed childish, petulant, but still it hurt. "If you wish."

"Fine, then. I have to use the head first." Preel got up, and Hemp was there to offer an arm. Her gait was far from steady, and I realized that she was indeed drunk.

When the quarter gallery door closed, Hemp cast me one of his looks. He was worried for Preel. Well, he had company.

I looked to Miko. "You've got the wording down?"

"I think so. Just the nearest place that will best allow us to destroy the scourge."

"Maybe not 'best'. It's ambiguous. Maybe easily, instead."

"I don't think anything about this is going to be easy, sir."

"Well, relatively speaking. Most easily, then. I'm just thinking that if we go to this place, but we need a wizard along to cast some spell or something, we're fucked."

"Wouldn't that be considered part of 'we', sir? I mean, we don't *have* a wizard, so if destroying the scourge needed one, we'd already be fucked."

"Or we'd need to find a wizard."

"Which would ruin our question for a destination."

"Bugger!" I ground my teeth and shook my head. "No. We're overthinking this. Destination first, then we'll work out the details."

"Aye, sir."

The quarter gallery door opened, and Preel stumbled out. I started to get up out of reflex, but stifled the impulse to help her. Hemp was there. Preel looked a little ill, and I wondered if she'd been sick. I refused to ask; my concern wouldn't be welcome.

Hemp took her robe and helped her into bed.

Preel breathed deeply and nodded. "Ask."

Miko cleared her throat. "Where is the nearest destination we can go where we can most easily destroy the magical scourge currently in this cabin?"

Preel stiffened and arched, her eyes wide and rolling up until only the whites showed. Her voice, as always when her talent was invoked, sounded nothing like her.

"The center of the Serpent's Eye." She collapsed, breathing hard; the answer had cost her.

It cost me, too. *The Serpent's Eye...* "Check her, Hemp. Make sure she's okay."

"Aye, sir." Hemp hurried to the bedside, but I could see from here her ashen pallor and labored breathing both already subsiding.

"Bloody hells and demons, sir! The Serpent's Eye!" Miko sounded near panic. "How in all the Nine Hells—"

"No questions!" I snapped, rising from my seat. "We'll talk on deck. Hemp, see to Preel. Lights out. We're going to be evading our pursuers soon. If you need anything, just send word."

"Aye, sir."

Miko followed me on deck. I was already trying to think of our options when she asked, "How in hell are we going to sail into the Serpent's Eye without being deformed by the magic, sir? And there are bloody *dragons* in there! It's impossible!"

"It can't be, Miko." I mounted the steps to the quarterdeck and nodded to Kivan. "Change the sails out to black. We're altering course soon, and we need a dark ship. Smartly now. The moon'll be up in three hours, and I want to be over the horizon by then."

"Aye sir! Rauley, black sails aloft!"

"Aye, sir!" My sailors hopped to, scrambling aloft to replace white canvas with dark.

"So, why can't it be impossible, sir?" Miko was not one to be put off, and it was a valid question.

"Because Preel gave an answer. You asked for a place we could go; if we couldn't go there, she wouldn't have told you."

"Good point, but that doesn't mean we'll be human when we get there."

"True, which has got to be our next question."

"What's that?"

"How do we *safely* sail into the Serpent's Eye?"

Kivan caught her breath, and murmurs broke out from the sailors within hearing. I cursed under my breath; morale had just taken one on the chin.

"And how do you know it *can* be done safely, sir?"

"I don't, but we have a gods-damned *truthsayer*, don't we?"

"True enough." Miko didn't sound convinced. "So, where are we going?"

"The one place in the Blood Sea where we're most likely to find someone to help us delve the Serpent's Eye. If there's anyone who knows how to safely do that, it's got to be one of the dragonlords. They're *obsessed* with dragon magic, and there are more dragons in the Serpent's Eye than anywhere."

"Valaka?" Again, she looked dubious. "What about Brekka?"

"Well, I hadn't planned on sailing right into the harbor." I pulled a chart from the deck locker and pinned it to the lid to keep it from blowing away. I tapped the long craggy shore of Valaka Isle. "We can anchor to the southwest out of sight. We'll be able to ask Preel another question when we get there."

Miko grinned ruefully. "You've just got answers to everything, don't you sir?"

"No, Miko. I'm making this shit up as I go, but I'm used to having a truthsayer at my disposal." I couldn't dismiss her concerns, but I also had to salvage some morale out of this. There were too many ears listening. I quickly plotted our position and calculated a course for Valaka Isle. "There's *nothing* we can't answer, and there's *got* to be some way we can do this, or we wouldn't have gotten this answer in the first place."

"All right. I see your point, sir."

"Black sails are all bent, sir!" Kivan reported.

"Excellent! Now, lights out! Not even a candle showing, and I want the binnacle light shuttered." My orders were relayed and the ship went dark. I rolled my chart and put it away. I scanned the deck and spotted the glow of a pipe forward. "No smoking on deck, there! Not so much as a live coal!"

Wix growled an epithet, and the pipe went out.

I checked over the taffrail and found the stern gallery windows dark. A scan of the starlit horizon showed me the lights of four ships strung out in a line behind us. Our pursuers had to run with lights to keep from running into one another. *Perfect.*

I gave the order everyone was waiting for. "Hard to starboard, Kivan! Course, two one zero."

"Two one zero, sir! Helmsman, hard to starboard. Wix, trim for a broad reach!"

Scourge veered to starboard, and my crew responded like the professionals they were. Well, most of them did. A few voices rang out from forward, cursing the newcomers.

"No bells, no calls, and no lights until dawn, Kivan. Keep an eye on *Golden Harlot* and plot their bearing every quarter hour. If they alter course to follow, wake me. Quiff for the midwatch, and Miko for the morning. I'll be in the guest cabin. My gods-damned feet are killing me." So was my leg, but I'd forced myself not to limp.

"Aye, sir!"

Miko followed me below. Inside the sterncastle, Bert met us with a lamp turned low and her medical bag over her shoulder. Her face said something was wrong. "What?"

"Wybly passed away about an hour ago, sir. He never woke up. Just stopped breathin'. I'm sorry."

"Bloody buggering hells!" Guilt and worry crashed down like an avalanche. There went morale, right out the scupper. The newcomers would be a problem, and I couldn't blame them. I'd delivered them out of the frying pan right into the fire.

"Not your fault, sir," Miko said. "He could have died a hundred different ways on the streets of Haven, none of them as kind as a blow to the head that he never woke up from."

"Aye, but tell that to his friends." I nodded to Bert. "Thank you. We're running dark, so no lights on deck."

"I got the word, sir. I still need to check your feet and that leg, and I need light for it. Where do you want to do this?"

I didn't relish the thought of her probing my injuries, but knew she was right. "The stores locker. It's below the waterline."

"Aye, sir." She ambled toward the companionway to the lower decks.

"Get some sleep, Miko." I followed my cook and tried not to dwell on Wybly. "I need you sharp as a tack when the sun rises."

"Aye, sir!" She saluted and went to her cabin.

Down two decks, I followed Bert into the storage locker. She pointed to a crate and moved another next to it.

"Boots off, and put your feet up." She handed me a cylinder of rolled leather pocked with the teeth marks of previous patients.

I sat down and worked off my boots, then leaned back and put my feet up. The bandages had soaked through, and were likely stuck to the scabbed wounds. I put the leather between my teeth far enough back to avoid the ones still sore from Preel's kick, and bit down.

Bert began peeling off the bandages. It hurt like hell, but somewhere deep inside, I felt like I had earned the pain.

Chapter Five
Vanished

Managing failure is an invaluable skill.
The Lessons of Quen Lau Ush

From the journal of Jhavika Keshmir –
Kevril Longbright is, without a doubt, the bane of my existence. If he has taught me anything, it's to trust my instincts. When he managed to escape the scourge's enchantment, my first impulse was to kill him. When I stole Preel, I refrained from having him assassinated against my better judgment, thinking I needed him to recruit my pirate navy. And now, my suspicion that he was leading me on a merry chase has been confirmed. I must learn to think with my gut, not my head.

Glaring into the morning sun, I tapped my pike hand on the leeward rail of the quarterdeck as the cutter from *Golden Harlot* maneuvered close enough for their message to be heard. I'd suspected what that message would be the moment word of the cutter's approach reached me, so it came as no surprise. A sore disappointment, but not a surprise.

"*Scourge* has vanished, your ladyship!" the young officer bellowed from the small craft's cockpit. "They went dark and evaded us in the night!"

That wily bastard! Just as I'd suspected, Kevril had been stringing us along, keeping us from dispersing, feigning difficulties until the time was right. Two questions rang out in my mind: why now, and where would he go? *If only I had my truthsayer, I could find him in a heartbeat!*

With that thought, the answer to the first question hit me like a thunderbolt. *Preel!* I counted the days since I'd last asked a question that invoked her talent. It seemed like a lifetime ago, but had, in fact, only been four days. Kevril had delayed shaking our pursuit until he could ask her a question. That suggested he had needed her answer to decide where to go.

But where? What the hell did you ask Preel? What are you looking for, Kevril? I both needed and dreaded the answers to those questions.

"Pull a small-scale chart, Captain Niland," I ordered.

By the time I reached the deck locker, he had a chart of the entire Blood Sea tacked down, our position denoted by an X and the time of our last fix. Realistically, I had no way to surmise what direction Kevril had gone. He could be in an expanding circle of ocean two hundred miles across. If he required Preel's help to discern his destination, there was no way I could divine it.

There were, however, only so many options.

Kevril might have sailed for the open sea, but I didn't think so. He knew the Blood Sea too well; these were his hunting grounds. Faced with an overwhelming force—my seven ships to his one—I felt confident that Kevril would try to recruit allies. With a fleet of pirates on his side and the promise of Haven as payment for their loyalty, he would be invulnerable. He could even make good on his threat of blockading Haven and starving my kingdom into submission. He might recruit those allies from anywhere in the Blood Sea. In fact, which pirate to approach first would have been a very good question to ask Preel.

I had only one advantage: my armada. Seven ships, seven destinations. Wherever Kevril went, we would find him and converge.

I had no illusions that *Scourge* couldn't outsail any one of my ships, and perhaps outfight some of them, but if we came at him from every direction, he'd be trapped and overwhelmed. I'd already considered where to search if we lost him, so I had my deployment long since figured out. Now we just needed to find him before he could assemble a fleet.

"Captain Niland, have your navigator plot a course for Twin Capes. We'll send our two cutters to the rest of the fleet with the following orders." He began scribbling frantically as I spoke.

I sent *Summer Violet* to scour the coast north to Hyko, and *Jasmine* coastwise south to Sariff. I thought neither of those destinations very likely—the former due to the danger of the god-emperor's truthseekers finding out about Preel or the scourge, and the latter because Kevril had a death sentence on his head in Sariff—but other pirates might lair in any one of dozens of hidden coves along the mainland, and I couldn't dismiss any possibilities. If they found no trace of *Scourge*, they were to send word, then continue north and south to Toki and Mati, respectively. *Hyacinth* I sent to search the small isles north of Twin Capes. *Peony* would scour Black Point, and *Bluebonnet* Ton Chi. *Golden Harlot* I sent to Valaka. The fastest ship to the farthest destination seemed prudent, though I didn't think it likely Kevril would go there after his falling out with the alchemist, Brekka.

I stipulated that they were to search tirelessly for any sign or word of *Scourge*, sending people ashore at towns and villages, and questioning all other ships. Reports of success or failure, as well as requests for help, were to be sent to their nearest allies by cutter. All reports would be relayed to me at Twin Capes, unless they received further instructions as to my movements. All ships would first search the leeward sides of their assigned islands, then, if they found nothing promising, the windward sides. The latter was not likely to yield results, since there were few safe anchorages on the windward coasts. If Kevril was searching for allies, he would focus on population centers.

My orders set up a moving relay of information that would best cover the areas most likely to yield results. It would take time, but we would slowly cut off every hiding place until we found them. I also stipulated that, if anyone found them, they were to take *Scourge* with minimal killing, and bring the survivors to me. There was no point to wasting people, and I couldn't risk Preel.

"Do you have all that, Niland?"

He nodded. "I believe so, your ladyship."

"Repeat them to me." There was no margin for error here.

He did, and I judged them close enough.

"Good. Copy and send those immediately and take us to Twin Capes. Lookouts aloft at all times! Find me that gods-damned pirate!"

"Yes, your ladyship!" Niland shouted orders, and sailors scurried to comply. The cutter from *Golden Harlot* received my written orders in minutes, and set off to the southeast toward their distant ship. Our own two cutters splashed into the sea and their masts were hastily stepped. Sailors, some of my more seaworthy guards, and provisions piled aboard, and they set off for our escorts. Finally, *Tiger Lily* wore around on her new heading to the northeast and Twin Capes.

I found myself tapping the quarterdeck rail with my pike hand, gouging the finely polished teak as if prodding the ship onward by sheer force of will. I had fought for so long, and now, only days after gaining my kingdom, I stood on a precipice. I could lose it all with one misstep. Only three things did I now long for in all the world: my scourge, my truthsayer, and Kevril Longbright's head on a pike.

Chapter Six
To Delve the Eye

Words, like serpents, may come back to bite you.
The Lessons of Quen Lau Ush

From the journal of Preel Longbright –
I've been a slave my entire adult life, abused and punished for insignificant infractions. After so long, I have even grown accustomed to it. One breath of freedom, true or false, changed me forever. I wish now that it had never happened.

I woke with a raging hangover and the echo of my own answer ringing through my head. I also had an urgent need to urinate.

My aching back stabbed me as I lurched out of bed and hurried to the quarter gallery. Scorching daylight stabbed through the windows into my eyes, searing my brain. Hitching up my nightgown as I stumbled through the quarter gallery door, I sat and relieved myself.

As the urgency eased, my answer to Miko's question hammered through the haze of headache and nausea.

The center of the Serpent's Eye? Gods and devils... I blinked into the morning sunlight streaming through the quarter gallery windows, and realized we'd changed course. We were sailing south, toward the Eye.

He's insane! He'll sail us right into hell!

Dread rose up from my gut, pushing my nausea over the edge. I whirled around and threw up into the commode. I retched until I had nothing left to expel, then retched some more, tears streaming and bitter bile burning my throat. Finally, the bout ceased and I staggered to my feet. Water from the wash ewer eased my throat and cooled my fevered face.

A light tap at the door startled me. "Lady Preel, it's Hemp. Please tell me you're all right."

"I'm okay, just sick." I swallowed more water. "My robe, please."

"Aye, lady." A moment later he tapped again. "Here you are."

I opened the door and took my robe, flinging it on. "Tell me we're not sailing into the Serpent's Eye, Hemp. Tell me Kevril's not *that* insane!"

"Oh, no, lady, he ain't that crazy. Not crazy at all, if you ask me true, but..." He looked uncomfortable. Hemp still idolized Kevril, the poor deluded fool. "Well, I'm sorry yer not feeling well. A spot of breakfast will put you to rights. I'll go tell Bert."

"Where are we going, then?" I staggered out into the cabin, rubbing my eyes. From the angle of the sun it was late morning. My answer had cost me dearly, as they often did when magic was involved.

"Valaka. Be there in three more days if the wind holds true." He smiled and ducked out of the cabin.

"Valaka..." That was almost as bad as the Serpent's Eye. Brekka would try to steal me away, and if any fate brought more dread to my already tortured mind than remaining in Kevril's clutches, it was becoming that creature's tool. She wanted me not for the answers I could provide, but for my magic itself. She would bleed it from me drop by drop.

I sat at the table clutching my tumultuous stomach and rubbing my aching head. If only Nala were here to massage away the pain. *Nala, Binsh...* I wondered what had happened to them. Had Jhavika punished them for failing to protect me? My poor sister, what torture she must be going through. Had she become the monster I dreaded, the woman I hated and planned to murder? The conflicting emotions and memories resumed their battle within my skull, like caged birds beating against their prison bars from the inside. I forced myself to think, to focus on something besides that which threatened to drive me mad.

Valaka. Why Valaka?

I knew the island lay on the edge of the Serpent's Eye, the last habitable land before the wild magic of the maelstrom began to transform living tissue into abominations. Even there, some were born with horrific malformations: the Serpent's Children. Only dragonkind were unaffected by the magic, and the Eye attracted them like a flame attracts insects. But why would Kevril take us there? We couldn't sail into that maelstrom of magic without being killed or transformed into monsters. Could we?

Hemp knocked and entered bearing a huge tray. "Feelin' better?"

"Not really."

"Well, this'll set you to rights!" He placed dishes before me: an omelet an inch thick, dribbling cheese; a bowl of fresh papaya, banana, and mango; a steaming cup of blackbrew; a tall cup of cool orange juice and another of water.

I downed half the glass of water in one draught and sighed. "Why are we going to Valaka?"

Hemp looked at me worriedly. "Um, well, to find some way to destroy that...the scourge."

"Sorry. I'll shut up." I tried a bite of the omelet and my mouth exploded with flavors. I hadn't even been hungry, but my appetite ignited like a pile of oil-soaked rags.

"Oh, no need, lady. We can dance around the sore spots." Hemp began bustling around the cabin, making up the bed, tidying things that didn't need to be tidied, and polishing gleaming brass. "Captain's thinkin' that someone in Valaka must know how to delve the Eye without gettin' turned into anything horrible, like. I suppose that'll be the next question he asks, but we got days to figure it out. We lost them sorry slugs in the dark, so we're free and clear!"

Jhavika... My stomach clenched on the food I'd already swallowed. *Kevril lost them, and they don't know where we're going!* Thinking it through, I couldn't decide if that was good or bad. I longed to see Jhavika, to explain, to hold her in my arms and tell her it would all be all right, but I knew it wasn't possible. I also knew it was a lie, magic compelling me to feel love that wasn't true. I drank down a swallow of blackbrew, forcing my mind to the task I'd agreed to undertake. *Destroy the scourge, then you'll know the truth from lies.*

But how?

The center of the Serpent's Eye was the key. There had to be a way to delve it without harm, or my answer wouldn't have directed us there. Or would it? Recalling the question Miko had asked, I realized that our wellbeing hadn't been part of it. Magic is a fickle thing, literal and unforgiving. *The center of the Serpent's Eye...* Something about that phrase plucked a string of memory. I'd heard it before, but where?

I ate absently, forcing my mind to task. "Hemp, could you bring paper and pen, please? I need to make some notes."

"Aye, Lady Preel." He fetched parchment, quill, and ink in a flash. "I see you found yer appetite!"

I saw that most of the omelet and half the fruit were gone. "Blame Bert."

"Oh, aye, she's a treasure and a curse, she is!" He patted his stomach, poured more blackbrew, and grinned. "Them newcomers fair worship her."

"Newcomers?" That took me aback. Kevril hadn't taken anyone new aboard in months, largely to keep the secret that he had a truthsayer.

"Oh, aye. He recruited near a dozen of 'em the night...well the night we left Haven. Scrawny and filthy lot they were, but they're shapin' up." He frowned. "Well, most of 'em are."

His tone boded ill. "Most of them? What happened?"

"Well, you remember that horrible lee lurch the other day?" Hemp resumed his bustling about. "The one that near put us on our beam ends?"

"Yes." I remembered it because we'd been warned it would come, as if it was planned.

"Well, it was a ruse to convince those slugs behind us that we was caught by the lee, you see. Rauley rigged the mizzen top to get carried away in a squall, so we'd look crippled, just so we could keep the chase close, you know. Captain's a fox for tricks like that."

The Pirate's Bane

And for manipulation, lies, and... I bit my tongue on the thought of all the myriad things he was so very, very good at. The sweet memories would clash against what I knew for the truth.

"So, when all hell broke loose, a block fell and cracked one of them newcomers square in the head. We thought he might pull through, but he passed just last night. His mates are right sore about it, but... Well, the captain's givin' the poor bloke a send-off this very mornin'. Full honors."

"How *magnanimous* of him," I said without thinking. I caught Hemp's look of reproach and bit my tongue again. The one subject on which we differed was our opinion of Kevril Longbright. "Sorry."

"Not yer fault, lady." He resumed his work and his story. "Anyways, the bloke's name was Wybly. His mates are all out of sorts, but they'll come around. Livin' on the streets of Haven, they know life's a gamble one day to the next."

Not just on the streets of Haven, I thought, returning to my notes to stave off the looming battle of memories versus emotions. *The scourge. It's all about the scourge. To destroy it we have to delve the center of the Serpent's Eye, but how?*

Again, that phrase caught me up. *The center of the Serpent's Eye.* Where had I heard that before, and what did it have to do with the scourge? I remembered the words as if from a dream, uttered by a coarse voice, but familiar. Then it came to me.

A blood pearl weighing four ounces collected from the depths of the Serpent's Eye.

The voice had been mine, the answer to a question about the scourge itself. One of the components of its making had come from the Serpent's Eye. The maker of the scourge had gone there, delved the depths, and apparently returned unscathed or, at least, unscathed enough to craft the scourge. However that had been accomplished might be the linchpin to the destruction of the vile thing.

If they could do it, so can we.

My heart pounded faster, and excitement banished any remaining nausea from the previous night's excesses. I had the strand of an idea, one that might just save my sister's soul.

Chapter Seven
Quiet and Questions

A common enemy is a blessed thing.
The Lessons of Quen Lau Ush

From the diary of Kevril Longbright –
Seeing Preel honestly working to help us destroy the scourge mended my shattered heart somewhat. She was trying. We had a common enemy, and it wasn't Jhavika; it was a braided piece of dragon flesh.

We sailed *Scourge* into the secluded cove with all caution: lead lines plumbing the depths in quick succession, lookouts poised, and the high afternoon sun shining down into the crystalline waters. I had good charts of the leeward shore of the island, but had never anchored in this particular spot. Valaka Isle was off the beaten trade route, and few ships ventured here on purpose. A barrier reef to the southwest and a craggy cape to the northeast offered a protected bay, but the mountainous terrain made the winds fluky. We were becalmed one moment and buffeted by shrieking gusts the next, which made maneuvering a delicate operation. Courses flapped and flagged, then snapped full, heeling us over hard, while topsails and topgallants cracked and strained.

"Furl the courses and forestays'l before we break something, Rauley. She's making too much speed, anyway."

"Aye, sir!" He relayed the orders, and my topcrew scrambled to the yards.

The lookouts called out bearings and distances to shoals, and my leadsmen counted off the shallowing depths. I bit a fingernail.

"Plenty of peace and quiet, at least, sir." Miko scanned the shore, a black sand beach wide and smooth. "Be a lovely spot for a picnic. Now all we need is—"

"If you say 'wine, women, and song,' I'll have you scrubbing the bilges, Miko." I knew she was just trying to diffuse my tension, but I was having none of it.

"Sourpuss," she muttered, drawing a chuckle from the helmsman.

I scanned the shore and couldn't disagree with her assessment. It was deserted and idyllic, a steep wooded hillside framing the beach, and even a small trickling stream. A jumble of rotted wooden frames at one end of the beach suggested an abandoned fishing village, but there were no other signs of civilization. It was just what we needed.

"There's fresh water and likely game. Some venison wouldn't go amiss. I'll send out shore parties when we're settled."

"I volunteer for the first one," Miko quipped. "I could use the exercise."

"And some time away from your surly captain, no doubt." That drew another chuckle from the helmsman, but it was true enough. I was in a foul mood, primarily due to my inability to decide what question I should next ask Preel.

"By the deep, eight fathom!" the leadman cried. A moment later came the reading of the bottom type from the waxed cup at the base of the lead. "Fine black sand!"

"That'll do nicely, Master Rauley. Up tacks and sheets, and furl everything but a riding sail. Lower the best bower."

"Aye, sir!"

The sails flagged as the sheets were eased, and we slowed. The huge anchor splashed, and the thick rode burned through the hawsehole. Wix paid out eighty fathoms before snubbing the line. Our momentum took us in until the anchor set with a jerk, the hawser standing out straight and squirting water as we wheeled around. *Good holding; one less thing to worry about.*

I had plenty to keep my mind busy, not the least of which was the tenuous morale situation. Word had spread that our quest pointed us into the Serpent's Eye, and I had little doubt that my crew would string their captain up from a yardarm before they'd sail into a cyclone of magic and dragons. I couldn't blame them. I would have done the same.

To allay their fears, as well as my own, I needed to figure out how best to proceed. Miko and I had spent hours discussing possible questions for Preel, but, as yet, we'd come up with only poor options. Asking which, if any, dragonlords had safely delved the Serpent's Eye might yield a list of twenty names or none, and would give us no information about how they'd done it or where to find them. And the dragonlords weren't renowned for their philanthropy, so seeking help there would be a chancy prospect. Likewise, asking Preel how to safely delve the eye might yield an impossible list of methods or none, and wouldn't tell us how or where we might pursue those methods.

We settled the ship, and I gave the crew an extra ration of grog for their performance. It wouldn't help the morale situation in the long run, but might raise the newcomers' opinion of me. The burial of Wybly at sea had been a grim affair, and I was afraid my words of solace had fallen on deaf ears. One of his comrades, a sharp-witted girl named Doria, had broken down in tears as we slid the canvas-wrapped body into the sea, and I had wondered if they'd been related. The newcomers' appointed leader, Spike, had astonished me by wrapping one arm around Doria's shoulders in an effort to give comfort. I don't know why it surprised me. Perhaps it shouldn't have.

We all take solace where we can find it.

I posted lookouts and double watches—we were still being hunted, after all—and accompanied my first mate to the wardroom, much to the chagrin of my junior officers. Having the captain take his meals there had put a damper on their conversations, but I needed to talk, and they might have some ideas that had evaded me. We'd barely taken our seats and served out grog, however, when an unexpected voice interrupted us.

"Captain, sir?"

I turned to find Hemp in the doorway, looking tentative. "Yes, Hemp? What's afoot?"

"Lady Preel asked me to tell you she wants you to ask her a question straightaway."

"So soon?" It hadn't been much longer than three and a half days, which pushed her abilities to the limit, especially when our questions delved magical subjects. "I haven't quite nailed it down yet. I'd planned to do it tonight."

"I know, sir, but she says she's got the question all figured out, and that time is against us. She's right chompin' at the bit."

"Well!" I exchanged a glance with Miko, but she just shrugged. If Preel had come up with a better question than we had, which wasn't unlikely, I would count myself lucky. That she was actively trying to help us lifted my spirits from the bilges as well. "Very well, then. Miko, I think it would be best if you came along."

"Aye, sir!" She downed her grog and rose to follow me.

Quiff, Kivan, Rauley, and Boxley watched us go, their faces anxious. Perhaps they sensed my trepidation.

In the passage, I put a hand on Hemp's shoulder and lowered my voice. "How is she, Hemp?"

"Not good, sir. She's in a state, I don't mind tellin' you. Always pacin' and frettin'. She's gone through a whole roll of parchment makin' all kinda notes, mutterin' this and that. And she's still drinkin' too much by my reckonin'."

"Do you think I should pull all the alcohol from the cabin?" I'd already considered and rejected the idea, but valued his opinion. After all, he was spending more time with Preel than anyone.

He shook his head miserably. "Oh, that'd probably be bad, sir. She's gotta have somethin' to take her mind off things. You, of *anyone*, knows that."

Indeed, I did. In fact, Preel had coaxed me into tempering my drinking when I was troubled. Her philosophy then had been to consider that things could be so much worse. I tried to imagine that now, and couldn't. Perhaps she couldn't either.

"All right, then."

Hemp tapped on the door to the great cabin, and we entered.

Preel sat exactly as she had the last time we'd visited, in bed, her back against the headboard, wearing a robe over nightclothes, a glass of wine beside her. She didn't look at us, but her knuckles were white upon her clenched hands. The scene was eerily familiar, and I stifled the impulse to mention it offhandedly. Any comment from me would be unwelcome.

A single sheet of parchment, a pen, and an inkwell sat upon my navigation table. I went to the table and glanced at the paper. A single line was written on it in Preel's elegant hand, a question.

> By what means was the blood pearl that is currently part of the magical scourge in our possession safely procured from the Serpent's Eye?

"A tot, sir?" Hemp asked.

I desperately wanted one, but denied that impulse as well. "No, thank you, Hemp." I passed the page to Miko to read, then glanced over at Preel. "Why did you choose the pearl?"

"Because it's the logical next step, and it's specific." Preel didn't look up, but reached for her glass. "Whether you've realized it or not, the crux of our problem is ambiguity. There may be dozens of different ways to delve the Serpent's Eye without harm. If we ask a general question, the answer will be equally general, perhaps even pointless. A specific question will yield a specific answer."

"But we don't know how long ago the blood pearl was procured, or by whom." Miko put the parchment down. "However it was done might not even exist anymore."

"Perhaps. There is no certainty. We might also ask *who* procured it, but that person is likely dead."

"I was thinking about what you said earlier, about the maker of the scourge being dead. They might not be if the scourge was made for someone else. Wizards *do* make powerful magical devices for kings and emperors, after all."

"The blood pearl was procured from the Serpent's Eye, which suggests the scourge was probably crafted nearby, not half a world away. There are no kings or emperors closer than Toki or Mati, and haven't been since ancient times."

"The gnomes founded Haven, and they had a ruler," I countered. "Maybe the scourge was made for them. Maybe they abandoned the place fleeing enslavement."

Preel's gaze slid sideways to me, the wineglass trembling in her hands. "Then, by all means, craft your *own* damned question if you find mine foolish!"

I bristled, stung by her venom. "I don't find it *foolish*, Preel. I was trying to *discuss* it with you."

She looked away and downed her wine without a word. Hemp took the empty glass, casting me a cautionary glance. I rubbed my eyes and sighed, reminding myself that the way Preel felt about me was neither her doing nor mine.

"The question does solve the ambiguity problem, sir," Miko offered. "It'll point us in one direction, and we can work out the details of who and where later."

Later... Time was not on our side, but this would at least give us a goal.

"Fine. Thank you for helping us, Preel. Frankly, your solution is far better than anything we've come up with." I stood without looking at her and pushed the paper and pen across the table to Miko. "You ask the question, Miko, and be ready with the pen in case the answer is complicated. Hemp, before we ask, see to the lady's needs. She may be asleep for a long time."

"Aye, sir." Hemp escorted Preel to the head.

I stared out the barred windows, cursing my sharp tongue. Miko remained studiously silent.

Shortly, Preel emerged from the quarter gallery, and Hemp helped her with her robe and the covers. I didn't look at her, but watched her reflection in the windows. She lay with her hair spread out upon the pillow in a wreath of onyx curls, her hands folded upon her breast.

Finally, she took a deep breath and nodded. "Ask."

Miko cleared her throat. "By what means was the blood pearl that is currently part of the magical scourge in our possession safely procured from the Serpent's Eye?"

Preel stiffened and arched, and I could no longer keep from turning to watch her. Her voice came in that wrenching, familiar rasp.

"The dragonship."

She collapsed, again breathing hard.

"The..." I checked myself and looked to Miko, my eyes wide.

"Well, *that's* interesting!"

"Indeed." I strode toward the door, crooking my finger for Miko to follow. "See to Preel, Hemp. Let me know immediately if she needs anything." I paused with my hand on the latch, staring back for a moment at the woman I loved, the woman who despised me. "And maybe water her wine a little."

"Aye, sir. I'll see to her wellbeing. Don't you worry none."

Don't worry about the woman I loved under a spell that made her hate me? That wasn't likely to happen, and he knew it, but I appreciated his assurance. We made our way back to the wardroom. I wanted to talk this over with my people and desperately needed a drink.

My officers looked up hopefully as we entered, and I tried to put on a positive face. "Ladies and gentleman, we have something to discuss. Lady Preel has posed a most interesting question, and we have a definitive answer, but it's one that will require some thinking to put to practical application." I took up the grog pitcher and filled cups as I told them of her question, her reasoning behind it, and finally the answer.

"Um...pardon me, sir, but what the bloody hell's a *dragonship*?" Quiff asked, clearly perplexed.

"I've not the foggiest idea, but it's how whoever made this damned thing got the blood pearl from the Serpent's Eye without being affected by its wild magic." I took the scourge from my belt and dropped it on the table. "If *they* can do it, so can we."

"But that could have been eons ago. Do you know how old the scourge is, sir?" Kivan asked.

"No idea. I don't even know where Captain Kohl got the thing. He *said* it was plunder, but from where, who knows. Such things don't just fall into the hands of pirates." I quaffed grog and stifled a cough, unused to the harsh beverage that the crew drank by the pint. Rotgut rum, lime juice, sugar, and water was a far cry from fine spiced rum, single malt whisky, or the vintage wine I usually drank. "Why is that pertinent?"

47

"Because if it was made, say, *thousands* of years ago, this dragonship isn't likely to be still seaworthy, is it? I mean, my old da used to always say every ship is sinking from the moment it touches water, some just sink slower than others."

I coughed a laugh; the old adage was true enough. Even the best-tended ships eventually succumbed to rot and age. "I suppose we should ask if it still floats, then."

"But sir, this ship's *got* to be magic, don't it?" Boxley asked. "I mean, to sail safely into the Eye... If the magic don't touch it, maybe the elements don't either. Like that thing." She pointed to the scourge.

"That's a thought," I agreed. "What else?"

"Well, where the hell it *is* would be a starting point," Miko put in. "If it's halfway around the globe, we'll have some sailing to do."

"If it's halfway around the globe, we'll have to find some other way to safely delve the Eye," I countered.

"And there's the whole *dragon* part." Quiff tapped the table with a finger and sipped his grog. "Dragons aren't affected by the magic of the Eye. That's why there's so many dragonlords on Valaka, right? They're all mad for dragon magic."

I nodded, following his train of thought. "Yes, and if this dragonship is somehow enchanted with dragon magic, maybe that's what makes it impervious to the magic of the Eye."

"And dragons live thousands of years, don't they?" Quiff looked to Kivan.

She furrowed her eyebrows at him. "Why ask me?"

"Because you read for *fun*!" Rauley grinned and nudged Quiff. "And *he* only reads when he can't avoid it."

We all chuckled. The mirth felt good for a change.

"So, if this dragonship is enchanted with dragon magic, it *might* still be seaworthy," I reasoned. "Unfortunately, the only way we can find out is to ask Preel."

"I still think we should ask her where it is first." Miko persisted. "Remember, if it's halfway around the globe, we're already buggered and have to find some other way."

"Good point."

An uneasy silence fell, and I could see that we'd all reached a similar conclusion; we had no other source of information about this dragonship and couldn't ask another question for four more days, maybe three and a half.

And we were being hunted by Jhavika Keshmir. Eventually, she would come here looking for us.

Chapter Eight
Broken Wings

One's own mind can be the worst enemy.
The Lessons of Quen Lau Ush

From the journal of Preel Longbright –
Why I am what I am is a question that has long plagued me.
I've begged former masters to ask me this, but it would
probably have yielded no answer. I am, in essence, a magical
creature, after all. But *why* am I? What entity bequeathed this
magic? Or am I a freak of nature like the Serpent's Children?
The question scores me like a lash.

My eyes opened to darkness, and I wondered for a fleeting
moment if I was blind. I raised my left arm, golden manacles glittering
in faint starlight. It was night, quiet save for the muffled lap of waves
against the hull. I remembered where, who, and what I was. I recalled
my question and the answer—another puzzle. The scourge, Kevril,
Jhavika, and the raging battle of memories against emotions surged up
within me then, and despair returned.

Please, Gods of Light and Darkness, turn me to stone, make me inert... I closed my eyes, pleading, but my prayers went unanswered.

For a time, the war raged in my mind, myself against myself. *I am the ouroboros, devouring myself endlessly.* Despair wracked me, and tears seeped beneath my clenched lids. I couldn't live like this, but I had no means to end my suffering. Even that solace had been denied me. I was a slave to myself, to my own curse, the lie of freedom and love, and the enchantment of the scourge.

The scourge... Destroy it and you'll know the truth.

Though I could have sworn I heard the voice, there was no one here but me. It had to have come from within my own mind, but it sounded like Kevril. *A memory, a haunting, or a delusion?* It was startling to me, the first pattering rain of a looming deluge of insanity. *I'm succumbing*, I thought. *I'm losing my mind.*

Surging out of bed, refusing the madness that hammered the inside of my skull, I lit a lamp and turned it up high, then another, then all of them, as if I could banish the voices as I banished the darkness. I had to do something to occupy my mind.

Destroy the scourge. Find a way. You're one step closer to the truth. Come on, Preel, think! Dragonship! Dragons. Magic. What must the next question be?

I cast about the cabin and my eyes fell on the bookshelf. Poetry, philosophy, Chen history, nautical almanacs, but scant few tomes on the arcane. *Oh, for my second master's library!*

"What a fool I am!" I searched the spines one at a time. "A magical creature that doesn't have a single book about magical creatures!"

Finally, I found something close to what I sought. *An Analysis of the Maladies Plaguing the Serpent's Children of Valaka: Theories Pertaining to the Causes, Treatments, and Reversals.* Kevril had actually bought it for me when we were in Valaka, a lie to occupy my suspicions, but now, perhaps, useful. I delved the precious pages.

Some limited success had been achieved using dragon's blood as a base for a potion to cure the mutations. Yes, dragons were immune to the effects of the wild magic in the Serpent's Eye. So, might a ship somehow imbued with dragon magic possibly confer immunity to those who sailed it? It was a stretch, but possible. I searched the tome from cover to cover, but found no details about how any enchantments or potions might be distilled from dragon blood, let alone how anyone might actually procure blood from a beast large enough to swallow a wagon whole.

"Damn it!" I dropped the book on the table and searched anew, pulling down each volume and setting it aside to make sure I didn't miss anything. Most of them, of course, were Kevril's, and I quashed the impulse to throw each and every one out the stern gallery windows. I wiped my hands against my robe with the thought that he had touched them. Many, I had read and enjoyed myself. A few I'd even purchased for him during my forays into Haven.

Freedom... I'd been free. Free to love...

But no. It had been a lie. I'd always been under guard, a prisoner under escort. Jhavika had said so.

Believe me... Her subtle command stung me like a lash.

Jhavika... Kevril... Lies... Truth...

"Stop it!" I clenched my fists in my hair hard, to the edge of pain, but unable to do any more. My manacles and Jhavika's commands wouldn't allow me to hurt myself. A slave denied her only chance at freedom.

Whirling away from the bookshelf, I cast about the cabin. Darkness outside drew me to the stern gallery windows, my own disheveled reflection, dark eyes wide with panic, then, as I focused beyond, the stars incongruously beautiful. We were anchored near the shore. I couldn't hurt myself, but perhaps there was a way to escape. I tested the bars, but they were solid and closely spaced. I could barely fit my head between them; my hips would undoubtedly thwart any further attempt. Both quarter galleries had been similarly barred. From the starboard-side one, I could see the wooded shore in the light of a crescent moon. So near, but I couldn't reach it. And even if I could escape, to what end? To wander the wilderness until I was devoured by wild beasts? Blunder into Valaka City and get scooped up by Brekka?

I paced the cabin, clenching and unclenching my hands, looking for something—anything—to help me, to occupy my mind, to alleviate the raging conflict.

Eventually, my eyes fell on the liquor cabinet.

Oblivion in a bottle, mine for the taking.

I snatched up the closest bottle. The label displayed two swordfish with their bills crossed under some Northlands script I couldn't read. I didn't know what it was and didn't care. I poured a measure, the aroma of peat and charcoal rising in a pungent cloud. I sipped and choked at the strong flavor. Cutting it with water helped, and I drank it down. I took the bottle and started for the bunk, then shied away. *Too many memories...too many lies...* The chart table then. I sat and drank and read and reread the single book I had that even mentioned dragons. There had to be an answer here somewhere.

By the time the eastern sky began to lighten, I was too drunk to read, and my mind was spinning in circles. The bottle was down by half, and I couldn't even taste it any longer. Still, I slopped liquor into my glass and gulped it down.

Oblivion... Please... Turn me to stone...

"Lady Preel?"

I lifted my eyes to a blurry figure coming into the cabin. Hemp. I opened my mouth to ask him something and hiccupped. I couldn't remember what I wanted to say. "I'm...sorry."

"Sorry?" He approached, and my eyes focused haphazardly. He looked worried. "You're drinkin' whisky for breakfast."

I looked at the bottle, then back at him. "Whisky? It tastes like ashes." I slurred the last badly and lifted the bottle to pour. I couldn't decide which glass to pour into, which seemed strange. I only remembered one, but I saw two. I tried the left one and missed.

"Here, lady. Let me have that." Hemp gently pried the bottle from my grasp, and took away the glasses, too.

"Please, Hemp." I looked after him and remembered what I'd wanted to say. "Turn me into stone."

"What?" He looked distraught. "Lady Preel, you're drunk as a stink weasel. Let me help you to bed."

"Not sleepy. I jus' woke up! I don't *want* to..." I fumbled at his grasping hands, but it proved useless.

"Here you go." He pulled me up from my seat.

My legs folded, but I never hit the floor. I floated up as if I lay on a magic carpet, then realized the Hemp was carrying me. I tried to push him away. The room started spinning. I clenched my eyes closed, and it spun worse.

"Stop spinning! I'm gonna..." Saliva flooded my mouth and I choked. "I'm gonna..."

"Hold fast there!" He put me down on the bunk and snatched up a dustbin in time to catch the flood of sour vomit. One hand deftly held back my hair, while the other held the receptacle. He obviously had experience with this. "There you go, lady. Get it all out. No worries now. We all been there before."

I found a scant measure of solace in his concern for me. When I could speak, I slurred, "Sorry. I'm sorry."

"No need to be *sorry*, you poor thing. Just lie back and let old Hemp take care of you." He lay me back and wiped my chin with a towel, then pressed a cup of water to my lips. I took a mouthful and tried to swallow, but most of it dribbled out. He had the towel ready. "That's okay. You just lie back and rest. You been through hell, and there ain't no shame in tyin' one on. Done so myself on plenty occasion."

"Hemp," I slurred, blinking to focus. "Help me, *please*."

"I'm tryin' as best I can."

"You *can* help me. It's *easy*." Suddenly it was clear to me. My escape hovered before me like a delivering angel.

"How's that?"

"Ask me a question." I reached up and tried to grasp his shirt, but my fingers didn't want to work. "Please!"

Horror painted his blurry features in a caricature of misery, a clown's painted face in the rain. He knew what I wanted him to do. "I *can't*, Lady Preel. I *won't*. You don't know what you're sayin'. You just lie back and sleep. You'll feel better. I promise."

"No, I *won't!*" I closed my eyes, but the cabin resumed spinning. "I'm going *mad*, Hemp. I'm hearing voices and I can't... I can't *do* this anymore!" Tears came in a torrent, wracking sobs shaking me like convulsions, hate, love, and memories a tornado in my drunken mind.

Strong arms enfolded me, holding me tight, kind whispers in my ear. "You just hold fast, Lady Preel. You can do this. You're the strongest person I know, you are. Just think what it'll be when all this is behind us. We'll be free, you and me both. Just think on that."

He didn't understand that I would never be free. I would always be a truthsayer, a slave to my own curse. I clutched him close and wailed my misery into his shoulder until I had no voice left. One simple question would have ended my pain.

Chapter Nine
A Transfer of Flag

Soldiers do not lose their tempers in battle.
The Lessons of Quen Lau Ush

From the journal of Jhavika Keshmir –
I left the pirate life for greater opportunities, and here I am,
risking my life on the deck of a ship again. Without my
scourge, however, I find myself constantly wary. I'm not used
to being around people who are not under my control.

I leaned on *Tiger Lily*'s quarterdeck rail, restlessly scratching long
lines in the teak with my pike hand. Our search of the southwest coast
of Twin Capes Isle had revealed nothing but empty coves and black
sand beaches. Continuing north along the coast, I'd grown ever more
frustrated and the crew ever more nervous, passing me with lowered
eyes or avoiding me entirely. Now we approached the city of Twin
Capes. We would find some other ships here, certainly, and I was
chomping at the bit for information. I shaded my eyes against the
blazing morning sunlight, squinting at the distant anchorage as the bay
opened before us.

"Three ships at anchor!" the lookout called down. "None of them is *Scourge!*"

"We should be so lucky," I muttered, raising my spyglass and panning it over the anchorage: one low-slung smuggler, a small junk, and a beamy galleon. But just because *Scourge* wasn't here now didn't mean she *hadn't* been. "Anchor the ship and launch boats, Captain. We question the ships for any word of *Scourge*, then send fifty of my people ashore to question the locals."

"Aye, your ladyship!" As Niland gave the orders, I bided my time, scanning the city.

The only true city on the isle of Twin Capes was an anachronism, hardly what most would call a proper city at all, but still, a city-state in its own right. The local government was rumored to be chaotic and adversarial—numerous tribal chiefs vying for supremacy—but hailing from Haven, I knew this wasn't antithetical to success. Near ten thousand islanders inhabited the vast conglomeration of bamboo, wood, and thatch structures. Though most buildings were smallish, many towered over their neighbors, vast community lodges with peaked roofs reaching high toward the sky. There were no fortifications, but the islanders were vicious and proficient fighters when provoked.

Despite the rapidly shallowing bay that deprived the city of deep-shore access for shipping, Twin Capes City was a thriving port. All cargo was ferried out to ships in long, sturdy canoes sporting fearsome figureheads. I watched a small fleet shove off from the sandy beach even before we dropped anchor. The canoes were crewed by smiling men and women and heavily laden with everything from pigs to fresh fruits and vegetables. They surrounded *Tiger Lily*, shouting out greetings and offers for trade, lifting their goods high for inspection. The islanders were disappointed when they found out all we wanted was information. I, in turn, was disappointed with their answers.

"No *Scourge*, fine lady!" The dark-skinned islander stood at the prow of his canoe, shrugging sadly, his words lilting with the local accent. "Not for some months! You trade for nice pig, banana, mango, maybe some pretty to share your bed?"

I eyed his muscled torso and considered for a moment. A distraction would be welcome, but we had no time for pleasure. "No.

You're sure you've seen no sign, heard no word of *Scourge*? Maybe from another ship? A pirate ship?"

"No see, no word." He shrugged again. "We see pirate, yes. *Crimson Hawk* come here sometime. Trade plenty! Trade and drink and spend gold."

I knew *Crimson Hawk*, a sleek three-masted corsair with a crew of seventy or so. Captain Bikka Patak—a half-islander, half-Morrgrey buccaneer I'd met a few times while serving under Captain Kohl—was both ruthless and intelligent. Just the type of pirate Kevril would recruit.

"You know where *Crimson Hawk* lies?" If they frequented the city for pleasure, they might lair nearby and pick off merchantmen passing from Toki to Hyko. Some pirates had become so regular in their pillaging of trade ships that their tactics had evolved to resemble tithing. They took payment in gold and let the ships go so they could be fleeced another day.

"I might know this, if you trade some, fine lady." The man grinned again.

I gritted my teeth. "Te-shan, put an arrow into that canoe's figurehead."

"Yes, your ladyship."

The islander's eyes widened as my komei strung his great bow and drew back an arrow. Before he could protest, the arrow quivered in the serpentine figurehead.

"Tell me where *Crimson Hawk* lies or the next one pierces your heart!" I warned.

The man glared at me, then pointed north. "Twenty miles, a cove with fresh water. That's where *Crimson Hawk* anchors! You go now! No trade, you go!"

I considered for a moment what to do. My first priority remained finding information about *Scourge*. However, *Crimson Hawk* posed an interesting opportunity.

"Captain Niland, change of plans. We question the other ships only, and quickly. If they've seen no sign of *Scourge*, we haul anchor." All things considered, this was the best news I'd had in a week, and I wasn't about to let it go to waste.

It didn't take long for the boats to return with no good news. None had espied *Scourge* or heard recent word of Kevril.

"Captain Niland, secure our boats smartly and haul anchor. Set course around the western cape and north along the coast as close inshore as you deem prudent." We still had to survey the coves north of Twin Capes City. Besides, skirting the shore would keep us hidden from any anchored ship until we were right on top of them.

We shipped anchor, set sail, and made our way around the western cape under tautly trimmed sails. We rounded the cape in gusty winds without a single mishap; hardly the lackadaisical merchant style of sailing I'd found when I came aboard. Captain Niland and his crew were shaping up. All they'd needed was the proper encouragement.

Training of additional crew was also going well. I'd gone through my soldiers with a fine-toothed comb, rooting out anyone who had even an inkling of nautical aptitude, and commanded them to learn all they could in the handling of the ship. Not that *Tiger Lily*'s crew needed their help, but when we took *Scourge*, I intended to keep her, which meant putting a prize crew aboard. Haven still needed a proper navy, after all. For that, I would need able sailors.

While we made our way north in the fluky inshore breezes, I pondered strategy. At the outset of this trip, I'd advised Niland of what to expect if and when we encountered *Scourge*, and how to prepare his crew. He'd paled at the word 'battle', but didn't argue. But now I had to consider that we might encounter both *Scourge* and *Crimson Hawk* at the same time. That would take more finesse.

My first step was clear; I would focus on *Scourge*. That was where my treasures would be found: my scourge and Preel. *What must she be going through?* I wondered, captive of the man she had loved but now believed to have manipulated her. *Torture... It must be torture.* Would she be of any use to me, other than her truthsayer abilities, when I got her back?

First things first, Jhavika...

Kevril had a head start, but not enough to have procured many allies yet. Pirates were notoriously distrustful. It would take days of negotiation for him to convince Patak to join him. Given the proper time and incentive, I'm sure he would; in fact, I had counted on it when I assigned him the task of assembling my navy. But I wasn't going to give him that time. Patak was a hothead, but he wasn't stupid. I expected he'd cut and run if we attacked *Scourge*.

But what if I only found *Crimson Hawk* at anchor? That bore some thinking. I lusted for a more seaworthy and spritely ship than this lug of a merchantman. A corsair would fit the bill nicely. Not to mention that every pirate ship I commandeered was one less for Kevril to acquire as an ally. Yes, I wanted *Crimson Hawk* whether they had information on Kevril or not.

But how? Take them at anchor, parley and ask if they'd seen Scourge*, then betray them, or play some kind of ruse?* I glanced around *Tiger Lily*, noting her corpulent lines and sluggish handling, obviously a merchant. No pirate would parley with a merchant; a predator doesn't negotiate with prey. *Well, that could work to our advantage.*

"Captain Niland, if by chance we find both *Scourge* and *Crimson Hawk* together, we'll engage *Scourge* directly, bringing *Tiger Lily* alongside, grappling, raking her deck with crossbow fire, then boarding her. They'll give us no quarter, but any of their people who lay down arms or are found unarmed will be spared." *Waste not, want not*, I thought, and there was always Preel to consider. *If some overzealous sailor killed her...* I refused to allow myself to think on that. "Relay those orders and prepare your people."

"Yes, your ladyship." He paused, then asked, "What if it's only *Crimson Hawk*?"

"That'll depend on how things unfold, Captain. Until we see what's what, keep all soldiers and weapons below decks. I don't want to tip our hand heedlessly."

The hours passed slowly as we proceeded along the coast, the tension building as we passed one empty cove after another. I paced the quarterdeck, Te-shan at my heels with one hand resting on his katana. I'd begun to think that the disgruntled islander in Twin Capes City had lied to me when the call came.

"Masts beyond the point!" the forward lookout cried. "Ship at anchor! Two...no, *three* masts!"

"Just *one* ship?" I snatched a spyglass from a sailor.

"One ship only!" the lookout replied.

Three masts... That told me nothing, really, since both *Scourge* and *Crimson Hawk* bore three masts.

"Orders, your ladyship?"

"Until we know what we're dealing with, sail on!" The cove opened up off our starboard bow to reveal a single ship at anchor. Careful examination through my spyglass confirmed it was *Crimson Hawk*—her elaborate winged figurehead was unmistakable. Several figures on deck sprang into action. They'd spotted us. If we tried a direct attack, they'd be bristling with steel by the time we could lay alongside. I had little doubt we could still take them, but it would be costly. However, they *were* pirates, and they had no notion of what surprises *Tiger Lily* held. They saw a merchantman, fat and low in the water with full holds.

A slow smile spread across my lips. "They'll try to take us for plunder, Captain, and I mean to let them."

"What?" Niland gaped at me.

"Wear ship, but do it sloppily. Let the spanker jibe freely. Tangle the braces, and sheet the headsails like a lubber. We want them to think we're panicked."

"Yes, your ladyship!" He relayed the orders, and I hardly thought his panic feigned.

We came around, and the spanker jibed hard. A jib sheet flew free, the sail flapping uselessly before it was slowly taken under control. Aloft, our yards were at all angles. I raised my glass and watched *Crimson Hawk* let go her anchor rode on a buoy and set sail, her long, black pennant unfurling from her mizzen.

"She's coming after us, Captain. Well done." I gauged the situation. To an uninformed eye, the pirates had all the advantages: a faster, more maneuverable ship, the weather gauge, and apparent surprise. *Perfect.* "When *Crimson Hawk* closes, we will fly a flag of surrender. Your sailors are to back away from the rail with their hands raised when they lay alongside. Once the pirates board, the soldiers below will surprise them with a volley of crossbow fire, then rush up on deck and overwhelm them."

"Yes, your ladyship," he replied, a little steadier.

There was only one more thing I had to do to make sure Captain Patak bought the ruse. "Te-shan, I need you to go below. Stand just inside the sterncastle until the pirates come aboard, then return to my side with all haste."

"Your ladyship..." His eyes widened behind the gruesome mask of his helm, then narrowed as his gaze shifted to the other sailors and officers around us. "I obey, but..."

"Don't worry, Te-shan," I raised my voice just enough to be heard. "If anyone harms me in your absence, you will come back up here and slaughter them all. Do you understand?"

"Yes, your ladyship!" He bowed, turned on his heel, and left the quarterdeck.

Gods, how I could use a thousand like him. I fantasized about an army of komei under my banner as I stormed the god-emperor's palace.

Focus, Jhavika!

I rested my left hand on the hilt of my cutlass and paced the quarterdeck as if I hadn't a care. Of course, I did. Aside from being stabbed in the back, there was a corsair full of pirates bearing down on us. I recalled my last sea action and smiled grimly; that had been the day I got the scourge and lashed Kevril Longbright across the face.

Oh, if I had only known then the power I wielded...

I gauged *Crimson Hawk* through my spyglass, the row of grinning pirates on the rail, grappling hooks in hand. The few crossbowmen in the tops had their weapons lowered, expecting an easy catch. I suppressed a grin of my own. They had no idea.

"Bring it on, Captain Patak," I muttered beneath my breath, tapping my pike hand on the rail. "I've got a surprise for you."

Crimson Hawk came in on a steep intercept course, her pirates roaring challenges, threats, and bawdy epithets. Hubris would be their downfall. I had Niland make a show of panicked flight, but when the outcome was clear, I called it.

"Let fly sheets and hoist a white flag!"

Niland complied with alacrity. The crew of *Crimson Hawk* cheered in premature victory as they bore in and lay along our windward side. Twenty grappling hooks flew across the gap, and the ships came together with a delicate groan of timbers and the hemp bumpers they'd placed over the side. Pirates swarmed aboard casually, weapons in hand, but with little menace, confident they had already won. As our sailors backed away, hands raised, I recognized Captain Patak at the fore of the pirates, a boarding axe in each hand.

Time for a little distraction.

"Captain Patak! Well met!" I called out, waving from the quarterdeck rail. Te-shan raced up the leeward steps to my side as the pirate captain's eyes fixed on me. "It's been quite a long time!"

His eyes widened. "Keshmir? What the fucking hell are you—"

A roar from below our decks cut him off. From the twin hatch coamings lunged a score of crossbowmen. They fired into the boarders from only yards away. Several pirates fell, but the others reacted as I'd predicted, bellowing in rage and charging. Dozens of my soldiers boiled up from the hatches, and dozens more streamed from fore and aft, boarding pikes leading the charge. Even faced with these overwhelming numbers, however, the pirates didn't waver. Steel clashed, and screams rose on the air.

It was a glorious, bloody mess. To their credit, Patak and his crew fought well, but the end was never in doubt. We took them in a span of ten hard-fought minutes, and I didn't even have to draw my sword. Two intrepid pirates did manage to gain the quarterdeck, but Te-shan cut them both down with lightning efficiency. When the outcome became evident, Patak ordered his crew to retreat and cut the grappling lines free, but my soldiers pursued and drove them away from the conjoined rails. When the last of the resistance had been quelled and the ships were hove to, I strode down and across our blood-soaked deck, vaulting over the rail onto *Crimson Hawk* where the surviving pirates were being held on their knees, my soldier's swords at their throats. Miraculously, Patak was still alive, though he bore two crossbow wounds and a deep gash to his wrist that bled freely.

"My apologies for the ruse, Captain." I sidled up to him with a condescending smile. "Not very sporting, I know, but...well, I guess I *am* still a pirate at heart."

"Jhavika Keshmir! You sniveling little bilge cunt!" Patak spat blood, ignoring the blade at his throat. "Who are you fucking now to better your position? I heard you went ashore in Haven to ply your trade with the lubbers!"

"Really, Bikka?" I rested the tip of my pike hand on his chin. "I'm *Queen* of Haven now, and I have you under my sword. You think belligerence is going to work well for you?"

He grinned through bloody teeth. "Kill me and be done with it, whore! If you want groveling, you've come to the wrong shop!"

"Kill you?" I laughed and leaned down close. "Oh, I'm not going to *kill* you, Bikka. I've got a *use* for you. Haven needs a navy, and you'd be a perfect recruit. Now, if you want to keep your testicles, tell me if you've seen the corsair *Scourge* recently, and where."

"Fuck off, Jhavika!"

I sighed and stepped back. "Well, if you value your balls less than a little information, so be it. Te-shan, bring me Captain Patak's testicles, please."

"At once, your ladyship!" He stepped around me and drew his wakizashi.

"Wait!" Patak bellowed as my komei bent down, blade in hand. "Jhavika, wait!"

I could have stopped Te-shan with a word, but didn't. For the insult alone, Patak had earned this, and he didn't need testicles to command a ship for me. His bellow of protest went shrill in the end, and he collapsed writhing to the deck.

Te-shan turned and bowed, proffering a bloody lump of meat in one hand. I hooked it with my pike hand and flicked it overboard.

"You there," I commanded one of my soldiers, "bind the captain's wounds and take him aboard *Tiger Lily*. Chain him below. He can serve me later as a eunuch. Now, who's next?" My eyes scanned the remaining few officers. "Oh, come now, one answer shouldn't be worth so much pain. Have you seen *Scourge* or Kevril Longbright, and, if so, where and when?"

Silence at first, then one younger officer spoke up. "We haven't seen *Scourge* in months. Last we heard, Longbright was workin' for you."

"That's true, he was." I stepped up to the officer and leaned down, resting the tip of my pike hand upon his chin. "You're *sure* you haven't seen them?"

"Absolutely sure. We been workin' the main trade routes for half a year, sellin' our booty at Twin Capes and livin' high. Last time we saw *Scourge* was maybe four months ago."

"Very well." I left him and assessed my new ship. *Crimson Hawk* was hardly kept in fine trim, but she was a seaworthy, weatherly, and fast, far better for my purposes than a merchant galleon. "Captain Niland! Take these pirates and chain them below aboard *Tiger Lily*. Start transferring provisions and people over to *Crimson Hawk*. I'll be leaving you a skeleton crew, along with a dozen of my most capable soldiers. You'll take your ship back to Haven and await me there. My people will have orders to dismember you slowly if you don't follow my commands to the letter."

"Yes, your ladyship!" He started barking orders with a will, evidently pleased to be soon out of my presence. I honestly couldn't blame him.

The crew got to work, and I went aft to explore my new cabin. Petak wasn't much for luxuries, but he did enjoy some comforts. His liquor cabinet was well-stocked, and he even had a bookshelf, though there wasn't anything there I would have been caught dead reading. I was going through his personal things when a crewman knocked at the door.

"Your ladyship, a cutter flyin' Haven colors has been sighted to the north, inshore working south. They changed course toward us."

"Excellent!" I went on deck, my heart pounding with the thought of word about Kevril.

The cutter came alongside, and a young officer I didn't know swarmed up the boarding ladder to salute. "Lady Keshmir! Lady Brilla Balshi sent me to report to you." He handed off a waxed packet.

I wondered how Brilla could have completed her search of the islands to the north of Twin Capes before I completed mine, but then recalled our starting point and angle of wind. *Hyacinth* would have sailed three points north of our course, almost a beam reach compared to our close-hauled beat. Even an advantage of two knots would have left her plenty of time for a search before sending the cutter to find me.

"Any sign of *Scourge*?" I took the packet and cut it open.

"No, your ladyship. No sign at all."

"Bugger it!" I read the report quickly. As the young officer had said, they hadn't sighted *Scourge*, and were proceeding to search the windward shores of her assigned islands pending further orders. I called for a pen and scrawled left-handed on the back of the same letter.

Brilla,

Continue your search of the windward shores of your islands, then head south and search the windward shore of Twin Capes. If you don't find *Scourge*, take up station at Twin Capes City. From there you will receive and forward on to me any messages from our other ships. If you don't receive word from Yorish within a week, dispatch a cutter to Hyko to find him. I have captured and assumed command of *Crimson Hawk*, a three-masted corsair (which your young cutter officer will now recognize), so don't send anyone looking for me aboard *Tiger Lily*. We will begin searching the islands to the south of Twin Capes, so forward all reports to me there.

Jhavika

I handed the packet back to the officer. "Here. Take this back to Brilla with all haste."

"Yes, your ladyship!" He tucked the packet away and scrambled down the ladder into the cutter. They shoved off, filled their sail, and bore off northward.

"Captain Niland, wrap things up here quickly! I want to be underway before the damned sun goes down!"

Chapter Ten
An Enemy's Counsel

Trust is a rare commodity, worth more than gold.
The Lessons of Quen Lau Ush

From the diary of Kevril Longbright –
Negotiating from a position of strength is easy. I'll respect the hell out of anyone who can do it well when their opponent holds a better hand, and both parties know it.

Waiting has never been my strong suit. If I have something to keep myself busy, I'm fine, but idle time wears on me like torture. Our third day at anchor, I was beside myself and driving my crew to distraction. Not being able to spend those idle hours with Preel tormented me.

My feet and leg were healing slowly but cleanly, thanks to Bert's evil-smelling salve. I resumed my daily exercise of pacing and even started sparring again, but I couldn't spend more than a few hours a day on my feet. Reading presented the problem of having to send someone into the great cabin to retrieve a book, which disturbed Preel. Hemp had informed me that she'd had a breakdown after waking from her last question. Alcohol seemed to be her only solace, which worried me, but Hemp told me flat out that cutting her off would only make things worse.

As a distraction, I took an interest in the ballista Kivan was building on the quarterdeck. We set up floating targets and rotated crews for practice. I made it a competition; the winning team won a bottle of my best rum and became the new ballista's permanent crew. I also continued to press my younger officers in navigation, mathematics, and seamanship. As my sole midshipman, Boxley bore the brunt of my attention; I pushed her so hard in her schooling that I thought she might stab me. I'd learned from Quibly that the newcomer Doria could read, write, and had an aptitude for figures, so I asked her if she had any interest in becoming a midshipman and working toward a higher rank. She was young enough to be trainable, and I thought that it might be good for the morale of the newcomers to see one of their own rise in the ranks. She had the temerity to laugh in my face. I tried not to spend too much time in the wardroom, but there was no place else for me to go. Sitting alone in the guest cabin left me thinking about my own cabin and its singular occupant, my wife, who despised me.

Dwelling on Preel, I knew, would lead me to madness.

As far as our goal of destroying the scourge went, I'd discussed potential courses of action with anyone whom I thought might have ideas, including Wix, Quibly, Bert, and even Hemp. Nobody aboard knew anything of a dragonship. Sailors trade tales like trollops trade the pox, so if not one of a hundred had ever heard of it, it seemed likely that whoever possessed it kept its existence a secret. Kivan volunteered to take a boat to Valaka City to delve the bookshops and search for any sages who might know anything at all about the dragonship. I considered it, but postponed the trip. It was only one more day until I could ask Preel another question, and, unless she came up with a better question, I intended to ask her where the dragonship lay. If I got a reasonable answer, I meant to leave immediately, and didn't want to delay until Kivan returned.

I was sitting in the guest cabin with my feet up, trying to read, when a cry of "Sail ho! East, nor'east!" came almost as a reprieve.

Dropping my book and jamming my feet into my boots, I snatched up a jacket and cutlass and hurried up to the quarterdeck. Miko had beat me there, and looked grim as she handed over a spyglass. I didn't need one to spot the small galleon rounding the point. Even as I raised it, the lookout confirmed what I suspected.

"Haven flag! Two-masted galleon! Looks like *Golden Harlot*, sir!"

"It's Tan!" I slapped the spyglass closed and stuffed it through my belt. There was only one thing we could do. "We've got to take them, Miko! If they escape or get a cutter off to Jhavika, we're sunk!"

"Aye, sir!" She cupped her hands and shouted, "All hands, man your stations! Wix, cut the anchor free! Rauley, topcrews aloft and make all sail! Kivan, man your ballistae!"

My crew scrambled to their stations, and Wix bellowed for boarding axes forward. I clipped my cutlass to my belt and assessed the sea, wind, and the ships' relative positions. We had the weather gauge, but it all boiled down to getting off anchor and underway before Tan raked us with arrows, set our sails afire, or lit out for a rendezvous with Jhavika. If she ran, we'd chase her down, but we couldn't do that if she managed to damage *Scourge* first. If we could force an engagement, I was confident we would win. The smaller *Golden Harlot* couldn't support as large a continent as I had, my pirates were experienced in fighting at sea, and Kivan's ballistae could wreak more havoc from a farther distance than Tan's best bowmen.

Tan knew all of this as well as I did, so when *Golden Harlot* turned upwind, cross-sheeted her jibs, and let fly her main sheets, my jaw dropped.

Heaving to? What the...

"Heaving to?" Miko made a rude noise. "That's stupid."

I frowned. "Tan might be a merchant captain, but she's not stupid."

"A ruse then? Luring us in until the rest of her fleet comes around the point?"

"No. That wouldn't make strategic sense. Jhavika would spread her fleet out to search for us. I think Tan just happened upon us." I hoped so, at least, but I wasn't going to bet our lives on it. "Lookout! Watch for the approach of any other ships."

"Aye, captain," the voice replied from above.

Canvas fell from our yards, snapping in the breeze above the sound of axes thumping into the thigh-thick anchor rode.

"Captain!" Boxley called breathlessly as she dashed up the quarterdeck steps. "She's hoisting a white flag!"

"Wix! Avast there!" I raised my spyglass again and beheld the long, white banner of parley. This was the last thing I'd expected. Tan was either surrendering or wanted to talk. "Rauley, slack sheets and furl the squares. Wix, splice the anchor rode. Boxley, get up to the foretop and keep a sharp eye on *Golden Harlot*! Sing out if they put a cutter in the water or fall off the wind."

"I still think it's a trick." Miko had her own glass focused on *Golden Harlot*, but spared me a suspicious glance. "If she gets a boat away..."

"Then we'd best be ready. Rauley, splash a longboat on our starboard side and step its mast. Lieutenant Quiff, if we have to chase down their cutter, you'll take the longboat after them; pick a crew."

"Aye, sir!" He grinned and bellowed for volunteers. Quiff might not be my sharpest officer, but he dearly loved a fight.

"On deck!" Boxley called, and my throat tightened. "They're lowering a skiff!"

"A skiff or a cutter?"

"A skiff, sir! Three people boarding, oars only!"

"So, looks like Tan wants to talk." Miko lowered her glass and gave me a sidelong look. "Best not mention our last meeting."

"I won't. She'll never forgive me for burning her ship."

She flashed me a sly grin. "I was thinking of your rude interruption of her tryst with Maurice Malchi, but I imagine she's still pissed about *Yellow Blossom*, too."

"I'll keep the conversation on a professional level, rest assured." I drew a breath to call for my steward to fetch a presentable jacket, and remembered I'd given over my steward to Preel. Straightening my patched jacket and cursing under my breath, I stepped to the taffrail and watched the small boat row over.

"You don't think Jhavika's aboard, do you?"

I looked at Miko sidelong. "Aboard the smallest ship in her armada? Not a chance. She'd surround herself with the biggest force she could put afloat."

"Can't argue that."

They stopped within easy hailing distance, and a young officer stood and raised a hand. "Captain Longbright!"

"Yes!"

"Compliments from Captain Tan, sir, and she would like to speak to you on neutral ground."

"Do you think she's one of Jhavika's slaves?" Miko asked quietly.

"No." I'd already thought about it. "I imagine Jhavika has commanded her people to kill me on sight. Parley sounds more like Tan."

Miko's grunt didn't sound convinced.

Raising my voice to address the skiff again, I pointed to the long strip of black sand. "The beach, then. I'll build a fire and bring the wine."

"An escort of two only. In one hour," the officer said.

"One hour. Tell Captain Tan she can anchor in our lee."

"With respect, sir, we'll stay hove to."

"Very well." I sketched a salute and turned away.

"She doesn't trust you," Miko muttered low.

"Would you, in her position?"

"I'm not sure I trust you in *my* position." She grinned and nodded to my jacket. "You may want to put on decent clothes, sir. You don't want Tan to think you don't respect her."

"True." I did respect Tan. She had guts to call for parley with a captain who commanded a superior force and faster ship. I certainly didn't want to offend her. I needed to know what Jhavika was doing. "Rauley, splash the jolly boat and call up Tansy and..." I thought for a moment. "...and Spike. Thirty minutes!" Adding the leader of the newcomers might help their morale, since my attempt to recruit Doria had fallen flat.

"Aye, sir!"

"Sure you don't want Wix along?" Miko asked.

"No, I'm not sure, but he's too intimidating." I nodded to *Golden Harlot*. "Keep an eye on things."

"Always, sir." She saluted as I went below.

I asked Bert to put together a basket for my meeting with Tan, and went to the guest cabin. As I shook out a decent shirt and jacket and spit-polished my boots, I missed Hemp yet again. I shaved, combed my hair, dressed, clipped a cutlass to my belt, looped the scourge to my hip, and went on deck. The jolly boat was ready, Tansy at the oars and Spike seated in the bow clutching a basket and small folding table. I boarded and manned the tiller.

Thankfully, there was no surf, so we landed without getting soaked. After dragging the jollyboat up on the beach, I took the basket and table from Spike and ordered them to collect some driftwood for a fire. It wasn't cold, but I needed one for other reasons. Bert had included a small white tablecloth in the basket—an elegant touch— and I set the table with wine, a plate of cheeses and biscuits, two fine crystal glasses, and a bowl of olives. Lastly, I poured a bottle of oil onto the pile of driftwood and lit it.

"Skiff coming," Tansy said, shading her eyes.

"Good." I squinted, but couldn't tell if the uniformed figure in the stern was Captain Tan or not. "I want both of you to mind your manners. This is a parley. Draw no weapons unless they do first."

They both agreed, though Spike grumbled. He wasn't used to rules. I watched the skiff near, and finally recognized Captain Tan. She didn't look happy. Well, I supposed I didn't either.

Two burly seamen pulled the skiff ashore, then followed their captain up the beach, hands resting on the hilts of weapons. I kept my hand away from my cutlass, and assessed them professionally, but it's impossible to know how good a fighter someone is just by looking at them. Tansy was deadly with a cutlass, and Spike had been street fighting his entire life. I felt confident we could at least hold our own.

Tan stopped several strides away, glanced at the table, then fixed her eyes on me. "I didn't come here to socialize, Captain."

"Neither did I, but I see no reason we can't be civil." I worked the cork from the bottle and poured. "Please, join me. I'd very much like to hear the latest news from Haven. I'm afraid I left in a hurry."

"You mean you *fled* after murdering five council members!" she snapped.

"Murdered five—" I fumbled the bottle and spilled red wine across the white linen cloth. Biting back a curse, I put down the bottle, heaved a calming breath, and stared straight at Tan. "I murdered no one, Captain. I admit that I tried to kill Jhavika Keshmir, but that attempt failed. The other council members were alive and well when I left Lord Balshi's party."

"That's not how Jhavika tells it." Tan stepped closer, her escort at her heels. She glanced down at the mess I'd made of the table, then back to me. "Why should I believe you?"

"Because there's no way in *hell* I could have killed five council members alone, and even less of a chance that I could have gotten a big enough force to do it into Balshi's palace! He has hundreds of guards, for Odea's sake! There would have been a pitched battle, and I *still* would have failed." I picked up a glass and stepped back from the table, wondering what other lies Jhavika had spread about me. Would I ever be able to return to Haven? "Who were killed?"

"Balshi, Fa-Chen, Tinworthy, Hatsu, and Temuso."

"Temuso? Gods and devils!" So, he had arranged for his own death in the event of my failure after all. I felt like I'd thrust a dagger into the heart of a friend. I drank down my wine and cleared the lump from my throat.

Tan cocked her head as she considered me. "You make a valid point, captain, and to tell you the truth, I've grown skeptical of Jhavika's story."

"Believe me, Captain, Getashi Temuso was my friend. He saved my life at that party and was very much alive when I left. Jhavika's lying. She had the others murdered. It must have been part of her plan all along."

"Well, then her plan was successful; she now controls the Council of Lords and has labeled *you* a traitor."

I narrowed my eyes at her. "So why are you here talking to a traitor, Captain?"

Tan remained quiet for a moment, gazing out to the ships, then she picked up the other glass and sipped. "Because I want to know the *truth*. Did you cut off Jhavika's hand, or is that another lie?"

I barked a laugh. "Oh, no, I did that. But I didn't kill anyone."

"Brilla Balshi, Ursula Roque, and Tambris Matesh all corroborated Jhavika's story, and Fa-Chen, Tinworthy, and Hatsu's heirs are backing her as well. Are they *all* lying?"

"They're saying whatever she tells them to say, Captain." I shook my head. "But if you were so suspicious, why did you follow Jhavika's orders?"

"I work for the Council," she said flatly. "Jhavika *is* the Council now. I had little choice other than to go along."

I shook my head. "You *always* have a choice. You could have sailed away."

"It wasn't quite that easy." Tan shot me a scathing look. "Jhavika commandeered every decent ship in the harbor. A few captains refused, and she had them executed." She downed her wine. "I thought it best to follow her orders, at least at the time." She reached for the bottle. "So, are you going to tell me why you tried to kill Jhavika?" She filled her glass and held the bottle out to me.

"Let's just say it was a business disagreement." Taking the bottle, I filled my glass.

"That's bullshit. You weren't even working for Jhavika at the time. You were working for the Council." She plucked an olive from the bowl and followed it with a slice of sharp cheese. "You're many things, Captain Longbright, but I know from personal experience that you don't slaughter people needlessly. Jhavika, however, sailed from Haven with three ship's officers dangling from her foremast yardarm. She's acting likes she's a gods-damn *queen*! I don't know why the others are backing her every word, but her story doesn't ring true."

I sighed. *She believes me.* It was time to tell Tan the truth, or at least most of it. "They're backing her because of *this*, Captain." I patted the scourge at my hip, which drew a curious look from Tan and glares from her escort. "This will be hard for you to believe, but Jhavika Keshmir has been enslaving people with this scourge for years. It's magic. I know because I used to be ensorcelled by it. Anyone she lashes with it has to follow her commands."

Tan's eyes widened, then narrowed. "You're right; it *is* hard to believe. If you're spelled, how did you attack her?"

"I broke the enchantment six months ago. I thought that I could still work with her, that we could still be partners. I was wrong." I downed my wine and put the glass down on the table. "Jhavika kidnapped and enslaved my wife to pressure me into doing her bidding. I got her back the night of the party, but she's been commanded by Jhavika to despise me, and...she does." *Preel...* "I'm going to destroy the scourge. It's the only way to beat Jhavika."

"Why haven't you done it already?"

"It's not so easy."

Tan looked dubious. "Why not?"

"Because it's virtually invulnerable to harm." I plucked the scourge off my hip and tossed it into the blazing fire. It sat there atop the coals, not even blackening in the heat.

Tan stared at the scourge for a long while, then filled both our glasses. She downed hers in a single swallow and put the glass down, her icy blue eyes fixed on me. "So, how are you going to destroy it?"

"I'm working on that, but I don't know if I should tell you." I shrugged. "You *are* working for Jhavika, after all."

"I don't work for Jhavika, Captain Longbright, I work for the Haven Council of Lords. And I now believe that Jhavika has usurped the Council. I'd say that voids my contract."

"Still, if she got her hands on you, you'd tell her everything you know."

She shrugged. "Probably true. I could lead her astray for you, if you like. Tell her I scoured Valaka from one end to the other and saw neither hide nor hair of you."

I shook my head. "Too risky. If she caught you lying to her, you'd be the next one to dance on her yardarm."

"True." Tan turned to the fire and prodded the scourge with the toe of her boot. It remained unburnt. "Gods-damned magic..." She turned back to me. "Then the best I can offer you is to sail away, I'm afraid."

I nodded. "I'd suggest Mati. If I can destroy the scourge, there might be a Haven to return to, but if I can't, you should tell the Mati parliament what's happened. Also tell them that Jhavika's enslaved their ambassador to Toki. His name is Fawahah. He's undoubtedly spying for her." I pointed to the scourge atop the burning brands. "If Jhavika gets that thing back, there'll be no stopping her short of war."

The muscles at Tan's jaw bunched and writhed. Finally, she nodded. "All right." Stepping forward, she extended a hand. "If you're lying to me, Kevril Longbright, I'll see you in hell."

"If I'm lying to you, Captain Tan, may Odea send me there herself." I shook her hand. "Fair winds to you."

"And to you." Tan started for her skiff, then stopped and turned back. "What are your plans if you *do* manage to destroy that thing?"

I opened my mouth, but realized that I didn't have anything to say. The truth seemed prudent. "I'll be happy enough to get my wife back. I don't have any plans other than that. Jhavika's as much a slave to the scourge as her thralls are to her. I'm not in this for vengeance."

She nodded, then said, "Still, she's not likely to thank you for destroying her secret weapon. She'll still be out for your head."

"Probably, but she won't have an army of slaves behind her. In fact, they'll probably lynch her. If I hear that that's happened, I'll sail back to Haven and start looking for allies."

"If you free the Council of Jhavika's influence, you'll earn their gratitude. Haven would still need a navy. You could still end up an admiral."

I chuckled. "Or dead."

She shrugged. "Well, if you survive, send word. I'd be willing to sail under your pennant, Captain."

My jaw dropped. Even after I'd burnt her ship and embarrassed her in front of her crew, Tan not only believed me, but would sail under my command? She was more forgiving than I would have been. "I... Thank you, Captain."

Tan saluted me. I returned it and watched her walk back to her skiff. I poured another glass of wine and sipped it as they rowed back to *Golden Harlot*, my opinion of Captain Tan even higher than it had been before.

"A wise woman indeed..."

"Nice job, that, sir." Spike jerked his head toward the departing skiff. "You sure got a way of bringin' folks over to your side."

I nodded vaguely, told Tansy and Spike to pack up, and nudged the scourge out of the fire with a stick. When I picked it up, the leather wasn't even warm. I hooked it back to my hip and prayed to Odea that it could, in fact, be destroyed.

Chapter Eleven
Location, Location, Location

Sometimes, there is no joy in victory.
The Lessons of Quen Lau Ush

From the diary of Kevril Longbright –
I would sooner have thrust a knife into my own gut than torment Preel with my presence, but we had no choice. She was our only weapon, our only path to the destruction of our common bane. I prayed constantly that she understood.

The following evening, when Miko and I stepped once again into the great cabin, my determination almost failed. Preel sat exactly as she had before, wearing the same robe over nightclothes, a glass of wine nestled in the cubby beside the bed. The cabin hadn't changed that I could notice, either.

The only difference was Preel herself.

Her dark eyes were vacant and red-rimmed, staring blankly at her feet, her cheeks sunken and complexion sallow. The knuckles of her clenched hands shown white, trembling, her lips pressed together hard, jaw muscles flexing as if holding back a hysterical scream. Preel wasn't just broken, she was shattered.

Seeing her like this undid me. I didn't know any other way to describe it. I longed to go to her, take her in my arms, comfort her, promise her everything would be all right, but I couldn't. I'd promised not to touch her, and I couldn't bear the rejection. Forcing my gaze away from her, I staggered to the navigation table and sat down.

"Somethin' to sip, Captain?"

I looked up at Hemp, surprised. I hadn't even noticed him. "No, thank you, Hemp." I cleared my throat. "Thank you for agreeing to discuss this with us, Preel. You're better at questions than anyone else aboard."

She didn't respond, but reached for her glass. Her hand trembled so badly that I feared she'd spill it, but she pressed it to her lips and downed its volume by half.

"I know you're in a state, Preel, but please, we need your input. If you could ease up on the wine a bit, just long enough to talk to us."

Preel's vacant eyes shifted to me. "You have no *notion* of what I'm going through! Right now, alcohol is the only thing keeping me marginally sane." Her words were slurred, but cutting.

I didn't want to argue that I actually *did* know what she was going through, and knew firsthand that drinking myself into a stupor hadn't helped me cope. What *had* helped me come to grips with my slavery to Jhavika was the kindness of another slave, the very one who now stared at me with bridled hatred.

"I'm concerned for your health, and we need your cognizant opinion, Preel."

She downed her wine and threw the glass across the room. It shattered against the bookcase. "My *cognizant* opinion is that you need to stop fucking with my head! Ask your fucking question and get out!"

Hemp blanched white, and I stared at Preel in shocked silence. She sat there trembling, apoplectic with rage, fear, and who knew what else. I couldn't see her like this.

"Miko, please. You know our options as well as I do."

"Yes, sir. We thought to ask the location of the dragonship next, but we're not sure if that's the best way to go. If it's at the bottom of the sea, that doesn't do us much good. However, if we ask who owns it, or if it's seaworthy, that might not put us any farther forward either. If it's halfway around the world, we're back to square one. If it's nearby, at least, we might scout it out or get some information from Valaka City before asking you our next question. The city has a very long history, and dragons are, of course, a huge part of it. The dragonlords are obsessed with dragon magic and the Serpent's Eye. It's a good bet that someone like this is involved. We'd...like to know your thoughts, Preel."

"My...*thoughts*?" Preel coughed a tremulous laugh, then forced calm. A quaking nod. "Yes. Location first, but ask for a precise one."

"We were thinking a precise latitude and longitude would be best." Miko flicked me a questioning glance, but I could only offer a shrug. Every time I spoke, I tormented the woman I loved, so I decided to keep silent. "Unless you can think of a way to include any other details."

Preel shook her head sharply. "No. Just location. If the ship is enshh— If it's magical, I probably won't even be able to give you that."

"Bugger! That's right. I hadn't considered that, and should have." Asking Preel specific details about enchanted items or creatures often received no answer. I clenched my fists hard. "If this ship can sail into the Serpent's Eye safely, it's safe to assume it's magical. We need to craft the question around that, like we did with the scourge."

"Then ask about something *not* magical that is closely associated with it, or where its owner has chosen to keep it," Preel said.

"Assuming it has an owner," Miko said. "If it's lost or sunk..."

"If it's lost or sunk, so are we," I countered. "Maybe not *owner*, but keeper. Something like this might not be anyone's property, but I'll wager someone's taking care of it."

"Not keeper," Preel said, a little steadier now. "Ships have masters, captains, even if they're not owned outright by a single person. Ask for where the master of the dragonship is keeping it. That should work."

"Okay. Good." I nodded to Hemp. "Pen and paper, Hemp. Miko and I will settle on the exact wording while you see Preel to the quarter gallery."

"Aye, sir." He fetched a paper, pen, and ink, then helped Preel to the head. She needed the assistance.

"So, I think exact latitude and longitude where the master of the dragonship is keeping it." I dabbed the pen and jotted down the question. "That's specific and avoids asking about something magical or anyone's intentions."

"Maybe 'the vessel' instead of 'it,' sir," Miko suggested. "Ambiguity, you know."

"Right." I corrected the question and reviewed it, trying to think past my raging emotions. "That ought to do it, I think."

"I hope so," she agreed. "I feel like we've been anchored here too long. I know it's only been three days, but..."

"I know how you feel." It had actually been three and a half days. We'd asked Preel a question upon our arrival, and were pressing her hard by asking again so soon, especially considering the subject matter. In her current state, I could only pray that she would hold up under the strain.

Preel emerged from the quarter gallery looking even worse than before, her face wan and sheened with sweat. Hemp took her arm and guided her to the bed. I looked away as he helped her out of her robe and tucked her in.

She folded her hands over her stomach and took a deep breath. "Ask."

I nodded to Miko.

"What is the precise latitude and longitude where the master of the dragonship used to safely sail into the Serpent's Eye has chosen to keep the vessel?"

Preel convulsed violently, her back arching and her eyes rolling. I'd never seen her jerk so severely, and it brought me to my feet.

"Twenty-four degrees, eighteen minutes, five seconds south latitude by two hundred seventy-four degrees, seven minutes, thirty-two seconds longitude." The words tore from her throat as if wrenched from her very soul, harsh and grating.

I went to the bedside to check on Preel, but remembered my promise and kept myself from touching her. Her breathing was ragged, her pulse pounding at her neck, and her color was bad, her lips almost blue. For a moment I thought we'd killed her, but her breathing gradually slowed, and her color returned somewhat.

"Tell me you got that, Miko."

"Got it, sir. It's not far, but we need a chart."

"Yes." I longed to brush the sweat-damp locks of hair from Preel's face, but again refrained. "Take care of her, Hemp. Whatever she needs. Anything at all."

"Aye, sir." Hemp sounded miserable. "She...um did ask me..." His voice trailed off and he wrung his hands, clearly reticent.

"What, Hemp. What did she ask?"

"She wanted me to ask her a question, sir. She was soused, and not thinkin' straight, but..."

I staggered back a step, feeling ill. Preel wanted to die.

"Don't worry, sir. I'll keep her safe. She's stronger than she thinks. I'll think of somethin'."

"Thank you, Hemp." I cast one more glance down at the woman I loved, who would now rather die than suffer my touch, and fled the cabin. "Send word when she wakes."

In the wardroom, my officers already had a chart laid out on the table. Miko rattled off the latitude and longitude, and Kivan walked it off with a pair of dividers. She scratched an X on the chart and stepped back.

"Damn! That's close!"

I stepped up and peered down at the mark she'd made. It stood on the southeast coast of Valaka, about ten miles northeast of the island's southernmost cape. We were anchored half way up the island from the same cape, but on the leeward side. "Double check it."

She did, and I watched closely. It came up the same.

"The *windward* shore?" Quiff sounded skeptical.

"Maybe there's a hidden cove that's not on the chart," Miko said.

"Only one way to find out." Suppressing my growing excitement, I focused on the task at hand. "Splash both longboats. Kivan, pick a crew to take yours to Valaka City. Find out whatever you can about this dragonship. Books, sages, rumors, legends, whatever anyone can tell you. I'll give you plenty of money to loosen tongues. Boxley, you and Rauley will take the other longboat around the southern cape and scout out this location." I tapped the chart. "If there's a port of any kind, you'll reconnoiter without going ashore. Whatever you find, you'll report back to me here as quick as you can."

"Sir," Quiff interrupted. "Send me. Boxley's..." He looked at her and shut his mouth.

"Sir!" Boxley's face turned beet red. "Request permission to inform Lieutenant Quiff that I'm *quite* capable of commanding a *longboat*, and that while my seamanship might not match his own, I'll have our sailing master aboard to help."

"Stand down, Boxley. Quiff, I need you here. I want a competent officer on deck at all times. I trust that Captain Tan's on our side, but another of Jhavika's ships might happen upon us."

"Aye, sir." He spared a sympathetic glance to Boxley. Sailing an open launch around the southern cape of Valaka would be wet and miserable. "I understand."

"Good. We've not a minute to spare, so I want you both underway at first light. Boxley, that should put you around the point the next morning, and you should be able to reconnoiter and get back around to leeward by nightfall." Rounding the point in the dark would be far too dangerous, both for the lack of light and the increased nighttime trade winds.

"Aye, sir!"

"Both of you start getting ready, then get some sleep. You won't get much underway."

They saluted and left the wardroom.

"What about moving the ship, sir?" Miko asked. "If Tan gets caught..."

"Maybe if Kivan gets back early we'll haul anchor and move down the coast, but not until. She's beating to windward in the morning."

"Aye, sir."

We stared at the chart, and I tried to imagine sailing a ship into the Serpent's Eye. I couldn't. I didn't even have decent charts of the Eye. *First things first, Kevril,* I told myself. *You need to find this bloody dragonship.*

Chapter Twelve
A Modicum of Solace

Inner peace is oft the most fleeting.
The Lessons of Quen Lau Ush

From the journal of Preel Longbright –
I don't know why I didn't think of it myself. My entire adult
life, I've dealt with adversity: slavery, punishment, and abuse.
Prior to my time with Kevril, only one thing ever brought me
peace.

I woke feeling like shit, but that seemed almost normal now. I
rolled out of bed, stiff and sore, and staggered to the head. The light
of mid-morning streamed through the window. I'd been abed for
more than twelve hours. Despite the simple answer, it had cost me.

After washing my face, I stared at the creature in the mirror, a
disheveled scarecrow of the young woman I had been. I didn't care,
not even enough to brush out my hair. My stomach rumbled, but I
drank some water and managed not to throw up.

Out in the cabin, I heard Hemp clattering about. I had begun to
suspect that he slept with an ear to my door. I found his attention

comforting, but also irritating. I remembered the glass I'd thrown the night before, and felt guilty for making more work for him. He'd offered me consolation when I needed it most. A little gratitude seemed warranted, but I wasn't in the mood. He'd refused the only request that would truly have ended my torment.

I stepped out of the quarter gallery to find Hemp standing there with my robe held out for me, his eyes carefully averted. A flash memory of Nala and Binsh gave me a shiver.

"Mornin' Lady Preel. Breakfast in two shakes."

"Thank you, Hemp." I shrugged into the robe, but didn't bother tying it. It didn't matter. "Just tea this morning, please. My stomach is a bit queasy."

"Tea and a biscuit, then. Nothin' like Bert's biscuits to settle a stomach." He hurried out.

I walked to the windows and stared out through the bars of my prison, glaring at the placid bay, the green hills, and the black shoreline, the vibrant colors mocking me. Why couldn't it be raining, storming, ugly? It would better fit my mood.

I thought of my answer from the previous night. The numbers meant nothing to me. Despite six months aboard *Scourge*, I wasn't a sailor. But they'd certainly mean something to Kevril. *So why aren't we underway?* Surely, he would race off to commandeer this dragonship and tear off into the Serpent's Eye. If I was lucky, he'd never return.

Memories crashed in: leaning back against the windowsill where I now stood as Kevril made love to me, pressing me against the hard corner, my nails and heels grasping, pulling him into me... That moment, so sweet, was now poisoned. I realized suddenly that I'd worn the very same robe then that I wore now, and a knot of nausea rose up from my gut.

No, no, no! I shucked out of the hated garment and cast it aside, then went to my hanging locker to pick out a different one. Pulling it on, I tied it tight and folded my arms over my stomach, willing the revulsion to subside. *Just don't think about it. Focus on something else.*

The door opened, and Hemp entered with a tray. His eyes swept the cabin, spied the robe on the floor.

"Somethin' wrong with that robe, Lady Preel?" He put the tray on the table and started placing a plate of biscuits, a bowl of porridge, and a tea service.

"Yes. I don't want to touch it. Please take it out of here." Ignoring his raised eyebrows, I didn't explain why, but took my seat. I hadn't asked for porridge, but found my mouth watering at the aroma of spices and cooked grains. I took a sip of tea, perfectly lightened with goat's milk and flavored with a hint of ginger. Hemp knew just how I liked it.

"As you wish." He scooped up the robe and headed for the door.

Guilt. "I'm sorry, Hemp. It's not the robe. It's me."

"No worries, Lady Preel. I understand." He left and came back a moment later to begin his morning ritual of tidying up.

"And I'm sorry for throwing the glass last night. I'm afraid I lost my temper."

He barked a laugh and grinned. "If I had a copper penny for every time I had to clean up broke glass, why, I wouldn't need to pirate anymore. Ain't no trouble at all."

"Thank you." I tried a biscuit, and my stomach accepted it. The tea was soothing as well. "So, why are we still anchored here? What's being done?"

"Oh, well, it so happens that the fix you gave the captain is just a hop-skip away, round the south point on the windward side of Valaka! Captain sent Boxley and Rauley in a longboat to have a look-see, and Kivan off to town to have a look through the book shops to see what she can learn about that there dragonship. Two birds in two opposite direction, ya know. Saves time, and probably a couple of questions."

"Boxley? But she's just a little girl!"

"Oh, she's tougher than you think, and this is a good shakedown for her. First command, you know. And Rauley could take a longboat across the whole Blood Sea with his eyes closed. Three days in a longboat'll put hair on her...um. Pardon, Lady Preel, I mean, it'll make a proper sailor out of her."

I kept forgetting the trials these youngsters went through. Boxley was the same age I'd been when I was sold into slavery. I sampled the porridge and found it delicious.

Kivan alone in Valaka also brought worries to mind. Kevril had said it was a dangerous city. What if Brekka found out?

And then there was *Scourge* itself. What if Tan betrayed us to Jhavika? *Poor maimed Jhavika, my dear sister...* Her wrath would be terrible. Would she slaughter the entire crew? Enslave them? What about Miko and Bert and Hemp? What would happen to them? Love and hate, memories and emotions, my husband, my sister, my life...

I felt my mind spiraling toward oblivion once again and pushed away my breakfast.

"Pour me a glass of wine, please, Hemp."

"Lady Preel, it's barely mid-morning, and you ain't even finished your breakfast yet."

His whining tone set my teeth on edge. My temper flared, and I lurched to my feet, hands clenched. "Take it away." I stalked toward the liquor cabinet.

Hemp stepped in my way, his hands up, his face imploring. "Preel, listen to me, please! I'm tryin' to *help* you."

"Help me by pouring me a gods-damned drink!" I tried to step around him, but he moved into my path again. "Out of my way! I can't *do* this! I'm going fucking mad!"

"I'll pour you anything you like if you just stop and *listen* to me for two *bloody* seconds!"

I stepped back, stunned for a moment. Hemp had never once raised his voice to me, but now he was well and truly angry. He might be a steward, but he was also a pirate, wiry and tough as old shoe leather. In fact, if anything Kevril had ever told me was to be believed, Hemp, not his captain, had killed my former master, Captain Nightspinner. If it came down to it, he could overpower me in a moment.

I folded my arms and glared. "Fine. I'm listening." At least being angry with him took my mind off the war raging in my mind.

"Booze ain't the answer. You need somethin' to keep yer mind busy. A book or some puzzle or somethin'."

"I've tried reading, Hemp. I can't keep my mind on anything. Everything in this cabin makes me think of Kevril!"

"Then let's *change* things! How about we paint the place, or hang drapes, or get different carpets?"

I stared at him dubiously. "I'm going mad, and you think *redecorating* will help?"

"Well, what about some sewing or crochet or painting? What about your journal or your exercises?" His eyes widened. "You ain't done your exercises *once* since you came back aboard! You said they used to calm you, right?"

"Yes, I did." Yamshi did help me with my anxiety, and I wondered why I hadn't been doing it. Then I remembered the last time I'd performed my exercises, when I'd been teaching Jhavika, the day she commanded me to love her like a sister.

Was that memory tainted, just as my memories of Kevril were? Would it only remind me of my dilemma? But it might give me something to do, a distraction for as long as I could keep it up. I knew five routines, and I had books that described half a dozen more in detail. I could teach myself new routines, make up my own, try them in different combinations, do them faster, blend them with the ancient martial arts I'd studied. Perhaps therein lay sanity, peace, solace.

I nodded to Hemp. "Would you please pull out one of my old outfits? I think I *will* try to exercise."

"Bloody good!" He grinned and dashed for my locker.

The strangest trepidation came over me then. Would the exercise provide a diversion for my mind or would it only remind me of Jhavika? Could I even concentrate enough to perform the routines at all? There was only one way to find out.

Hemp handed over one of my old pairs of pantaloons and wrap tops. I took them, the silk smooth between my fingers, familiar, comforting even. I hurried to the quarter gallery and changed, the motions automatic, unthinking. When I stepped out, Hemp had cleared the floor, moving the dining table aside and rolling up the rug.

"Thank you, Hemp." I stepped to the center of the space, my footsteps tentative.

"Thank me by gettin' better, Lady Preel." He smiled again and backed away.

I considered which routine I should do. Not the basic *ton-chi*; that had been the one I had been teaching Jhavika. *Gie-wa then*, I decided, taking up the opening stance. My body and limbs settled into the familiar posture: weight centered, knees slightly bent, hips forward, feet shoulder width apart with equal pressure on my toes and heels. Arms relaxed, fingers poised, head straight...all the tiny details occupied my mind and eased my soul.

I raised my arms and *greeted the sun*.

Chapter Thirteen
No Rest for the Wicked

Toil wins as many battles as swords.
The Lessons of Quen Lau Ush

From the journal of Jhavika Keshmir –
I've become soft. As a youth, I remember endless days of toil
for little gain. I remember the bosun's lash, a knotted piece
of rope. I had forgotten the squalor aboard ship, the roaches
and rats, the moldy food and weevil-ridden hardtack. I must
relearn what it truly means to be a pirate.

The morning of the fourth day after taking *Crimson Hawk*, we
sighted our third pirate ship. The second one had been at sea. Ignoring
our signals for parley, they'd just kept sailing past us as if we didn't
exist. I realized then that sailing a corsair has its disadvantages; I could
no longer pull the hapless merchantman ruse. Perhaps they even
recognized *Crimson Hawk* and had no desire for an encounter with her
famously irascible captain. The winds didn't favor us, so I didn't
pursue. They'd likely mistake such a move for aggression, and I
couldn't afford the casualties a battle would incur.

This third ship, the *Devil's Doubloon*, we found at anchor at one of the innumerable small islands southwest of Twin Capes. They spotted us immediately and manned battle stations. We were still a mile away, and I hadn't yet decided what to do, when they hoisted a flag of parley. Warily, I dispatched a boat to ask if they'd seen any sign of *Scourge*.

The reply came back terse and negative. Yet another disappointment.

"Haul the cutter aboard and get us underway!" I strode to the deck locker to glare at the chart pinned there and consider my futile search for *Scourge*.

Two days ago, we'd rendezvoused with *Peony*'s cutter, which bore a thick packet of reports relayed from my southbound ships. None of the news had been good. Ursula Roque had completed her search of Black Point and come up with nothing. Matesh had nearly lost his ship in a battle with a pirate ship. Fortunately, the superior force of soldiers aboard *Bluebonnet* had prevailed, though barely. Matesh had anchored in an isolated Ton Chi cove to repair his ship. To make matters worse, the surviving pirates all denied having seen our quarry for months. Busashi's report was short and concise: "No sign or reports of Captain Longbright or *Scourge*. Continuing south to Mati."

The only captains I hadn't heard from yet were Yorish and Tan. Brilla already had orders with regard to Yorish, so that left Tan. I tapped the chart, inadvertently piercing the parchment at Valaka with my pike. Granted, Valaka was the largest and farthest of the islands, but still, I should have heard *something* by now. *Desertion?* I wondered, then immediately dismissed the thought. Tan was loyal to the Council, and hated Kevril for destroying *Yellow Blossom*. No, I didn't see her as a deserter. It was far more likely that she had difficulties while asking questions about Kevril in Valaka City, or had found *Scourge* and been destroyed.

"Where in the Nine Hells and Seven Heavens did you *go*, Kevril?" I was beginning to think I had been wrong about his tactics. Thus far, no pirates had admitted to seeing Kevril in months. But if he wasn't amassing his own pirate navy, then what the hell was he doing?

I clenched my good fist. Searching the Blood Sea didn't seem to be working. I had to think like Kevril, distill his actions down to motives, then predict his next move.

Preel... It has to be about Preel. He rescued her, but she despises him. That will drive him mad. He'll try to free her from the enchantment. But where? Not Valaka, I was sure, recalling Preel's story of Brekka's death threat. Perhaps he'd asked Preel for an alternative location where they might procure a cure for her enchantment. The problem was, that answer could have sent him anywhere.

I pulled a smaller scale chart from the locker and traced a finger across it, ruminating on the possibilities. Monsoon season intensified the trade winds and brought on the possibility of hurricanes. If he set off for a far destination, it would have to be to the north, or south. Considering the trade winds, it would be easiest for Kevril to head south. Busashi would find him if he'd sailed to Mati. Farther south, the lands of the Roo offered no cities or safe harbors, nothing but unfriendly natives. Any farther south and Kevril would encounter the ice winds of the Great Circle Sea; no ship could round the Cape of Storms westward against those perpetual storm-force winds and mountainous seas.

So, to the north then. Scourge might find safe harbor in Chen, but they'd first have to pass through Toki waters, and even Kevril wasn't crazy enough to sail a pirate ship there. The god-emperor's navy routinely stopped ships in transit, and they often carried truthseekers in search of any sort of magic. Kevril would be hanged as a pirate, and the god-emperor would confiscate both Preel and my scourge. The only other option was to cross the Great Western Sea on the northern trades to the Northlands. *Fengotherond, maybe?* There was certainly magic aplenty to be found in the domed city, perhaps someone with the knowledge and skill to break Preel's enchantment.

"Your ladyship."

I looked up into the face of my appointed first officer, the former bosun of *Tiger Lily*, an invaluable seaman, but hardly officer material. I honestly hadn't taken the time to remember his name. He looked worried. I could almost taste the pending bad news.

"What is it?"

He clenched his jaw, eyes fixed over my shoulder. "Respectfully, your ladyship, the crew needs rest."

"Rest?" I faced him and clenched my hand on my cutlass. Te-shan sidled up at my side. "Gods and devils, what makes you think for one *second* that I'd be inclined to give them rest when we've accomplished exactly *fuck*-all toward our goal?"

"It's not a matter of goals, your ladyship, it's a matter of survival." He seemed undaunted by either my ire or my bodyguard. *Brave or foolish*, I thought. "They're exhausted, and they're still learnin' how to manage this ship. She's a far cry from the *Lily*. Exhausted crews make mistakes, and, in these waters, that could put us on a reef or up against a lee shore in the dark. One day's rest ain't too much to ask."

My temper surged, not only at the man's impudence, but with the frustration that I couldn't simply murder him. Other than myself, he was the most competent sailor aboard, though his navigation skills were sorely lacking. We'd been searching shorelines during the day and transiting between islands at night, so no one got much rest. My people were learning, but one does not make a seaman overnight, and *Tiger Lily*'s sailors bore the brunt of the work. Consequently, everyone was exhausted. I didn't give a damn for their health or welfare, but I would need them all alive and reasonably healthy when we found *Scourge*. And running *Crimson Hawk* up on a reef would quickly end our mission and our lives.

Damn if the impudent bastard wasn't right.

"One day." I whirled back to the chart. "Here!" I stabbed the desolate island directly to our south with my pike. "Dunnhaven Rock. There's a fair anchorage on the leeward side. Set course. If there's no other ship there, we'll anchor and broach a cask of rum."

"Aye, your ladyship! Thank you, your ladyship!"

"Thank me by following my orders and teaching these lubbers proper seamanship!"

"Yes, your ladyship."

I considered the chart and the deployment of my armada. I'd previously sent orders for Ursula Roque to start searching the islands northeast of Black Point while I explored north to south from Twin Capes. I'd intended for us to meet eventually in the middle. Dunnhaven Rock was as good a spot as any.

"Also, since we'll be sitting on our *arses* for a day, send our fastest cutter to find *Peony*. I'll draft orders to Lady Roque to rendezvous with us at Dunnhaven."

"Aye, your ladyship!"

"When the crew's *rested*, we'll continue to scour every single rock, isle, cove, and reef between Dunnhaven and Valaka Isle. Do you understand me?"

"I understand perfectly, your ladyship!"

"Good. Carry out your orders! The deck is yours. I'll be in my cabin."

He saluted and whirled away, bellowing commands.

I strode to the great cabin with Te-shan at my heels. Inside, I found my steward fussing about with a brush and bucket in an endless attempt to scrub the cabin free of mold. The odor of lye was strong enough to make my eyes water, but it might at least dissuade the roach population. I'd put some of my less-seaworthy soldiers to work scrubbing the bilges. With luck, they'd reduce the rat population out of self-defense.

"Stop that fussing and get me something from the galley!" I snapped. I hadn't eaten yet, and my inability to sleep soundly was taking its toll. I had to remind myself to eat and rest, but I was used to fine cuisine, a soft bed, and sleep induced by the attention of a bevy of skilled pleasure slaves. I'd brought no such amenities with me, and cursed my lack of forethought.

My steward dashed out, mumbling apologies.

I paced. My absent right hand reached for my absent scourge, and I cursed beneath my breath. *Gods damn you, Kevril Longbright...*

The door opened, and Te-shan drew his katana. He refrained from decapitating my steward, and allowed the miserable fellow to put the tray down on my chart table. He bowed and hurried out.

I glared at the dismal fare. We'd run out of fresh provisions and were down to hard tack, salt pork, and dried peas. My breakfast consisted of a single bowl of ship's gruel, a pasty porridge of crushed ship's biscuit and small beer brought to a boil and cooked overnight. The weevils added protein to the vile stuff, but their bitter flavor turned my stomach. A dollop of molasses made it edible, barely. A pot of blackbrew and a tankard of beer rounded out the meal. The ship's water supply was only fit for soaking salt pork.

"Disgusting," I muttered, but I needed food.

I sat and forced myself to eat the gooey mess. The gruel hadn't been cooked thoroughly; some of the weevils were still moving. I swallowed quickly and washed it down with beer and blackbrew, considering various forms of punishment for the ship's cook. I finished every bite, got up, and resumed my pacing.

My missing hand flexed on the haft of my missing scourge while I paced. *My missing soul...* My crew would get their rest, but for me, there would be none until I had my scourge back.

Chapter Fourteen
The Curse of Hope

Do not dwell on false hope. Truth is the kinder fate.
The Lessons of Quen Lau Ush

From the diary of Kevril Longbright –
I remember now why I had once eschewed love. Leaving home broke my heart, for I loved my mother and siblings. I even loved my father, which is why he survived my departure. I swore to myself that freedom came with the price of solitude. I think now that I had the right of it.

The endless waiting for Kivan and Boxley to return was driving me insane. If I was ever stranded alone on a deserted island, I swore I'd slit my own throat before the first week was out. Thankfully, good food, a loyal crew, and immersing myself in my duties kept me from plunging over the brink. I'd begun a rigorous sparing schedule, and Wix had given me lessons in humility along with a set of new aches and pains.

My mood was also buoyed by good news from Hemp. Preel had eased off on her drinking and plunged into a demanding yamshi regimen, exercising at least five hours a day—often in middle of the night—to the point of exhaustion. Hemp complained about the heaps of laundry he was doing, but his ire was tempered with relief. Preel was sleeping soundly, her appetite had improved, and she'd had no more breakdowns. Tomorrow we would ask her another question, though with information from Kivan or Boxley still pending, we had not yet decided what to ask.

Even so, I felt like celebrating, so, in the interest of morale—primarily my own—and exerting my authority as captain, I planned a dinner for my officers and senior crew. We sat down to a feast for no other reason than we needed a dose of camaraderie. Wix, Miko, Quibly, and Quitt rounded out the table in the wardroom, and Whinn served us wearing Hemp's white steward's jacket. No venison, but a saddle of mountain goat wreathed with wild mint, fresh breadfruit, fried plantains, several fresh snappers that the crew had caught on hook and line from our jolly boat, and a massive plum pudding for dessert. I'd cracked open a case of my finest wine, and we were all in high spirits.

We ate, drank, told tales—some of them even true—and toasted our cook, conferring upon her the title of Goddess Roberta, Wielder of the Golden Cleaver and Silver Spatula. Her cackling laughter reached us from the galley and drew smiles all around the table.

The highlight of the evening, however, had nothing to do with my celebration.

"Captain!" One of the newcomers, a skinny woman named Bathilda, stepped into the wardroom with a wide, gap-toothed grin. "Longboat comin' back from the northeast! It's Kivan!"

"Excellent!" I downed my wine and lurched up from my seat. "Whinn, don't clear the table. Kivan's going to be hungry."

Everyone stood and followed me out.

"She made damn good time!" Miko sounded more worried than elated. "She either found what she was looking for or ran into trouble and high-tailed it back."

"If she'd run into one of Jhavika's ships, she'd have been back yesterday," Wix reasoned. "Day there, a day in the bookshops, and a day back. She's right on time."

"I just hope she found something useful."

We burst onto the deck, and I ran up the steps to the quarterdeck. The sunset blazed orange and red to the west, distant squalls slashing black along the horizon. Tansy had the watch and handed me a spyglass.

"Just west of the point, sir." She pointed. "So far, no other sails sighted."

The notion that Kivan might have a ship chasing her dwelled on my mind, but I doubted she would lead them back here if she did. Still, caution seemed prudent. "Sharp eyes aloft and prepare a buoy in case we have to cut the anchor free." I raised the glass and focused. The longboat was running well, heeling with the cape-effect winds, her three crewmembers leaning out from the windward rail to even her keel. Kivan leaned on the windward side of the transom, tiller in hand, her long hair flying. She'd either lost her hat or stowed it.

"She's cracking on," Quiff said with a grin.

"That she is." I shifted my view to the eastward point, half expecting the bowsprit of a ship to emerge from beyond at any moment.

"Maybe she's being chased," Miko said, echoing my thoughts.

"Or maybe she just smells Bert's cookin'," Wix said.

"Knock wood, scratch a stay, and think *positive*, Miko." I kept my eye fixed on the cape.

"I'm *positive* I'll be positive if she's not being chased, sir." Her knuckles rapped the rail and she reached up to scratch the backstay.

We all watched the longboat approach, alternating with glances toward the distant cape. The wind eased as they neared, and the boat slowed. Close enough to see their faces through my glass, they didn't look overly concerned, and weren't looking over their shoulders for pursuit. They did, however, look exhausted, salty, and worn thin with toil.

"Port-side boarding ladder, Wix, and ready to haul the longboat aboard."

"Aye, sir!" He strode forward, shouting orders.

I held my tongue as I watched them come alongside; I'd know soon enough if she had found anything. When my lieutenant clambered aboard clutching a bulging waxed canvas bundle under one arm, I knew she'd had some success.

I trundled down the steps to the middeck. "Lieutenant Kivan, you look positively done in. Tell me you found something worthwhile."

"Some interesting things, yes, sir." She handed over the bundle. "Not many details, but I made some notes and sketches. Sorry about the salt, but we wanted to make it back before dark, and had some gusty winds." She was crusted white from head to toe, and her three crew members were already laving their faces and hands with fresh water.

"Well, it just so happens I put on a little feast for supper. You're just in time to tuck in. Have a bathe and join us in the wardroom. We're full up on fresh water, so indulge yourself."

"Thank you, sir! I'll be there in two shakes." A crewman stood by with a bucket, and she shrugged out of her coat. "Pour," she ordered, pointing to her head. He complied, and the crew laughed as she gasped and sputtered.

We returned to the wardroom, and I poured wine for everyone, instructing Whinn to plate hearty portions of everything for Kivan. I sat and untied the string on the packet, delving the contents with trepidation. Pages of tightly written notes and sketches spilled out onto the table.

The first drawing took me completely by the lee.

"What by Odea's sweet tits is *that*?" Miko asked.

"A ship...I *think*." A closer look confirmed that it was, but like none I'd ever seen in my three decades on the sea.

The hull was wide and flattened like a wedge, as if it was made to skim over the surface rather than push the seas aside. The deck was flat from the curved stem to the wide, square stern. Twin keels, if that's what they were, stuck down like daggers from the port and starboard chines of hull, mirrored by twin rudders just as deep.

"Is that an *elvish* design?" Miko asked.

"Damn me if I know."

"Looks more like one of those boards the islanders use to ride the waves," Quiff commented.

I couldn't disagree. Then I flipped to the next page, and my wonder redoubled, for Kivan had sketched the vessel's rigging, and it made no sense to me at all.

"Mother Odea's green garters, where are the *masts*?" I squinted, wondering if I'd had too much wine. "And what are these arched things?"

"Something, isn't it, sir?" Kivan came in with her hair still dripping, but wearing clean, dry clothes. Her face, though drawn with fatigue, glowed with excitement. "I'd never seen anything like it."

"I don't see how it could even sail!" Miko said.

"Search me," I muttered, staring at an odd circle seemingly suspended above the deck between two long arches fore and aft.

"I'm not sure exactly how the rig works myself. The drawings I found weren't very detailed, and I may have made some errors in my sketch, but it's the materials that really gave me pause."

"Materials?" I handed Kivan a glass of wine and gestured her to a chair. "Sit down and eat. We haven't read any of your notes yet, but these drawings..."

"I *know*, sir." Kivan downed half the glass of wine and stuffed a huge slab of goat into her mouth. She groaned in bliss and spoke as she chewed. "Evidently, the reason it's called a *dragonship* is because it's actually *made* out of a *dragon*! That page there outlines it. Some dragonlord several generations back built this thing out of dragon bone and sinew. The sails are dragon wings, though I didn't find any illustrations of those or information on how the damn things are set. Whoever designed it obviously wasn't any kind of a naval architect, but it's *supposed* to be able to sail into the Serpent's Eye without the crew being affected by the wild magic. I don't see any way to rig trisails other than one or maybe two forward. As for square-rigged sails, there are no gods-damned *yards*, so... She might be able to hoist a spanker and a spinnaker, but the rest would be rigged from those bows and that circular...thing. I don't know what the hell to even *call* it."

Neither did I. Trying to imagine how to rig sails on the thing, I failed. "I don't see how it even sails without flipping over," I admitted.

"I'm thinking that the keels are solid metal, sir," Kivan said around another mouthful, "so her center of mass is balanced perfectly. As she heels, the upper keel comes out of the water and weighs it down more. If it ever *did* flip, it'd never right itself, that's sure."

"Like sailing a bloody pancake," Wix muttered.

"The designer was either a genius or a lunatic," I agreed, poring over her notes. I didn't understand half of what was written; Kivan's sense of engineering surpassed mine.

"Maybe both," Miko said. "I wonder if it's still seaworthy."

"A good question, and one we might very well ask Preel."

"Or who owns it or claims it, and if they'd be willing to let us borrow it," Miko added.

"And show us how the hell to *sail* the fool thing!" Quiff put in with a snort of derision.

They were all good questions. I dreaded discussing the options with Preel, but saw no alternative.

"Is Boxley back yet?" Kivan looked around as if noticing her shipmate's absence for the first time.

"Not yet. Maybe tomorrow." I filled Kivan's glass and continued to study the drawings and notes. "I don't want to move the ship until we find out if there's anything useful where we're going."

"And if there isn't?" Quiff asked.

I bit my lip and sighed. "Then we'll have yet another question to ask Preel, won't we?"

Chapter Fifteen
Venom Unwarranted

Anger breeds contempt. Let it not consume you.
The Lessons of Quen Lau Ush

From the journal of Preel Longbright –
I know now what assails me; the venom of the scourge runs
through my veins. It gnaws at me constantly, turning every
thought, every memory, every feeling to poison, changing me
into something I'm not. I feel myself slipping into a well of
corruption from which I'll never escape.

Someone knocked as I slipped from *dragon swoops low* into *crane
spreads wings*.

I ignored the interruption, pivoted my foot on the sweat-damp
deck, and contorted my arms and legs into *serpents embrace*.

The knock sounded again, followed by Hemp's tentative call,
"Lady Preel, it's time."

Time... Time for a question.

I dreaded seeing Kevril—hearing his voice, remembering his
touch, his scent, his tenderness, his manipulations—but I had agreed

101

to help. Truths or lies, I had no way to discern, and it didn't matter; I believed what I believed. If I didn't, if I let the conflict rage within me, I would go mad. I'd found my balance, my center, and I dared not lose it.

"Come in." I relaxed my stance as the door opened.

"Got your bath water hot and ready." Hemp entered with two brimming buckets.

I snatched up a small towel and wiped the dripping sweat from my face, heaving breaths to calm my pounding heart. "Fine."

Hemp put the buckets down inside the quarter gallery and stepped back, holding out a thick white towel. I took it, stepped inside the tiny compartment, and closed the door. Peeling off my soaked halter and pantaloons, I opened the door a crack and handed them out. Hemp took them with his face averted.

I almost laughed at his continued discomfort around me. He'd held my hair while I vomited and embraced me when I broke down, yet still averted his eyes. Part of being a steward was discretion, and there were invisible lines he absolutely refused to cross. I'd suggested he simply hang my sweaty clothes to dry instead of laundering them every time I exercised, and he'd just looked at me like I'd told him to cut off his own testicles.

I ladled hot water over my head and sighed in bliss. Yamshi had once again saved my life, giving me focus, respite, peace, strength, if only for as long as I continued to exercise. I'd never pushed myself so hard, and my muscles ached. Hot baths, a luxury aboard ship, eased the strain.

Clean, I rubbed the towel briskly across my skin, then hung it in the quarter gallery window to dry. Teasing the tangles out of my damp hair, I considered the woman in the mirror; not so much the haunted scarecrow of a few days ago. At least I was sleeping, albeit the sleep of exhaustion.

Sleep... Soon I would sleep for twelve hours straight, but first...Kevril.

A strange irony settled upon me as I steeled my nerves for our discussion. I remembered my second master who had insisted I learn yamshi. He'd saved my life with that command, yet punished me for every infraction. I loved and hated him, much as I now loved and hated Kevril, loved and hated Jhavika, loved and hated my parents. I wished I could insist that Miko alone attend me to discuss the questions, but couldn't justifiably change our arrangement now. And there was no doubt that they needed my help in crafting the questions. Kevril had become adept at wording, but he often missed key elements that could confound my talent or introduce ambiguity. And we couldn't afford any delay.

I needed the scourge destroyed. Only then would I know the truth.

I donned a nightgown and robe, stepped out of the quarter gallery, and went straight to the bunk. Hemp had already placed a glass of wine in the cubby, bless him. I sat with my back to the headboard, my legs folded tailor-fashion, and reached for the glass. I had cut back on my drinking, but I still needed its soporific influence to face Kevril.

A knock at the door startled me, and I nearly spilled my wine. I reduced the volume by half, stilled my trembling hands, and nodded to Hemp to open the door.

Kevril and Miko entered. I clutched my glass in my lap, refusing to allow my eyes to go where they wished, to look upon him, to stir my memories like a hot iron stirring a banked fire to life. *Trust your memories, those are real.* Kevril's own words. But all of my memories were now poisoned, all the good turned rancid, all the love transformed to hate.

"Thank you for agreeing to discuss this with us, Preel. I'm glad you're feeling better."

His conciliatory tone felt like salt in a wound. I bit back a cutting reply. "I agreed to help. Stop thanking me for keeping my word."

He ignored my comment, or at least didn't react. I kept my eyes fixed on the foot of the bed while he and Miko sat at the navigation table. They declined the wine Hemp offered, a subtle rebuke for the glass in my hand, no doubt. I drained it out of sheer defiance and held it out for Hemp to refill.

"I see you went through Kivan's notes. What did you think of the dragonship?"

Kevril seemed to be trying for a conversational tone now, which irritated me. We weren't here to chat. "I think it doesn't really *matter* what I think. I'm no sailor. It only matters that it'll sail into the Serpent's Eye safely, and we already know that it will."

"Actually, we don't." He sighed, and I heard his frustration there. I knew him so well...too well. "We know that it did at one time, but not that it still can. Unless you can think of a more pressing question, we thought to ask if the ship is still seaworthy. So far, our questions haven't answered that."

He had a point, damn him. For all we knew, the dragonship could be a rotten hulk at the bottom of the sea. My answers had only told what it had done in the past, not what it was currently capable of doing. I tried to think of a better question, but couldn't. I'd been too preoccupied with my yamshi to consider much else. Staying sane had become my full-time job.

I looked pointedly at Miko and asked, "What about Boxley?"

Miko shook her head. "We'd hoped she'd be back by now with more information, but she hasn't returned yet, and seaworthiness seemed important to know first anyway. If the ship won't sail, it's useless to us and we have to figure out some other way. If it *is* seaworthy and Boxley actually sees it, we can then ask who owns it or if they'd be willing to barter for the ship's use."

"Yes, that seems logical." I drank more wine, considering the other questions. When Miko spoke, I could think through my hate. "You should be careful about asking the willingness of the ship's owner to cooperate. As we learned with Brekka, asking about intent is dangerous. We asked for someone willing to barter for breaking the scourge's enchantment, and she was. We had no way of knowing that the only thing she'd accept in trade was *me*."

"Actually, there was one other thing she would have accepted."

I couldn't help but stare at Kevril. "What?"

"The scourge. She told me that if I brought it to her, she'd trade it for the potion." He shrugged.

My temper surged; he'd never told me that. "Nice to know you valued the *scourge* more than you did *me*."

"Preel, there was no way we could get the scourge from Jhavika without first getting the cure to the enchantment. I offered to do exactly that, but Brekka wouldn't trust me to keep my end of the bargain."

I downed my wine and glared at him. "My opinion of *Brekka* just went up! At least *she* had the sense not to trust a pirate! More than *I* had."

Kevril's face flushed, the muscles at his jaw bunching. My taunt had scored. He looked away from me and stood. "Ask the question, Miko. I'll be in the wardroom. I'm only upsetting her."

"Aye, sir." Miko watched him go, her dark features a blank. When the door closed, she looked at me, and I could tell she was angry. "Why do you do that?"

"Do what, tell the truth?" I put my glass in the cubby. "It's my only *function*, remember?"

"Kevril freed you, Preel. He loves you. I *know* the scourge has—"

"Lies!" I lurched out of bed and glared at her, my fists clenched at my sides. "I was *never* free! He bartered me like a piece of plunder for that potion, so *he* could be free! He only manipulated me to get me into his bed!"

"That's not true, Preel." She was angry with me, but controlling it better than I was.

"Oh?" I shook my left arm at her, the golden manacles and chain rattling. "Here I am, chained! Bars on the windows! I was never allowed to leave this damned ship without guards! I was *never* free!"

"You were never confined against your will. The guards were for your protection. You *know* that!"

"I don't know anything of the kind! You believe him because you think he's your friend! You buy his relentless bullshit because he's manipulated you, too! It's what he *does*!"

"Preel, I've known Kevril my entire adult life. He's not what Jhavika's told you to believe he is. *Those* are the lies. He would have taken you anywhere you wished to go and left you free to seek your own life."

"To be scooped up by the first warlord to realize what I am?" I snorted in disgust. "That's not freedom. That's just leaving one master for a worse one." I waved a hand at the confines of my prison. "I was permitted the *illusion* of freedom. Pretty clothes, jewelry, comforts... nothing but a gilded *cage,* as long as I remained his truthsayer whore!"

Hemp drew a sharp breath at my tirade, but held his tongue.

"His *whore?*" Miko's features hardened, her eyes narrowing in cold fury. "Can you tell me honestly, *truthsayer*, that Kevril *ever* touched you without your consent?"

I froze. Being a truthsayer didn't prevent me from lying, but this wasn't a lie I could tell; Kevril had never touched me without my consent.

"He *manipulated* me into consenting! He's no better than Nightspinner! At least *he* didn't *lie* about keeping me as his whore!"

Miko's face darkened dangerously. "Maybe you would *prefer* that we'd left you with Captain Nightspinner."

Memories of waking up sore, even bleeding, turned my stomach. A hundred violations revisited me, clear as crystal in my mind, but none as painful as the memories of Kevril's seductions. "Nightspinner only used me when I was *unconscious*! At least I don't have to remember *him* inside me!"

Miko stepped up to me, her fists clenched at her sides, her expression livid. For a moment I thought she might hit me.

She didn't. Instead, she asked abruptly, "Is the dragonship that was used to acquire the blood pearl that's now part of Jhavika's scourge still seaworthy?"

My legs folded. I crumpled the floor as the convulsions took me. My head hit something, and the room spun, then went black as my eyes rolled up. The answer tore up from my chest as if my heart was being ripped out.

"Yes."

The voice that was not mine sent me into oblivion.

Chapter Sixteen
Inconclusive Findings

When faced with inconclusive information, decisive action is more valuable than inaction.
The Lessons of Quen Lau Ush

From the diary of Kevril Longbright –
I don't know how much longer I can do this. When being in the presence of the woman I love only throws her into fits of rage, I ask myself why I do it at all. I fear that, when this is over, there will be nothing left of her. Even sane and whole, the hate will have poisoned her soul. Who will Preel be when she is finally free? The question terrifies me.

"Sorry we're late, sir!" Boxley clambered over the rail, salt-rimed and stumbling with exhaustion. "Our first try to round the cape didn't go so well."

"Got our asses kicked and damn near lost the mast, we did," Rauley agreed. "And Foist lost the skin off one hand tryin' to take in a wild sheet."

Foist raised his bandage-wrapped hand in evidence, though it was so crusted with old blood and salt, I wondered if the dressing was doing more harm than good. His face was pinched and pale.

"Off to Bert with you, Foist." As he hurried off, I faced my midshipman. "So, the cape effects are substantial, I assume."

Boxley snorted. "To put it *mildly*, sir. Maybe gale-force gusting higher, and *hellacious* seas. We had to tack miles to the south to round it to windward. Even so, currents and leeway damn near put us on the rocks."

"Well, it speaks well for your seamanship that you're alive, anyway." Conditions like that in an open boat weren't just dangerous, they were deadly.

"Thank Rauley, sir! He's a fookin' genius." Boxley accepted a bucket from a crewman and promptly dumped it over her head. Rauley grinned and did likewise, and the two started shucking salt-caked clothing. Their skin was mottled with salt sores, abrasions, and bruises.

"Just tell me what you found, then you can finish cleaning up and join us in the wardroom for breakfast."

"A keep, sir, but no harbor and no ship of any kind." Boxley winced as she scrubbed the salt from her abraded neck. She looked like she'd been hung. "Just bare rock cliffs with little more than a stone beach, and the surf's a right *bitch*. I wouldn't want to take a longboat ashore there. You'd likely end up smashing it to kindling. Mooring a ship against that lee shore would be suicide."

"But there's a keep and someone living there, you say?"

"Aye, that's sure. We saw lights in some of the windows, and smoke."

"All right, then. Lieutenant Quiff, stow the longboat, haul anchor, and haul ass. Make our course southwest. We'll look for someplace to anchor as close to the southwestern cape as we can find, but we've got to get there in daylight. All the canvas she'll bear."

"Aye, sir!" Quiff bellowed orders, and crewmembers rushed for their places on the capstan and scrambled up the ratlines.

"Boxley, Rauley, join the rest of us in the wardroom as soon as you've cleaned up and shifted your clothes. Kivan returned yesterday. She discovered some things about the dragonship, and we know from Preel that it's seaworthy. Now that you're back, we can plan our next step."

"Aye, sir!"

I left them to it. In the wardroom, I found Bert scraping Foist's palm with a straight razor. He sat tied to a chair, two stout sailors restraining him. His face was beet red, and tears streamed from his clenched eyes. A muffled scream escaped around the leather bite block clamped between his teeth.

"How is he, Bert?"

"The wound went bad. He'll be right as rain in a few days, but he won't be haulin' on a line for a while. Lucky it's his *left* hand." She continued her work without looking up.

"Hold fast, Foist. She'll set you to rights in no time." I left Bert to her work, knowing from experience that it wouldn't take her long. I woke Miko and Kivan, informed them that we were getting underway, and that Boxley and Rauley were back and would be joining us in the wardroom for breakfast and discussion. I tapped on the great cabin door, and Hemp opened it, his face grim.

"How is she?"

"Still out like yesterde's bilge water, sir. Not to worry. She'll wake soon, and I'll take care of her."

"Thank you, Hemp." I gripped his shoulder hard. "I'll never be able to repay you properly for this, you know."

"Already did, sir. Trustin' me after what I done..." He looked suddenly uncomfortable, and shook his head, probably suppressing the urge to cut his own throat again. "Best not speak of it."

"We'll speak of it when this is all done with, Hemp." I left him and started back for the wardroom.

Bert was bandaging Foist's hand now, and he sipped an ample tot of rum with his free hand, both to kill the pain and as a reward for being a good patient.

"All secure!" Bert tied the last knot and clapped her charge on the shoulder. "Now keep the damned thing *dry*, Foist, or I'll be fittin' you for a hook!"

"Aye, Bert!" He stood, wobbled a bit on his legs, and saluted me as he left the wardroom.

"Boxley and Rauley are back, Bert. I'll breakfast here with them, Miko, and Kivan. We'll be underway in…" The ship lurched to leeward, and Wix bellowed overhead. "…well, right now."

"No more injuries?" she asked, stowing her supplies in her big leather bag.

"Just salt sores and some bumps and bruises. Nothing serious."

"Good. I'll bring a salve for the sores. Breakfast in two shakes, sir!" She grinned and waddled past me.

I blessed my lucky stars for the thousandth time that I'd found Bert, and sat down. My officers trickled in. Miko was still in the surly mood she'd descended into last night. She didn't volunteer what had set her off and, when I asked, only said, "Just one of those things, sir. I'll get over it."

Boxley and Rauley arrived together, staggering with exhaustion and still damp from their baths. Whinn delivered blackbrew, and I spiked their cups with rum.

"You two are off duty until this evening. Right after we talk things over, I want you in your bunks."

"Ain't gotta tell *me* twice, sir!" Boxley yawned and downed half her blackbrew. "Only thing I need more than sleep is food! I could eat a *sea drake*, scales, claws, and all!"

"It was too rough to cook, sir, and the bag of hard tack got soaked." Rauley's eyes slid sideways to Kivan. "Heard you found out somewhat about our dragonship?"

Kivan was the bright spot of the group. She'd spent hours poring over the sketches she'd done of the dragonship, trying to work out various sail plans. Now she delved into her satchel, bubbling with enthusiasm, and slid one of her sketches over. "Just have a look at this thing! It was made by a dragonlord, crafted from dragon bone and sinew. The rig's…well, I'm still trying to figure it out."

Rauley's eyes were drawn to the sketch like a magnet. "What the...
Looks like a nautical architect's *nightmare* to me!"

"We're hoping that whoever owns the ship at least knows how to
sail it," I said.

"Breakfast!" Bert arrived bearing a massive platter of fried
potatoes, onions, peppers, and sausage. Whinn placed plates, a platter
of fresh bread, and a pot of sweet butter. The aromas hit my nose and
traveled to my stomach like a runaway coach.

"Bless you, Roberta!" I started serving.

"Bless me by eatin' every last bite, you pirate!" She left with a
mirthful cackle.

Boxley and Rauley ate like starved wolves, though my sailing
master kept one eye fixed on Kivan's sketches. Once they had time
between bites to speak, I had them relate their findings to Miko and
Kivan. When they finished, everyone fell silent for a moment.

"So, without a harbor or even a place we can land a longboat, I
think our only option will be for a small team to trek overland. *Scourge*
and the rest of the crew will stay anchored on the leeward side of the
island." I ate and considered my officers, thinking ahead on the
decisions I would have to make. "I'm not happy about splitting up our
people, but I don't see the alternative."

Miko looked just as unhappy about the prospect as I felt. "We
could drop off an overland team, then take *Scourge* around the point
and heave to east of this keep."

"We could, but I don't really see the advantage. If we can't land,
whoever's aboard will be no use to those onshore if there's trouble." I
turned to Boxley. "How bad was the surf on the beach?"

"Bad, sir, and it ain't sand. It's rocks about the size of
cobblestones. You've got maybe six-foot breakers in the lull and ten
footers at the peak of the sets. You can hear the rocks rumbling when
the waves break. Might land a boat if the waves settled, but not this
time of year." She looked to Rauley.

Rauley nodded in agreement, his mouth too full to answer.

"And no sign of a ship at all?" Miko asked.

"None that we could see, sir," Rauley said after swallowing hard. "Just a big, ugly block of a keep. Not like a castle; it didn't have any battlements or crenellations. Just black stone. Looked gnomish."

"Magic?" I speculated, looking from face to face. "Could this dragonlord hide a whole *ship* with some kind of illusion?"

Everyone shrugged. What we knew of magic wouldn't fill a thimble, and the only person aboard who *did* know anything on the subject hated my guts and refused to talk to me.

"All right, then. If there's no better idea, we'll find an anchorage before sunset, and I'll pick an overland expedition to leave at first light." I finished my blackbrew and got up. Rauley opened his mouth to speak, but I held up a hand. "I'll decide who comes along and who stays, and inform everyone of my decision tonight."

"Yes, sir." He didn't sound happy.

I left the wardroom and went up to pace the quarterdeck. Quiff thanked me for taking over his watch and hurried below for breakfast. Wix ambled up to join me.

"I talked to Foist, sir." He spat over the leeward rail. "Overland?"

"Looks like."

"No other way, sir. That sounds like a bitch of a lee shore."

"Yes, it does. It'll be at least a two-day trek overland, *assuming* we can find a trail."

"Aye, and who knows what's in them mountains." He glared up at the craggy peaks and spat another stream of tobacco juice over the leeward rail. "Who you takin' with ya?"

"I haven't decided yet."

"Aye." He lifted a knuckle to his forehead and ambled off.

It was decision time, and I mulled over my options. I'd already chosen the first two: myself and Preel. With Jhavika searching for us, there was no way I was letting her out of my sight. But one thing was sure: Preel wasn't going to be happy about it at all.

Chapter Seventeen
The Price of Defiance

Never risk more than you can afford to lose.
The Lessons of Quen Lau Ush

From the journal of Preel Longbright –
I don't like the person I'm becoming. Even if I'm ever truly free, if I'm still this person, I don't think I can live with myself. I'll always remember my spite, my hate, my loathing of the man I remembered loving. Will the truth wash away the poison? I pray it'll be so, but I harbor little hope.

This wasn't the first morning I'd woken in soiled clothes upon a sodden mattress, but it's a thing one never gets used to.

My temper flared as I surged out of bed. "*Damn* you, Miko!"

Stiff muscles and a lurching deck sent me staggering unsteadily to the quarter gallery. The ship was underway. Of course, it was; my answer had confirmed that the dragonship was seaworthy, and Kevril was hightailing to find it. Knowing him, he'd take it by force, pitting his pirates against the arcane might of a dragonlord, if necessary. My conscience told me I was lying to myself, but I ignored it and shifted my ire back to my venomous argument with Miko.

I'd never seen the first mate so incensed. She hadn't hit me, but asking the question without allowing me a trip to the head had been punishment enough for my rancor. That and the lump on the back of my head. *Would that I had landed harder and dashed my brains across the deck!*

I seemed to be alienating my friends among the crew one at a time. I hadn't seen Bert since she tended the abrasions on my wrists, and now Miko hated me. Who knew what the other officers thought of me. They idolized the captain, so it couldn't be good. I had little doubt that rumors were spreading about my episodes of raving lunacy.

They all probably despise me now. Tears threatened as I sagged against the bulkhead and leaned my aching head against the cool wood.

"Bath water, Lady?"

All save Hemp.

Embarrassment heated my face; he'd obviously been listening at the door for me to wake up, and most likely was the one to put me to bed last night. Hemp would also be the one to pay the price for my argument with Miko, cleaning my soiled clothes and the bedlinens, and replacing the mattress. Guilt surged up.

I cracked the quarter gallery door wide enough to speak to him face-to-face. "Yes, please. Thank you for putting me to bed. I'm sorry for the mess. I've made a lot of work for you, I'm afraid."

"No worries, Lady Preel." He smiled and called out the door for bath water, then started gathering up the soiled bedlinens. "You play with matches in a flour mill, there's bound to be an explosion eventually. Just glad you weren't hurt."

I noticed how he didn't blame Miko for the mishap. "Well, thank you, anyway." I closed the door and stripped out of my wet robe and nightgown.

There was enough water in the ewer for a quick splash, but it was bracing cold and barely enough to rinse away the odor of urine. A bar of scented soap did, however, and by the time Hemp knocked on the door, I was suds from neck to toes. Shivering, I cracked the door, reached out a soapy arm, and took the steaming bucket.

"Bless you, Hemp." I glimpsed his studiously averted face, his neck glowing red, and felt guilty again for embarrassing him. "Sorry."

"Not a problem at all, lady."

I closed the door and rinsed the soap from my body, the steaming hot water banishing my shivers. Clean and warm, I toweled dry, gazing out the window at the sea racing by. Living aboard for half a year had taught me how to read the motion of the ship and the passing of the waves. We were on a port tack with the wind abaft the beam, racing along under a large press of sail. My simple answer had prompted concerted action. We were cracking on, but to what destination?

"Clothes, Lady Preel?" Hemp asked through the door.

I wrapped the towel around myself and cracked the door. "Thank you, Hemp."

"Breakfast in two shakes." Still, he kept his eyes averted as he held out my neatly folded clothes.

As I put on the pantaloons and wrap halter—he'd anticipated my desire to exercise—I wondered about Hemp, and not for the first time. He treated me with such deference, even though I was a slave, even after all my venomous raving. He alone understood what I was going through.

Hemp took great pride in his job as Kevril's steward, though I didn't know why. The captain could be insufferably ungracious. I owed Hemp a debt of gratitude for helping me through my bouts of madness. His concern for me, unquestioningly honest and true, gave me comfort. I vowed to pay him back, though I had no idea how I could.

I emerged from the quarter gallery to find the bunk completely stripped and Hemp scrubbing at the underlying wood with vinegar. More work I'd made for him.

"You should let me do that, Hemp. It's *my* mess."

He looked at me as if I'd suggested he strip naked and jump off the ship. "Oh, *no*, lady. I could *never* let you do that! Why I'd perish of embarrassment if anyone found out!"

"But it's my mess," I reiterated.

"Aye, and it's my job to keep this cabin in trim. I'll not hear of it. Now, you do yer stretches or read or whatever you like until breakfast, and let old Hemp do his job." He went back to scrubbing, the matter settled.

"Well, all right, but I hate making so much work for you." I started some slow stretches to alleviate the aches of being abed for so long, forcing myself to focus on each muscle, each motion, working through the pain, abolishing it by concerted effort. Once again, though my answer had been simple, the question had concerned a magical thing, and had taxed me considerably. "What's the hour?"

"Comin' up on four bells in the forenoon watch. You were out for quite a spell."

"Yes, I was." I twisted my back, and vertebrae popped in sequence. "We're underway. Where are we going?"

"The southwest end of Valaka Isle." Hemp dunked his brush in a bucket and shook it out, then began meticulously wiping the wood down with a dry towel. "Mister Boxley come back this mornin' with news."

"Oh?" I'd forgotten about Boxley's ordeal, and felt bad for my lapse. Kevril had put her life at risk. "Is she okay?"

"Oh, she's fine, though it was a trouncy trip by all accounts. Foist took the skin off his hand tryin' to tame a wild sheet, and the youngsters got knocked about some when they rounded the southern cape. They made it 'round finally and scouted out the windward side, hove to for a night in the teeth of the trades, then rounded the cape again downwind and sailed coastwise through the night to get back at first light." He began flogging the wood dry with the cloth.

"And did they find the dragonship?" I raised one leg to stretch my hip and struggled for balance on the moving deck.

"Nope, but she found a keep right on the shore there. Probably some dragonlord's place. Since Kivan found out that a dragonlord built the ship, it stands to reason that it's there somewheres. Hid by magic, mayhap. There's no anchorage or harbor at all near the keep, so the captain's gonna anchor on the lee side and trek overland come first light tomorrow."

Good, I thought, lifting my other leg for the opposite stretch. *I won't have to see him for a few days.*

A knock at the door announced breakfast, and Hemp interrupted his work to bring the tray to the navigation table. He'd already dismantled the dining table and stowed it away to make room for my exercises, and the smaller one was more comfortable underway.

Unless Kevril had guests, we had generally eaten our meals there, the two opposing benches close enough that our feet got tangled up beneath.

My mind dredged up a memory: sitting in our robes, sipping blackbrew, lazily running my toes up Kevril's leg under the table, looking up to find his eyes shining at me. The recollection almost brought a smile…before I remembered to hate him.

Stop it! Just stop thinking about him! I sat at the table as Hemp uncovered the dishes: an omelet, toasted bread, crispy fried plantain, and blackbrew. More than I would usually eat, but I'd be exercising all day and welcomed the energy the food would give me. The longer I could continue my yamshi, the longer I could stave off the madness.

Take pleasure where you can find it. I thanked Hemp and tucked in, the fabulous aromas and flavors distracting me from my plight.

By the time I washed down the very last bite with a swallow of blackbrew, Hemp had finished flogging the wood dry, and the cabin smelled strongly of linseed oil. Wrinkling my nose, I got up and resumed my stretches.

"Sorry about the smell, Lady Preel. I'll just take the dishes and see to the laundry. That oil's got to dry before the new mattress goes down, anyways." He stacked the dishes and left, his stride as straight and easy as mine would have been on solid ground, a sailor to the core.

A sorely deluded one, I reminded myself as I finished stretching and assumed the first pose of the *gie-wa* sequence. The entire crew idolized Kevril Longbright; he'd manipulated them all into loving him, just as he had me.

Forcing my mind to task, banishing all thoughts but those concerning the placement of my hands, feet, hips, and spine, I started the routine. Challenging enough on solid ground, I found myself fully occupied with every pose just to keep my balance. I worked into a rhythm with the motion of the ship. The seas weren't bad in the lee of the island, and the leeward rolls weren't violent. Even on one foot, I could keep my balance, but it required deep concentration, exactly what I needed. I finished the sequence in a light sweat, breathing deeply and evenly, centered and at peace. Hemp had put out a pitcher of water, so I downed a glass and immediately started the even more challenging *teh-wa* routine. I stumbled twice, but kept my focus, and finished drenched and breathing hard.

Another cup of water eased my breathing. The last of my aches and pains had long been banished, replaced by a languid fatigue. My hair was plastered to my face and neck, distracting, so I wound it in a tight bun and tied it back with string. Now it tugged at the lump on the back of my head, reminding me of my tirade and Miko's petulant revenge. I truly wished she would have hit me. I felt like I somehow deserved it for directing my hatred of Kevril at her. Another friendship destroyed.

"Stop it!" I wiped my dripping face with a towel and launched into *gie-wa* again, faster this time, adjusting the poses to the roll of the ship, hardly pausing between them.

Hemp came in with a tray, but I barely noticed him, so focused was I upon my routine. The aroma of food, however, invaded my concentration and brought an image to my mind: Bert, her face livid and flushed at my scathing rant the night of my abduction. I'd destroyed that friendship as well. She'd always doted on me, cared for me aboard *Hymoin* when Nightspinner's abuse left me bruised and bleeding. *Gone...* Her love, her tenderness, was gone.

I stumbled with a leeward lurch of the deck and fought for control. *Focus! Feet, hands, legs, hips...* As I moved into c*rane strikes deep*, my rear foot found a wet patch of wood. I slipped and went down, my hip hitting the cabin sole hard, my concentration shattered. I swore and bit down as pain lanced through my leg.

"Lady Preel! Are you all right?" Hemp was there to help me up, his hands sure and cool.

"Yes, just clumsy." My leg supported my weight, but twinged. My hair had come undone and clung to my face. I brushed it aside in frustration. "I'll be fine."

"Mayhap I should put a rug down. With the deck lurchin', you could take a bad spill."

"I'd only wear the rug to tatters and sweat all over it, which would be even *more* work for you." I took a breath, reveling in the aromas of fresh bread, garlic, onions, and mutton. "I'll break for lunch."

"Very good." He waved me to the navigation table and lifted the cover from the plate to reveal a bowl of hearty stew, bread, a smaller bowl of fruit, and a cup of juice. *Hardly crew fare*, I thought, wondering why I deserved such care. Hemp poured water and handed me the glass.

"Thank you." I sat down and drank deeply, my stomach growling despite my recent breakfast. As I ate, the spicy stew biting my tongue, I noticed Hemp laying out some of my clothes along with a sturdy duffle bag. "What's all this?"

"Just packin' up, Lady Preel." He smiled and began wiping up the spots of sweat from the cabin sole. "Dunno where I'm gonna find a pair of boots to fit ya, but I swear I will if I have to cut off someone's legs to get 'em!"

"Boots?" I choked on a half-chewed bite, coughed, and recovered. "Why are you packing for *me*, and why would I need boots? Where am I going?"

He looked at me askance. "Why, overland to that dragonlord's keep, lady. I told you, the captain's gonna be settin' out at first light tomorrow. It'll take two days to get there, and two to get back."

"With *me*?" I lurched out of my seat, panic extinguishing my appetite. "I am *not* trekking across Valaka with Kevril Longbright! Tell him I refuse! I *won't*!"

An expression of pure misery crossed Hemp's homely face. "Oh, but you *gotta* go, Lady Preel. Captain *needs* you along."

"Why? Why does he need me? I'm not a pirate! He can take this damned dragonship and sail off into the Serpent's Eye on his own!"

"Ah, well, there's the gettin' the ship, part, lady." He rolled up a pair of my pantaloons and tucked them in the duffel. "This dragonlord may just tell him to piss up a rope. Captain's gotta have somethin' to barter with for that ship, and your talent... Well..."

My temper surged. Days hiking over mountains with a man I despised, just so he could use me as barter. "Oh, of *course*! Once again, I'm nothing but his bargaining chip! Does he plan to trade me to the dragonlord like he traded me to Brekka?"

"Lady Preel, it's not like that. He may need to *ask* you somethin'. You're the only advantage we got."

"I'm a *truthsayer*, not a pack mule!" Enraged, I launched into yet another yamshi routine, forcing my mind into the discipline to no avail. *Faster! Focus!* I stepped up my pace to twice the rhythmic roll of the ship, fast enough that the fluid poses resembled the original martial discipline far more than the relaxing exercise. My feet squeaked on the deck, my hands whistling through the air, fingers poised like claws. My loose hair whipped around into my face as I spun, distracting me. I cursed, my concentration broken, and fought my unruly curls back under control.

"Let me help you there, Lady Preel. I'll fix a knot that'll never come out."

"Thank you, Hemp. I can't seem to—" A memory assailed me— Kevril running his hands through my long hair. A sudden need for retribution struck me. I couldn't refuse to go on this mad trek across the island, but I could make my displeasure known. "Cut it off, Hemp!"

"What? No, Lady Preel. You got *beautiful* hair!"

I whirled on him. "Why does it matter? There's no one who cares what I *look* like! I'm only valuable because I'm a truthsayer! I want you to cut my hair short, Hemp. Now!"

He looked miserable, but finally nodded. "All right, Lady Preel, but you gotta sit still and let me do a proper job. I won't have nobody sayin' I just hacked off your hair with a cutlass."

"Fine." I retrieved one of the chairs he'd set aside and sat. "Get the scissors!"

He went to the vanity and got his barbering tools, returning with a sour look. "You sure about this?"

"I'm sure, damn it! And I want it *short*! I'm sick of it!" I folded my arms as he draped a towel over my shoulders, my chest heaving with my raging temper. "*Short*, Hemp!" I was tempted to have him shave my scalp completely, but refrained. It would be cold trekking over the mountains.

"All right, Lady Preel. Just hold still now."

The razor-edged scissors snipped, and a foot and a half of sweat-soaked black hair fell to the deck.

Chapter Eighteen
A Concerted Effort

Only a foolish commander is a tyrant.
The Lessons of Quen Lau Ush

From the journal of Jhavika Keshmir –
Years under Captain Kohl taught me many things. I learned much about seamanship, to be sure, but even more about people. I also learned to use all of the tools at my disposal to manipulate them. Gaining the scourge made that simple. Now, without it, I am having to relearn.

"Why in the Nine Hells wasn't I called up earlier?" I mounted the quarterdeck and accepted a spyglass from a hapless sailor. "Where away?"

"One of ours, right northwest, your ladyship." The sailor pointed. "She's beating hard. Lookout recognized *Peony* as soon as she came hull up."

"About gods-damned time!" I focused on the distant ship. Her yards were slightly askew, and her sails weren't trimmed perfectly, but she was making good headway. They'd arrive at our anchorage in an hour, at most. "Once they drop anchor, signal for Lady Roque to come aboard *Crimson Hawk*. I need to speak with her in private."

"Yes, your ladyship."

I handed back the spyglass and went below, fighting my impatience. I needed information and cooperation, and I needed it now. Waiting around while my crew rested had worn on me like sandpaper on an open wound, leaving me unable to sleep.

In my cabin, my hovering steward was hard at work. He'd finally cleaned the great cabin to my satisfaction, and learned my habits. He had blackbrew waiting on the chart table, and some cheese and ship's biscuits as well.

I tossed my hat to him and started pacing. "Lady Roque will be joining me in an hour or so. Cool a bottle of decent wine and find something not entirely vile for us to eat."

"Yes, your ladyship." He hung my hat and hurried out, circling as wide as he could around Te-shan.

My komei stood there like a statue, unmoving, alert, silent, and obedient. I'd become so accustomed to his constant presence that I barely realized he was there most of the time. He even stood beside my bunk in the rare event that I slept. As far as I knew, he never slept himself. He practiced an ancient Chen discipline that allowed him to rest while standing and alert. I'd ordered him to teach me, but he'd said it would be impossible to teach to someone of my age; it took years to master. I had bristled at being denied, but in the end, I realized there were some things I could never have.

Old dog, I thought, resuming my pacing. *No new tricks.*

I drank blackbrew, considered my charts, my pending meeting with Ursula, and the evolving deployment of my armada. There were vanishing few places left where Kevril could be hiding.

Finally, my guest arrived.

"Lady Roque, your ladyship," my steward announced, ushering Ursula into the great cabin.

"Ursula!" I turned with a genuine smile. "It's good to see a..." I hesitated, then finished with a careful lie. "...a familiar face."

I barely recognized the woman I knew. She looked like a wraith of her former self, thin and drawn, her already prominent cheekbones now skeletal, her eyes sunken and dark-circled. Haggard, worn, and exhausted, she seemed ready to topple over at the merest whisper of wind. Ursula Roque wasn't handling her slavery very well.

She curtsied stiffly, her hand white on her rapier. "Jhavika."

"Come and sit down. You look exhausted." I motioned her to the chart table, and she sat down, her motions jerky, like a puppet, which of course she was. But my puppet was very nearly broken, and I still needed her. "Tell me, haven't you been getting any rest at all?"

"No. How could I? You commanded me to search for Longbright tirelessly, so I've done nothing else since we parted company. There's been no sign of him in Black Point or the smaller islands you had us search." Her voice trembled, taking on a hysterical note. "No one in Black Point City has seen or heard from him in months. The windward side of the island doesn't have anyplace he could moor, even temporarily. We searched everywhere. I *swear* it!"

I didn't remember commanding her to search *tirelessly*, but I well could have in a fit of temper. If so, it had been a sore mistake. I knew better than to give commands like that. As my conscribed second in command had pointed out to me, exhaustion was deadly while navigating the Obsidian Isles.

I sat and motioned my steward forward. "Ursula, have a glass of wine and relax. You need to take rest when you're exhausted. If you don't, you'll run your ship up on a reef."

The steward presented a tray of sliced cheeses, sausages, and smoked fish, then filled two glasses with a deep-red wine before backing away.

"Yes, that's what the sailors said." Ursula drank some wine and visibly relaxed. Of course, she had no choice but to do as I commanded. "Here are the messages I've received from the others since my previous packet." She delved the satchel at her hip and pulled out a waxed canvas packet of letters. "Matesh is still repairing damage. They lost their mizzenmast and a number of sails were burnt. More than half of his crew were injured, most by fire, and they have no surgeon aboard. I haven't heard from Busashi since he left Sariff for Mati."

I glanced through the correspondence and frowned. It boiled down to one hard fact: nobody had seen *Scourge* or heard of Kevril for more than a month. I shifted through the letters, looking for what wasn't there. "No word from Tan?"

Ursula shook her head wearily. "Nothing."

Damn! "Very well, Ursula. Well done." I ate some cheese and sausage and washed it down with a swallow of wine, then made a decision. I didn't know that had happened to Tan, but I wasn't about to sit here on my ass and wait for word that might never come. "Since Valaka is still unknown, you and I will look into it." I tapped the chart with a finger. "We're well situated to search the island. I want you to sail directly to Valaka City and start asking questions about Kevril and Captain Tan. Be thorough, but be careful, too. Kevril's been there before, and made enemies. I know one's an alchemist named Brekka, but that doesn't rule out others." I wasn't about to tell her that Kevril had broken his enchantment with a potion from Brekka; there was no sense in putting notions into her head. "If you find nothing, then start searching along the leeward coast. I'll search down the windward shore, since it's more dangerous and I've got the more weatherly ship." I was also much more of a sailor than Roque or her conscriped captain, and the last thing I needed now was for *Peony* to fetch up on the rocky coast due to inexperience or exhaustion. "I'll round the southern cape and start working my way back up the leeward coast. We should meet somewhere along the way. But if you spot *Scourge* or find word of Kevril, immediately send a cutter down the coast to find me."

"Yes, Jhavika." Ursula started to get up, but I put a hand on her arm.

"Sit and finish your wine, Ursula." I needed to find out what had put her in such a state. If she didn't take care of herself, she was useless to me. "Once *Peony* is underway, I want you to take some rest. You've at least a full day of open-sea sailing before you reach Valaka. Get some sleep and eat something. You're no good to anyone if you collapse of exhaustion and malnutrition."

Ursula looked a little surprised as she sank back into her chair. "Thank you." She sipped her wine and ate some cheese and sausage, her motions stiff, her eyes still wide and haunted. There was something going on with her, more than simple exhaustion.

"What's *wrong*, Ursula? You're obviously upset about something. I need you to tell me what's bothering you."

124

"*Bothering* me?" Her eyes flashed wide, and she started to shake. "You... You'll punish me if I tell you."

"Punish you?" Suspicion rose up in me. Something was very wrong. "Tell me right now what's got you in such a state, Ursula."

"It's you! You've enslaved me, controlled me with magic somehow. I can't break it, and it's driving me mad! It's that scourge of yours! The one Kevril took! You lashed me with it during that party at your place! I can't fight you, I can't kill you, and I can't even kill *myself*!"

She was ranting now, and I realized my error. I hadn't had the time to fully indoctrinate Ursula, and she was chafing at her bonds.

"Ursula, calm down. I'm not going to punish you. Yes, I'm controlling you with magic, and there's nothing you can do about it. But you needn't fear me. You *enjoy* serving me. You shouldn't think about it. Just do as I say and let go of the notion that you want free will. You don't need it. Nobody's free, anyway. We're all slaves to one thing or another. You'll feel calm and relaxed as you carry out my wishes, and you will take *care* of yourself. You'll do as I say because you *want* to." I patted her arm. "Now, relax, calm down, and enjoy this bottle of wine and this food with me. Then we'll go on and find Kevril together. When that's done, we can both go home to Haven. Okay?"

"Okay." Ursula sipped wine and ate some more, smiling with induced pleasure, considerably more relaxed. "It's...hard to get used to. That's all."

"I know it is, but in time, you'll realize it's a freeing thing to take pleasure in serving another. You just need to accept it." I drank my wine and motioned for my steward to refill our glasses.

The man's hand shook so badly as he poured that he spilled wine onto the chart.

"Clean that up!" I snapped.

"Sorry, your ladyship!" He dabbed at the spill, but the wine left a purple stain on the chart. His hands were still shaking.

I realized then just how much he had overheard. The original crew of *Tiger Lily* already knew I had utter control over my people, but not how. I wondered if keeping the secret really mattered anymore, but old habits die hard.

"Te-shan, take my steward up on deck and execute him. Find me a new one."

"Yes, your ladyship."

The steward's eyes widened in horror for a moment, his mouth gaping. He whirled and dashed for the door, but Te-shan was there. A sharp blow from an armored fist dropped the man like a pole-axed steer in a slaughterhouse. Te-shan gripped the collar of the man's jacket and hauled him out.

I sighed in frustration and sipped my wine. "Just when I had him trained properly, too."

Ursula smiled at me from across the table, sipping her wine and nibbling the food happily.

Well, at least I'd solved one problem.

Chapter Nineteen
The Wilds

Love is a two-edged sword.
The Lessons of Quen Lau Ush

From the diary of Kevril Longbright –
Hiking through the wild country of Valaka brought back memories of my youth. The long hours I spent in the forests of Tira evading my father's temper had not been ill spent. The outing might even have been enjoyable, but it's difficult to enjoy beauty in the company of someone who hates you.

Making unpopular decisions is part of a captain's job, but I thought I might have a mutiny on my hands when I told Rauley that he wasn't going on the trek across Valaka. Kivan's sketches of the dragonship had intrigued him to the core, and he wouldn't get to see it. He accepted my reasoning, but that didn't make him any happier about staying behind.

In the end, I decided on a small group. I considered leaving Miko in command of *Scourge* in my absence, but I needed her for moral support as much as for her sharp wit and sharper blade. I wouldn't have left the ship without Wix at my side for all the sunken gold in all the seas of the world, which was why Rauley had to stay behind. After my bosun, no one else knew the sails and rigging as well as my sailing master. I put Kivan in command, with Quiff as her second and Tansy as acting bosun. The four youths together could sail *Scourge* well enough. I asked Boxley along because she'd seen our destination before, and I would have had to tie her to the mainmast to keep her on the ship, which wouldn't have been good for morale. Wix asked for volunteers, so we had ten more stout pirates along for protection.

We packed warm clothing, food—Bert made several dozen meat pasties that would travel well—water skins, weapons, and some gold and baubles for barter, though I didn't know if a dragonlord would want or need money. I'd long ago learned how to pack light, so when Hemp came on deck lugging a duffle big enough to carry a side of beef, I confronted him.

"That's too heavy, Hemp. We're only packing for a few days, at most."

He gave me a look of utter stubbornness. "With respect, sir, I'll pack how I like, and I'll carry it myself. Lady Preel ain't used to such treks, and you ordered me to take care of her as best I could. This here is both my stuff and hers."

"If you say so, Hemp, but if you slow us down, I'll—" My voice failed me as Preel stepped onto the deck. She wore pantaloons tucked into stout boots, a sturdy shirt, her silken gag, and a wide leather belt. It wasn't her garb, however, that brought me up short. It was her hair, or the lack of it.

The beautiful waves of onyx that I so adored were gone, her hair cut so short that it made her look boyish. The top was barely long enough to ruffle in the breeze, and only a short fuzz remained above her ears and neck. Thought skillfully done—obviously Hemp's work—and not unattractive, it completely transformed her appearance. Her bare neck seemed unnaturally long, her ears more prominent, her skin darker. Not the woman I knew at all.

Appropriate, perhaps.

A number of the officers and crew caught their breath at the sight of her, and a few even swore quiet oaths. I opened my mouth to say something, then thought better of it. I wondered why she'd done it, what in the world could have prompted such an action. Asking, however, would only provoke her ire. I couldn't think of any other reason than to spite me. She knew I loved her hair, and cutting it denied me that simple pleasure.

I turned to my officers. "Lieutenant Kivan, you're in command. Keep a sharp lookout. If you spot one of Jhavika's ships, cut your anchor free and run for open sea on your best point of sail. You will *not* engage, even if you have the advantage. Do you understand me?"

She snapped me a brisk salute. "Perfectly, sir!"

I returned it. "Good. If we can buy, beg, borrow, or *steal* this dragonship, I'll send a messenger to let you know. If not, we'll probably be back in four or five days." I leveled my most serious stare at her. "Take care of my ship, Captain."

She blushed at the honorific. "I will, sir! Good hunting!" She stuck out a hand.

"Thank you." I shook it firmly, nodded, and turned to Miko. "Let's go."

"Aye, sir! Wix, get them aboard."

We boarded the two longboats and rowed ashore. Hemp and Preel sat in one, with Miko at the tiller, while I took the other. The surf was negligible, so we got everyone and our baggage ashore without even wetting our boots. That was fine by me. We were in for a long trek, and wet boots would rub my still tender feet raw. I was glad they had healed well enough to handle the upcoming strain, but the wound where the crossbow bolt had pierced my leg still ached. We all shouldered our packs, and my sailors hefted loaded crossbows. The longboats pushed off, and the crews rowed for the ship.

I sighed and looked up at the heavily wooded hills. "Wix, I want you breaking trail. Try to find the easiest path you can. We should be on a heading of east southeast." I pulled out a hand compass, took a bearing, and pointed to a distant mountain top. "There's a good landmark. Let's not climb right over the top of it, though." The last drew a few nervous chuckles from my crew.

"Aye, sir." Wix drew a broad-bladed cutlass and strode forth.

We all followed in single file. Miko fell in behind me, with Preel and Hemp behind her, then Boxley, and finally the rest of my pirates.

"So, what do you think we'll find, sir?" Miko asked conversationally.

I shrugged. "This far from Valaka City, I don't know. A dragonlord would be my best guess."

"I hope they don't mind visitors."

"So do I. If they built a keep this far away from civilization to avoid human contact, we could have a problem."

"Is it true that some of the dragonlords are mad?" Boxley asked.

I resisted looking back at her, unwilling to meet Preel's eyes even accidentally. "I don't know that either, but it's my guess that the rumors are exaggerated. From all I've heard, they're just wizards and scholars obsessed with dragon magic or the Serpent's Eye itself."

"It's the *wizard* part that's got my knickers in a bunch," Miko said. "I've never met one who didn't seem a *little* mad. Maybe it's the magic itself that makes them that way."

"From what little I've heard, magic's a bit like black lotus: intoxicating and addictive as hell. Wizards might sometimes go mad trying to push their knowledge ever higher, but the magic itself isn't the cause."

"Except the magic from the Serpent's Eye that mutates people into monsters," Boxley said.

That drew worried mutters from the rest.

"Well, if we do find a dragonlord, let's hope it's a sane one," Miko added.

"We can only hope, I'm afraid." I recalled all too well my reticence in contacting any of the dragonlords when we were searching for a cure for my own enchantment. There was a reason why people left the dragonlords alone.

We began the steep climb, Wix hacking a path through the jungle. My pirates cursed and growled with every step. Though as strong as apes and fit from ceaseless labor, they weren't accustomed to long treks. Neither was I, and my healing thigh burned with every step. In no time, we were all dripping sweat.

I began pushing my hands down on my knees as we ascended, biting my tongue on my own complaints. Farther down the line, Hemp huffed and puffed, but trudged on without a word, the quietest, in fact, that I'd ever heard him. I guessed that we were both carrying heavy burdens on this trip. *Well, if he can suffer in silence, so can I.*

I reflexively glanced back and inadvertently caught Preel's gaze: hard, dark, and as sharp as twin chips of obsidian. I looked away. Gagged with her enchanted binding, she couldn't complain. *At least I don't have to listen to her sharp tongue*, I thought, and immediately felt guilty for my venom. The gag was in place for her safety, not my comfort. I resolved to call frequent rest stops. I could always claim my leg was hurting, which was true enough.

The pain in my leg, however, paled in comparison to the less tangible agony of Preel's hatred for me. With difficulty, I forced my thoughts away from her. Perhaps the woman I knew was gone forever, irreversibly poisoned by the magic of the scourge and Jhavika's spiteful commands. It didn't matter. I would destroy the scourge anyway. Only then would I know if I'd made a mistake in rescuing her from Jhavika. I wondered privately what I would do if Preel continued to hate me after the scourge was gone.

To that, I had no answer, and it was one question I would never put to the truthsayer.

Chapter Twenty
Staring into the Eye

Fear is natural. Denying it is foolish.
The Lessons of Quen Lau Ush

From the journal of Preel Longbright –
I don't know what I expected, but the foreboding I felt when I first gazed upon the Serpent's Eye took me by surprise. As a magical creature, I couldn't help but wonder what might happen if my talent came under the influence of that maelstrom of wild magic. I find myself both worried and intrigued by the prospect.

I woke shivering. Despite the two blankets and a weather cloak atop me, the earth beneath had leached every last bit of warmth from my bones. After a moment's disorientation, I remembered where I was—Valaka, halfway across the island. We had camped at dusk along the upper edge of the leeward tree line. Wix had found a path of sorts, and then a pass through the mountains, but we hadn't reached the crest before darkness settled in. It wasn't yet light, but my teeth were chattering, and I knew the only way I would get warm was to move.

Moving, however, proved painful. I wasn't used to sleeping on hard ground.

Every muscle seemed intent on torturing me as I forced myself up. My right leg cramped, and I fought to force it straight. I would have screamed had I not been wearing the gag. I staggered to my feet and clutched my boat cloak close, stretching slowly to alleviate the pain and work some blood into my limbs.

Around me, pirates huddled under blankets, some snoring, obviously better inured to hardship than I. Two figures sat at the center of the camp, smaller Boxley dwarfed by Wix's hulking form. They both looked at me, but said nothing, and it was too dark to see their faces clearly. There was no fire, no warmth to be shared. The jungle had proven perilous enough. Twice our piratical escort had dissuaded the interest of misshapen creatures with volleys of crossbow bolts. One of the creatures had fallen from a tree beside the trail. A twisted caricature resembling both monkey and pig. Huge tusks protruded from its lower jaw, and its long, prehensile tail twitched as we hurried past. None in our group knew what might prowl the higher forest at night, so Kevril had ordered a cold camp for safety's sake.

Kevril... I couldn't discern his shape from the others, and quashed the fleeting temptation to sneak a dagger from someone's belt and stab him in his sleep. It was a foolish thought, I knew; Kevril was the only hope I had of being freed of the scourge's enchantment. But my hatred was all I had to keep me sane, and I clung to it like a lifeline in a storm.

I moved away from the snoring shapes and began to stretch in earnest. Muscles protested, and my feet ached inside my boots. Eventually, I stopped shivering. Assessing the faint light over the crest of the mountainous pass, I estimated we still had at least an hour before full dawn.

Awake and too thoughtful for my own good, I faced east, *greeted the sun*, and launched into the *te-wah* routine. The fluttering cloak interfered with the fluidity of my exercises, but it was cold this high in the mountains, and a chill breeze whipped down from the ridge crest. My exposed ears felt numb. By the time I finished the routine, the sky had brightened, my muscles were warm, all aches and pains had been banished, and my breathing came in deep, hungry lungfuls. I hadn't broken a sweat, but I was panting from the thin air. I wondered how high we were. Turning in a slow circle, I drank in the stark beauty of the wind-twisted trees and rocky outcrops.

"Blackbrew, Lady Preel?"

I turned to find Boxley holding out a steaming tin cup. My face must have registered my confusion.

"No fire," she explained, "but Bert sent along a heatstone, so we got blackbrew at least. No milk, but it's warm."

I took the cup gratefully and tapped the gag, turning for her to untie it.

"Sure." Boxley slipped the knot and handed me the gag with a smile. "I like your hair, by the way. Makes you look different, younger." Her face flushed. "Not that you looked old before, but..."

"I..." Her compliment took me aback—*She doesn't hate me*—and my fingers brushed my foreshortened hair. "Thank you." I didn't know what else to say, so I turned my attention to the blackbrew. Cradling the cup in my hands, I sipped. It was warm, but not hot, and strong enough to wake the dead.

An uncomfortable smile twitched the corner of Boxley's mouth. "There's food, if you're hungry." She gestured back to the camp.

Wix had begun walking around, nudging sleeping forms none too gently with the toe of his boot. His deep-throated chant—"Rise and shine, my lovelies! We're burnin' daylight and my boot's up yer arse if you're not on your feet my next time 'round. Rise and shine!"—silenced the snores and elicited curses.

I realized that I was hungry and nodded. "Please." Downing the tepid blackbrew and following her, I traded the empty cup for a strip of jerky, a wedge of cheese, and a slab of day-old flatbread wrapped in a kerchief.

"Here, you can take some for Hemp." Boxley handed me another bundle and dipped my empty cup in a simmering pot, handing it over full.

"Thank you, Boxley." Maybe one friendship hadn't been destroyed. I tried to smile, but my face refused. Turning to find Hemp, I spotted Kevril rising stiffly from his blankets and remembered why I never smiled anymore. I ducked my head and hurried to my abandoned bed. Hemp was already stowing our things in his pack. I felt guilty about his carrying my gear in addition to his, but he'd insisted. The least I could do was fetch him a meal. I held out the food and cup. "Here. Breakfast."

"Blyme, Lady Preel, you shouldn't be servin' me. That's *my* job!" He took the cup and bundle with a pained smile.

"Shut up and eat." I ate my own tasteless fare mechanically, knowing I would need the energy. By the time I finished, the camp had been struck, and we were ready to go.

"All right, my lovelies, fall in or we leave you for the buzzards!" Wix hefted his pack and a crossbow and started uphill without another look back, tireless and indomitable.

"Let me just fix that for you, Lady Preel." Hemp gestured to the gag dangling from my belt.

Kevril had insisted that I wear it for my own safety, but I knew it was just to protect his only bargaining chip—me. I nodded and handed the strip of silk to Hemp, turning my back for him to tie it.

"There you are, safe and sound." He hefted his pack, and we joined the line of muttering pirates.

We emerged from the sparse trees into a scrubby, lichen-strewn landscape, stark and beautiful, but unforgiving. A hawk screeched high above, and I spied a pair of them soaring free on the wind. Oh, for that freedom... Then one stooped, plunging to the earth with talons outstretched, and the wailing cry of some small animal among the rocks pierced the air. *Freedom...to kill or be killed, live or die, love or remain safely alone.* Banishing my torturous thoughts, I concentrated on placing my feet as the rocky path steepened.

Within half an hour, everyone was breathing hard, even the tireless Wix. We were nearing the peak of the pass, a slash in the range between a craggy spire to our south and another farther away to the north. The track—a narrow path worn into the earth by mountain goats, humans, or who knew what other kind of creature—switched back and forth as it climbed higher and higher. A straight path would have been shorter, but far too steep to manage without scrambling on all fours. Despite all my recent exercise, my legs were burning as we approached the crest and Kevril stopped our procession.

"Five minutes. Drink some water, everyone." His voice sounded foreboding, even fearful. He stood staring to the east beside a stone cairn, a sure sign that we were on a man-made path.

When Hemp and I topped the crest, I understood his trepidation. I might have blamed the chill that shivered my spine on the wind that howled over the ridge, but I would have been lying.

"Behold, the Serpent's Eye," the captain intoned prophetically.

I would have called it melodrama but for the view.

The Serpent's Eye blotted out the horizon to the southeast, the maelstrom of wild magic backlit by the muted glow of the rising sun. Clouds swirled in every hue of the rainbow, a stationary hurricane that defied nature. Despite the haze, I spotted islands jutting from the ocean, craggy and menacing in the fringe of the storm. From this height, the seas looked calm, but that was deceptive. I stared for a full minute, feeling that there was something wrong with what my eyes beheld. Then I realized; the trade winds blew hard from the east, propelling black squalls in a constant westward march. The Eye, however, rotated in a clockwise direction, the magical mists swirling in opposition to the prevailing winds.

"Well, bugger me if that ain't somethin' you don't see every day!" Hemp's irreverence cut through my rapt attention. He held out a water skin and untied my gag.

"Unless you live in that keep we found," Boxley countered. "It'd be passing odd to have *that* outside your window every morning."

"Aye, true enough," Hemp agreed. "Gotta admit, it's quite a view."

I accepted the skin and drank the water greedily. The arid air up this high seemed to leach the moisture from my body, drying my sweat before it even formed. As soon as I lowered the skin, however, my eyes were drawn back to the Eye. I couldn't disagree with Hemp's assessment; the view was indeed awe-inspiring.

Lightning flashed within the storm, but like none I'd ever seen before; blue and green, red and black, purple and orange bolts streaked the sky like streamers at a Chen carnival. And in the maelstrom, above the peaks of the nearest isles, something flew.

"Want a closer look, Lady Preel?" Boxley held out a spyglass.

"Please." I took it and raised it to my eye, focusing on the distant shapes. Huge wings beat the air, utterly unlike those of the hawks I'd seen earlier, long and leathery, like those of a monstrous bat. "Dragons," I muttered, my chest suddenly tight, my head spinning. I heaved in a lungful of chill air; I'd forgotten to breathe. I'd known that dragons existed, but knowing and actually *seeing* were two totally different things. They soared along the magical winds as easily as vultures on an updraft, but on an immensely larger scale. I couldn't believe anyone would willingly venture close to such creatures, but that was evidently our captain's intent. *Into the magic…among dragons.* I didn't know whether to pray for his success or his demise.

"They weren't lying about one thing," Miko said. "The Eye seems to draw dragons like flies, doesn't it?"

I couldn't tear my eyes away. Five of the massive beasts swooped on the thermals above one island. As I watched, lavender lightning flashed and struck one of them, but it merely arced and crackled harmlessly along the dragon's wings. In fact, the dragon shimmered, seeming to bask in the magical energy. Nothing mortal would fare so well. Only a creature of magic could withstand such an arcane barrage.

"A creature of magic…like a truthsayer," I whispered to myself.

"Whassat?" Hemp asked.

"Nothing, just musing." I handed back the spyglass and held out the gag to Hemp. "Please."

"Sure, Lady Preel."

As he tied the binding, the Eye drew my gaze as surely as it drew those soaring scaled beasts of legend. Wild, uncontrolled magic, its source unknown, its effects indeterminable. I couldn't help but wonder what would happen if I entered the storm. Would it augment my innate talent, amplify it? Would I see the future, know the answers to all the questions ever asked? Would the dormant voice of my talent burst forth unprovoked? Would it destroy me?

We started down the other side of the pass, our pace thrice what it had been on our ascent. Watching my feet to ensure that I didn't slip on the steep, rocky trail, I snatched furtive glances at the maelstrom, fascinated. Despite all my recent doubts and insecurities, I felt certain of one thing: if we did find this dragonship and venture into the Serpent's Eye, my questions of truth or lies, love or hate, would be answered without anyone having to ask.

Chapter Twenty One
The Dragonlord

Expect the unexpected, always.
The Lessons of Quen Lau Ush

From the diary of Kevril Longbright –
Never having met a dragonlord, I suppose I should have known better than to have preconceived notions of what one might be like. I know firsthand that legends grow in the telling and are rarely accurate.

Years of pacing the quarterdeck had not prepared me for a two-day trek across the mountainous terrain of Valaka. Even wearing the best pair of boots I owned, my feet were killing me by the first night, and the descent down the windward side of the mountains left my knees quaking and my healing thigh burning. This forest was wilder than the one of my youth, but I found similarities nonetheless. The thin air of high altitude, the green of the tree tops against the blissfully clear blue sky, the sharp woodland scent of decay and growing things—so different from the salty tang of the sea—dredged up long-distant memories of the months after I left home. I'd lived rough in the wilds, camping under the trees, working my way ever southward, hunting and fishing, alone and free, seeking a new life.

Now, I sought to reclaim that life I'd carved out for myself, a life paid for with scars, toil, and pain. I sought to recapture the dream I had lived for half a year with Preel, the best months of my life. But there was yet toil and pain to endure, perhaps more scars to earn.

At least our pace increased going downhill. By midday we had reached reasonably level ground, and the track we'd been following had widened into almost a road. The pain in my thigh eased somewhat, and my knees stopped shaking. My feet hurt, but the tender healing skin had not blistered, thanks to the supply of good wool socks that Hemp had darned for me. I occasionally glanced back at my former steward toiling along under that massive pack without complaint, always within reach of Preel, his eyes ever watchful should she miss a step. Hemp seemed a changed man, no longer a surly scallywag, but an utterly devoted companion. I watched him and wondered if that devotion was to me or Preel.

The bleat of a goat announced the first sign of civilization.

"Hold up, Wix," I ordered, and our ragtag column came to a stop. I spotted one goat, then another, cropping the short turf that covered the windswept hills. The swards were grooved with their paths. "We're getting close."

"Aye. What's the plan, sir?" Wix sounded ready for a frontal assault, but that probably wasn't our best option.

"I want a closer look at the keep itself before I make a decision, but we need to make some simple preparations." I looked over our people. "No loaded crossbows, and keep your hands away from weapons. If there's trouble, we're not going to be the ones to start it."

"Best news I've had all day." Miko slipped the bolt from her crossbow and slung it over her shoulder. "Bows and blades probably won't do much good against a dragonlord anyway."

"Wizards bleed, sir," Wix countered, following my orders with visible reluctance. "Just sayin'."

"That they do, but the tricky part is encouraging them to bleed before they reduce you to a pile of charred bones, so no nonsense from any of you." I raked them all with my sternest gaze. "We're here to barter for the use of this dragonship, nothing else."

My people grumbled assent and put up their crossbows. Then I spotted Preel, sticking out like a beacon in our midst, the swath of enchanted silk and the stark tattoo on her forehead marking her as unique and valuable. Keeping her nature a secret was paramount. I'd only reveal it if absolutely necessary.

"Hemp, please ask Preel if she'll allow a veil, headscarf, and a bit of makeup to cover her tattoo." I turned to scan the hillsides, more to avoid her obsidian-sharp glare than any interest in the goat population. "It's for her safety, but it's her choice."

"Aye, sir," Hemp said.

I raised my spyglass and scanned the hills, counting goats. Most were the everyday variety, brown or white and four-legged, but some sported bizarre deformities like those seen in the Serpent's Children. One bore eight legs instead of four. Another had no legs at all, but slithered along the ground like a slug, leaving a trail of slime in its wake. Shuddering, I shifted my gaze.

To seaward, the greensward ended in abrupt cliffs of the black stone that had given the Obsidian Isles their name. Beyond lay the sea ruffled with white caps, a dark squall building to the northeast, and the rainbow mists of the Eye to the southeast, our ultimate destination.

"Ready, sir!" Hemp said.

I turned to find Preel now garbed in a colorful sea-blue cloak with matching headscarf and veil. The tattoo on her forehead had been covered by a careful application of makeup. She seemed to me transformed once again, this time back into the woman I knew and loved.

But her eyes harbored little doubt that my feelings were neither appreciated nor reciprocated.

"Thank you." I looked over my crew one more time and nodded to Wix. "Let's move out."

Over the next half hour, we sighted additional signs that we were nearing the keep: even more goats, a goatherd who seemed more curious of us than wary, and a man so intent on cutting firewood from a grove of scraggly trees that he remained oblivious to our passing. Finally, we rounded yet another grassy knoll and beheld the dragonlord's keep.

"That's it," Boxley said as I called another halt. "Can't see the rock beach from here, but that's the keep proper. Couldn't see those other buildings from the sea, though."

"Not quite what I expected," I said. Actually, it didn't resemble any keep I'd ever seen.

The main structure was little more than a cube of quarried stone, undoubtedly gnomish in design, sporting three short towers pocked with windows and topped with steep cone-shaped, slate-shingled peaks. The low slate roof atop the main building was fitted with an impressive gutter system for collecting rainwater. An iron-bound wooden door, barely wide enough to fit a cart through, protected the entrance, but at the moment stood wide open. The outbuildings included a cow byre, a shack abutting a goat pen, chicken coops, an impressive woodshed, and a well-equipped smithy. The surrounding acres were cultivated in orderly gardens, and people worked among the rows of beans, corn, potatoes, and tomatoes.

"Not built for defense," Wix commented.

"Which means they don't need it." Miko eyed me sidelong, then raised her spyglass. "Wizard, remember."

"Aye, when you've got a wizard in residence, arrow slits and battlements aren't really necessary, I suppose." I motioned us forward. "The people don't seem overly concerned about us either."

"You're right, sir, they're not concerned, or at least, they're not showing it." Miko lowered her spyglass and gave me one of her looks. "Maybe the dragonlord's expecting us?"

"Maybe." The thought gave me pause. If we would be dealing with someone who could see the future—Odea only knew what kind of magic was practiced by the dragonlords—there was no point in attempting any deceptions. I cast a worried glance at Preel. "I hope not."

As we approached, a few of the laborers wandered into the keep, their movements casual, but their eyes lingering on us. Several sported the mutations of Serpent's Children. By the goatherd's shed, a girl crouched next to a barking sheepdog, hugging it with arms that bifurcated at the elbows, stroking it with four hands. As we neared the keep proper, a stout fellow ambled from the smithy, his leather apron much scorched, a smith's hammer held easily in his hand. He regarded us with narrow eyes.

"You're a bit off the beaten track here."

"We are." I nodded to him and stopped. "My name's Kevril Longbright. I'd like to speak with your master, if I may."

He frowned. "No masters here, Kevril Longbright, and if you mean trouble, you'll find more than you can manage."

Wix snorted, but I shut him up with a glare. "We mean no trouble. I'm here to ask the master or mistress of the keep some questions, and hopefully barter for their services."

"The shepherd's busy. We don't take visitors and don't offer services."

Shepherd? I wondered. I hadn't seen any sheep, only goats. "We're willing to pay for their time."

"Shepherd's not interested in money, either." The man waved his hammer at the surroundings. "What's to spend it on out here?"

"Then we'll barter services and information." Still perplexed, I was through talking to the keep's blacksmith. "We seek the master of the dragonship."

Finally, a reaction. The fellow's eyes widened and his mouth dropped open, his knuckles whitening on the handle of his hammer. He closed his mouth and nodded once. "Stay here."

"Fine." I crossed my arms and watched him hurry to the door of the keep.

"That was dangerous, sir," Miko said low. "If this lord's a wizard, he could kill us with a wave of his hand."

"They better be a fucking wizard if he can sail a ship into that." I nodded at the looming Serpent's Eye.

"Agreed, sir, but we would have been safer to get *inside* before you told them what we wanted."

"We'll see." I eyed the other laborers still outside, seemingly unconcerned as they went about their work. "They're not afraid of us. That seems strange. Even if their lord *is* a wizard, it seems strange."

"Aye," Wix said. "Don't like it."

"Just hold fast for now," I warned.

"It's your funeral, sir," Wix quipped, eliciting a few nervous laughs.

In time, the blacksmith returned with another fellow, swarthy with short, dark hair, dressed barely better than any of the laborers in a plain woolen shirt and sturdy pants and boots. A set of keys dangled from his belt, but no weapon. He regarded us with curious eyes, looking me over from head to foot, then at Wix, then past me. I didn't look over my shoulder, but would have bet he was examining Preel. My hand longed for the hilt of my cutlass, but I kept it lax at my side.

To my surprise, he simply nodded and said, "Follow me."

I traded a glance with Miko, but she just shrugged. We followed.

The inside of the keep was even less impressive than the outside. The entry hall struck me as stark, even minimalist: comfortable and clean, but with no adornment, not even a coat of arms or house banner. *So much for the legendary egos of wizards.*

Our guide stopped and gestured to an alcove. "You may leave your bags and cloaks there."

He didn't mention weapons, so we kept them. Divested of our knapsacks, we followed our guide once again, this time into a wide hall with an arched ceiling lit by glow crystals and warmed by a coal-burning hearth. Comfortable enough, but again, not a single adornment or sign of luxury. Sturdy wooden tables sat in rows with simple wooden chairs without cushions. There was no head table, no raised dais, no sign that any single seat differed from any other. It looked more like a communal dining hall than a lord's feasting hall.

"Wait here," our escort intoned without a hint of welcome. "The shepherd will meet with you shortly."

"All right." I nodded to my people as our guide departed, and they took seats on the chairs closest to the hearth. I was as footsore as they undoubtedly were, perhaps more so, but I remained standing. When the lord of the keep arrived, I didn't want to be seated. Rising when he entered would be too deferential, whereas remaining seated would be impertinent. I wanted to begin this relationship as respectful equals. I tried not to grimace as I flexed my sore feet.

"Not a single weapon or guard, sir," Wix said quietly, fidgeting with the spiked bronze guards of his daggers as he glanced warily around the room. "Downright bizarre, it is."

"They obviously don't feel the need." Miko propped her feet on the hearthstone and leaned back with a heavy sigh.

"Which either means they're fools or they *don't* need them," Wix continued. "Which, assumin' this lord or shepherd or whatever ain't a fool, the neighbors and nasty beasties from the wilds have learned not to fook with 'em."

"Shepherd… No sheep, so I don't think it's a literal title." I held my hands out to the fire. "Perhaps an honorific?"

"Maybe he's a priest of some sort," Boxley suggested, her eyes taking in the unadorned walls. "You know, like shepherd of a flock of worshipers? The place has the look of a monastery, don't it? Kinda...austere."

"Austere," I looked at her with appreciation. "That's *exactly* the word I was looking for, and not a bad theory, either. Thank you, Boxley." I reexamined our surroundings and nodded.

"You're welcome, sir."

We fell into a contemplative silence. Turning to warm my backside, I surreptitiously glanced at Preel. She sat with her eyes cast down, staring at her hands clenched in her lap. Her knuckles were blanched white. I wondered if she could feel the magic of the Serpent's Eye, if its chaos threatened her own arcane talent. *Or maybe she just doesn't want to be anywhere near me.*

"Captain." Miko's warning tone broke my morose thoughts, and I turned to find that we had visitors.

Three robed figures approached. Boxley's theory of a religious order seemed more likely by the moment, as they reminded me of monks. They appeared startlingly similar, clad in unadorned gray, bare-headed, even sporting the same haircuts, simple and barely neck length. Only the hues of their hair differed: one dark, another sandy, and the third brown dusted with gray. Oddly, I couldn't have said if they were male or female. None sported facial hair or any sign of it, and their robes revealed no hint of their underlying physiques.

Each bore a simple wooden platter—meats and cheeses, bread and a crock of butter, a pitcher and cups—which they placed on a table. The elder of the three turned to face us while the other two backed away.

"Kevril Longbright?" The elder's emotionless gaze fixed on my own.

The voice also provided no hint of gender, the timbre higher than a man's, but deeper than most women's. I might have guessed elvish, but they had neither pointed ears nor other distinguishing facial characteristics.

"*Captain* Kevril Longbright," I said with a respectful bow, "of the *Scourge*, out of Haven. And you're the lord of this keep?"

"There are no lords here, Captain. Call me Shepherd."

I cocked my head. "But you're a *dragonlord*, right?"

"Dragonlord?" The corner of the elder's mouth twitched with what I hoped was amusement and not annoyance. "A grandiose title, but some might call me that. I prefer Shepard." Shepard poured pale green liquid from the pitcher into the cups, took a cup and sipped, then gestured us forward. "Please, refresh yourselves."

"Thank you," I stepped forward and took a cup, a little uncomfortable with the restrained hospitality of our host.

The liquid turned out to be lightly fermented goat's milk, sweetened with honey and tinged with an herbal flavor I couldn't place. I found it cloying, but motioned the others forward. My people didn't need a second invitation, given the pitiful trail rations we'd been eating. While we all partook, Shepherd looked us over, eyes lingering on me, Miko, and, most of all, Preel.

"We don't get many visitors here, Captain, and I must admit, I'm both curious and startled to find that you know so much about us." Shepherd's mouth twitched at the corners again, not a smile, perhaps in annoyance. "Tell me why you've come."

"I know next to nothing about you, Shepherd, only that you possess a ship that can safely delve the Serpent's Eye."

"That's not an explanation. I'm *busy*, Captain. Tell me what you want." Impatience burred Shepard's voice.

I'd known there would be questions, and steeled myself to provide only enough information to get what we needed. I hoped it would be enough. "We need to sail to the center of the Serpent's Eye, and I learned that the dragonship could do so while protecting its sailors from the wild magic. I'm willing to pay, trade, or barter for the use of your ship."

"The dragonship is not mine, per se, Captain Longbright, but I am its steward." Shepherd sipped again and regarded me with narrowed eyes. "I *might* consider your request if you tell me how you came to the knowledge of the dragonship and its location. And please do me the courtesy of not lying to me."

An omission isn't necessarily a lie. I resolved to keep Preel's talent a secret as long as possible. Fixing my eyes on the Shepherd, I said, "I learned these things through the services of a truthsayer."

"A *truth*sayer." Shepherd's eyes widened. One of his two escorts actually gasped, but Shepherd's raised hand forestalled any further outburst. Those inscrutable eyes snapped to Preel, then back to me. One eyebrow slowly rose. "And why, Captain, does your veil-clad companion wear enchanted bindings over her mouth and left wrist?"

I shot a glance over my shoulder. Preel still wore the veil over the gag, and her sleeve covered the manacles. I gaped back at the Shepherd. "How did you...?"

Shepard waved a hand dismissively. "I can sense the magic about her just as easily as I can sense that the whip coiled under your coat is enchanted, and that your friend's katana is magical, a komei weapon if I don't miss my guess. I'm attuned to magic in all its forms, Captain. Living nearly my entire life so close to the Serpent's Eye, studying arcane lore, experimenting, and, yes, delving the maelstrom itself, have given me certain...abilities. I'm not omniscient, however. I could tell there was something unique about this young woman, but not exactly what. Your reaction provided the confirmation." The Shepherd's eyes remained fixed on mine. "Now, tell me why she's bound by magical restraints."

Bugger! I had no recourse but the truth—the whole truth—this time. "For her own protection, Shepherd. She is under an enchantment, a compulsion, as is my steward, Hemp." I waved toward Hemp, and he nodded in confirmation. "The manacles keep Preel from hurting herself. Hemp was commanded to slit his throat under certain conditions, and we want to prevent the same with Preel. The gag keeps her from speaking. If she's asked any question to which she doesn't already know the answer, it'll invoke her talent, which taxes her severely. A careless question could kill her."

Shepherd stepped past me then, staring rapt at Preel. She didn't look up at him, her eyes fixed on her clenched hands. Miko and Wix both put hands to hilts and shifted toward them, but I held up a hand.

There was no malice or greed on Shepherd's face, only curiosity. If we were to have any chance of using the dragonship, we'd have to offer some sort of compensation. As much as I hated the idea, Preel remained our best opportunity to offer something the enigmatic dragonlord might value.

"This enchantment of compulsion..." Shepherd turned to me, eyes bright. "...how was it achieved, who cast it upon her, and what is she compelled to do?"

I gritted my teeth, wondering how far I should trust the dragonlord. If I detailed the powers of the scourge, would Shepard try to take it? It was, after all, a powerful magical artifact made from actual dragon flesh and components from the Serpent's Eye. Just because it couldn't be wielded until Jhavika's death didn't mean Shepherd wouldn't covet it. And, if I revealed that we sought to destroy the scourge, might he try to stop us rather than help?

I shook my head. "That's not pertinent. What's important is that the enchantment can only be broken by sailing to the center of the Serpent's Eye, and you have a ship that can safely make that trip. So, will you barter for its use or not?"

My defiance elicited a bark of sardonic laughter from our host that set me back on my heels and brought a dangerous rumble from Wix's throat. But the smile on the Shephard's face was one of amusement, not malice or contempt.

"We *are* bartering for the use of the dragonship, Captain Longbright."

I blinked at Shephard in confusion. "I'm sorry?"

Again, that smile. "Let me explain. I'm called *Shepard* because I'm a Shepard of Knowledge. That's the *purpose* of this place, all these people, all my apprentices, all my predecessors, and the dragonship itself." Shephard downed the contents of his cup and sat in a chair, leaning back and gesturing for me to take the seat opposite. "We seek only to *learn*. *Knowledge* is our goal, not power, riches, comforts, or dominion over others. I came here long ago seeking knowledge of dragon magic. Eventually, I inherited this place from my predecessor. I'm the *twelfth* Shepherd of this keep, and the eleventh steward of the dragonship. The line of Shepherds goes much farther back. Each steward of the ship has used it to further our collective knowledge, sometimes sailing into the Eye to discover on our own, and sometimes taking others into the Eye in exchange for knowledge. Knowledge is the *only* currency accepted for the use of the dragonship. So, if you want to travel into the Serpent's Eye on the dragonship, you will provide us with the knowledge we seek."

"I see." The news both thrilled and worried me, for I possessed a dove that laid diamond eggs of knowledge. I had planned to use Preel's talent—specifically, the answers to a limited number of questions—to barter for use of the ship, but if I wasn't careful, Shepherd might choose to bypass the eggs and claim the dove for their own. "Forgive my lack of trust, Shepherd, but living in Haven for so long has taught me to be wary. What assurance do I have that you won't murder us in our sleep and take Preel to assuage your limitless thirst for knowledge?"

"A fair question." Shepherd sighed and made a face, eyes shifting to Preel, then back to me. "Consider, please, for a moment, our position here. We're not without some power to defend ourselves, but we couldn't stand against an army. That's why we keep the location of the dragonship a secret. What do you think the God-Emperor of Toki would do if he learned we had such a vessel?"

"You'd have an armada on your doorstep," I said.

"Precisely. And here you come knocking on our door asking about the dragonship. We would be foolish *not* to wonder how our secret was discovered and who else might know of it. Common knowledge of the ship would bring many more visitors, most of them much more *adamant* than you."

I thought of Kivan and Rauley's obsessive interest in the dragonship, and had to admit that Shepherd was right. Our host was as much concerned with keeping their secrets safe as we were with keeping ours. We had to balance our mutual interests for our mutual benefit.

"So," Shepard continued, "we will offer you the use of the dragonship to enter the Serpent's Eye in exchange for answers to certain questions, and at least *one* question to Preel that will invoke her truthsayer talent. I'd also like a simple conversation with her. I've never had the opportunity to converse with a truthsayer, you see. We can barter further, if you dislike those terms."

I noted that Shepherd called Preel by name, not "your truthsayer." He saw her as a person, not a thing, not a slave. That single glimpse into the dragonlord's character finalized my decision.

"Very well, Shepherd, we can discuss these terms, but I'll not answer an endless string of questions, and neither will Preel. She needs four days of rest between the employment of her talent, and time, I'm afraid is not on our side. If you agree to those terms, we're on an even playing field."

Shepherd nodded in acquiescence. "Agreed, Captain. Now, please, tell me of this enchantment that compels Preel and your steward."

I reached under my coat and plucked free the scourge, holding it out for examination. "They were both lashed with this scourge, which compels them to obey the commands of its master. I seek to destroy the scourge and free all who've been enslaved by it. There are certainly hundreds, perhaps *thousands*."

"And to do that, you need the dragonship."

"Yes. Preel's talent has informed us that the nearest place it can be destroyed is the center of the Serpent's Eye."

"And how did you *specifically* learn about the dragonship?"

"Preel, again, of course. We had no idea how to delve the Eye safely, but knew it had been done before. The blood pearl in the pommel was procured from the Serpent's Eye through the use of *your* ship."

Shepherd's eyes lit up at my mention of the blood pearl, and widened further at my every word. When I finished, those eyes flicked up to mine, filled with amusement. "Oh, the *irony*, Captain Longbright! Ha!"

"Irony?" Once again, Shepherd had taken me by the lee.

"That you should come to me with your request. Have you heard of the great dragon, Noethrex, Captain?" Shepherd's grin widened as my jaw dropped. I remembered the name from Preel's lips. "The very same dragon whose heartstrings, claws, and sinews went into the crafting of *that* scourge, unwillingly donated bone, sinew, and hide toward the crafting of our dragonship!"

"What? How could that be? The ship was *used* to procure the pearl!"

"Yes, it was, by the crafters of the ship itself." Shepherd sighed and chuckled. "Great dragons don't just fall from the sky willy-nilly, Captain. They're magical creatures, all but immortal, and when one is slain, every scale, every tooth, every shred of tissue is priceless. The first Shepherd of this keep perished under the claws of Noethrex, but his four apprentices prevailed, and...split the proceeds, so to say. Three of them in concert built the dragonship, while one began crafting the scourge you now hold. The others knew not what enchantments the scourge would gift its master, but agreed to help procure the blood pearl. That was the maiden voyage of the dragonship, you see, and it resulted in a sore falling out between the four apprentices. The crafter of the scourge sought not only knowledge, but dominion over others. The thirst for power corrupted him, and the scourge itself corrupted him further. The other three apprentices banded together and cast him out. Now, it seems, the scourge has returned to its origins."

"Sonofabitch." I downed my disgusting drink and reached for the pitcher. A thought came to mind as I poured. "You'll help me destroy it, then?"

Shepherd's lips pursed. "I'll consider it. The more information you can give me, the more likely I am to aid your efforts. Preparing the dragonship for a voyage is no simple task, and sailing into the Eye at this time of year is...challenging."

"Where is the ship?" I asked, sipping my drink. I was either developing a taste for the stuff or my taste buds had been inured to the cloying sweetness.

"Safe," Shepherd replied, reaching for the pitcher. "Who is the master of the scourge now? Clearly not you."

"No, not me. Jhavika Keshmir, one of the Lords of Haven. She's used it to gain power and now controls most of the Council of Lords."

"Sir?" I turned to find Hemp looking miserable, sweat beading on his brow. "Might I be excused? The...um..." He scratched the scar at his neck.

"Ah! Sorry, Hemp." I looked to Shepherd imploringly. "I'm willing to answer any questions you have within reason, Shepherd, but I have to ask that my steward not be present. His compulsion is to commit suicide should certain subjects be discussed in his presence."

"Really? That's *fascinating*! How did... Oh, sorry!" Shepherd stood, looking suddenly stricken. A wave brought the other two robed figures forward. "I'll arrange quarters for your people, Captain. You'll forgive me, but sometimes I can't help but ask the next question. Occupational hazard, you see."

"Yes, I see." Shephard was indeed obsessive about knowledge, and not just dragon magic either. I wondered why the dragonlord hadn't insisted on asking Preel more than a single question. For now, I deemed it wise that she went with Hemp, if only to ease her discomfort with my company. "Thank you, Shepherd. Miko, see that everyone's settled."

"Aye, sir." Miko and the others stood, and the other two robed figures—Shepherds-in-training or apprentices, I supposed—gestured for them to follow.

"If anyone wants to stay, they're welcome." I glanced at Preel, but she was already standing to follow Hemp, her gaze averted. Boxley dropped back into her seat, her insatiable curiosity piqued, and her bottomless appetite not yet sated. She sat and watched us, stuffing bread and butter, meat and cheese into her mouth, washing the food down with the pale green drink.

"Now, Captain," Shepherd continued, "tell me about Jhavika Keshmir and how you managed to take the scourge from her. I know that the master will not give it up willingly."

"I intended to kill her, actually, but that didn't work out so well. I ended up cutting off her hand to get the scourge." I cringed at the memory of the scourge and Jhavika's severed hand dangling from mine. The look of rage on Jhavika's face visited me in my nightmares. Even without the impetus of the scourge, she would chase me down to her dying day. "She's hunting us with an armada. That's why we're in a hurry. Once the scourge is destroyed, her entire power base falls apart."

"I see." Shepherd's lips pursed again, a sign I was learning meant a pending question. "And how did you cut off her hand without being lashed by the scourge?"

"I didn't." I raised my scarred left hand in evidence, the marks from the lash still vivid. "I didn't know it at the moment, but I'm immune to the effects of the scourge."

Shepherd looked astonished. "And how did you manage *that* trick?"

"It's a *long* story."

"And I'll hear it, Captain. Every detail." Shepherd stared at me, implacable and holding all the cards in this game.

So, with no recourse, I told the tale from the beginning, from learning through Preel that I'd been Jhavika's unwitting slave to Jhavika discovering Preel's nature and kidnapping her.

"That was the final straw." I avoided Shepard's rapt gaze by refilling my cup once again. Boxley's eyes brimming with tears at my tale nearly undid me. Reliving our history only made me miss Preel all the more. "I concocted a plan to kill Jhavika and rescue Preel. I didn't honestly expect to survive, and things didn't go exactly as I'd planned, but we got Preel out. But now...well, Jhavika filled her with so many lies that she now despises me."

"Yet another vested interest in destroying the scourge." Shepherd's mouth pursed again. "Forgive me, Captain, but I knew it had to be more than a crusade for justice that drove you. You don't strike me as the philanthropic type. You're in *love*."

I bristled at Shepherd's tone. "Yes, I am. What of it?"

"Love is the most insidious of emotions, Captain. Nothing personal, but I'm happily rid of it."

"Rid of it?" I blinked at my host. "What do you mean?"

"I mean that we, the shepherds of this keep, have divested ourselves of human desires. You see, our predecessors learned a lesson from that coil of dragon flesh you now bear. Avarice, ruthlessness, desire, and spite corrupted the crafter of the scourge, Captain. So, when we become shepherds, we divest ourselves of most human desires. We seek only knowledge, not love, sex, power, dominion, devotion, or riches." Shepherd shrugged. "It simplifies our lives, eliminates distractions, and makes us incorruptible."

"Does it?" I smiled ruefully, thinking to myself that the services of a truthsayer might indeed corrupt the shepherds' insatiable thirst for knowledge.

Shepherd smiled back. "Well, *mostly*. We do tend to be rather...single-minded about our pursuits, but we don't squabble over the petty things in life."

"Good for you." I didn't want to say that I thought such a life barely worth living. "We're all slaves to one thing or another, I suppose. I'd rather be a slave to love than knowledge, if given the choice."

"To each his own, Captain."

"Yes," I agreed.

"So, tell me about Preel. I know little of the talents of the truthsayer, and she seems...troubled."

I sighed, preparing myself for a long question-and-answer session. Evidently the bartering had just begun.

Chapter Twenty Two
I Shall Not Want

Temperance in all things is a virtue.
The Lessons of Quen Lau Ush

From the journal of Jhavika Keshmir –
I find it incomprehensible that I miss Preel's company as much as I miss my scourge. Simple, honest companionship was one thing my life had lacked. Even though her friendship was compelled, after a fashion, losing it troubled me more than losing my hand.

"After this squall passes, work us to seaward a few miles and heave to." I glared at the wall of black clouds and slashing rain to windward, then at the fading sunset beyond the looming mountains of Valaka to the northwest. I pointed to the lights within two high keeps high upon the cliffs. "Use the lights of those keeps to stay on station. Let the off watches rest, but keep enough people on deck to handle weather." I looked over craggy shore, unforgiving and menacing. "If you need sea room, bear off southeast, but not too far. The last thing we want is to wake up tomorrow morning in the Eye."

"Aye, your ladyship!" My second in command touched his forehead with one knuckle, then called for shortened sail and slacked sheets to handle the squall.

The distant flash of colorful lightning on the southeastern horizon gave a good point of reference to the Serpent's Eye, but also caused concern among the crew. They wanted nothing to do with the maelstrom of wild magic, and neither did I. Kevril insane enough to sail into it to escape me, though he might hide somewhere near the Eye in the hope of avoiding my armada.

Sheets of rain swept toward us, so I hurried down the steps from the quarterdeck, ducking into the sterncastle as the deluge struck. Teshan closed the door against the gusting wind and torrential rain. As *Crimson Hawk* heeled beneath the force of the squall's winds, I took off my weather cloak and worked my way aft. The reek of simmering pork, beans, and dried peas nearly turned my stomach as we passed the galley.

"Wine," I called out as I entered the great cabin. I needed rest, and there was nothing else for me to do. Our search, so far, had been uneventful: no harbors, no coves, and no *Scourge*.

My new steward, a former guard from my garrison, poured wine and handed me the glass. "Anything else, your ladyship?"

I eyed him; not a bad-looking fellow, really, but hardly to the standards I was accustomed to. If I couldn't sleep again, I might consider him for a distraction. For now, however, I'd try wine and food. "Supper, when it's ready. And help me off with this jacket." I emptied my glass and put it down, silently cursing my one-handedness. I hadn't considered the difficulty of sleeves when I had my armorer fashion my boarding pike hand. The hook tended to catch.

"Of course." He helped me, refilled my glass, and hung my jacket. "I'll check on supper."

I sat down and laboriously removed my boots, sipping wine and welcoming the dulling warmth it offered. The howl of wind and roar of rain against the deck overhead foretold a significant blow, but nothing dangerous. Before my steward even returned, I found myself pacing again. The frustration wore on my already tattered nerves. My missing hand ached, and I couldn't keep from reaching for the scourge with it. I glared at the bottle of wine and considered getting well and truly drunk, but that would be dangerous. If something went amiss in the dark with a lee shore, being impaired wouldn't do.

Supper arrived, and I ate because I knew I needed food. The largely tasteless fare reminded me of what I was missing: home, comforts, Ty-lee, my physician, my sage, my chef, my bevy of pleasure slaves... *Preel.*

Getting up from the table, I started pacing again, a caged wolf. I had to figure out some way to divert my ceaseless need for the scourge. I hadn't brought any distractions with me, unfortunately. I tried to remember the last time I truly felt relaxed, and suddenly stopped short.

"Preel!"

"Your ladyship?" My steward stopped, the tray with my half-eaten meal in hand, a stricken look on his face.

"Nothing." I waved him out, dredging up the memory of the last time I saw Preel.

She had finished teaching me the yamshi routine. I'd felt peaceful, contented, focused, physically and mentally at ease. Looking around the cabin, I wondered if I could do yamshi here, on the pitching deck, without Preel's assistance. Did I even remember the routine? It had been weeks.

I turned to my komei bodyguard. "Te-shan, are you familiar with the discipline of yamshi?"

"Yes, your ladyship. Several routines."

Thank the gods! "I've been taught the basic routine, *ton-chi*, and I want to try it, but I may have forgotten some of the postures or the sequence. I want you to help me through it. Just name the next pose in sequence, and adjust my stance if I do anything incorrectly."

"Yes, your ladyship." He bowed respectfully, but didn't move from his position.

"Excellent!" I took off my cutlass, changed into a pair of drawstring pajama bottoms, and assumed the beginning stance, or as closely as I could remember it.

"Greet the sun," Te-shan said, and I raised my arms, exhaling as I brought them back down.

"Receive the morning."

Rotate heel and toe, slight turn, lean and cup the arms.

"Align your spine and hips with your rear leg, your ladyship," Te-Shan said.

I did, concentrating on feet, legs, hips, spine, and relaxed as I settled into the proper balance. *Peace...* I moved into the next pose at Te-shan's prompt, then the next, and so on, each successive posture one more step toward solace.

This, I thought, as my body and mind settled into one. *This is what I need...*

Chapter Twenty Three
The Proposal

Never surrender unconditionally.
The Lessons of Quen Lau Ush

From the journal of Preel Longbright –
How can I be expected to make such choices when my
emotions are not my own? I cannot help but wonder if this
isn't yet another manipulation. One does not ask a slave what
she wants, after all.

"This place gives me the willies, it does." Hemp cleared the plain
wooden dishes from the small table and piled them on the floor beside
the door. "Like a bloody monastery. Not a picture on the walls, not a
pattern on the blankets or rugs, not even so much as a carved bedpost
or frilled collar anywhere. It ain't natural."

"It is strange," I agreed. The room we'd been given was small and
blank, but comfortable, with two sturdy beds, a table and chairs, a
small desk, and cabinets for hanging clothes. There wasn't a single
adornment to be found anywhere. Even the food had been bland,
nutritious and filling, but without the spices and flavors that I'd grown
so used to. Austere, Boxley had called it. Rising to gaze out the narrow

window at the distant flashes of multi-hued lightning in the Serpent's Eye, I shuddered. Austere, maybe, but I found the keep downright comforting compared to the prospect of sailing into *that*.

"And them shepherds..." Hemp tidied up as he spoke, though there was little to tidy. His nervousness might also have been related to the prospect of sharing sleeping quarters with me. "Can't rightly figure if they're men or women."

"Not exactly what you expected from a dragonlord, is it?"

He snorted in derision. "Dragon *monk*, maybe. I wonder if they're eunuchs."

I'd wondered the same, but Shepherd and the two acolytes, if that was what they were, didn't have the look of eunuchs. I'd had eunuch guards in the past, a jealous master's assurance that none but he would violate me. Memories of Kevril's subtle manipulations and violations, and my willing compliance, welled up within me. My hands clenched hard at my sides, nails biting into my palms.

"I need to exercise, Hemp. Would you please move the table aside?"

"Happy to, lady." As he started to do so, however, a knock sounded at the door.

Hemp froze and looked at me.

I shrugged and nodded to him. "Probably just coming for the dishes."

"Right." He answered the door, but instead of one of the servants, the lord of the keep stood there.

"Preel." A short bow and a plaintive smile, not what I considered lordly behavior at all. "I'd like to speak with you, if you'll allow it."

"The captain—" Hemp began, but Shepherd raised a hand.

"I'm here with the captain's blessing. He thought it would be better if I came to speak to you without him. You witnessed our bargain. Captain Longbright has fulfilled his portion of the agreement, but he wouldn't agree to the rest without your consent, Preel."

"*My* consent?" I scoffed. "My talent isn't voluntary, Shepherd. If Kevril bartered my services for the use of the dragonship, I have no say in it. Slaves don't *get* choices."

"Both true and not true. The captain assured me that you agreed to help him in his effort to destroy the scourge. I wish to speak with you as part of our agreement, and ask one question that will invoke your talent, but since *I* am not the master of the scourge, you *do* have a choice." Shepherd shrugged. "I gave the captain my word that I'd not ask a question that would invoke your talent without your foreknowledge and consent."

A lie? A manipulation? One more twist of the knife? "And if I refuse, you can ask anyway. If I refuse to speak with you, you withhold the use of your ship. That's not a choice, Shepherd, it's coercion."

Shepherd's smile faded slightly. "Is a merchant's bartering with the customer coercion, then? No, Preel. Your mind has been assaulted; this is clear to me. If you don't wish to speak to me, I'll still help Captain Longbright destroy the scourge. Though he seeks primarily to set you free from your enchantment, much more than your personal freedom is at stake while the scourge exists. After you're free of its influence, I may petition you again for the use of your talent, but it'll be up to *you* whether you'll answer or not. You are *not* a slave except to the will of the master of the scourge."

"I'm a *truthsayer*, Shepherd. I'm a slave by definition."

"By *that* definition, I'm also a slave, Preel." Shepherd made an all-encompassing gesture. "I'm a slave to knowledge, but I sacrificed much to put those chains upon myself. I have no name, no gender, no pride or spite. I willingly gave them up. They're distractions from my calling, my pursuit of knowledge."

"And I'm a bottomless *pit* of knowledge," I countered, still unconvinced. "Tell me, Lord Shepherd, why have you not slaughtered Kevril and his people with your magic and claimed me for your own? Or are you like a cat, playing with your prey before you kill it?"

Shepherd looked mildly shocked. "You truly *are* troubled, child. I'll show you exactly what it is to be Shepherd of this place, if you'll allow it, but let me assure you that I'll commit no violence unless it's in the defense of myself or my charges. You're a guest in this place, therefore *you* are in my charge. You're *safe* here."

You're safe here... Jhavika's words rang in my mind, a lie I was compelled to believe by the magic of the scourge. But she'd been wrong; Kevril had stolen me away. My clenched fists trembled at my sides as truth and lies, feelings and memories, all waged war in my mind.

"Please, Preel, give me the opportunity to show you what our single-minded pursuits have wrought here. I assure you, we learned our lesson from the very scourge that has poisoned you. We harbor no avarice, no deception, no desire for dominion. There is no *slavery* under this roof. We only seek knowledge, discovery, learning, and the free exchange of ideas." Shephard held out a hand. "Let me show you. Walk with me."

Gods of Light and Darkness, help me. Shepherd's words felt like a lifeline in the midst of a raging storm, a promise of neutral territory, a sanctuary impossible to refuse. "All right, but understand that a careless question will invoke my talent."

"I understand."

"And I'd like Hemp to come along."

"Of course."

Warily, I put my hand into Shephard's. It was warm, welcoming, and held mine carefully, as if I might break. So comforting, in fact, that I had no desire to break our clasp. *Magic?* I wondered. With my other hand, I beckoned for Hemp to follow.

We walked down a corridor and descended a curved stair, Hemp two steps behind us, silent and nervous. Strangely, I felt more relaxed than I had in weeks, and my curiosity won out over any reluctance I might have had in speaking to Shepard.

"Do you think the scourge *can* be destroyed?" I asked. "We only discerned *where* it could be destroyed, not exactly *how*. My talent doesn't always work when I'm asked about magical things or beings."

"So the captain told me." An enigmatic smile graced Shepherd's features. "It's my belief that the magic that binds the elements of the scourge together will fail when exposed directly to the wild magic at the core of the Eye."

"And…I'll be free of its enchantment?"

Shepard shrugged. "If the component parts become unbound, its power *should* fail, and all those poisoned by it released from their compulsions."

Poor Jhavika, I thought. Her people would rebel. They'd kill her. How could I do that to my beloved sister? I shuddered at the conflicting emotions the thought elicited.

"What troubles you, Preel?"

"Part of my...compulsion is to love the master of the scourge like my sister. I know it's the scourge making me feel that love, but I can't *not* feel it. I want to be free of the enchantment, but I know what will happen to her if the scourge is destroyed, and it's tearing me apart."

"Ah, yes. Love. The most dangerous of emotions." Shepherd squeezed my hand gently. "As chaotic and unpredictable as the magic of the Serpent's Eye. Such emotions are a weakness, distractions from reality. Yours have been twisted into chains by the master of the scourge. We shepherds expunge ourselves of the most divisive of emotions, our most intense desires, in order to focus solely on our work."

"Convenient," I mumbled, considering the concept. What had my emotions ever done but torture me?

I allowed myself to be led along by Shepard as I imagined an existence without desires. I'd resigned myself to a life of misery as captive to my curse and my masters...until Kevril found me. For a few months I reveled in my love for him, nurtured my hatred for Jhavika. But now I hated *him* and loved *her*, a slave to my emotions and the scourge. How would that change with the scourge's destruction? *Would* it change with the scourge's destruction? *Oh, to be made of stone...*

We descended many stairs until we stood before a blank wooden door bound with lustrous black metal. There was no keyhole, no latch, and no visible mechanism, but when Shepherd placed a hand upon the door, it swung open freely.

The air within was dry and smelled slightly of beeswax. Warm light bathed my face as we entered a chamber perhaps a hundred feet across and carved deep into the living rock beneath the keep. My hand slipped free of Shepherd's, and I stepped forward to a curved railing of the same lustrous black metal to gaze out and *down*, transfixed by the sight of countless shelves of books.

"Oh...my...lord."

"This is the charge of the Shepherds of Knowledge." Shepherd waved a hand out at the unfathomable collection. "One million, two-hundred eighty-two thousand, four-hundred and six tomes, books, scrolls, and manuscripts dedicated to every subject one can name, and some as yet unnamed. Art, science, engineering, arcana, religion, philosophy, politics, and myth, to mention but a few. We are the stewards of this archive, and to it we ceaselessly add whatever worthy findings we can procure or author ourselves." Shepherd's hand settled on my arm, tightening for a moment, and I turned to face the dragonlord's rapt countenance. "It is to *this*, and this alone, that I am a willing slave, Preel."

"Why here?" I asked for the lack of a better question. "Why not in a city where it can be shared?"

"To avoid the greed of others, but also to delve two areas of learning that have been sorely neglected: dragon magic and the phenomenon of the Serpent's Eye. The Shepherds of Knowledge didn't originate here, Preel, but here we've found a refuge." That enigmatic smile again. "So you see, while I am *indeed* interested in your truthsayer talent, Preel, herein lie the answers to more questions than you could be posed in a lifetime."

I gazed out at the library again, down at the interminable levels below until I lost count. The warm light bathed everything, sourceless, magical. A desire welled up in me that overwhelmed even the war raging within my soul. The irony of my truthsayer talent was that I couldn't ask myself a question, couldn't satisfy my own curiosity, couldn't feed my own hunger for knowledge. I relied on books, and here were more than I could read in a lifetime. I could die happy in this room, old and gray and filled with knowledge. A sudden thought struck me so hard that my knees quaked beneath me. Here was a solution to all of my problems.

"I could help you!" I whirled to face Shepherd pleadingly. "Whatever answers can't be found here, I could give you...if you make me like you, without emotions! Please!"

"Lady Preel!" Hemp interjected, but Shepherd raised a forestalling hand.

Shepherd smiled. "So, only minutes ago you spoke of slavery with venomous acrimony, and from first-hand knowledge of all the horrors you have personally experienced. Now you would willingly put chains upon yourself again." The warm hand on mine squeezed hard. "No, Preel. You cannot make that decision now, not while your mind is assailed by the scourge. Afterward, when your will is your own again, when you're free to feel what and who you truly are, *then* I'll consider your petition. Then, if you still wish it in your deepest heart, with clear conviction, we will accept your help."

"But...you can render the power of the scourge moot. If you take away my feelings, make me as you are, then I'll be free."

"Ah, but we would remove part of *you* in the process." Shepherd smiled kindly. "You're still in love with Kevril Longbright, and he's in love with you. Even though it's been tainted by the magic of the scourge, we will *not* destroy that out of hand, not without the consent of both of you. When you're free, then we'll consider it."

I nodded reluctantly. I would remain conflicted until we could destroy the scourge, but the opportunity to join Shepard and his associates shone like a golden prize in my mind, more than I had ever hoped for. "Very well. I agree to make the choice once I'm free, but I must warn you, Shepherd. Kevril's a pirate. He won't let me go easily. He bartered me for a cure to his own enchantment, then stole me back."

"I know. He told me of it. He's agreed to honor whatever decision you make once you are freed from the influence of the scourge."

"He's *lying* to you." I felt a sliver of pride that I had managed not to scream it. From behind me, Hemp muttered low, but I disregarded his assertion of loyalty to Kevril. I knew better.

"Perhaps." That smile again, knowing, almost mirthful. "Perhaps not. We'll discover the truth in the end."

The irony smote my heart. "Your question. That's *it*, isn't it? You want to know if Kevril's lying to you."

Shepherd's bark of laughter caught me off guard and echoed around the vast chamber. "Ah, no, Preel. I mean to ask you the location of a misplaced tome, a treatise on gnomish herb lore. I can't seem to find it anywhere, you see."

"A *book*?" I stared at Shepherd, dumbstruck. "You have a *truthsayer* at your disposal, and you wish to ask the location of a lost book?"

Shepherd looked back at me in bafflement. "Why, yes. Why is that strange to you?"

I burst into helpless and honest laughter for the first time in weeks.

Chapter Twenty Four
The Dragonship

Timing is indeed sometimes everything.
The Lessons of Quen Lau Ush

From the diary of Kevril Longbright –
The first time I saw the sea, I fell in love. It spoke to me of freedom. Then I spent four years throwing up. My love never died, but I learned to temper my ardor.

We were awoken and summoned to breakfast early. The shepherds had no blackbrew, so Boxley brewed a pot using Bert's heatstone. Hospitality be damned, the alternative would have been too grim to face. The meal was bland fare again: potatoes, onions, and the seemingly ubiquitous goat meat fried up in great greasy mounds. Only Preel and Hemp were missing, I assumed because Shepard had posed a question to her last night, which meant that Preel was cooperating. I'd half expected her to deny the request just to spite me.

As we finished, Shepherd entered the hall with his two apprentices.

"Captain Longbright, I trust you slept well."

"Well enough." Actually, I hadn't slept well at all, staring sleepless at the ceiling of my chambers, listening to Wix snore like some cranky gnomish contraption, and fretting over the deal I'd struck with this enigmatic dragonlord. "I trust you had a productive conversation with Preel last night." I stood and downed the last of my tepid blackbrew.

"I did. May we…" Shepard motioned toward the corner. "…discuss something privately?"

Breakfast suddenly soured in my stomach, but I followed our host out of earshot of the others. "What's wrong?"

"Nothing is wrong, Captain," Shepherd assured me, "but I would like you to know that Preel asked me if she could remain here at the keep after our mission is complete, to become a seeker of knowledge."

"What did you—" My hand slipped toward the hilt of my cutlass.

Shepard held out his hands in a calming gesture. "There was no coercion on my part, Captain. You can ask your steward; he was with us. Though I won't deny that Preel would be an invaluable asset for our work here, I don't believe her capable of making such an important decision at this time. I told her that her decision would have to wait until after the scourge was destroyed, once she was free of her compulsion. She agreed. The question is: will you abide by her decision?"

I released my held breath and clenched my hands. Much hinged on Preel's state of mind after the influence of the scourge was broken, but what choice did I have? I'd never force Preel to do anything against her will, even if it meant losing her. If she still hated me after the scourge was gone, at least she'd be safe here.

"I offered once to take her anywhere she wished to go if she didn't want to stay aboard *Scourge*," I said. "That offer still stands. She's not a *possession*, Shepherd."

"No, she's not." Shepherd nodded respectfully, then smiled that quirky smile. After hours of answering the dragonlord's questions the previous afternoon and evening, I was getting a little tired of that smile. "If you and your people have broken your fast sufficiently, I believe we have some work to do."

"Indeed." Shepherd had told me that readying the dragonship would take some work, and I was eager to get to it. At least it would get my mind off of Preel. "We're ready."

"Then follow me."

So we did, along with a number of the keep's people. Shepard led us downstairs one floor and along a wide corridor that appeared to have been hewn out of the living rock, the smooth walls seamless. Chambers opened up here and there along its length, workshops of various sorts, but I couldn't discern their purposes as we passed. At the end of the tunnel stood a massive door bound with black iron.

"No latch," Miko whispered at my side, and I saw that she was right. The door had no visible mechanism, but opened readily and quietly to Shepherd's touch, admitting daylight and the scent of the sea.

"Magic, or something hidden, maybe," I whispered back with a shrug.

We stepped through behind Shepherd's people and were immediately blasted by the sea breeze. A long, steep stairway had been cunningly hewn into the windward cliff face, a rough stone wall hiding it from seaward view. Tremors vibrated through the soles of my boots as the wild surf pounded the rocky beach below, each wave tumbling black cobblestone-sized rocks. The sound reminded me of horses' hooves on the cobbled streets of Haven.

I saw no ship.

We descended the smooth, regular steps, the aching muscles of my legs complaining again. The overland trek had taxed me as I hadn't been in years. I was fit, but even eight-hour watches on deck in gale conditions weren't the same as toiling up and down mountainsides. It was no better at the bottom of the stair. The footing on the beach was difficult, the rolling rocks threatening to turn ankles.

Still no ship.

Miko shot me a concerned glance. Wix and the rest of my crew didn't look any happier.

Shepherd led us to a cleft in the rock that proved much deeper than I'd guessed at first glance. Inside resided a massive windlass, not unlike a ship's capstan, but mounted horizontally. A chain as thick as my ankle ran through the large, toothed gypsy, one end dropping down into a deep well, the other trailing through a hawsehole in the stone. My gaze followed the chain's direction, onto the beach and down toward the water, the heavy links cleverly hidden beneath the hefty rocks.

The location of the dragonship became clear to me. "It's *sunk*?"

"Intentionally, yes. Hidden beneath the waves." Shepherd looked at me quizzically. "What better place?"

"What about rot, corrosion, pestilence? Even a *month* underwater can do irreparable harm to a ship's seams."

"Not *this* ship, Captain." Shephard motioned, and his people took up long rods. Fitting them into the windlass, they began cranking. Ponderously, the chain lifted from the rocks, pulled tight, and began clattering through the gypsy and down into the well. "The dragonship is untouched by the elements, rot, and the invasive vermin of the sea. It sits in a cradle not unlike those you've undoubtedly seen in shipyards. The cradle rides on rails hidden beneath the rocks of the beach. The materials of the dragonship's construction are all heavier than water, so it rests securely in the cradle when submerged. To store the ship, we open several seacocks that allow it to fill with water as the cradle is lowered down the rails, then drain it out when we raise it."

My crew muttered oaths, sharing my skepticism. I couldn't imagine ever getting the salt and damp out of a ship so long submerged. We would have to wait and see.

The going was slow, but finally Boxley called out and pointed. "Captain! Look!"

In the midst of the pounding surf, the tip of a spar rose above the waves and slowly emerged inch by inch. My hope rose even as the ship did. As we stared in anticipation, however, a horn sounded from above, one long note followed by three short ones.

"A ship!" Shepherd held up a hand, and his people stopped cranking. "That's highly unusual. No ships save your own small boat have ventured this way in years."

"Bugger!" I stepped into the open and scanned the horizon, but saw nothing. "Boxley! Up the steps quick! Where away?" I tossed her my spyglass.

"Aye, sir!"

She dashed off, and I turned to Shepherd "This could be one of Jhavika's armada. I'd recommend they not find out we're here."

"I'd rather *no* one saw any evidence of the dragonship. Everyone, stand clear!" Shepherd made another motion, and one of his people hauled a lever on the massive windlass.

The mechanism spun free, slowly at first, but picking up speed, the links rattling like thunder through the hawsehole and across the stones. Thankfully, they had only hauled in about a hundred feet of chain. The tension eased quickly, and the chain came to rest on the black-stone beach. The black-iron links matched the hue of the stones well, but the chain had dug a trough that would be visible from the sea.

I opened my mouth to suggest something be done about that, but Shepherd's people were already dashing out of the cleft with wide-tined rakes. As they hurried across the uneven footing to the surf line, Boxley's call reached my ear.

"East nor'east! Three masts above the bluff! Corsair! They'll round the point in a minute, sir!"

"Corsair?" Miko looked at me askance. "Jhavika didn't *have* any corsairs in her armada. They were all slogging merchantmen. This is a bit off the regular seaways for a pirate, though."

How or if Jhavika had added a corsair to her fleet, or why a pirate might be coasting by, were questions I couldn't answer yet. All we could do was to assume the worst and hope for the best. "Hide your people, Shepherd! You have less than a minute."

"Yes!" Shepherd stepped out onto the beach and withdrew something from his cloak. "Everyone under cover!" As Shepherd's people raced for the cleft, the dragonlord reached down to touch the massive chain with a slim silver wand.

The chain seemed to come to life, writhing like a huge iron snake among the stones, burrowing down. When it settled, no sign of the chain could be seen.

"Why didn't you do that to begin with?" I asked as the last of Shepherd's people hurried into the cleft.

"Because magic is not without *cost*, Captain." The dragonlord's voice came out ragged, and one glance confirmed that a price had indeed been paid. Shepherd looked drawn, as if some great weight had just pressed down upon those slim shoulders.

"I'll remember that," I said with a nod of acknowledgement.

"Rounding the point now, sir," Miko said from the edge of the cleft, her spyglass leveled toward the northeast.

"Do you recognize her?" I moved to her side, but dared not show myself to look.

"She's familiar, but the angle..." Miko went quiet.

I knew the ship would pass abeam of our position, giving us a better vantage, but I could barely keep from snatching the spyglass from Miko's hand and looking for myself. I clamped down on my impatience and entrusted her to tell me know as soon as she knew anything useful.

Long minutes passed.

My teeth worried a fingernail, but I kept my mouth shut.

Finally, Miko turned and handed me her spyglass. "She's *Crimson Hawk*, Captain, but the pennant's not Patak's."

"What?" I took the glass and traded places with her, leaning out just enough to level it at the dark-hulled corsair skimming down the coast. I recognized *Crimson Hawk* readily enough from the winged figurehead, but the pennant... A shiver crept up my spine like a chill serpent. A red scourge on a black field—Jhavika Keshmir's coat of arms. I swept the deck with the glass and focused on the quarterdeck. A slender figure topped with bronze-blonde hair stood by the rail. With a spyglass in her left hand, she scanned the shore.

"Fuck!" I ducked back. "It's Jhavika. She must have taken *Crimson Hawk*."

"Jhavika? The master of the scourge?" Shepherd looked at me as if I'd committed a deliberate betrayal.

"I *told* you she was hunting us. I've no doubt she's scouring every island one by one."

"Or that fookin' Tan ratted on us," Wix growled.

I would have sworn that Tan would never have told Jhavika bout us, but perhaps my trust had been misplaced. *If only I'd asked Preel about Tan's intentions*, I thought, but I'd had more pressing questions at the time.

"If she spots anything suspicious…" Miko didn't have to finish that thought.

If Jhavika thought for a moment we were here, she would storm the beach and to hell with the danger of landing in such surf. Hell, she might even run *Crimson Hawk* ashore to reach us.

I turned to Shepherd. "Can you defend the keep?"

"I can *secure* the keep, Captain, but defend it?" A shrug told the tale. "As I said, not against an army, and you said this Jhavika Keshmir has one under her control. The master of the scourge won't be easily dissuaded."

"No, she won't. Pray she doesn't spot us." I risked another peek around the edge of the cleft without the spyglass, wary of the eastern sun glinting off anything shiny. *Crimson Hawk* continued on her course. *Go on, Jhavika, nothing to see here. Just a dragonlord's keep. You don't have time to mess with a dragonlord.* Slowly, far too slowly for my comfort, *Crimson Hawk* continued southwest and finally vanished around the headland.

I breathed a sigh of relief. "She's gone."

Miko grabbed my arm hard. "Captain, she'll round the southern cape and start up the leeward side! She'll find the ship! Kivan and the others!"

"Shit!" I did the math. Jhavika would round the southern cape this afternoon and probably either find an anchorage on the leeward shore or heave to offshore. Either way, tomorrow she would start working her way back northeast and find *Scourge* at anchor. "And with *Crimson Hawk*, she might be able to take them before they can escape."

"We've got to send warning!" Miko insisted. "Send me, sir!"

"No." Again, I did the math. If we had any hope of getting someone to Kivan in time, it had to be someone fast. I recalled our slog up the leeward mountains, my assessment of my people at every stop. "No, I'll send Boxley. She's fastest. Wix, pick one more. Who's lightest on their feet?"

"Sauncey, sir." He dragged the slim crewman from our midst. "Part mountain goat, this one."

The young sailor snapped a salute. "Aye, sir! I'll run the whole fookin' way!"

"Good!" I ventured out of the cleft just as Boxley leapt down the last of the stairs.

She looked stricken. "Sir! I saw... It was Jhavika's pennant."

"I know. We've got to warn Kivan. Grab just enough food and water to keep you alive and go! Go *fast*!"

"Aye, sir!" She handed me my spyglass and dashed up the steps, Sauncey at her heels.

I watched them go, again doing the math in my mind. I didn't like the answer I got.

"Think they'll warn them in time?" Evidently, Miko had done the same calculations and didn't like the answer any better than I did.

"Maybe. We've got to try." The rest of my grim calculations revealed one more unpleasant truth. I turned to Shepherd. "If they take my ship and crew, they'll learn where we went and why. We've got maybe three days. It's too dangerous to round the cape in the dark, so...yes, they could be back here the evening of the day after tomorrow at the earliest."

"Then we must be away before they arrive, Captain!" Shepherd turned and waved his people into action, and I ordered my own to help as they could.

With the extra hands, the windlass turned faster this time, and the chain came taut. Slowly, the dragonship rose from the waves.

The tip of one mast emerged first, rising higher and higher. I squinted skeptically until I finally conceded what I was seeing; the mast was, indeed, curved. Another mast emerged farther forward, arched the opposite direction, just like in Kivan's drawing. The ship's broad stern broke the surface, the waves pounding upon the wide, flat deck. Foot by foot, she rose, and I could see that the two masts were, in fact, the two ends of a long open arc affixed at its midpoint to the deck. Suspended between them by a web of stays hung a circular metal ring the height of two men, encompassing another, smaller ring within. It looked for all the world like a great staring eye, and I could fathom no possible use for it.

Perhaps a hundred feet from stem to stern, the ship looked like none other I'd ever seen. Her hull was flat and wide, nearly as broad at the transom as she was at middeck, then narrowing to a sharply pointed bow with a long bowsprit. Her hull didn't draw much water, with barely enough depth for a single level below the deck. Twin dagger-like keels angled out from the bottom like a shark's pectoral fins, and twin free-standing rudders thrust down from the stern almost to the ground. The ship was secured by cables to a heavy metal cradle atop a wheeled carriage, plow-shaped wheel guards pushing aside the beach stones as the grooved wheels ascended the rails.

Finally, the contraption rumbled to a stop, the ship's stern facing up the beach, and the bow pointed out to open sea. Water streamed from the open seacocks, ejecting several fish that flopped about on the stony beach. However, true to Shepherd's word, not a single barnacle or scrap of weed marred the hull.

"Smaller than I thought," Miko commented with a grimace.

"Aye. I don't imagine she was built for comfort. Hell, she barely looks as if she was built for *sailing*."

"She was built for only one purpose, Captain." Shepherd motioned us out toward the ship as his people hurriedly wedged blocks under the carriage's wheels. "To sail into the Serpent's Eye."

Which is exactly what we're going to do, Odea help us. Cold resolve settled into my gut. "And we need to have her seaworthy in forty-eight hours. Put us to work."

Chapter Twenty Five
Blood and Betrayal

One never fully knows a man's heart.
The Lessons of Quen Lau Ush

From the journal of Jhavika Keshmir –
I'll never understand how Kevril Longbright instilled such
loyalty in a crew of ruthless pirates. I suppose I've lost the
knack; five years with the scourge in my hand. All things
considered, I'd rather rely on magic than the hearts of men.

I leaned on the rail, gazing blankly at the seemingly endless
expanse of lush, green hillsides ascending steeply to rocky, windswept
peaks. I felt as if we'd been searching for *Scourge* for months, not
weeks. *And what do I do if we don't find them?* I wondered. *Search again or
head back to Haven?* I controlled the Council, true, but without my
scourge, I couldn't expand my army, which would shatter all my
carefully laid plans for the Blood Sea and beyond.
Damn you, Kevril!
An errant gust from between two of the lofty peaks heeled the
ship, but she quickly righted. A least we were out of the tempests and
wild seas of the windward shore. Rounding the southern cape had left

my entire crew near collapse, with rocks to leeward and the chaotic maelstrom of the Serpent's Eye looming to the southeast. All, myself included, had been relieved to finally round the southern point, however trouncy, and heave to for the night in the lee of the island.

And what did we discover for all our effort? Nothing but a totally inhospitable shore and a handful of stony keeps. I gouged the railing with my pike hand and cursed my foul luck.

"SHIP!"

The lookout's call snapped me out of my morose musing.

"Where away?" I grabbed a spyglass and focused it up the coast. Had Roque finished her inquiries in Valaka City and progressed down the leeward shore already? If so, she'd made amazing time. "Is it *Peony*?"

"Three points off the starboard bow! Anchored near shore beyond the headland! I can just see the tips of her masts!"

"What pennant?"

"Can't tell. It's slack; no wind inshore. But not *Peony*. Pennant is black."

My heartbeat quickened. Only one type of ship bore a black pennant. *Pirate!* I dared not hope too much lest the fickle gods dash them.

The spyglass trembled in my hand as I focused it off the starboard bow, but the anchored ship was still hidden behind the headland from my lower vantage. Slowly, ever so slowly, the tops of the masts emerged above the dwindling headland. A black pennant hung limp. Then a momentary breeze stretched it out, and I caught my breath. I didn't need to hear the lookout's next call.

"Black pennant! Dragon skull and crossed scourges! She's the *Scourge*, your ladyship!"

"YES!" My face stretched in a triumphant grin. "Battle stations! Make all sail! Smartly, damn you all!"

Sailors and soldiers jumped to obey. The flying jib soared up the outer forestay, and topgallants cracked and filled. I hooked the starboard rail with my pike hand and leaned out to fix my quarry in my spyglass as we cleared the headland.

There she lay, anchored in a snug cove. I had *Scourge* dead to rights. Only by some miracle could Kevril escape now.

The wind shifted and strengthened as we rounded the headland, staggering *Crimson Hawk* for a moment. Then we steadied, gaining speed.

"Helmsman, bring her upwind as close as she'll bear. Sheets and braces close-hauled! Lookout, keep a sharp eye! If they cut their cable and make sail, call out!"

"Aye, your ladyship."

We cracked on as close to the wind as we could manage, two full points closer than *Tiger Lily* could have sailed. The corsair might be a slovenly ship, but she was weatherly, and her narrower hull gave her far better sailing to windward. Maybe even as good as *Scourge*.

"I've got you now, you sonofa—"

"REEF!" The panicked call dropped from above. "Dead ahead!"

"Bear off!" I ordered, snagging the rail with my hook to keep from toppling over with the sharp maneuver. A reef slipped by less than half a ship-length off our starboard side. Though easily spotted in the noonday sun, all eyes had been focused on our quarry, not our surroundings. The lapse nearly cost us our ship…and our lives. "You there!" I jabbed a nearby sailor with my pike. "Get aloft and watch the water." She scrambled up the ratlines, and I turned back to my prey.

I could now see figures scurrying aboard *Scourge*, sailors in the rigging, out on the yards. A jib shot up the forestay, and the bow began to pull downwind to the south. The most likely scenario played out in my mind. They had the weather gauge, but being tucked so far into the cove limited their wind. I'd hoped to pin them inside the cove, but avoiding the reef had forced us farther offshore. Still, they had to get past us to reach open sea and any hope of escape. *Scourge*'s best point of sail was a broad reach, which meant southwest or northwest. We would block their northwest escape if we continued on our current course.

"She's cut her cable and set her courses!" my lookout cried.

I raised my glass. They had come around to the southeast. I scanned the water, but the angle of the sun was wrong for me to see the reef. Was there a gap they were intending to sail through, or would they simply skirt the tip of the reef? Either way, they'd be in open sea if they escaped the cove, and our advantage would vanish.

"Like hell you will," I snarled, gouging the rail with my pike hand. "Have we cleared the reef?" I bellowed aloft.

"Aye, Captain! Well clear!"

"Tack ship!" We came around. Not as smartly as I'd hoped, but far quicker than *Scourge* was able to set sail and start making headway. They were still heading southwest, but I had an angle to intercept them. I smiled; I hadn't lost all my tactical skills in five years ashore, and I knew all Kevril's tricks.

Settling on our new course, we were now closing on *Scourge* at a steep angle. We had the advantages of speed, greater sail area aloft, consistent wind, and momentum. They, however, still had the upwind advantage. I raised my spyglass. The scenery beyond *Scourge* crept from their stern to bow; we were gaining on them. We would cut them off. The reef prevented them from angling farther south, so, to avoid us, they would have to wear ship and head northwest. The question was, when? Too early, and we would simply match their maneuver and cut them off again. Too late, and we'd collide. Of course, if they didn't change course at all, we would close to grappling range, but Kevril would most certainly try to evade. He must see that I had greater numbers.

I fixed my spyglass upon *Scourge*'s quarterdeck, but spotted neither Kevril nor Miko, just a dark-haired young woman in a blue officer's jacket. *Who the hell?* She was definitely in command, pointing, shouting orders, and watching us closely. *Where are you, Kevril?*

The Scourges were arming themselves, and a dozen crossbowmen climbed to the tops. Two groups readied the two siege engines Kevril had recently installed.

I frowned. The siege engines had seemed an inspired idea when Kevril worked for me; now, they were going to be a problem. With better range and penetrating power than crossbows, they might damage our rigging or steering before we could touch them. The heavy weapons were ungainly and difficult to aim, and presently pointed away from us. But when they wore ship…

"Be ready to come about, hard to port on my order!" We had to get alongside straightaway. Every minute's delay gave them time to rake us with those ballistae. "We'll board from our starboard! Grappling hooks ready! Smartly, you gods-damned laggards!"

A round of ayes, and my boarders surged to starboard, heeling the ship another strake.

"Remember, I want *prisoners*, not corpses! Take their officers alive if at all possible!" Kevril and Miko still weren't on deck, and I needed to know why.

I sensed Te-shan stepping closer, standing protectively at my shoulder. I kept my eye trained on *Scourge*'s quarterdeck. *Closer...* The dark-haired commander shared nervous glances with a young man also in blue. *Gods, they're young! Where the hell is Kevril?*

Finally, the commander barked an order, and *Scourge*'s helmsman hauled on the wheel.

"Tack ship!" I bellowed.

"Helm's alee!" the helmsman shouted, and we came about.

I could see the surprise on the young commander's face as I matched her maneuver. Her inexperience showed; she wasn't thinking far enough ahead. She bellowed another order as we both came around on the same tack, then stepped away from the binnacle. Before I could wonder what she was doing, she strode to the ballista mounted on the quarterdeck and leveled the deadly engine right at me.

"Shit!" Before I could react, a blur of motion jumped in the lens of my spyglass. Something struck my left shoulder hard enough to knock me reeling and send my spyglass clattering to the deck.

Panic struck as hard as the impact. *I've been hit!*

I slammed my pike hand into the rail to catch myself, visions of torn meat and shattered bone spinning through my mind. I looked down, expecting to find my arm missing and my lifeblood pumping out onto the deck. My limb hung there intact. I flexed my fingers, confused. *If not the ballista bolt, then what hit me?*

"Your...ladyship!"

I whirled at the groaned words, the voice familiar, but the distress in it uncharacteristic. Then I saw... I had been spared; Te-shan had not.

He'd apparently pushed me aside, and the wrist-thick bolt had torn through him like a paper doll. He still stood, as if he didn't notice the two massive wounds in his chest and back, the blood pouring from the gaps in his armor. The komei drew his katana, took one step forward, and toppled over like a felled tree.

Damn it! I drew my cutlass and whirled around. Would the crew revolt, try to cut me down now that my bodyguard was gone? All eyes, however, were on *Scourge*.

A second crack from their bow ballista, and the bolt smashed through our binnacle, probably in an attempt to foul the steering or kill the helmsman. Sheer luck saved both, though one spoke of the wheel had been shattered. The siege engine crews worked furiously to reload their weapons.

I wasn't going to give them the chance for another volley. *Scourge* bore up as close to the wind as she could, sails flat as boards, sheets singing tight. I ordered my understandably rattled helmsman to steer upwind, but we couldn't quite match their angle. *Damn, they know how to trim sails!* But we still had more speed, and barely fifty yards separated us.

"Lay us alongside! Let her luff if you have to, but put us within grapple range! We have to board before they fire those ballistae again!" It was a risky move; luffing would slow us, and if we missed grappling, they might just escape.

We veered closer. The square sails luffed, but the jibs and trisails still drew. A shrill command rang out from *Scourge*'s quarterdeck, and a hail of crossbow bolts raked our deck. Several of my people fell, and two bolts narrowly missed me. I accepted the losses; putting archers aloft meant fewer to fend off when we came rail to rail. *Closer...* Another volley raked us, one bolt buzzing past me so close that I felt the draft of its flight. I ignored it as I gauged the progress of the two ships. Our speeds were almost even now as we drew abreast. *Closer...*

I filled my lungs to give the order to heave grapples.

"Rauley! Now!" *Scourge*'s commander screamed, and the helmsman heaved the wheel to port.

"Sonofabitch!" I lurched back from the rail as their bow turned directly toward us, barely a ship-length away.

It was the most insane maneuver I'd ever seen. Did they intend to smash straight into us? A collision might break off their bowsprit and fell their foremast, perhaps even damage their hull, but it would definitely snap our aft stays, topple our mizzen, and maybe fell our mainmast. But *Scourge*'s bow continued its sweep; they were turning, not ramming us. If their bowsprit didn't snag our mizzen shrouds, they might actually break free.

I had only one chance to prevent their escape. "Hard to starboard!"

The helmsman—one of my own soldiers under the scourge's compulsion, thank the gods—spun the wheel without hesitation, and we rounded up into the wind. *Scourge*'s bowsprit scythed past perilously close to *Crimson Hawk*'s starboard quarter. I cringed and braced myself for the impact, watched the tip of the spar clear our mizzen shrouds with mere feet to spare, so close that their bobstay chain shaved splinters from our taffrail, and their forestay struck the tip of our mizzen boom. Their helmsman was either mad, very skilled, or both.

Barely twenty feet separated the two ships, our square sails backfilling, while theirs cracked full. If I didn't stop them now, they were as good as gone. "Grapples away!"

At my command, fifty iron hooks flew across the gap. All but a few found purchase, most in wood, some in flesh. The lines came taut with a horrific jerk, staggering both ships. Several of the lines parted, cracking like coachwhips, and a few were cut by *Scourge*'s crew, but the ships were drawn together by their own momentums, wheeling around one another like two massive dancers.

The rails smashed together hard enough to knock half the sailors off their feet.

"Boarders away!" I bellowed even as *Scourge*'s commander ordered her pirates to repel.

Crossbow bolts raked our deck, but we outnumbered them two to one at the rail. My soldiers poured over the gap, deflecting boarding pikes, and forcing the *Scourge*'s crew back before they could cut the grappling lines. A bolt clipped my hip, scoring a line of pain. I stepped behind the mizzen mast for cover. Without Te-shan at my side, I wasn't about to join the fray.

"Take prisoners!" I bellowed, peering out to gauge the mayhem.

It was a bloody mess. My soldiers overwhelmed the Scourges by a sheer press of bodies, but a slim young sailor managed to leap from *Scourge*'s foredeck to *Crimson Hawk*'s quarterdeck. Cutlass in hand and screaming a battle cry, he charged me. I dodged, keeping the mast between us, and slashed at his sword arm. He swung at my face, and I felt a sharp sting, then his blade struck the mast. I pinned it there with my pike hand, stepped in, and smashed the guard of my sword into his nose. He reeled back, and I jammed my pike through his sword arm. His blade clattered to the deck. He reached for a dagger, but I kicked him squarely between the legs. He folded to the deck groaning.

I ducked back behind cover, but the heat of battle had already cooled to isolated pockets of stubborn resistance. In short order, we had most of the Scourges backed up against the far railing and a blade at their commander's throat. A few still fought against the overwhelming odds, and would have been mercilessly cut down except for my order to take prisoners.

"Hold!" I cried out, cursing the loss of so many from both crews. "If you drop your weapons, I swear we'll let you live!"

"Don't!" their commander screamed, despite the steel that drew a thin line of blood across her throat. "She'll slaughter us like cattle!"

"NO! No, I *won't!* I *need* you all, every single one of you!" I hurried down the steps from the quarterdeck and crossed to *Scourge*, picking my way across the deck slick with blood and littered with dead and wounded. "I need every able-bodied sailor I can get my hands on! You won't be harmed if you just give me Kevril Longbright and Preel!"

"She's lying! She'll—"

"Gag her!" I roared. As my soldiers stuffed a rag in her mouth and lashed it in place, I leveled my cutlass at the rest of the *Scourge* crew. "Now, drop your weapons. I swear on my name that I'll transport you safely back to Haven. If you fight, you die! Drop your weapons, and you live!"

First one, then a few others, and finally every single one of the Scourges disarmed. The ship was ours.

"Secure their weapons and hold the prisoners here on deck. You," I stabbed a finger at one of my soldiers, "get a detail together and see to the wounded. The rest of you, search the ship and secure everyone."

As my soldiers complied, I scanned the faces of the captured crew. Still no Kevril or Miko, and no Wix. Dread crept through my gut like a burrowing rodent. Why would the captain abandon *Scourge* with his most-trusted officer and bosun, leaving the ship in inexperienced hands? Had they taken *Golden Harlot* from Tan and sailed away? *No, I* realized. Kevril might put a prize crew aboard a captured ship, but he would never leave *Scourge*.

"So, where the hell are you, Kevril?" I tapped two of my soldiers on the shoulders with my pike hand. "You two, come with me; guard me from all harm." They weren't komei, but better than nothing. At least they alleviated that itch of vulnerability on my unprotected back.

I strode into the sterncastle where my people were already searching cabin by cabin. Two held the ship's fat cook and two scullery swabs at bay in the galley. At the great cabin, I motioned for a soldier to open the door.

My escort peered inside, then stepped aside. "All clear, your ladyship."

I edged into the cabin, wary of an ambush, but it was empty: no Kevril, no Preel, and no Hemp. Bars had been installed on the windows. *He kept her here*, I realized. *My truthsayer. My Preel.* The clothes press was full of gowns that I could picture her wearing, and the starboard quarter gallery had been converted into a dressing room. Kevril's locker was surprisingly empty. There were signs of habitation, but there was no one here.

A low growl escaped my throat as I hurried back on deck. The prisoners knelt in two rows along the port-side rail of the middeck, perhaps fifty at a glance, many of them injured. My people stood over them with bared weapons while a squad of soldiers tended the wounded from both crews. The severely injured lay moaning on the deck, their injuries hastily bandaged. One severed arm had been tied off, the end cauterized with a torch. I wrinkled my nose at the stench. The dead were being unceremoniously dumped overboard. The sharks and crabs would feed well.

Such a gods-damned waste... I found the dark-haired commander kneeling with the rest, and sliced off her gag with my pike hand. She spat out the wad of bloody cloth and glared at me.

I smiled and positioned the hook of my pike under her chin, its tip barely piercing her flesh. "Where is Kevril Longbright? Where has he taken Preel?"

"He flew away on the back of a fucking dragon, you maniacal bitch!"

I laughed and pressed the hook's tip into her chin. She grimaced, but didn't scream. "You tried to *kill* me, little girl. Now you think *defiance* is going to earn you an easy death?"

"I'll die a *thousand* deaths before I tell you anything!" she raged through bloody teeth.

"Oh? You think so?" I longed for my scourge. One lash and I would get everything this defiant whelp knew. I quelled the urge to drive my pike into her eye. Killing her wasn't the answer. I hadn't lied when I said I needed every able-bodied sailor, and this young woman had proven herself more than capable. I didn't, however, need her undamaged. "Nail her hands to the capstan and strip off her shirt. I think it's time for a little *discipline* aboard this ship!"

As my soldiers hauled her up, the prisoners grumbled and swore. I kept my eyes on their faces as the hammer struck, tearing a scream from the young commander's throat. Some glared with rage, others averted their eyes, and a few even shed tears. Good. The officer might not talk, but someone would. The hammer fell silent, but curses still flew from the young woman's mouth. Turning, I watched impassively as they cut off her jacket and shirt, laying bare her back.

"Now, we will see..." I stalked up to her, brandishing my pike hand.

"Wait!" A young man stood up from the midst of the prisoners, and I recognized the helmsman. His face was flushed and streaked with blood and tears. "Don't! I'll tell you—"

"Stand *down*, Master Rauley!" the commander screamed. "You tell her *nothing*!"

"Oh, on the contrary, Master Rauley, *do* tell me." I fixed him with a cruel smile. "Tell me where Kevril took Preel, and I won't harm another hair on your commander's head. Tell me," I raised my pike hand, "and I won't flay the skin off her back!"

The young man blanched. "I..."

"Shut the *fuck* up, Rauley!" the commander raged.

The helmsman's jaw clenched. "Aye, Captain." He looked down at his feet.

"Very well, then. Let's begin." I caressed the pristine skin of the young woman's back with the blade of my pike hand, but didn't cut...yet. She shivered, and I turned to face her crew. "This doesn't have to happen. Tell me where Longbright went, and I'll let her go."

They grumbled, many looking away, others glared at me defiantly.

"Your choice." I slowly sliced a long gouge down her back, not deep enough to damage muscle, but blood flowed freely. She screamed, of course, a long, throat-tearing sound, exactly what I needed from her.

Still not a word from her crew.

"Such unwavering loyalty for Kevril Longbright, the coward who abandoned you to *this*?" I cut another furrow parallel to the first, eliciting a second scream that choked off with curses. The crew, however, remained silent. I worked the tip of my blade beneath the skin at the top of the parallel cuts and freed a flap. Switching from pike blade to hook, I snagged the flap of skin. "Hold fast, dear. I'm afraid this might sting a little."

"*Fuck* you, you piece of—"

I pulled, and her raging curses rose into a wailing scream. The young commander writhed as I peeled the flesh downward, straining at the nails that pierced her hands, arching and kicking. There was less blood from this wound, the whitish connective tissue peeling away in a clean sheet. I'd been right about it hurting, though.

"Stop!"

I paused and turned to find a different man standing among the kneeling prisoners, slim and pox-scarred, his hair patchy and thin.

"You want to say something?"

"Shut your mouth!" my victim raged, spitting blood. "Don't you say a fucking word!"

"No, *you* shut *your* mouth!" the man snapped back, cold fury in his eyes. "I'm *through* taking orders from the likes of *you*!" He fixed me with narrow eyes and a grim expression. "I got no dog in this fight, yer ladyship. Me and mine was pressed into this here crew. I don't owe Kevril Longbright a fuckin' thing!"

Several Scourges muttered curses and glared at him.

I dislodged my hook from the young woman's flesh and raised it to point the pike at him, the tip dripping blood. "Then tell me where he went."

"He took a dozen of his crew and that wench he stole from you, and trekked off overland." He pointed to the mountainous peaks that ridged the island. "He was goin' to the windward side, to some dragonlord's keep or somethin'."

"A keep?" I stepped toward him. We'd passed several keeps on the windward side of Valaka—I remembered one clearly from the previous morning, perched on a cliff above a black stone beach. There'd been nowhere to land on those windswept, rocky shores, and even if there had been, I'd seen no need to question any of their inhabitants. I'd never dreamed Kevril would leave his ship. "Why a dragonlord?"

"Shut up, you *traitor*!" The young commander strained at her nailed hands.

"No, I *won't* shut up," the man replied, his voice edged with scorn. "They was goin' to get some ship that would sail into the Serpent's Eye."

A murmur swept through my soldiers and crew.

A chill gripped me as I recalled those swirling rainbow mists, the mystical maelstrom that was every sailor's nightmare. "And why would they want to do that?"

"To destroy that scourge he took from you. They said it was magical."

I caught my breath, panic clenching my heart in a vice. "*What? How?*"

"Dunno how. Longbright don't tell us everything. That wench of his told him, they said."

Preel! He asked Preel how to destroy the scourge! My scourge...

"Motherless son of a..." My panic burst into desperate action. "Chain the prisoners below! Put a prize crew aboard, just enough to sail her back to Haven! Everyone else, back aboard *Crimson Hawk*!"

"What about her, your ladyship?" One of my men pointed at the bleeding wreckage nailed to the capstan.

"Pull the nails and chain her with the others! We don't have time to dally here!" I glared around the deck, wondering what I could salvage. I'd lost at least a score of my people, and Te-shan to boot, but I couldn't trust any of Kevril's. I needed all the advantages I could get if I was going to tackle a dragonlord. Then my eyes fixed upon the siege engines mounted fore and aft. "Cut the mooring lines on those ballistae and hoist them aboard *Crimson Hawk*! Move, damn you all, or I'll flay the hide off *your* backs next!"

Chapter Twenty Six
Skin and Bone

Manual labor builds character.
The Lessons of Quen Lau Ush

From the diary of Kevril Longbright –
I'm no stranger to hard work. Growing up on a farm, then learning to ply the seas, taught me how to pace myself and work efficiently. Never in my life, however, have I felt the urgency that drives me now. Hope is a potent drug indeed.

"This is the weirdest fookin' rig I ever *seen*, sir." Wix spat over the railing, earning a curse from a man standing on the rock beach below. He leaned over and cringed. "Sorry, mate!"

I rubbed my sore hands together and lifted my gaze to the dragonship's bizarre rigging. "Can't disagree with you there, Wix."

My crew and Shepard's people had been working non-stop for nearly thirty-six hours to ready the dragonship, eating on our feet and resting only when exhaustion forced us. We'd first rinsed every interior surface with fresh water, flogged everything dry, and rigged wind scoops to air out belowdecks. As I'd suspected, there was only one lower deck, sparse accommodations above shallow bilges. It would be tight and uncomfortable, but that was to be expected; our voyage into the Serpent's Eye wasn't going to be a pleasure cruise.

I inspected the vessel for seaworthiness and came away impressed by the overall condition of the ship. All of the fittings were forged from a lustrous black metal that, despite being submerged for who knew how long in sea water, remained untarnished and free of any fouling. Blocks and tackles of the same black metal ran smoothly with no grease, and winches turned without a snag or squeal. Braided cables of dragon gut served better than any manila or cotton line I'd ever used, thin, but strong as iron, and as pliable and smooth as silk. Now we were hoisting the most curious sails I'd ever seen.

Dragonhide sails.

My crew had stared in open-mouthed shock when Shepard's people hauled the massive mainsails down the stairs from the workshops—two actual dragon wings. The base of each wing, where the joint would have attached to the dragon's body, fit snugly into a black-metal recess in the deck that rotated and swiveled like a gimbaled compass. The mainsails towered above the middeck at seventy-degree angles to port and starboard, wing bones serving as battens to reinforce and stiffen the sails. Dragon gut shrouds connected the bone luffs to the circular metal hub that hung suspended amidships, and then outboard to pullies along the cap rail. They could be spread wide for downwind sailing, or pulled in vertically for hauling close to the wind.

Right now, the enormous sails luffed and flapped in the steady winds that blew in from offshore. Smaller quadratic sails fluttered fore and aft, and a tiny, crescent-shaped jib that stretched from the bowsprit to the curved forward mast shuddered violently in the occasional gust. Canvas sails would have shredded with the constant abuse, and I kept expecting these to fray or split.

Shepherd noticed my consternation and laughed gently. "Relax, Captain. The sails are quite impervious. Go ahead and try to damage one, or cut one of the stays or halyards with a blade."

I wasn't about to deliberately attempt to damage the ship, but Wix took Shepard at his word and thrust one of his daggers at the sail. It rebounded without marking the sail in the slightest.

My bosun squinted at the gray hide and nodded. "Fookin' weird, but I gotta admit, they're tough."

I reached out to run my fingers over the sail. As smooth as silk and as light as strong canvas. I imagined *Scourge* outfitted with dragonhide sails and sighed in longing.

"And she's seaworthy in rough weather?" I asked.

"Eminently seaworthy, Captain, though I'll admit that she's not a very *gentle* ride." Shepherd gestured to the wide, flat deck. "She tends to heel severely on a close reach, and doesn't sail very close to the wind. Her lighter displacement decreases her speed with a head sea. Downwind, she fairly flies, but close-hauled she tends to plunge."

"Well, I don't suppose she was built for comfort."

"No, Captain, she was not."

The breeze chilled as the sun set behind the lofty mountains to the west. There would still be light enough to work for hours yet, and we could work into the night under the light of glow crystals, but dusk was fast approaching.

Turning toward the hold, I called down, "Miko! How's the provisioning coming?"

She shrugged and gestured toward the piles of blankets, foul weather gear, medical supplies, fresh foodstuffs, pots, pans, spare cordage, and all other supplies. "Four or five hours, maybe."

"Bugger." I'd hoped beyond hope that we'd be ready to leave before nightfall, but the final preparations below decks had to be seen to, and we had not yet heard back from Boxley. I squinted into the trade winds at the distant glow of the Serpent's Eye. "Shepherd, might we launch in the dark? One tack, and we've got open sea to the south."

The dragonlord frowned. "No, Captain, we must wait until dawn. Launching the dragonship is tricky at the best of times. Nightfall brings higher winds and seas. Though the ship may be resilient against *most* damage, she may still be dashed to pieces upon the shore."

I cursed again silently, but resigned myself to the inevitable. "First light it is, then. Wix, take over getting the provisions loaded and stowed." I turned to Shepherd. "Would you mind going over our route one more time?" We'd done so once the previous evening, but I wanted our course fixed in my mind.

"Not at all, Captain."

I leaned over the main hold coaming again. "Miko, meet us in the mess. I want to look over the charts some more."

"Aye, sir!"

My first mate met us in the ship's mess, the largest compartment besides the main hold. Here, Shepherd's cook bustled about stowing provisions, but one table had been dedicated to a copious array of nautical charts. Drafted by shepherds over the centuries, the charts were amazingly detailed and, the dragonlord had assured me, accurate.

Weighing down the curling parchment with polished bronze wedges that had been enchanted to remain fixed in place until moved by a hand, we pored over the intricate maze of landmasses and notations denoting currents, winds, and shoals. There was no direct route to the center of the Eye, but Shepherd had plotted out a course. With its endless mists, navigating the Serpent's Eye would depend solely on dead reckoning. Maneuvering through the maze of islands and islets would require that precise speeds and headings be constantly logged, positions continually plotted. Thankfully, Shepherd possessed a precision gnomish chronometer that I would have given my eye teeth for. In the Serpent's Eye, the smallest of errors could prove fatal.

"We'll be constantly navigating a lee shore in heavy fog." Miko ran a finger nervously over our proposed course, a circuitous route zig-zagging through the islands.

"Except here the fog's deadly and there are dragons above and below," I pointed out.

Miko leveled a cold stare at me. "You're a *font* of reassurance, sir."

"Fear not," Shepherd assured us. "I've sailed the Eye dozens of times and lived to tell the tale. One must be cautious and vigilant, certainly, but it's far less dangerous than it sounds."

Miko turned to Shepherd. "What *about* the dragons? Don't they try to...um...eat you?"

Shepherd's lips curved into that infuriating smile. "Actually, no. The inherent magic of the ship interacts with that of the Eye. To a dragon, the ship appears as just another dragon, or so I was told." Shepherd shrugged noncommittally. "I've no reason to disbelieve that. We've never been attacked."

Miko and I stared at one another, then at the dragonlord, neither one of us truly comforted.

A hollow pounding on the hull startled me. The dragon bone planks and framing resounded like a thin, fragile drum. Suspecting trouble, I shot up the companionway onto the deck. Hurrying to the rail, I squinted down through the twilight at one of Shepherd's apprentices. "What's wrong?"

"Nothing, Captain Longbright. Your young officer's returned. She requested to speak with you, but I bade her stay in the keep and take rest. She's utterly exhausted and awaits you in the dining hall."

"I'll come." I turned back and called down the companionway to Miko. "Boxley's back!"

"Good news or bad?" she asked as she climbed up the companionway steps.

"I don't know. She's knackered, waiting for us in the dining hall."

"More bloody stairs," she muttered, but we descended the ladder, picked our way across the stony beach, and started up the cliff-side stairway.

We found Boxley and Sauncey seated at a table wolfing food and downing hot drinks.

"Sir!" Boxley vaulted to her feet. Her face was drawn, eyes red, and she quaked with fatigue. She looked to have run the entire way across the island and back. "Sir, I saw—"

"Sit down before you fall down, Boxley, and catch your breath. I need a report, but I need it slow and accurate, not rushed and incoherent." I was tired myself, but Boxley looked ready to pass out.

"Aye, sir." She collapsed into her chair and heaved a ragged breath. "No easy way to say this, sir. We saw Jhavika take *Scourge*."

"Fuck!" I'd been dreading the news, hoping that perhaps Jhavika had continued on straight to the south. Hearing Boxley voice my worst fear felt like a knife stroke across my soul. "Burned?"

"No, sir. Kivan damned near got away! Boldest move I ever saw, but...well, Jhavika's crew grappled and took the ship. I couldn't see much more than that, except that she's got *lots* of people aboard. We were still way up on the slope. I don't know who's alive or dead, but *Crimson Hawk* took them lock, stock, and barrel. I saw—" She hiccupped and caught her breath. "I saw bodies being thrown overboard afterwards. Then it looked like Jhavika put a skeleton crew aboard and sent *Scourge* off to the northwest."

"What about Jhavika?" I asked. "Where did she go?"

"Last I saw, *Crimson Hawk* sailed off southeast the way she came. I had to get back to tell you, sir. My guess is they..." She dragged another deep breath in, choking back tears. "...probably learned were we went and are headed back here."

Miko swore under her breath.

Learned where we went. A kind way to say that Jhavika tortured information out of my crew. My knuckles popped on the hilt of my cutlass.

"The best thing we can do for our friends is to destroy the scourge as soon as possible." I stood and put a hand on Boxley's shoulder. "I need you to rest. We're leaving at first light. We can't launch in the dark—these seas and shores are too dangerous—but that works two ways; even Jhavika's not crazy enough to round the cape at night. Then she'll have to beat against those headwinds you encountered. She won't be here until tomorrow afternoon at the earliest. We'll be long gone by then."

"Aye, sir." Boxley looked from me to Miko, then back. "What about Lady Preel? Is she coming with us into the Eye?"

I'd thought long and hard on that question, but Boxley's information made the decision for me. "I'm not leaving *any* of our people behind, least of all Preel. Not as long as Jhavika's still alive and this," I shook the scourge, "isn't destroyed."

"Aye, sir!" Boxley gave me a tight smile, grim with the need for retribution. She and Kivan had become close over the last half year. "I'll be ready, sir."

"Good." I nodded to Miko, and we strode out of the hall.

"You want me to tell Preel that we're leaving at first light?" Miko asked.

She was reading my mind again. "Yes. I'll ask Shepherd to arrange a cabin for her and Hemp. She shouldn't have to even see me."

"Aye, sir." She nodded and cleared her throat. "I'll tell them what happened."

"Be careful, Miko. She's..." I didn't know what words to use: insane, beside herself, not in her right mind? I felt like *I* wasn't in my right mind. "She's fragile."

"I know, sir. Don't worry. I don't hold it against her. It's not her, it's the scourge."

"Yes. Thank you, Miko."

She shot me a narrow-eyed glance. "Well, *somebody's* got to deal with the women in your life! You don't have a very good track record."

I snorted at her gallows humor, but it broke the tension. "No, I certainly don't." I clapped a hand to her shoulder. "And get some sleep. We set sail at dawn."

"Aye, sir!"

I strode away, but knew I wouldn't be sleeping that night. I'd be recalling the faces of the crew I'd left behind, wondering who had lived and who had died, who had been tortured, and who had been broken. I should have told Kivan to sail for the horizon, but I'd had no way to know if our expedition to find the dragonship would succeed. Now I wondered whether I'd ever see any of them again, and, if so, whether I'd be able to look them in the eye.

More scars, I thought, rubbing the ones down the side of my face. But these weren't even scars yet; these were open wounds.

Chapter Twenty Seven
Don't Kill the Messenger

Sorrow bleeds the soul.
The Lessons of Quen Lau Ush

From the journal of Preel Longbright –
I know not what I expected. I should have known that Kevril
Longbright would drag me to hell with him.

I heard the knock on the door clearly enough, but refused to let
the sound distract me. I refused to let anything distract me.
Concentration was my key, my *only* key to sanity.

*Sun chases moon, clouds obscure sun, eagle stoops to sea, dragon rises from
waves...* I proceeded through the sequence quickly, my feet squeaking
on the smooth stone floor, arms and legs ablur.

Hemp shuffled to the door without a word. I ignored him,
pressing my concentration away from the madness, my body and mind
together, my shield against the screams, staving off the raging conflict
between memories and feelings, love and hate, Jhavika and Kevril.

Dragon strikes eagle, eagle's talons rend, dragon's jaws close... Faster, faster,
my hands claws, my nails teeth, my feet talons...

Voices low behind me. I pushed them away, pushed the whole world away. *Breathe, move, feet, spine, legs, arms, neck, mind...*

"Lady Preel," Hemp interrupted, his voice apologetic, but firm. "Miko needs to speak with you."

I paused the routine, holding my pose—*eagle's wings fold*—my breath heaving with exertion. I was streaming sweat, near exhaustion, near release from the torture of my mind. The last thing I needed was an interruption. I turned my head to glare at them. "I'm *busy*." Miko already hated me, so a sharp retort wasn't likely to add fuel to that fire.

"I see that." Miko stepped past Hemp, her dark eyes alight with determination, but no hatred. "And I'm sorry to interrupt, but I'm busy, too. We're *all* busy, and I've got news you need to know. Jhavika took *Scourge*."

Hemp gasped and muttered an oath.

Jhavika...my sister. What have you done? I relaxed my posture. "Kivan, Quiff, the others?"

"We don't know who lived and died, but she must have...gotten information from them." Miko's voice broke, the muscles at her jaw flexing and bunching.

"Information... Torture, you mean." *Oh, sweet sister, what have you done?* My knees trembled, fatigue and despair invading my mind, my body, my soul.

"We don't know what happened, but...yes, it's likely." Miko cleared her throat. "She sent *Scourge* off to the northwest with a skeleton crew, then sailed back to the southeast. She's likely coming here."

"When?" The question was out of my mouth before it even registered in my mind. What would Jhavika do if she took Shepherd's keep? What horrors would she commit, my dear deranged sister? I didn't need a truthsayer to know the answer. *Blood, fire, rage, revenge...*

"She can't round the cape in the dark. It's too dangerous. She'll probably be here by tomorrow afternoon. The dragonship's ready, and we're leaving at first light."

"*We?*" I had known, but denial came easy. "I'm not going."

"The captain isn't leaving anyone behind. Shepherd and some of their people are going with us, of course—it's their ship, after all, and they know how to sail it. The rest will secure the keep, then head into the hills. If Jhavika thinks we're inside the keep, she'll waste time trying to take it. She won't stop until she gets what she wants."

"Meaning *me*." I shivered and told myself it was the cooling sweat on my skin. It wasn't.

"Yes, and the scourge. Don't worry; she won't get either. By the time she realizes were not in the keep, we'll be long gone. She may figure out that we've sailed into the Eye, but she can't follow. So, get some sleep; we're leaving early."

My teeth chirped as I ground them together. I had no choice. I was a slave. "We'll be ready at dawn. Now, please leave." I resumed my pose.

"Preel, I'm...sorry for what I did the other night. You didn't deserve that. I was angry."

I stopped and looked at her. *Miko's not my enemy.* She had done what she did out of misguided loyalty to Kevril. I couldn't blame her for that. "I provoked you. You should have hit me. I deserved it."

"No, you didn't." Tears swam in Miko's eyes. I'd never once seen her cry, even when she'd been shot through the chest. "None of us deserved this, but we have no choice. There's no other way."

"No other way..." She had no idea, and my anger surged again. "You know what will happen to Jhavika when the scourge is destroyed, Miko. If I'd been left where I was, none of this would have happened. Our friends wouldn't be dead. My sis—" I clenched my teeth on the word, on the lie I'd been forced to believe. My knees began to tremble from the strain of holding my pose. "Jhavika wouldn't have to die."

"And she'd have you *and* the scourge, and she'd be Queen of Haven," Miko countered, her dark eyes flashing. "She'd take every other lord on the Council eventually. Then she'd take the Obsidian Isles by force, then Sariff, then Hyko and Mati, then Toki. The god-emperor would fall, his magic would be hers, and she'd raze the Jungle of Nin, then sweep across Chen. She'd ride a wave of blood and destruction until every man, woman, and child in the *world* was enslaved to her will."

"You're saying death is the *kinder* fate?" I wasn't actually disagreeing. I remembered how I loathed Jhavika for what she intended to do…before I loved her. I wondered if, at her side, I could have prevented it. A moot question now.

"Yes, I am. I'm sorry, but yes. I'm sorry for all that's happened, that our friends had to die, for what you're going through, but it's not our fault. *Jhavika* started all this. We have no choice but to fight back."

"No, we don't. We're slaves. All of us."

"Maybe we are, but we're slaves to freedom." Miko nodded and left.

Slaves to freedom... Slaves to something I've never known. Not true, perhaps, but I believed it. I remembered being free, in love, happy, but I had been forced to believe it was a lie. My mind spun in circles.

I resumed my exercises, but found it impossible to regain my focus. The faces of all the people I knew aboard *Scourge* flashed through my mind's eye, their screams shattering my concentration. Finally giving up, I stared out the window of the keep. Multihued lightning flashed within the haze of the Serpent's Eye, painting the mists like a rainbow, a mocking invitation. More lights flickered upon the stone beach, illuminating the dragonship, a steed to carry me into the maelstrom. One *magical creature bearing another into the heart of magic. The dragon that will swallow me...*

"Lady?" Hemp stood at my shoulder, concern writ large on his face. "Don't worry for them aboard *Scourge*, Lady Preel. Kivan's a tough one, and she'd rather die than betray the captain."

"That's what I'm afraid of." Visions of whatever cruelties Jhavika might have perpetrated raged through my mind. *Blood, screams, madness...* I shivered.

"You best not catch a chill." He held out a weather cloak.

I coughed a laugh and realized that I was, in fact, chilled, the breeze from the window prickling my sweaty skin. "You're always looking out for me, aren't you, Hemp?"

"Well, it *does* keep me busy." With a crooked smile, he helped me don the cloak so I could change with a modicum of modesty. "Now, you get out of those damp things, and I'll get you some hot water. Prob'ly the last hot bath you'll get for a few days."

"Thank you." He left, and I shucked out of my sweat-damp clothes, shivering under the cloak. *More work for Hemp, my faithful steward.*

I wondered about Hemp a lot. He'd held me through my breakdowns, cleaned up my urine-soaked clothes and sheets, tucked me into bed, watched over me while I was unconscious, tended my every need, and not once had he taken a single liberty. Not a glance, not a stare or misplaced touch. He was a pirate and a whoremonger, but not a rapacious scoundrel at all.

A tear slid down my cheek, and I wiped it away. I wondered if I was crying for myself, for Kivan and the others, for Kevril, or for my dear lost sister. *All my fault... I'm the bane of the Blood Sea.* There weren't enough tears in the whole world to weep for all those my curse had destroyed.

Chapter Twenty Eight
Claws of the Hawk

A strategic withdrawal is not defeat.
The Lessons of Quen Lau Ush

From the diary of Kevril Longbright –
I thought I knew Jhavika Keshmir. I imagined that I could predict what she was capable of. I was wrong, and I will forever rue that mistake.

    I paced the deck of the dragonship beneath the brilliant stars in the velvety black sky, spying the rainbow-lit maelstrom of the Eye with each circuit. Down on the beach, workers were making final preparations for our departure. All but one of the mooring cables that secured the dragonship to its carriage had been loosed, the skids upon which the hull rested greased, and the rails cleared of stones to ease the ship's passage into the sea. Now all we needed was enough light to launch. From the faint pre-dawn glow in the east, I gauged we had about half an hour to wait. I had to step around klatches of sailors and Shepard's people on deck. There wasn't enough room for everyone below, even with the tiny ship's complement of only thirty or so. Many would be sharing their bunks with the other watches to save space, and almost all had already boarded.

But not all.

I stopped by the rail and looked toward the keep, but saw no lights that might indicate someone descending the stairs or crossing the beach in the darkness.

"She'll be here." Miko approached and leaned against the rail by my side. "Hemp won't let her be late."

"I know," I said, but I was far from sure of it. If Preel refused to come, my choices were equally impossible. If I ordered her brought aboard by force, she'd hate me even more than she already did. If I let her stay, she might fall into Jhavika hands, and I couldn't—*wouldn't*—let that happen.

"Shepard wants to review the launch process." Miko nodded toward the bow.

"Fine." I followed her toward where our host stood. At least it would provide a distraction.

The sky seemed lighter—pearl gray now—almost bright enough for a safe launch. Dawn would break soon, but the rising sun would be obscured by the northern edge of the Eye.

"I'm afraid the procedure is little more than a barely controlled plunge, Captain." Shepherd pointed to the rails extending down the beach and into the water. "You see how the rails are aligned some forty-five degrees south of east. The wind direction here is quite constant, so the angle allows us to actually *sail* into the surf as the carriage descends."

"That sounds dangerous," Miko said.

It sounded like sheer insanity to me, but I didn't want to insult the dragonlord. Besides, there was no turning back now.

"It is, but only for the persons aboard. The dragonship is quite resilient." Shepherd pointed to the sails. "It is *vital*, however that we adjust for a close-to-the-wind sail configuration as we launch. We must maintain the ship's momentum to clear the rocks to the southwest."

A close reach to weather the lee headland, I translated mentally. Shepherd knew his ship well, but he didn't use the nautical terminology I was accustomed to.

Shepherd smiled and continued. "I think you'll find the process exhilarating. Yet another reason I prefer dawn for this procedure is that the winds and surf are at their minimum. You and your sailors are welcome to work alongside my people, Captain, to get a feel for the ship."

"Yes, I—"

Motion to my right caught my eye, and I turned. Preel climbed over the rail with Hemp's aid. At that moment, the mists of the Eye thinned, and the sun broke over the horizon. A spear of golden sunlight shot across the sea to illuminate her face.

My breath caught in my throat. I hadn't seen Preel since our arrival at the dragonlord's keep; there was no reason to put either of us through the pain. The sight of her now struck me a blow.

Preel glanced up, squinting into the sun, and saw me. Her eyes widened, and in the light of the new day, her cheeks flushed above the enchanted ivory cloth that ensured her silence. I stared at her, unable to look away. Her cheekbones were more pronounced than I recalled, her short-cropped hair fluttering in the fresh breeze, dark eyes red-rimmed, hollow, and filled with pain.

I caused that pain. Me.

I opened my mouth to apologize, but she averted her eyes. I looked away, cursing myself.

"Are you all right, Captain," Shepherd asked.

"I'm fine." I cleared my throat, and pointed to the sunrise. "We've light enough to launch now, Shepherd."

"Agreed. We can—"

A horn sounded from the keep—one long note, then three short ones—the same sequence we'd heard before.

"A ship?" I shaded my eyes and scanned the horizon, praying that it was just a merchantman, though I knew that wasn't likely. *Odea, please…*

Shepherd's crew rushed forward, straining to see. Before anything came into view, the call I'd dreaded came from the top of the cliffside stair. "A corsair to the southwest, coming fast!"

"Shit! It's *got* to be Jhavika!" I reached for my spyglass, but the ship wasn't yet visible around the headland. "She weathered the southern cape in the *dark*!"

Miko gripped the rail beside me. "I can't *believe* it! That's suicidal!"

"We've misjudged her desire to regain the scourge." Shepherd put a hand on my arm, fixing me with a dire look. "We must launch and try to evade her at sea. If we flee to the keep, she'll take the dragonship."

"Not to mention the scourge and Preel!" I turned and spied Preel standing amidships with Hemp, her eyes wide with panic. "Hemp! Get her below!" I tore my eyes from her and fixed my gaze on Shepherd. "Launch now!"

"Very well, Captain." Shepherd called for everyone to make ready, and the last of his crew clambered aboard. "Prepare to release the windlass! Man the sails. Shore crew, remove the ladder and step away."

"Wix, help however you can! We'll be close-hauled on a port tack at launch!" I whirled to follow Shepherd aft.

"Aye, sir!" Wix might consider the dragonship an affront to his sense of nautical architecture, but he'd studied the rig and sails and consulted with Shepherd's crew; he knew what he was about. He barked orders, and my people moved with a will.

The dragonship didn't have a raised quarterdeck, only a couple of cuddy cabins to shelter the companionways leading below. The wheel stood as tall as Miko, made of black metal, the rim wrapped with dragonhide. It had no extended spokes to provide a grip, and was manned by only a single helmsman. I had to assume Shepard knew how to man their ship, but I would have preferred someone standing by to assist.

"Everyone ready?" Shepherd called out. At a round of yesses from Shepherd's people and ayes from mine, the dragonlord smiled and nodded. "Release the windlass! Adjust the sails! Everyone else, hang on firmly!"

A clang sounded from behind us, and the ship started moving forward, the wheels of the carriage rumbling down the smooth tracks. The crew hauled on sheets, drawing in the trisails and great dragon wings. The incessant flapping of dragonhide stilled, and the ship surged forward. The sea grew closer at an alarming rate.

The portside mainsail luffed a trifle, and I couldn't hold my tongue. "Wix! Sheet the port main! All hands, hold fast!"

"Aye, sir! All right, you fookers! Make this fookin' dragon fly!"

The sheets were hauled in, and our speed increased. The hull groaned against the carriage, but we couldn't heel; the carriage wheels were shaped to grip the rails and couldn't lift free. A single mooring line held the ship to the carriage, ready to be released the moment we touched water.

"Brace yourselves!" Shepherd called out.

Faster and faster we sped down the rails, racing toward the raging surf even as the waves raced toward shore. I watched the waves, trying to judge if we would strike one as it broke. The moment before we wetted our hull, *Crimson Hawk* nosed out from behind the headland.

We crashed into the sea like a plummeting osprey. The crewman assigned to the release cable slapped a hand down on the mooring line's restraint, and the dragonship leapt free of the carriage, plunging deep into an oncoming wave. Spray flew high into the air and doused the deck as the ship's flat hull punched through the curling sea, seawater streaming aft to drench us all. Wix howled in glee, his tusky grin wide.

Free of the cradle, the ship heeled so sharply that I feared we'd capsize, but we flew onward. The deck canted at an astonishing angle, the leeward rail dipping into the sea on the downward roll. I lunged over to lend a hand to the struggling helmsman. The wheel trembled under my grip, the ship a living thing, responding to every touch like a high-spirited horse. We roared beyond the surf in a heartbeat, making a good line to clear the rocks on the southern headland. Angles, seas, wind, and the course of the approaching corsair all ran through my mind in a torrent. The cape effect as we neared the headland would push us another point to leeward, and every second brought us closer to *Crimson Hawk*.

And damn, the dragonship wanted to round up into the wind. "Wix, she's griping like a bitch! Ease the mains a trifle!"

"Griping?" Shephard looked at me askance. "As in *complaining* in some manner? I don't—"

"Griping means the ship wants to turn upwind." I nodded at the wheel in my hands. "The point of effort on the mainsails is greater than the headsails, which impels the ship to twist to windward, forcing the helmsman to constantly steer downwind."

"Oh, yes." Shepherd looked up at the sails and nodded. "Alas, nautical jargon wasn't part of my education."

I grinned at the dragonlord. "And magic and dragons weren't part of mine."

Under Wix's direction, the mixed crew slacked the complicated mainsail sheeting system a bit. To my relief, the helm eased and our heel lessened. It would take some practice to learn how to tweak the rig for the best performance. She was a far cry from sailing *Scourge*, but the forces at work were the same.

The helmsman stopped straining and shot me a grateful glance. "We're not usually in such a hurry when we do this," he said.

"Well, we are now." I pointed to *Crimson Hawk*, sailing on a beam reach with an astonishing amount of canvas flying. "She's coming hard."

Shepherd frowned. "I'm not exactly sure what to *do* about that, I'm afraid. We don't have any weapons that can stop a ship."

"Can't you...um..." I waved a hand at *Crimson Hawk* and wiggled my fingers.

Shepherd looked at me blankly.

"*Magic*, for Odea's sake! You're a dragonlord, a wizard! Can't you use *magic* to stop them?"

"I'm afraid I'm not *that* kind of wizard, Captain. I can't evoke lightning or fire from my fingertips, at least, not without considerable study. We must rely on evasion, I think. The dragonship is quite maneuverable." He looked dubiously at the approaching corsair. "What would you recommend?"

"*Recommend?*" I glimpsed the doubt in Shepard's eyes; it didn't engender confidence. "Shepherd, a ship can only have one captain. There's no time for discussion on tactics in situations like this."

"Yes, well..." Shepherd glanced nervously at the oncoming corsair, the forbidding headland to starboard, and the cliffs to the northeast. "I am the *steward* of the dragonship, Captain Longbright, but I have no experience in naval combat. In this situation...I will cede command to you...for our mutual benefit."

"Thank you!" I stepped behind the helmsman and surveyed our situation.

We would weather the headland easily enough. Once past it, we could bear off the wind for more speed, but *Crimson Hawk* was positioned to cut us off before we could get there. I couldn't allow them to come into grappling range. Jhavika's ship massed five times the weight of the dragonship, and who knew how many more people she had. If they boarded us, it would all be over except the screaming. We had to keep our distance.

"Miko, prepare to tack ship. The instant we have a wind shift at the headland, we come about."

"Aye, sir! Wix, prepare to come about for a starboard tack, close-hauled."

As Wix bawled orders, I turned to my only other officer. "Boxley, I want you on the helm station to assist if necessary. Get a feel for her. She's responsive like no ship I've ever sailed."

"Aye, sir!" I didn't think Boxley big enough to handle the helm on her own, but she had a deft touch.

I raised a spyglass and leveled it at my nemesis. I couldn't see Jhavika, but the deck was crowded. She had a full complement indeed. I moved to the binnacle and took a bearing on *Crimson Hawk*, then another bearing on the cliffs to the northeast. First, we had to get free of the lee shore, then get past the corsair. Once that was accomplished, I could see two possible strategies to evade Jhavika: outrun them downwind and lose them in the dark tonight, or beat to windward into the Eye and lose them in the mists.

First things first, I decided. *Get some sea room*. Once I didn't have a lee shore, I'd have more options.

The headland loomed off the starboard bow, waves crashing against the rocks at its base, the bearing slowly changing as we approached. Two points off our port bow, *Crimson Hawk* bore down on us, her bearing constant, a collision course. Jhavika had the weather gauge, and we had a lee shore. My teeth chirped like crickets as we closed the gap.

"Wind's clocking a trifle, sir!" Boxley called over her shoulder, one hand resting on the wheel, her eyes fixed on the sails.

"Ease your helm to keep her from luffing! Ready to tack ship!"

A chorus of ayes. The bizarre rig allowed me to watch my headsails from between the twin fore-and-aft rigged, dragon-wing mainsails. The jib shivered. The aft quadratic sail over my head luffed. We bore off a point, and both sails steadied. A gust heeled us over, the cape effect intensifying the already fresh trade winds. The jib shivered again.

"Now! Tack ship!"

"Helm's alee!" Boxley cried, helping the helmsman haul the wheel to port.

The dragonship snapped around so fast it took my breath away and drew an unexpected expletive from Boxley. We came about in less than a ship-length, sails cracking like ballistae shots. Wix howled and cackled like a madman, grinning like I'd never seen him grin before.

Miko looked at me wide-eyed. "Udea's sweet *tits*, this ship's quick!"

I couldn't help but grin. "That she is!" Even ready for the shift, I'd barely been able to keep my position without grabbing a stay. Shephard gripped the curved mast behind me with white knuckles. I checked our course and position, the northern headland ahead and our foe behind. Jhavika had already changed course upwind, her sails sheeted in tight. I watched for a moment and grimaced. "We're *still* not bearing as close to the wind as *Crimson Hawk*."

"Nor will we, Captain," Shepherd said. "The dragonship's designers were not mariners, but engineers and scholars. This close to the wind, I fear the corsair will outrun us."

"Well, at least they're closing slower at this angle. We can outmaneuver them." I brought the charts I'd studied to mind and began considering strategies. It seemed that everyone was doing the same.

"Once we get sea room, we could bear off southward and leave them over the horizon," Miko suggested.

"Yes, but I'd bet my best cutlass Jhavika knows where we're headed. She could beat up to the edge of the Eye and wait for us."

"Sail into the Eye, Captain," Shepherd suggested. "She will *not* follow us. She must know what would happen to them."

"Oh, Jhavika knows the legends of the Serpent's Eye. I just don't know if she's insane enough to follow us in there or not. I wouldn't have rounded that cape in the dark for all the magic in the god-emperor's vaults, but she did it. She did it to retrieve *this*." I patted the scourge at my hip, then thought, *And Preel*.

"Ah, yes; the magic of the scourge will not allow her to relent. But won't her crew mutiny?" Shepherd countered.

"I don't think they can. I'm betting that most of them are enslaved by the scourge."

"Of course." Shepherd frowned.

I glared at *Crimson Hawk* and considered our dwindling options. Our pursuers would catch us in an hour if we continued on this course. They were already to windward of us; if they got abeam, they'd have us pinned against a lee shore again. That would be our death knell. I looked aloft at the bizarre sails and reminded myself that I wasn't sailing *Scourge*. I knew we could tack far faster than *Crimson Hawk*, but not much else.

"Do you think we can outrun them downwind, Shepherd?"

"Yes, if we sail far enough downwind to set the large foresail."

"And how far downwind is that?"

"At least a hundred degrees off the wind."

"Okay. This ship comes about quickly enough that we'll gain distance every time we tack, but we lose it again when we beat upwind. We need sea room. That means getting past them to the south without getting grappled."

"Tack now, aim for the southern cape," Miko suggested. "Let *Crimson Hawk* try to pin us, then tack away again. Then, when she's coming about to the northeast, we tack *again*, and we're past them."

The course lines played in my mind as she spoke, and I nodded. "We just have to keep our distance."

"So, we stay at bowshot," Miko countered. "A few arrows won't hurt *this* ship."

"That's correct, Captain," Shepherd confirmed.

I nodded. "Let's do it. Prepare to tack ship."

Miko bellowed to Wix, and he bellowed to the crew. We were ready in moments. During our deliberations, we'd gained about a mile of easting. Once we passed *Crimson Hawk*, we'd have our sea room.

"Ready, sir!" Miko called.

"All right, then! Everyone, hold fast! Tack ship!"

"Helm's alee!" Boxley called. The dragonship came about, this time not so abruptly, but still carving a tight arc in the water. Our momentum didn't falter, and we heeled sharply when the sails cracked full.

I had to admit, it was an exhilarating ride. Six days of this might wear on my nerves, but right now, I was finding it hard to keep from smiling.

Crimson Hawk altered course until we were once again on intercepting paths, and getting rapidly closer. I raised my spyglass and spotted Jhavika's mop of bronze-gold hair streaming downwind. Light glinted off of something, and I knew she was watching us also, probably wondering what the devil kind of vessel we were sailing.

"Would you *please* give us a little warning before you throw the ship around!?"

I lowered my spyglass, blinking in confusion at the shrill complaint. Preel stood in one of the cuddy cabins, glaring at me, a livid contusion on her temple, her hands bloody.

"Gods, are you okay?" I took a step, then stopped myself. "Miko!"

"We're getting knocked about like beans in a tin cup!" Preel shrilled. "Hemp took a bad fall. What the *hell* are you doing?"

"Trying to stay alive. Best hold tight for a while. We'll give you warning if we can." I checked our position relative to our adversary. "We'll tack again in about ten minutes, maybe more than once."

Preel brushed away Miko's hand and glared anew. "Bloody damned pirate!" She whirled and climbed carefully down the companionway, leaving bloody handprints on the railing.

Miko shot me a sardonic smile. "Bloody damned pirate? That's not so bad."

"Indeed." After kicking me in the teeth and accusing me of seducing her into sex-slavery, bloody damned pirate seemed high praise. "Send someone below to help her out and put a crewman in the companionway to relay warnings. Then prepare to tack to port."

"Aye, sir." Miko sent Sauncey below and bellowed orders to Wix.

I raised my spyglass to examine our foe. I couldn't see *Crimson Hawk*'s deck, but there were people in the rigging and the windward sheets and braces were taut. They were anticipating our maneuver and preparing to tack to windward to cut us off.

Fine, I thought. *Catch me if you can, Jhavika.*

"Miko, we'll hold a northeasterly course just long enough to convince them to alter course. The instant they commit, we wear ship and come back around on a southerly course."

"Aye, sir!"

"I must ask you to explain your strategy and terminology once we're past them, Captain." Shepherd looked pained. "This field of knowledge is new to me. I realize now isn't the time, but..."

"Once we're in the clear, I'll be *happy* to explain."

Crimson Hawk bore down on us hard, now barely two hundred yards away. It was time.

"Everyone hold fast!" I took my own advice and gripped a stay. Sauncey echoed my command below for Preel and Hemp. "Boxley, tack the ship. Smartly now!"

"Aye, sir! Helm's alee!"

We came about in half a ship-length, sails cracking and the deck lurching so violently that my feet left it for a moment as we righted. A shrill curse sounded from below, and I cringed. A glance to my right confirmed that *Crimson Hawk* was changing course. Jhavika's crew handled the sheets reasonably well, though not to my own exacting standards. The maneuver put them on our upwind starboard quarter, giving them a secure advantage in angle, wind, and speed.

"Don't get used to it," I muttered quietly as I watched and gauged their progress. As soon as they were on the new course, but before they could pick up much momentum, I executed the second half of my trick. "Now, Boxley! Wear ship!"

"Aye, sir!" She and the helmsman hauled the wheel to port, and we came about in a tight circle. The dragon wing sails jibed, booming like thunder, first one, then the other, the whole ship trembling with the impacts. We surfed a swell for a moment, then heeled sharply to starboard as the crew sheeted in.

Crimson Hawk veered, trying to cut us off, but they had no chance. We were past them with perhaps seventy yards between us. I smiled grimly as I imagined Jhavika's frustration.

"Archers!" someone called from forward.

"Everyone, take cover!" I grabbed Shepherd and ducked behind one of the cuddy cabins as flaming crossbow bolts buzzed past. Some struck the ship and sails, and one even hit the binnacle, but not one found flesh, and nothing caught fire. Every single one bounced off like they'd hit iron. "A sound ship indeed!" I patted Shepherd on the shoulder.

"Yes, she certainly—"

Something struck the hull hard, the impact resounding through the soles of my boots.

"What in the name of—" I peered out from behind the cuddy. "Shit!"

A second ballista bolt shot past barely five feet away. It hit the leeward cuddy cabin and ricocheted off the dragon bone coaming. *She must have taken them from* Scourge, I realized, but that concerned me less than the wrist-thick line trailing from the bolt.

The line came taut, and the bolt jerked back across the deck. It struck the binnacle and knocked the helmsman from his feet, but Boxley was there to handle the wheel. Then the bolt's barbed iron head hooked the dragonship's port-side taffrail, and the trailing line snapped tight.

"Hang on!" I barely had time to grab the edge of the cuddy cabin.

The line jerked hard enough to knock people to the deck. The dragonship slewed to starboard, straining as the wind pushed it in one direction and the grapple pulled in another, but the stout line didn't part. I scrabbled to the taffrail, drawing my cutlass. The fine edge came down on the hardwood shaft, but barely left a nick.

"Boarding axe!" I glanced over my shoulder, but almost everyone was just getting to their feet. "Boxley! Downwind! Wix, bring a gods-damned boarding axe!" I slammed my cutlass down on the ballista shaft again, but still the wood didn't break. I couldn't reach the line trailing from its far end.

The line stretched bar-straight to *Crimson Hawk*'s deck. The corsair's sails had been loosed, flapping free, and sailors crowded around the capstan. They were drawing us closer. More sailors crowded the railing, grappling hooks in hand. Jhavika stood tall on the quarterdeck, grinning victory. I hacked at the bolt shaft again, to no avail.

"Somebody, bring me a fucking *axe*!" I bellowed.

"Sir! Stand away!" I turned to find Miko with her komei katana raised high in a two-handed grip, determination fixed on her face.

I stepped back as the blade came down. I didn't expect much; a katana isn't much heavier than a cutlass, after all. Consequently, when the blade sheared through two inches of hardwood like a knife through butter, I was unprepared. The line stretching to *Crimson Hawk* recoiled hard enough to whip across their deck. The dragonship shot forward, sending me up against the taffrail. I doubled over the rail, clawing for purchase. My boots slipped on the wet deck, and I tipped.

A hand grabbed my belt and hauled me back.

"Not a good time for a swim, sir!" Miko steadied me on my feet as she sheathed her katana.

"No, it's not." I caught my breath and scooped up my dropped cutlass. "Thank you, Miko."

"My job, sir." She grinned and nodded to the rest of the ship. "Besides, I don't want command of this lunatic asylum."

"Fair enough." I laughed and sheathed my cutlass, then glanced back at *Crimson Hawk*. We were well away, and they were still struggling to sheet in their sails. "Gods-damned ballistae. They must have taken them from *Scourge*."

"We'll have to keep more distance than we thought," Miko said.

"Agreed." I returned to the binnacle. "A point west of south, Boxley. We'll bear up when we clear the lee shore."

"Aye, captain!" She clapped the helmsman on the shoulder, and he turned the wheel.

"Sheet for a broad reach, Wix! Everything she'll fly!"

"Aye, sir!" Wix barked orders, and the huge flying jib soared aloft, cracking full and increasing our speed markedly.

Shepherd stood at the cuddy cabin, running fingers over the splintered dragon bone coaming. The ballista bolt had actually nicked it.

"Miko, have Sauncey check for water coming in. That first shot hit us squarely." I approached the dragonlord cautiously. "I'm sorry for the damage to your ship, Shepherd. I didn't think they would have ballistae."

"It can be repaired." Drawing the same slim silver wand I'd seen before, Shepherd touched it to the damaged coaming. The silver glimmered, and the dragon bone reformed into a smooth unblemished luster. "There. Healed."

"Handy." I worried that the hull had been damaged, but there was nothing to be done about it. If we weren't taking on water, the damage would have to wait for a shipyard. I gauged our angle, our speed, and our pursuer. We were still leaving the corsair behind, but our goal lay well upwind, and the farther south we sailed, the steeper our eastward course would have to be later. "Ease her upwind a point, Boxley. Wix, trim her! I want every inch of easting you can give me."

"You will want to take us east of the next isle to the south, Captain." Shepherd advised. "If you don't, it will add a day to our passage."

"I will, Shepherd. I just want a couple of miles on them before we start beating to windward again." I looked forward. The unnamed island stood at the edge of the maelstrom of magic, twenty miles or so distant. We would enter the Serpent's Eye in less than three hours. I suppressed a shudder. All my sailing life I'd been regaled with the dangers of sailing near the Eye. Now I intended to pierce it to the core.

"Do you think she'll follow us into the Eye?" Miko asked.

I raised my spyglass and looked back at *Crimson Hawk*. They'd finally gotten their sails squared away and were making way, sailing much farther to windward than we were.

"I think she'll try to cut us off, first. They're beating upwind. Jhavika knows we're going to have to work to windward and that she can beat us close-hauled. She's trying for the weather gauge. If we manage to get by her and into the Eye..." I shrugged, then lowered my glass and put it away. "Yes, I think she'll follow. This is going to be a long and dangerous dance, Miko."

"Aye, sir." She grinned maliciously. "But then, you've danced with Jhavika before and survived."

I barked a laugh at the memory of our dance at Balshi's estate. "Ironic, isn't it? We were trying to kill each other then, too."

Chapter Twenty Nine
The Mad Queen

Avarice is a lethal form of madness.
The Lessons of Quen Lau Ush

From the journal of Jhavika Keshmir –
Magic. It has been my greatest triumph and my most grievous
pain. I admit what I have known for some time; I am not the
master of the scourge, it is the master of me. It is my bane,
and will one day be the death of me. I cannot let it go.

What in the name of... I stared dumbfounded as our volley of
crossbow bolts bounced off the strange ship's sails. *What the hell is that
thing, anyway?*
   Leave it to Kevril to ally with a dragonlord and end up with a ship
so bizarre that I wouldn't have believed it existed if I wasn't staring at
it with my own eyes. The vessel skittered across the water like a bug
and turned like a startled cat. Hell, the sails looked like dragon wings.
How the thing had repelled our barrage, I had no idea. Ballistae, I
judged, would prove more effective.
   "Fire!"

The two ballistae cracked in quick sequence at my command, first from the bow, then the quarterdeck. The massive bolts flew through the air trailing stout lines. The bizarre ship might be quick, but one hit and we'd reel it in like a harpooned whale.

The first shot struck true, dead amidships in the craft's hull. I opened my mouth to cheer, but caught my breath. The bolt that would have pierced an eight-inch plank of solid oak had shattered as if the hull were made of iron.

What in the Nine Hells is that thing made of?

The second shot glanced off the coaming of one of the cuddy cabins. I cursed as the hardwood shaft clattered across the vessel's flat deck.

"Motherless son of a demon-spawned—" Then the shaft's barbed head hooked the ship's taffrail, and my heart raced anew.

"Seize that line and *haul*, you poxy whores! Make it fast to the capstan!" My crew jumped to action, and the line snapped taut, dragging the strange ship off course and pulling *Crimson Hawk*'s head around. I grinned. "Haul away! Grapples at the ready! I've got you by the *balls*, Kevril Longbright!"

My crew flung themselves onto the capstan bars, and it spun. The strange ship was nimble, but light. A figure struggled at their rail, but there was too much tension on the line to pull the barbed head free, and flailing at the hardwood shaft with a cutlass proved useless.

Kevril's frustrated bellow reached me over the distance, and I grinned. "I've got you, you bastard!"

Raising my spyglass, I watched him hack at the ballista shaft, his face contorted in panic. Then Miko joined him, a katana raised high. *That's not going to work either, fool!* I drew breath to laugh. Another ten yards and my grapplers would be in range.

Then Miko's katana fell, and the ballista shaft snapped.

My laugh turned into a scream of rage as the line lashed back across *Crimson Hawk*'s deck. The remnant of the hardwood shaft struck a crewman in the head, sending bone and gray matter flying. The bizarre ship leapt forward like a stallion from the starting gate. Kevril nearly toppled over the taffrail, but Miko dragged him back. I cursed both of their names and raised my spyglass. That cocky bastard Longbright stood there grinning in triumph, patting Miko on the shoulder as she sheathed her weapon. When he turned, I saw my scourge coiled at his hip.

My scourge... A need like I'd never before experienced tore at my gut.

"Trim sails, you useless swabs!" I raged. "After them! Trim to windward! We'll cut them off when they bear upwind!"

"Your ladyship! They're sailing into the Serpent's Eye!" My first mate sounded panicked.

As if I didn't know. They were going there to destroy my scourge. This I couldn't allow, no matter the cost.

"I said *after* them!" I faced him down. "I'll chase that bastard straight to hell if need be!"

"But the magic! It'll kill us or change us, make us into *monsters*!" His swarthy features had gone gray.

"I don't *care*!" I brandished my pike hand under his nose. "You'll follow my orders or I'll gut you like a fish!"

He swallowed hard, then nodded and backed away. "You're *insane*!"

I laughed at him. "Sail or die, you sniveling—"

Before I could finish, the man turned and leapt over the railing into the sea.

I gaped in shock for an instant. A mile and more from a rocky lee shore and pounding surf, he wasn't likely to survive. Before I could react, several more members of the original *Tiger Lily* crew also dashed for the rail, diving and leaping into the sea.

"Hold them! Clap them in irons! Don't let them get away!"

My soldiers complied, wrestling the few remaining sailors to the deck. A full dozen had abandoned ship. I watched their heads bobbing in our wake and cursed them to all Nine Hells.

Mutiny... So be it!

"Trim sails! Chain those mutinous dogs to the mainmast! I'll flog them myself!" As my faithful slaves followed my orders, I glared at the receding shape of the strange ship bearing Kevril Longbright and my scourge. *I'll chase you into the maelstrom itself*, I swore.

The Serpent's Eye...

I knew the legends, had seen the abominations, the twisted Serpent's Children in Valaka. Even now, I could see the dark shadows of huge winged beasts soaring within the mists. The dragons would kill us or the magic would change us, change me. It didn't matter. I couldn't stop, couldn't relent until I held my scourge in my hand once again.

Chapter Thirty
The Promise of Respite

Peace of mind is a gift from heaven.
The Lessons of Quen Lau Ush

From the journal of Preel Longbright –
I am a creature of magic. How ironic that I finally found
refuge from my madness at the hands of a magician.

Thankfully, someone had the foresight to pack medical supplies.
The gash on the back of Hemp's head was bone deep and bled like
hell. I pressed a wad of linen into the wound to staunch the flow.
Sauncey had helped me initially, but he'd paled so drastically at the
sight of Hemp's blood that I sent him back up on deck. An hour
passed until the bleeding finally started to ebb. Hemp hadn't quite lost
consciousness, though he was groggy and disoriented. Kevril seemed
to have finished throwing the ship around like a child's toy in a
bathtub, so I assumed we were safe.
Kevril...
The horror on his face at the sight of blood on my hands had been
undeniable. He'd been terrified, thinking that I'd been hurt. He truly

cared. I loved him and hated him with every breath. *Lies and truth, feelings and memories...*

Focus, Preel! I dragged my mind away from the battle raging within my own skull and concentrated on Hemp's. If I kept my mind busy, I could stave off the madness.

Hemp hissed as I pulled the cloth away to examine the wound. He'd flown across the cabin like a ragdoll when the ship tacked. So had I, but I'd managed to cushion my landing better than he. I'd have bruises, but that was all.

"The bleeding's slowed, Hemp, but there's a nasty gash."

"Take a stitch or three, I suppose," he muttered.

"Or *six*, and I'll need to wash it out." I put the sodden linen back in place and pressed his hand over it. "Hold that. I've got to get some water."

The dragonship still heeled to an alarming degree, pitching and shuddering with every wave. Recalling *Scourge*'s gentle roll, this felt like riding a war chariot compared with a hay wagon. The strange bunks in our cabin were hung on gimbals to rotate with the heel, but I'd been unable to crawl into one without being thrown. We'd settled for huddling on the deck with our backs to the hull, the rush of living water rumbling against our backs, only two inches away.

I carefully got to my feet and staggered to the cabin door, gripping handholds with every step. I'd never be able to do my yamshi aboard this ship. In the companionway, I braced myself against the bulkheads and worked my way to the galley, following the scent of cooking food. A single cook worked there, cutting potatoes and carrots into a pot upon a big gimballed stove. The compartment was sweltering, but he seemed not to notice, greeting me with a cautious smile, his eyes flicking down to my bloody hands.

"Help you, miss?"

"Yes, please. My friend's hurt. I need hot water to wash out his wound."

"Of course." He pulled a small pail down from a hook and poured steaming water from a kettle, his bare feet amazingly stable on the deck.

"You're experienced with this, aren't you?" I asked.

"Oh, yes. I've been on half a dozen such jaunts, though usually not quite so rough. Your captain sure knows his ports and starboards, he does! Drives this old girl like a hay wagon caught fire!" He handed over the pail and smiled.

Kevril...

I thanked the cook and took the water back to our cabin, struggling not to spill it. Hemp sat where I'd left him, the back of his shirt a bloody mess, his long ponytail sodden. He needed a proper wash, but I needed to stitch him up first. I'd never stitched flesh before, only cloth. How different could it be?

"You may as well take off your shirt, Hemp. It's a mess."

He stared at me, clearly mortified. "You shouldn't have to do this, Lady Preel."

"Well, there's no one else, and it'll keep me busy for a time. Now, stop complaining and take off your shirt. I've seen naked men before." I grabbed the hem and hoisted it up, forcing him to lift his arms.

"All respect, but you ain't seen *this* one naked."

"I'll allow you to leave your pants on. How's that?"

He snorted a laugh and muttered an oath under his breath. We worked the bloody shirt over his head, and I draped it over his shoulders. Hemp's back was crisscrossed with old scars from flogging. *From the scourge*, I realized, remembering Kevril's claim that Captain Kohl had applied the thing to every crew member, offense or no. The scourge had tasted my flesh, too, though I had no scars from it. I still wondered how Jhavika had managed that, for I'd inspected myself top to bottom for any sign that she'd lashed me and found nothing.

Jhavika... Memories clashed with feelings again, and I forced myself to focus on my task.

First, I washed off the dried blood with warm water and inspected the damage. The cut was only an inch long, but I could see bone.

"This will sting."

Hemp nodded and mumbled something around the sleeve of his shirt; he'd stuffed it into his mouth to stifle his groans and give him something to bite on.

The medical kit was well stocked. After dabbing the wound with gauze soaked with witch hazel, eliciting a muffled expletive and then an apology from my patient, I snipped the hair short around the injury and applied one of the tiny blades from the kit, shaving the hair away. The lurching deck made it challenging, but I managed not to cut him.

"I'll have to sew it up in layers, Hemp. Hold still."

He nodded again.

The kit had a plethora of needles and catgut threads, and I picked the thinnest I could find. My stomach lurched in protest of the grisly task, but I managed to sew up the muscle over the exposed bone with three quick stitches. I swabbed it with more witch hazel to stop the bleeding, then picked a heavier thread for the skin. Five stitches, and it was done. Hemp held remarkably still throughout the procedure.

"There. Good as new."

"Thank you, Lady Preel." Hemp promptly felt the stitches. "As good as Bert could've done, I'd wager."

Bert... I wondered how she fared, if she was alive. Feeling my thoughts beginning the familiar downward spiral, I began cleaning up. The bloody linens and Hemp's shirt I bundled into a ball and put aside to soak. I forced Hemp to hold still while I rinsed the blood off of his neck and out of his hair, then dried him off and allowed him to get dressed. Lastly, I washed my own hands thoroughly, digging the blood from under my fingernails with a pick from the medical kit. The work helped me focus, but when it was done, I had absolutely nothing to do.

"You should lie down, Hemp. I'm going to find out what's going on."

"You shouldn't go on deck, Lady Preel. The way this damned thing pitches around, you could take a spill over the side."

"I won't go on deck. I just need something to do." I urged him into his bunk, and he managed it without falling and splitting his head open again.

There were voices from the mess hall, but I worked my way to the companionway instead and climbed up. Spray slashed the deck with every wave. Kevril stood behind the binnacle, one hand on a stay, the other on Boxley's shoulder. Boxley was grinning, her hands sure on a wheel taller than she was. They didn't notice me, focused solidly on guiding the ship. I peered about.

To starboard I spied a rocky island barely a half mile to leeward. Shifting my grip to get a better hold on the wet hatch coaming, I squinted to windward and gasped. A looming wall of multihued mists swirled barely a quarter mile away. Lavender lightning tore a jagged line high above the sea, wreathing a winged shape with its eerie light. A dragon. We were angling into the Serpent's Eye.

The dragonship topped a swell, and I gripped the handrails hard to keep my place. From the vantage of the high wave, I glimpsed another ship behind us and to windward, a large black-hulled corsair.

Jhavika! Gods, no. She was following us into the Serpent's Eye, blinded to the danger by her need for the scourge. She'd die or be twisted into a monster by the magic, but she couldn't stop. *My poor sister...*

I swung back toward the binnacle...toward Kevril. He stood tall and steady, his eyes constantly sweeping the horizon, peering up to check the sails, his confident voice booming out commands that were instantly followed. They trusted him. My heart ached and raged, swelled with love and burned with hate, as I gazed at him. The scourge hung at his hip, secured there by a stout leather strap on his belt, just as Jhavika used to wear it. Jhavika was chasing us for two reasons: the scourge and me. If I gave her both, she might let Kevril go, abandon this suicidal chase.

But could I do it? Could I snatch the scourge from Kevril's belt and leap over the rail? *Crimson Hawk* was barely a mile away. They would see me jump. They would pick me up.

Maybe. Or I drown and the scourge sinks to the bottom of the sea.

I gripped the rail in an attempt to steady my unraveling nerves, trying to formulate a plan. If I went to Kevril and feigned a stumble, he would grab me out of reflex. I knew he would. He'd done it aboard *Scourge* dozens of times. When he did, I'd grab the scourge and break free. The enchanted manacles shouldn't interfere; I wouldn't be trying to hurt myself, only to escape. If it worked, I'd save both of them, and perhaps find some peace for myself. I would have a purpose.

Love and hate, memories and feelings, lies and truth, Kevril and Jhavika...

With a new sense of resolve, I took a step forward.

"Preel!" A hand on my arm, and I turned to find Shepherd beside me. "You shouldn't go on deck. It's not safe."

"I need..." What did I need? *My loved ones safe, my sanity restored... Priorities.* "I need to speak to Kevril."

"I'm afraid that's not possible right now. We're at a rather critical juncture."

"I *know* that! I need to..." I jerked my arm free and turned. Kevril had spotted us. Instead of tending to the ship, his attention was fixed upon me, pain clear in his eyes. "I need to *stop* this!"

Shepherd looked puzzled. "Stop what?"

"Stop us from sailing into the Eye! Stop Jhavika from being destroyed! I can't bear it!"

"Calm, child." Shepherd's blithe tone took me aback, the warm hand on my shoulder soothing me. "You are ensorcelled."

"I *know* that!" I caught my breath. "Please! Order your people to turn back. We can't do this! The magic will kill her!"

"Perhaps, but we have no way to stop the master of the scourge from pursuing it."

"Yes, we do!" I rounded on Shepherd. "She wants the scourge and me! Give her both. Let me *save* her!"

Shepherd considered me pensively. "You know you're being compelled by the scourge, don't you?"

"Yes! Of *course*, I do!"

"And you know what Jhavika will do if she regains it." It wasn't a question, but a statement.

"Yes! That doesn't change anything!"

"Interesting." Shepherd's brow furrowed. "Even knowing these things, you cannot stop yourself from loving her, from wanting to help her."

"*Yes!*"

"This enchantment is insidious, Preel. It has set your mind against itself." Shepherd raised a hand, soft fingertips brushing my cheek. "You must concentrate on what you *know*, not what you feel."

"*How?*" The panic in my voice sickened me. I trembled like a leaf in the wind.

"I can aid you, help still your mind, but you must trust me." Shepherd held out a hand, empty and welcoming, a promise of solace. "Please, let me help you."

I glanced back at Kevril, the scourge, and beyond to Jhavika. Hate and love warred within me, tearing me apart. But salvation, a chance for peace, waited at my back, the dragonlord's presence as warm and comforting as the glow of the sun. I turned back to Shepherd and nodded, not trusting myself to speak, afraid I'd start screaming and be unable to stop.

"Come."

I clasped the proffered hand and went.

In the cabin, Hemp stirred and looked at us with a wary expression. He didn't trust magic, and I couldn't blame him. My own had only brought pain and despair. I hoped that Shepard's grace would prove me wrong.

"What's afoot, Lady Preel?" He started to get up.

"Please, stay there, Hemp. Shepherd wants to help me." I took a breath and girded my nerves, swallowing my screams. "I'm not going to be able to exercise on this ship. It bounces around too much. I can't concentrate on anything. Jhavika's chasing us right into the Serpent's Eye, and I'm losing my *mind*!"

"Help you *how*?" I could have cut the suspicion in Hemp's voice with a knife.

"Magic, Master Hemp." Shepherd drew a slim bar of silver from a robe pocket and turned to me. "We shepherds have learned arcane skills that help to curb human emotions. This is part of how we prepare ourselves for our work. What I offer you, Preel, is a lesser form, temporary, similar to what our apprentices experience before they decide to devote themselves to becoming full-fledged shepherds. It will only blunt your emotions, not remove them. You'll still retain your wants and desires, but the conflict should be calmed somewhat, though probably not completely."

"I'm not sure—"

"Do it!" I insisted, cutting off Hemp's protest. "If you don't, I'll go mad."

Shepherd looked quizzically at Hemp, then nodded to me. "Very well. I'll cancel this enchantment when our mission is complete and you can discern truth from enchantment once again."

"Please." I closed my eyes as the silver wand raised to my forehead.

I expected to feel something—a tingle or pain, perhaps—but I didn't. Just a cool press of the metal against my skin, then...nothing.

No, not quite nothing. I felt calm. I felt tired. I felt hungry. But the love, the hate, the clash in my mind was muted. My memories and emotions lay like broken crystal shards ready for me to pick up, sharp and dangerous, but I could let them just lay there if I wished. I had no control over what Kevril was doing, or Jhavika either. I couldn't save them from themselves or one another. I could only save myself.

Peace...

A tear slid down my cheek as relief flooded through me. "Thank you, Shepherd." I sniffed and blinked my eyes open. "Thank you so much."

Shepherd smiled that enigmatic smile and nodded. "You are most welcome."

Hemp just grumbled something incomprehensible and narrowed his eyes at the two of us.

Chapter Thirty One
Into the Mists

Courage and desperation are oft confused.
The Lessons of Quen Lau Ush

From the diary of Kevril Longbright –
I had thought I had sailed in all manner of weather imaginable. Maybe I have, for the Serpent's Eye isn't really weather, it's magic. An old sea chanty about a ship of fools comes to mind. If I survive this, I swear to Odea that I will never sail in fog again.

"Squall!"
The forward lookout's warning drew a curse from my lips. The mists of the Eye were not as thick as I'd feared; we had about a half mile of visibility, despite the low light of dusk. Even so, the intermittent squalls of monsoon season plagued us. They swept down out of nowhere, giving us precious little time to prepare, and shot the hell out of our dead reckoning calculations.

"Ease sheets! Helm, try not to make quite so much leeway this time, and keep track of our heading. Run the log once we get into the thick of it, Boxley. Sauncey, log the time, heading, and speed!" Without a view of the stars, dead reckoning was our only means of navigation, so precise speed and course logs were vital. If I calculated right— *Please, Odea*—by morning we'd be within sight of an island by which I could fix our position. An error in calculations might run us aground during the night.

"This is why we don't venture into the Eye during this time of year, Captain." Shepherd ducked into one of the cuddy cabins as the deluge swept down on us.

"A sensible practice." *But desperation and sensibility don't mix*, I added to myself. "Please tell everyone below that we're weathering a blow."

"Yes, of course." Shepherd vanished below, which was fine with me. My nerves were frazzled enough without the dragonlord's criticism.

I glanced over my shoulder and marked *Crimson Hawk*'s position before I lost the pursuing ship in the squall. They were still holding a closer line to windward than we were, but had yet to gain enough to cut us off. I'd been trying to keep them on the edge of visibility, sacrificing a point of our eastward progress and a bit of speed to keep an eye on them. Better to lose some headway toward our goal than blunder into them unexpectedly in the mists. That strategy, however, was not without risks.

During a previous squall, Jhavika had used the gusty winds and concealing deluge to race down on us. When the curtain of rain cleared, *Crimson Hawk* was barely two hundred yards away. I'd learned my lesson. During the night, we would tack ship and hopefully lose them permanently. That would be Jhavika's death knell. Without accurate charts, she'd be forever lost in the mists.

The gusty winds at the leading edge of the squall hit us hard enough to lay the ship over at a frightening angle. Only my white-knuckled grip on a stay kept me in place. The leeward rail plunged beneath the sea's surface. Overhead, the flagging sails cracked like thunder, and we righted somewhat, but white water still raced down the deck. Rain slashed down so thick that I could barely see the foredeck, and only Wix's bellowed commands could be heard above the roar.

Then something rose from the sea beside the ship.

At my first gaping glance, I thought we'd run into a rocky shoal, but the 'rock' kept rising and paced along beside us. I closed my mouth to keep the deluge from drowning me as a massive, ribbed dorsal fin rose to half the height of our masts. Iridescent scales the size of dinner plates glistened and scintillated in rainbow hues as they shed torrents of sea water.

"Sea drake!" Wix bellowed. Cries of alarm shivered the air as my crew fled to the opposite rail. Curiously, Shepard's people barely reacted at all, glancing up at the huge creature with disinterest.

It rose, a truly massive creature, easily the length of the dragonship. The sea drake's head broke the surface, a bright lavender eye looking us over, teeth the length of scimitars edging a mouth that could swallow a longboat. The beast moved effortlessly, wings that rivaled the dragonship's sails beating slowly beneath the surface.

We'd seen dragons aplenty, but from a distance, and they'd ignored us. This one—the largest drake I'd ever seen—I could have hit with a tossed biscuit, and it was definitely taking an interest. "Helmsman, veer away from that beast!"

"Don't worry, Captain!" The helmsman—a burly islander named Callus, one of Shepherd's people—grinned over his shoulder at me. "She's just curious." He eased the helm a trifle, but not enough for my contentment.

"Curious about what? How we might *taste*?" The great head plunged, and the huge wings flapped underwater, creating a wake that rocked the ship.

"No. Just looking over another dragon." He laughed. "Maybe she's in love."

"Gods, I hope not!" I'd taken Shepherd at this word that dragons saw the dragonship as one of their own kind, but it lent me little comfort. It did make me wonder how *Crimson Hawk* fared, both with the dragons and the wild magic of the Eye.

The drake's head broke the surface again, and the long, flexible neck twisted upward. The jaws opened to the sky, the throat expanding.

"*Draco marinus iridensus*, the rainbow sea drake." Shepherd said from the port-side cuddy cabin. "She's drinking! They take in fresh water from rain."

"Of course, they do." I couldn't tear my eyes off those teeth.

"Twelve and a half knots, sir!" Boxley, at least, was keeping her attention on her duties.

"Thank you, Boxley. Sauncey, make sure you get all the numbers."

"Aye, sir!" Sauncey stood in the shelter of the starboard cuddy where the ship's log was kept. It was the most detailed record we'd ever produced; ship's speed was taken twice an hour, and data was logged any time our course or speed changed due to wind or conditions. *Mists, squalls, and gods-damned dragons. I must be insane.*

Our draconic escort arched her hill-sized back and dove, twin tails flexing like serpents. In an instant, she was gone. I breathed easier, but the majesty of the beast had not been lost on me, beautiful and terrible. I could understand the dragonlords' fascination with them.

The rain and wind eased as the squall passed, but the sky remained dark. Wix trimmed sails without my order, and the helmsman resumed our close-hauled course. We'd lost our daylight during the squall, or most of it. The sky still flashed intermittently with multihued lightning, but I hoped that would serve to confuse our pursuers rather than help them. I looked behind us and smiled; *Crimson Hawk* was no longer in sight.

Soon I'll lose you for good, Jhavika.

My smile faded as I spied an iridescent trail in the water behind the ship, not unlike the phosphorescent wake often seen in tropical waters. If Jhavika spotted it, she could follow it right up our ass.

Shepherd joined me. "Our passage disturbs the magic in the water. Beautiful, isn't it?"

"It is," I admitted. "But I've encountered many beautiful things that are deadly."

"Oh, no doubt, Captain, but danger doesn't lessen the wonder of it. Magic's like that, you know. Beautiful and dangerous."

"Don't I know it." I thought of the sea drake, then of Preel, who was resting finally. I'd thanked Shepherd a dozen times for easing her torment. "It's also a magnet for trouble. I often wonder why the god-emperor doesn't send a fleet to Valaka to take all the dragonlords' secrets."

Shepherd barked a laugh. "The law of diminishing returns, I'd wager. It would cost him more than he'd glean. *I* may prefer to avoid violence, but some of my peers aren't so reticent."

"Maybe."

I watched the glowing wake behind us, my eyes adjusting slowly to the darkness. Color flashed from the depths, and more luminous trails traced the paths of sea creatures. It made me wonder what lurked below, how the magic of the Eye might have affected the denizens of the sea. Remembering the Serpent's Children in Valaka, I shuddered and patted the rail of the dragonship.

Scanning the horizon behind us, denoted only by a line of fluorescence where the squall's rain hit the surface of the sea, I wondered how Jhavika and her crew fared. I watched for the better part of an hour, but saw no sign of *Crimson Hawk*.

"Do you think we finally lost them?" Shepherd asked.

"I hope so. Jhavika might have tacked to avoid the squall. Maybe that sea drake decided to have a snack." Silent lightning flashed overhead, magical static dancing on our sails. *Beautiful and deadly.* "Jhavika knows where we're going, but she can't run at night without charts. Come daylight, she can use the rotation of the maelstrom to calculate a course to the center. With luck, we won't see them again, but I'm not counting on it."

"Yes, keeping a sharp lookout would be prudent, and not only for our pursuers." Shepherd waved a hand at the impenetrable darkness. "There are other denizens of the Eye, mutations of indigenous life that may or may not pose dangers to us. I've found it best to avoid them whenever possible."

I raised my eyes to the sky in frustration. "You said the dragonship would protect us."

"From dragons and their kin, yes. But I never said that it would protect from *all* dangers."

"Wonderful!" *So much for getting through this alive.* Fatigue and stress were wearing me thin. "*How*, then, do we avoid these other denizens in this soup?"

"Cautiously." That enigmatic smile shone in the darkness. "As you can see, disturbances in the sea leave fluorescing trails at night. Watch for them and alter course to evade. Islands, of course, should be given a wide berth if possible."

Biting off an acerbic reply, I said, "Of course," then sent an order to Wix to keep a sharp lookout forward. I got an indignant and profane reply. He was already doing so, of course.

Oblivious of my distress, Shepherd said goodnight and went below, leaving me to my tumultuous thoughts. I scanned the darkness, the sky, and the depths around the ship, as much to stay awake as to maintain vigilance. It had been a very long day.

"Eight bells, sir!"

I turned to find Miko standing ready to take the watch, barely visible in the dim light of a shuttered lamp in the starboard cuddy. I yawned reflexively, more than ready for my bunk. I'd been on deck since dawn, fourteen long hours.

"Did you read the log?" I asked.

"Yes, and plotted our position, give or take a few miles. Good that we shook *Crimson Hawk*. When do you want to tack?"

"If our speed holds steady, at the end of your watch. If you spot anything—land, a glow in the water, whatever—don't wait. Maneuver to evade." I filled her in on a few details: the curios phenomenon of luminescence beneath the water, how the rainfall of the squall we'd passed left a line of light on the horizon, and Shepherd's warning about the non-draconic denizens.

"Lovely." Miko peered into the dark. "Fog, dark, and fucking dragons..."

"Well, I haven't seen any of them actually *fucking* yet, but the sea drake that surfaced beside us might have had romantic intentions." I laughed at her scathing glare. "Sorry. I'm punchy with fatigue. I need sleep."

Miko shook her head. "You do. It's good to hear you laugh, though."

"It feels good to laugh." I sighed and rubbed my bleary eyes. "Strange. I'm wound tighter than a watch spring, but I feel like we're finally on the last stretch. All we have to do is reach the center of the Eye, and it's over."

"And Preel's feeling better," she added. "Sleeping, at least."

"Yes, and that." Maybe, when this was done, she'd be the woman I knew again.

"Go sleep, sir. You're dead on your feet."

"I am. One of the dragonlord's apprentices is taking the midwatch, and Shepherd's taking the morning watch. Leave word to wake me at six bells in the morning watch, and I'll take the forenoon." Miko nodded, and I ducked into cuddy cabin.

Despite a weather cloak, I was soaked to the skin. I hung my jacket in the wet locker to air and made my way below. Cutting through the mess, I paused long enough to wolf down a wedge of goat cheese and a hunk of stale bread, washing it down with tepid tea, then staggered to the cabin I shared with Wix. He was already snoring, though he'd gotten off watch the same time I did. I kicked off my boots, peeled out of my wet clothes, donned a dry shirt, rolled into my bunk, and fell immediately and deeply asleep.

In my dreams, I heard a cry that chilled my blood.

Chapter Thirty Two
Bane

Only a fool fights in a burning house.
The Lessons of Quen Lau Ush

From the journal of Jhavika Keshmir –
Flesh is a tapestry woven by the gods. Magic unravels that tapestry and weaves it in new patterns. I see the truth now. We are all fraying at the edges. We will be made anew by the will of the Serpent. I seek that which is destroying me, and I cannot relent.

"Sail on, damn you!" I lashed the helmsman's back with my pike hand, laying open his shirt and the flesh beneath. Ahead of us, the strange ship bearing my scourge, my truthsayer, and Kevril Longbright heeled so hard with the initial gust of the squall that I feared it would capsize. If it sank to the bottom of the sea, I would lose everything. Moments later, though, it stabilized and vanished into the wall of rain. I breathed in relief and exhaled commands. "Slack sheets as the gust hits, then brace up! We'll use it to overtake them! *Move*, you laggards, or I'll have the flesh off your bones!"

My crew leapt to comply. Of course, they could do nothing less. Even without the incentive of the mutineers still chained to the base of the mainmast, the flesh of their backs torn and bleeding from my just punishment, they could not disobey. I was their queen, their goddess.

I'd taken no rest since we took *Scourge*. I needed no rest. I needed no sleep, food, or companionship. I only needed my scourge.

We'd been sailing through the Eye all day, following Kevril. The rainbow mists of wild magic swept across the deck, prickling like nettles on my skin, through my clothes, along my bones, burning like fire. It didn't matter. The scourge was within reach now. I would have it in my grasp before the sun rose again.

The squall hit us hard, laying the ship over, but I'd gauged its force well. We blew out one topsail, but the rest held, and *Crimson Hawk* righted after the initial gust. Rain blasted down so hard I could barely see. I opened my mouth and drank, soothing my raw throat. The liquid tingled on my tongue, shimmered on my skin, cool, magical.

"Cut that torn sail down and bend a new one, damn it! Ease to leeward a point and trim smartly!" Our quarry lay ahead somewhere, I knew it. They couldn't escape me. *Crimson Hawk* could beat them to windward, which gave me the only advantage I needed. That strange ship might be nimble, but I'd hook them eventually. "Load the ballistae, you laggards! We may come out of this within range, and I don't want to miss this time!"

Again, my crew leapt to, cranking back the siege engines and loading the hardwood shafts. I'd ordered grappling hooks lashed to the heads to increase the chances of hooking their rigging, and ordered my crews to aim high. If I hooked a mast too high for the crew to reach and cut free, I'd have them. *Kevril, Preel, my scourge...* On the other side of this squall, they might well be becalmed, lying helpless.

The shredded sail flew away to leeward, and crewmen hauled a new one aloft despite the howling wind and blinding rain. I squinted into the curtain of blackness, but could see nothing. Night was falling, and the shimmering iridescence of the sea seemed brighter, as if reflecting the magical lightning overhead. The whole ship glowed above and beneath me.

"Lookout forward!" I bellowed. "Keep a sharp eye or I'll pluck them out!"

The new sail was bent, unfurled, and sheeted. A scream from aloft, and I glanced up in time to see someone fall. They missed the deck and hit the sea to leeward. No one even suggested that we try to recover them.

Crimson Hawk strained forward, smashing through the choppy sea like a bull through a briar patch. The deck shuddered beneath my feet, the wood groaning. I put my hand on a stay and felt it tremble under my fingers. I was pushing her hard, but I didn't care. As long as she held together, nothing else mattered.

"SHIP!" someone howled from forward.

My heart leapt into my throat. "Ready ballistae!" I shielded my eyes and squinted into the impenetrable darkness. Something shimmered within the curtains of rain. "Where away, damn you?"

"Two points off the—" The lookout's voice fell silent, then rose in a shrill screech. "*Sea drake!*"

The shimmering shape coalesced, not a ship, but a massive winged form rising from the waves. It breached on a parallel but opposite course, clearing the water entirely, a baleful lavender eye gleaming in the massive head. The beast fairly glowed in the darkness as it plunged back down, wings like rainbow-hued sails splitting the sea, twin flukes the size of a ship's rudders thrashing.

I froze, not in fear, but in awe as it swept past us. *Ninety feet and fifty tons, at least. Such power...* It made me feel suddenly insignificant, a fly on the back of a bull while a hungry tiger prowled the grass. Well, this bull had horns, and if the beast came too close, it would feel them.

"Sail on!" I wasn't about to give up now. "Keep an eye on that thing and fire the ballistae if it comes at us! Sharp eyes, damn you all!"

We sailed on, every eye trained, every weapon ready.

"There! Starboard side! She rises!"

I whirled to stare at the ribbed dorsal fin rising from the sea. The drake's outline shone below, glowing from the magic in the water just as we shimmered from the mists. The massive head turned, looking up at us from beneath the surface.

"Ready ballistae, gods blast you!"

The crews fought to aim the unwieldy machines. I kept my eyes trained on the beast. It paced us easily, massive, yet effortless in motion. Breaking the surface again, its neck craned up to look at us, curious or hungry, I couldn't tell. The last thing I wanted was to provoke it.

"Don't fire unless it—"

The sinuous neck twisted, the saurian head turning sideways. I watched those jaws open…and knew.

"DOWN!"

I took my own advice and flattened myself on the deck. Teeth like swords flashed over my head, snapping closed on three hapless sailors too slow to evade. As it dragged its screaming prizes overboard, the beast's neck smashed onto the rail. Wood splintered, and the ship rolled with the impact, but it was over in an instant. The snapping jaws had miraculously missed the shrouds, whether by chance or intent, I had no way to know.

I scrabbled up to survey the damage. Only the bulwarks and a few deck boards were cracked. Blood smeared the deck, but the rain quickly washed it out of the scuppers. My gaze was drawn into our wake where the sea drake thrashed and snapped its jaws, swallowing its catch. Would it be satisfied? I thought not.

"Keep your eyes on the sea, for the gods' sake! Call out if you see that thing coming back! Ballista crews, reload with straight bolts. The last thing we want to do is *hook* that thing! Helmsman, hold your course or I'll flay you alive!" I resumed my position behind the binnacle, wondering how we might avoid the hungry denizens of this gods-forsaken sea.

My eyes fixed on the mainmast, the six mutineers chained there, and followed the trail of their blood as the rain washed it across the deck and out the scuppers. Blood. Like chumming for tuna and hooking a shark, we'd attracted something much too large to land.

"Damn!" It was too late to do anything about that now, but once we cleared the squall, I'd have to get rid of the bait.

"Astern!"

I whirled at the cry and stared at the sea behind the ship. In our wake, the beast came at us just beneath the surface, its bulk throwing a bulging wave, iridescent scales flashing and gleaming. We topped a swell and raced down the other side, and for an instant the sea drake swam within it, a great luminous bird silhouetted against the darkness. Its head broke the surface, lavender eyes blazing, tattered flesh flapping from between those horrific teeth.

"Stern ballista, come around." I rushed to help pull the unwieldy engine into position. "Wait for it to strike, then fire right down its mouth! If you hit its scales, you'll just piss it off!"

The drake submerged and came right at us.

I knew sea drakes were reasonably smart. It was a type of dragon, and dragons were said to be more intelligent than humans. Specifically what this one intended, other than to feed, I had no idea. To disable the ship, sink us, or just pluck us off the deck until it was sated, I didn't know or care. All I knew was that it was threatening my mission, keeping me from my scourge. That was a death sentence in my book.

"Wait for it!" I bellowed to the crewman clutching the ballista's release cord. "Wait until it strikes! If you miss, I'll feed you to that beast myself!"

"Aye!" He sounded steady, but there was blood trickling from his lip where his teeth clenched.

"Ready..."

The drake came at us, right up our wake. We crested a swell together, and the beast lifted its head out of the sea, the sinuous neck flexing, the jaws turning sideways and opening as it struck.

"FIRE!"

The ballista cracked, sending a six-foot, iron-tipped shaft right down that maw. A roar loud enough to knock us backward tore from its throat. The jaws snapped shut and struck the taffrail. Wood exploded from the impact, splinters flying. I gaped as the beast thrashed behind the ship, the wings whipping the sea to froth, the two tails lashing like great serpents.

The drake reared in the water, shaking its head and roaring, blood spraying from its mouth. Then it sounded, the great back arching, the fluked tails rising to drive it deep. The sea roiled in its wake.

Gone. And we'd survived.

"Well done!" I clapped the ballista crewman on the back. "Now, reload and—"

Something beneath my feet cracked, and the ship veered to windward. Even before I could utter an appropriate expletive, we rounded up.

"Helm! Steer downwind! Up tacks and sheets!" I whirled to the helm, but my helmsman spun the wheel to no avail.

"The helm won't answer, your ladyship! Something's broke!"

"Shit!" We were dead in the water and drifting downwind. "Furl the courses and topsails. Ballistae crews, keep your eyes open for trouble. Deck crew, follow me."

We hurried below, down into the bowels of the ship where the steering mechanism was housed. Here, we found the problem. The sea drake must have hit the rudder hard enough to dismount the controlling chains from the steering quadrat. The rudder shaft had wrenched its housing out of the overhead beam, splintering the hard oak. The wheel's controlling lines hung limp.

Until we fixed it, we weren't going anywhere.

Rage overwhelmed me. "Start taking this apart! Get it remounted! There've got to be tools somewhere! I'll send help." I dashed back up toward the deck, clawing my way up the companion ladders with my pike hand. On deck, it was pitch dark save for the thin luminous glow of the magical mists that flowed over every surface. My skin tingled anew.

"Anyone not doing something important, get below and help remount the steering quadrat! Find tools. Get to work, laggards!" My crew hurried to comply, but my rage remained unabated.

We were drifting abeam to the seas, rolling hard, losing miles of easting, losing my scourge. The deck damage was minimal, and the rain had washed away the blood, or most of it. Crimson rivulets still ran from the backs of the mutineers I'd flogged. More chum in the water. That wouldn't do.

It was time to cut bait.

I fished a key from my pocket and approached the chained prisoners. They slumped from the eyebolts, slack but alive. I worked the key in one manacle, and the man sprawled on the deck.

I flipped him onto his back with my hook and put the point to his nose. "Now, you can do as you're told or get off my ship. If you—"

I froze. The man's eyes clicked open, but instead of eyes, the faces of snakes peered from within his sockets.

"What the..." I backed up, wondering if my fatigue was causing delusions.

The man rolled over and heaved himself to hands and knees. The manacles had abraded the scales from his wrists. *Scales?* He coughed, and something slithered from his throat, a long, bifurcated tongue.

Before I could find my voice, he scrabbled for the splintered railing and over the side.

Snakes for eyes, scales, a split tongue... Wild magic.

I knew the tales of the Serpent's Eye, had heard the warnings of horrific mutations, but I'd assumed that such changes would take time, days or weeks, not mere hours. I had expected to have recovered my possessions and be heading back to Haven well before any magic affected my crew. I glanced around and saw that others had also begun to change, sporting feathers, twisted limbs, writhing fingers, teeth like the mandibles of a crab...

I reached out to steady myself against the mast and drew a ragged gasp. My right forearm bent midway between wrist and elbow, twisting and flexing as if it had no bones at all. The flesh at the end of my arm had grown into the metal base of my pike hand, veins pulsing blood through the steel. My left hand seemed normal, save for a chitinous growth that roughened my knuckles. Then I flexed my fingers, and claws unsheathed from the beds of my nails.

"Oh, dear gods..." I swallowed bile and strode for the splintered railing, glaring out at the swirling magical mists that were transforming me into a monster, reweaving the tapestry of my flesh. I gripped the rail hard, my pike hook and claw-like nails gouging splinters from the wood.

The rail shuddered in my grasp.

I looked down at the wood, at the broken planks, the cracked bulwarks, and gaped in disbelief. The wood was twitching and flexing, reforming, healing as if it were flesh.

"Wild magic..."

Crimson Hawk was coming to life beneath me.

Chapter Thirty Three
The Changed Queen

When faced with the impossible, improvise.
The Lessons of Quen Lau Ush

From the diary of Kevril Longbright –
I never thought to see such wonders, such horrors, dreams and nightmares made flesh. Sweet Odea, Goddess of the Sea, please let me never see them again.

"On deck, sir!"
I started from the midst of the most wonderful dream—*Preel... Oh gods...*—to blink into the betusked face of my bosun. *Hell of a way to wake up.* "Odea's green garters, Wix. I just got to sleep!"
"Nine hours ago. Shephard's called for you on deck. Out of that bunk or I dump you out!"
Gods, I'd slept. I muttered a curse and rolled out of my bunk. Bosuns will always be bosuns, no matter your rank. I pulled on pants, jammed my feet into my boots, and yawned. "I need blackbrew."
"And I need a week in a brothel. We're out of blackbrew."
I tried to speak, stuttered, then managed, "How in the Nine Hells can a ship *function* without blackbrew?"

"Well, sir, there's these things called sails, and when you put them up on masts, they catch the wind and pull the ship along." Wix laughed at my glare.

"Smartass." I followed him through the ship's mess, grabbing a wedge of goat cheese on my way. The cook was busy, the aromas of cooking meat and biscuits heavenly, but breakfast wasn't on yet. On deck, I peered out of the cuddy cabin to find Shepherd looking worried. It wasn't quite the dark of night, but not quite the light of day yet; I guessed two bells in the morning watch. We were surrounded by swirling eddies of multi-hued fog that had nothing to do with the weather. In fact, they drifted against the wind. *The Serpent's Eye. That's right...* I was still disoriented, fighting the last dregs of sleep. I dragged on my damp jacket and a weather cloak, and stepped out of the cuddy.

"Problem?" I asked, stifling another yawn. We were on a northeasterly tack, but my brain couldn't decide where that would place us on the chart. I hadn't looked at the logbook to check our position.

"Perhaps. A most curious sound on the wind. Listen."

I turned an ear to the wind and cocked my head. The sails thrummed, the rigging creaked, the hull groaned, all normal sounds to a sailor. Then, above the wind's howl, I discerned a high-pitched keening, an intermittent wail, like voices on the wind. "What *is* that?"

"I've no idea, Captain, but it's been moving with us, upwind, in approximately the same direction for the last half hour." Shepherd looked at me askance. "I've taken dozens of trips into the Eye and never encountered such a phenomenon."

"And you want *my* opinion?" I barked a laugh and rubbed my bleary eyes. "Shepherd, I can't even wake up without a pot of blackbrew in my belly, let alone hypothesize what some wailing wind might portend."

"Ah, I see. You're not yet fully awake. Here." Shepherd delved a pocket and withdrew a small dried leaf, about two inches long. "Chew this and tuck the pulp in your cheek. It'll invigorate you and sharpen your mind."

I took the leaf and peered at it. "What is it?"

"A miraculous medicine discovered by the fae of the Jungles of Nin. They use it in rituals and as a mild stimulant. Its effects are much like blackbrew, but more intense."

"Sounds perfect." I took the leaf in my mouth and chewed. It was bitter. "Let me read the log and fix our position. I'll be right back."

Shepherd nodded blithely. "Of course, Captain."

I ducked into the cuddy cabin and perused the log. Miko's notes were precise. She'd tacked the ship at the end of her watch, trimmed for a close reach, and handed the ship over to Shepherd's apprentice. Shepherd had assumed the morning watch almost two hours ago. Fixes of speed and bearing had been taken every half hour, each sequential dead reckoned position plotted on the chart with a small x and the time. Supposedly, we were sailing right up the slot between two islands. If we maintained our speed, we'd tack again in another eight hours or so and make a line close to the center of the eye.

I chewed the leaf to a bitter pulp and tucked it in my cheek. My tongue tingled, and my mind felt sharper already. *Quicker than blackbrew*, I decided, *but not as enjoyable.*

Back out on deck, I listened again. The howls and wails were at about the same angle and no louder. If there were words in there, I couldn't make anything out. I turned back to Shepherd. "No other sightings or encounters?"

"A few drakes and dragons, but nothing else."

"And you've never before encountered anything like this…this wailing?"

Shepherd shrugged. "Nothing so far at sea. Some of the islands have curious creatures capable of human-like speech, but they don't venture far to sea."

"I imagine the sea drakes feed on them. No wonder that one we saw was so huge."

"Indeed, they *are* voracious. The consolidation of dragons and their kin in the Eye has decimated the indigenous ecology, such as it was." Shepherd nodded to windward. "Concerning our mysterious phenomenon, I thought to tack the ship, but that would take us nearer an island. We might be able to weather the headland, but our position isn't certain, and I generally don't take that kind of risk, especially in the dark."

"I can understand why."

I looked aloft, longing for a high lookout, but the dragonship sported no ratlines and no crow's nest. All of the sails were raised and adjusted from the deck. I plucked my spyglass from my belt and scanned the mists to windward. A few flashes and indistinct glows, but nothing solid. The sounds, which reminded me disconcertingly of human voices, seemed to be coming from slightly abaft the beam, just south of the eye of the wind. I didn't like it. We had about fifteen miles of open sea to windward and leeward. Whatever the sounds were coming from, they were much closer than any potential land. I recalled Shepherd's warning from the night before, his recommendation that we evade anything unknown. A reasonable strategy.

"I'd say tack, sail southeast for two hours with a sharp lookout forward, then tack back to the northeast to finish this leg."

Shepherd nodded. "Very well. Would you like to take the deck now or wait? You still have almost two hours until your watch begins."

"I'd rather take *breakfast*, if it's all the same to you. Your leaf has me wide awake, but I could use a real meal."

"As you wish, Captain." Shepherd dismissed me and gave orders to prepare to tack the ship.

I went below. In the mess, the cook was handing out rations of stewed goat meat, mashed potatoes, and fresh biscuits with gravy to the groggy forenoon watch. The tables in the mess were set on gimbals to keep them level, which made meals rather like target practice with knife and fork. Hemp was there, loading two bowls, his head swathed in a bandage.

"Morning, Hemp. How's your head?"

A shout from above warned us, Wix's bellow loud enough to reverberate through the deck, and everyone grabbed something stationary. The dragonship came about relatively gently, but heeled hard at the first portside gust, sails cracking as they filled. The strain this rig endured astounded me. We settled quickly on the opposite tack.

"Fine, sir. Preel patched me up right as rain, she did." He grinned at me.

"How…how is she?"

"Still sleepin'. Needs it, poor thing." He must have seen my expression because his grin faltered and he rushed to assure me. "Don't you worry, sir! She's not all restless like before." He hefted the bowls and made for the door. "I knew we'd be tackin' soon, which is enough to wake the dead aboard this...vessel, so I thought to bring her breakfast. I'm gonna fatten her up if it's the last thing I do."

"Good plan." I took a bowl and a cup of tea, sat down, and ate, hoping that Preel had indeed found a measure of peace.

The fare was bland, but filling. I missed Bert, which elicited thoughts of my ship and crew. Despair clenched my gut and my appetite fled, but I needed food and forced myself to finish, eating mechanically, concentrating on the positive. Preel was stable, we'd eluded *Crimson Hawk*, and we hadn't been eaten by dragons...yet. As I chewed the last bite, Wix ducked hid head into the mess.

"On deck, sir! You need to hear this."

"Trouble?" I was up and headed for the door.

"Oh, aye, sir, all nine shades of the hells trouble." His words sent a ripple of murmurs through the rest of the crew.

I followed Wix up on deck and immediately agreed with his assessment. Though we still couldn't see anything through the mists, the wails were louder now, on our port aft quarter, and much more distinct. Voices. Howls of pain and anguish. And above them, a shrill cry of command, obscenities and epithets, curses and rages. I knew that voice.

"Jhavika!"

"Captain?" Shepherd looked at me sharply. "You're *sure*?"

"I know her. Yes, I'm sure." I would have recognized her fluent profanity anywhere.

"How could they have found us?"

I wracked my brain, asking myself the same question. "I have no idea. I'd say she'd been following us except that we've seen no sign of them, so they can't have seen any sign of us." I would have bet my last gold imperial that we'd lost her yesterday. "Jhavika's smart and experienced. She doesn't have detailed charts of the Eye, but maybe working off a small-scale chart is good enough. And *Crimson Hawk* can sail closer to the wind than we can. Maybe she beat upwind, then tacked and spotted our wake in the dark."

"And now they've changed course." Shepherd's brow wrinkled. "They must have heard us tack. I'm afraid the dragon wings are quite loud when they luff."

"True, but they might not know it's us. They're chasing phantoms. Call all hands, Shepherd, but *quietly*. If we can hear them, they can hear us. No bells, no calls." I looked at Wix pointedly. "If we're *quiet*, maybe we can slip past them."

"Next you'll be insistin' we all wear fookin' slippers and prance around in nightshirts," Wix muttered as he turned away, passing my orders along to the deck crew one by one.

"I'll call up the others." Shepherd went below.

I listened, took a careful bearing on the sound, and wrote it in the log. The rest of the crew came up on deck slowly, bleary-eyed from sleep, some still chewing their hasty breakfasts. Shepherd returned with Miko on his heels.

She gave me a questioning look. "Shepherd said you called everyone up because you heard *voices*?"

"Listen." I hooked a thumb in the direction of the noise. "It's *her*."

"How can you tell?"

"Her voice, the way she gives orders, remember?"

"Like tacking a curse on the end of every sentence?" Miko cocked her ear, listened intently, and finally nodded. "You may be right. What's your plan?"

"Sneak away like a thief in the night."

"It's daytime."

"A thief in the fog then."

"Good save." Miko cocked one dark eyebrow. "You need the whole crew for this sneaking?"

I narrowed my eyes at her. "Perhaps not, but in the unlikely event that I've made an error in my dead reckoning calculations, we may have to react with speed and decisiveness."

She gave me a sour look. "You mean if you fucked something up, you want us ready to bail your bacon out of the fire."

"Well, if you *insist* on putting it *that* way...yes."

Miko snorted a laugh.

Shepherd looked at us as if we were mad. "How can you find this situation humorous?"

"Gallows humor," I said. "It helps break the tension."

"Ah, I see." The dragonlord didn't look convinced.

"Miko, let's bear off a point. I want some distance. We can make it up later."

"Aye." She went to the helmsman and quietly gave the order.

We eased downwind ten degrees. I checked the bearing to the sounds, which remained unchanged, then the log to note our speed on the previous heading. A glance at the chart showed an island entirely too close for my comfort.

"Boxley, run the log. *Quietly*, mind you."

"Aye, sir." She took the log reel and the half-minute glass from the nook in the cuddy, and tapped a crewman to help her.

I turned back to Shepherd. "We're approaching a windward shore in fog. Not my favorite practice. I need to know if you're absolutely sure about the leeway this ship makes close-hauled, and that the data you've compiled on currents here is accurate."

Shepherd looked mildly affronted. "We've compiled, analyzed, and collated more than two *centuries* of data concerning the characteristics of this ship, as well as the currents, isles, and phenomenon of the Serpent's Eye, Captain. *Trust* me when I tell you, it *is* accurate."

"Good. Our lives depend on it."

Boxley returned, looking troubled. "Nine and a half knots, sir, and it seems to me we aren't heeling like we were. I think the wind's slacked some."

I frowned. That was a knot slower than we'd done previously on this heading.

"Log it." I looked up at the rig, then checked the inclinometer. Boxley was right; we weren't heeling quite as much, and the wind seemed to have slackened. "Windward shore, or just the morning calm?" I muttered.

"The seas have come down a bit as well, Captain," Shepherd added. "We should have at least ten miles of open sea to windward."

"*Should*, yes, but do we? If we erred in our calculations..." My teeth chirped as I ground them together. I spat out the wad of chewed leaf. I was awake and my nerves were singing like the strings of a harp. "Ten miles is a lot of distance to feel the effects of an island to windward. We could also be windward of a squall, but the air doesn't feel right for that." I breathed deep, but didn't smell land. "Hold course."

We sailed on. I sent the off watches down to eat. Wix took a sounding, but reported no bottom. Shepherd reminded me that the water shoaled very near shore here; we would likely see the island before the lead line touched bottom. The wind eased a few more knots, and the seas subsided even more. The screams in our wake faded.

Miko came back up on deck looking awake and fed. "Anything?"

"I think we may have shaken them. We'll tack as soon as we spot land. The water's deep near shore, and it'll give us a solid fix."

"Lighter air, though," she said.

"A respite from heeling twenty degrees day and night," I countered.

One of Shepherd's people raced aft from the bow. "Lookout reports surf sounds and other noises."

"Prepare to tack ship." I ordered. "Easy on your helm. Boxley, lend a hand there. Word to Wix, light touch on the main sheets. Keep it as quiet as possible."

We were ready just as the shadow of an island loomed out of the mist ahead of us. I gave the order, and the helmsman brought us around in a smooth arc. Wix cursed low as the starboard mainsail cracked loud before it was sheeted home. For the rest, we came about without a sound, the headsails cross-sheeted to backfill rather than letting them luff and flag. I nodded in satisfaction and looked to windward.

The sea was smooth save for a light wind chop, and the indistinct shadow resolved into a looming shoreline. The magical mists swirled and eddied among the rocks and malformed vegetation, sweeping in glowing streamers down the slope to the sea. Along the shore, kelp grew in thick rafts.

"There, Captain." Shepherd pointed to a distinct promontory, a jagged stone shaped like a great ship's prow. "We have a certain fix of our position." Beckoning me to the cuddy cabin, the dragonlord tapped the chart with a finger. "Here."

The distinctive rock formation was noted. I nodded in satisfaction. "We're about five miles east of our plotted position. Not bad for twenty-four hours of dead reckoning, but it's nice to know exactly where we are." I scratched a note in the log with the time. "Now all we need is a—"

"Captain!"

Miko's tone, cold as ice and hard as fresh-forged steel, brought me out of the cuddy cabin like a bolt of lightning.

"Port bow!" She pointed. "They've found us."

"Damn!" I raised my spyglass. *Crimson Hawk* loomed silently out of the mist, still on a port tack close-hauled. She looked to have been in a fight. "Her forecourse is blown out, and her starboard rail's stove in, but she's holding a tight line to windward."

"She's got better wind aloft," Miko pointed out. "Taller rig. But…something's not right about…" Her voice trailed off and lost its cold objectivity. "Gods and devils! Look at the figurehead! It's come *alive*!"

I refocused my glass and caught my breath. *Crimson Hawk*'s figurehead, a beautiful winged woman with fiery hair, was moving. Its wings had torn free of the hull, and the arms flailed forward as if reaching for something. The hair writhed like a nest of snakes, the mouth gaped in a silent scream. Then my gaze swept the deck, and my gut roiled.

"The crew! They're… The magic's changed them!" My unappetizing breakfast threatened to surge up my throat as I swept my view across the deck.

I'd thought the Serpent's Children in Valaka grotesque, but Jhavika's crew had been exposed to the full force of the magical maelstrom. Twisted flesh, scales, feathers, tentacles, and pincers abounded. Some of the crew struggled to perform their tasks with malformed limbs, while others fought amongst themselves or battled the ship itself as their mutated shapes allowed.

Shifting the spyglass to the quarterdeck, I spotted Jhavika. Sour vomit flooded my mouth, and I choked it back. I'd worked with Jhavika, fought with her, made love with her, cursed her, and even tried to murder her, but nothing prepared me for this horror. Her right arm flexed and writhed bonelessly, tipped with a broad-bladed pike head. She flailed with it at the backs of two crewmen chained to the wheel. Her hair flew about her head in the wind, her mouth stretching unnaturally wide as she shrieked out commands and curses.

I could barely muster a whisper. "She's *changed*."

"As we knew they would be, Captain." Shepherd sounded pragmatic about the revelation. "Likely the entire ship will be altered by the wild magic. Wood and canvas are formerly living tissues, susceptible to mutation. We must concentrate not on *their* fate, but ours."

"Good point." I swallowed hard and analyzed the angle of their approach for a few breaths. "We're beating them, but not by much. Can we beat up at all, Boxley?"

"Pinching it just about as hard as we can, sir. Maybe a half a point without losing headway. It'll take us perilous close to shore."

"Give me every degree to windward that you can." I cupped my hands and bellowed forward. "Wix, sheet to windward for everything we can get! We've got maybe three minutes before they're in ballista range! Sharp lookout forward!" I turned back aft. "Miko, bring up all our boarding axes and distribute them to the rest of the crew. I want you free to deal with anything that hooks us. That blade of yours..."

"Aye!" Miko patted the hilt of her komei katana and grinned. "Almost worth getting shot through the chest!"

Shepherd watched her hurry off, wide-eyed. "She was shot through the *chest*?"

"Well, it was a *glancing* shot, but yes. Long story." I kept my attention on *Crimson Hawk* as the crew made the adjustments.

We were beating *Crimson Hawk*, but only by a slender margin. The closer they got, the more evident it became that both ship and crew had been transformed by the wild magic of the Eye. The bowsprit flexed and twisted with every roll of the ship, and the figurehead's wings flapped as if to drive the hull forward. Several twisted figures were chained to the mainmast, their bodies so melded with the spar that it was hard to distinguish flesh from wood.

"Here, sir." Miko handed me a boarding axe.

"Thank you." I tucked it through my belt, leaned close and lowered my voice. "I don't like this, Miko. *Crimson Hawk* looks...alive, and some of the crew are actually growing *into* the wood."

"Maybe it'll foul their ballistae," she speculated.

"We can hope." I watched them come and shook my head. "We'll be within ballista range as we cross their bow."

"Then this will be interesting." Miko drew her katana and strode to the windward rail of the quarterdeck.

"They're tacking, Captain." Shepherd pointed.

"So they are." Jhavika and I had been trained aboard the same ship, so I realized her tactics as I watched them come about. She'd use *Crimson Hawk*'s better windward sailing to close the gap, pinning us against the shore. I couldn't allow that, but thwarting her would be tricky. "Boxley, I want you on the helm. If they fire ballistae, bear off downwind behind them. Don't wait for my order. By the time they come around, we'll have a quarter mile lead and sea room to run."

"Aye, sir!" My young officer shouldered aside the helmsman, who seemed more than willing to relinquish the responsibility.

"Sir?" I turned to find Miko pointing at *Crimson Hawk*. "What in the nine unholy hells is that?"

"Where?" I joined her at the rail.

"Aft, just below the water line."

I raised my spyglass. Something moved in undulating waves below the waterline from the quarterdeck aft. "Something attached to the hull?"

"Fins," Shepherd said, joining us. "Like a cuttlefish. The ship is indeed coming alive. This is *most* interesting."

Now it was Miko and my turn to look at Shepherd as if the dragonlord was mad.

"Well, from a *scholarly* standpoint, you see? The ship's evolution could provide a unique opportunity to study the effects of wild magic on formerly living, but currently inanimate, tissue."

I cleared my throat. "You're either *serious* or you've picked up a knack for gallows humor."

Shepherd blinked at us both. "Why *ever* would you think I was joking?"

"Well, you may get an opportunity to study it up close," Miko added. "They're closing on us."

She was right. They would be within range in moments. "Ready to veer, Boxley!"

"Aye, sir!"

"Reef!" The lookout called from forward.

"What?" Shepherd sounded indignant now. "There *is* no reef here!"

I didn't remember one from the chart either, but I couldn't doubt the lookout's eyes. "Bear off a point!" Though it would take us closer to *Crimson Hawk*, running up on a reef would be a death sentence. Even if the dragonship survived the impact, Jhavika could then pluck us off at her leisure. I raised my spyglass, frowned as I focused in on the patch of dark water that frothed and foamed like breaking waves. "It's…kelp." I flinched as several thrashing strands shot from the water to grapple a misshapen creature on shore that seemed half tree and half lizard. A battle ensued as the kelp dragged the creature into the water.

"Ah, yes, I was correct!" Shepherd smiled in satisfaction. "It's *not* a reef, but a mutated kelp forest. Quite vicious, but you need not fear it, Captain. It won't attack the dragonship."

A reckless plan clicked into my mind. "How deep's the water there?"

"Oh, ten fathoms or so."

"Bear up, Boxley! Belay the order to veer if they fire on us. Take us right through that patch of kelp!"

"You're *sure*, sir?" Miko pointed to leeward. "If we bore off and set the headsail, we could leave them behind."

"But we'd lose ground, and they'd find us again upwind. Jhavika's not a fool. We need to stop them now, and *that*," I pointed at the writhing mass of kelp, "is our chance without having to fight them!" I whirled to face Shepherd. "You're *certain* that stuff won't drag us down?"

"Well, there is no *certainty*, but we've encountered animated kelp beds before. The tendrils tend to recoil from the ship."

"Good enough for me."

Jhavika's cry of "Fire!" rang out across the misty distance between the ships.

I ducked reflexively and reached for the boarding axe at my belt. What shot out from *Crimson Hawk*'s foredeck, however, wasn't a ballista bolt, at least, not exactly. A long, ropy tentacle sporting a hooked tip lanced forth, but it hadn't the range of a real ballista bolt and fell a few feet short. The aft machine cracked also, but that shot fell even shorter. Jhavika screamed obscenities and ordered her crew to reload and prepare grapples.

"All hands, port rail! Weapons ready! Anything comes aboard, cut it free!"

Crimson Hawk edged closer. We were within bowshot of the rocky shore, just seaward of the kelp strands writhing in the lazy surf. The winds were fluky, but the dragonship was light enough to keep her headway. We were committed. If we veered off the wind now, we'd collide with *Crimson Hawk*.

Another shrill cry of "Fire!" brought me around.

More malformed projectiles shot forth, these writhing and flapping as they flew. The shot from the bow ballista struck amidships, its sucker-like pads sticking to the hull. The shot from aft soared over the our taffrail and struck the curved aft mast, wrapping around it and holding fast.

The dragonship jerked hard as both lines came taut, but Miko was already at the taffrail. One sweep with her katana severed the line, which apparently wasn't rope anymore. It spewed foul blood across the deck, while the dismembered tip fell to squirm and flop on the deck. Amidships, Wix whipped a line around his waist, tying a bowline one-handed as he vaulted over the side of the ship. Four stout crew members held the rope fast. I leaned out over the rail to watch him attack the animated grappling line with a boarding axe, his feet braced against the hull as the sea raced by below. Four solid hacks, and the tentacle fell away.

"Gods of *Light*, he's a badass!" I crowed.

"Glad he's *our* badass." Miko skewered the flopping dismembered grapple and flicked it overboard.

But despite our quick actions, the damage had been done. *Crimson Hawk* was close enough to grapple, at least from their bowsprit. Three malformed figures had made their way out onto the spar, each one holding a coil of line and a grapple. They threw, and the hooks snagged the dragonship. One of the figures fell as the *Crimson Hawk* bowsprit flexed and bent beneath his feet. He hit the water screaming, still clutching his own grappling line so that he trailed through the sea behind us.

"Cut them loose!" I bellowed, though it was hardly necessary.

Miko and several others were already there. The lines were severed, the trailing man lost under *Crimson Hawk*'s bow wave.

Closer, and more of Jhavika's enslaved crew edged out to throw grappling lines. She screamed orders and obscenities, flailing at her helmsmen with her serpentine pike hand, her face a mask of madness. The grapples found purchase, but they were cut the moment they touched the deck.

Still *Crimson Hawk* closed. I glanced forward; a quarter mile until we would reach the kelp. *Too far.* More grappling hooks hit the deck to be cut away, but soon there would be too many. Jhavika laughed and swore a blue streak, spitting oaths, promising torment.

Enough!

"Tack ship!" I ordered, and, gods bless Boxley, she responded without hesitation or question.

We snapped around so fast that half a dozen thrown grappling hooks missed us entirely. Wix sheeted to the port tack, and by the time Jhavika responded, we were well away. Of course, we were now aimed right at the rocky shore instead of parallel to it.

"Captain?" Shepherd sounded concerned.

"Trust me, Shepherd." I glanced over my shoulder. *Crimson Hawk* came around, Jhavika shrieking orders. "Just a little bait for the trap." I gripped the aft stay and stepped up onto the taffrail, then plucked Jhavika's scourge from my belt and held it high, howling at the top of my lungs, "Come and get it, you crazy bitch!"

A ballista cracked, and a ropy tendril shot right at me, the tip of the bolt a gaping serpent's head. I released my grip on the stay and leapt out of the way, hitting the deck hard even as the snake head latched onto the aft stay and clamped down. The ship jerked backward.

"A bit too much incentive, maybe?" Miko stepped past me and slashed the snake head free of the stay. The head released its grip and fell to the deck, snapping and gnashing its fangs. Miko skewered it with her sword and flicked it overboard, then reached down to help me up. "Now, how about we tack again before we run ashore?"

"Not yet." I gauged *Crimson Hawk*'s progress, our approach to the shore, and the seething mass of kelp that lay off the beach. "We've got to lure them in close enough to get entangled."

"If you pitch the scourge overboard in the middle of that kelp patch, maybe Jhavika would go in after it and get herself killed."

"Maybe, but Preel's answer was 'the center of the Serpent's Eye', and we're not there yet. If the scourge isn't destroyed, then something or someone could eventually pick it up again." I clapped a hand to Boxley's shoulder. "Well done, Boxley! Everyone, stay sharp! We tack at the edge of the kelp bed and run the shoreline."

"Your tactics are bold, Captain," Shepherd said, though not in praise. "Please have a care with *our* ship."

"I will, Shepherd. The *last* thing I want is to get stranded on an island in the Serpent's Eye!" I watched the line of kelp nearing, and clapped Boxley on the shoulder. "Now! Tack ship!"

We came about again, not quite as hard as previously, for the wind blew less briskly this close to shore.

Looking back, I saw that our pursuers had tacked already. Jhavika had guessed what I was planning. Hopefully, she hadn't guessed all of it.

Crimson Hawk began to close on us again, faster than I'd estimated. They were getting added thrust from the bizarre fins that had grown out of the hull. Still, I gauged we would make it, if only just.

I pointed to the wide swath of kelp in our path. "Take us right into that big patch, Boxley."

"Aye, sir." She sounded worried, but determined. She'd make a hell of a captain one day.

We were barely a ship-length from the edge of the kelp when Jhavika fired her ballistae once again. One fell short. The other slammed into our transom and stuck.

The jerk nearly took me off my feet, but the dragonship still strained forward, edging into the seething raft of kelp. The animated tendrils hissed and writhed along our hull, questing up, then recoiling. The drag slowed us slightly. I prayed to Odea that the stuff wouldn't foul a keel or rudder.

"Captain!" Miko called from the taffrail, her katana held one-handed as she clung to the aft stay with the other. "I can't reach it!"

"A line!" A quick crewman handed me a heaving line and I whipped a bowline around Miko's chest, just under her arms. "Careful!" I said, as she climbed over the rail.

"Just don't let go!"

We lowered her.

Crimson Hawk's crew hauled on the tether that bound the two ships together, more crewmen edging out onto the bowsprit, grapples in hand. The figurehead flapped its wings and gaped its silent maw, arms reaching out for us.

"Lower!" Miko yelled.

We lowered her, the thin, smooth line slick on my palms.

Crimson Hawk plunged into the mass of kelp, but the questing tendrils didn't recoil as they had from the dragonship. Instead, they crawled up the hull, grasping onto the rail and crawling aboard. *Crimson Hawk* slowed, and the ballista line groaned with the strain

Animated kelp entwined *Crimson Hawk*'s figurehead, which in turn fought the tendrils, but there were too many. Wood splintered, and the winged figurehead was torn away, thrashing for a moment before it was dragged under. The scar in the bow of the ship bled a greenish ichor, the raw wood-flesh pulsing.

"Shit!" Below, Miko kicked away several grasping fronds of kelp. Apparently, the dragonship's immunity didn't extend to those hanging over the side. With a desperate slash of her katana, the line connecting us to the mutated ship parted, snapping back, and we surged away from *Crimson Hawk*.

"Haul away!" We pulled Miko back up on deck, gasping and bleeding from several lacerations, her sword dripping greenish ichor. "Good to have you back aboard!"

"It was a near thing." Miko heaved breath. "Gods, you can *feel* the magic on your skin out there!" She shivered and wiped at the slime coating her blade.

"Well, we shouldn't have to deal with *them* again, anyway." I pointed behind us. Tendrils of kelp snaked up *Crimson Hawk*'s sides, her forward progress all but stopped.

"Thank Odea for that!" Miko said.

"Thank your captain," Shepherd said. "I would never have attempted such a thing."

"Well, we can bear off the wind now." I turned to the helm. "Boxley, get us some—"

A rending groan and an unearthly growl brought me back around.

"Shepherd! Look!" One of the dragonlord's people pointed at *Crimson Hawk*.

"Interesting!" Shepherd raised a spyglass.

I just stared open-mouthed.

The ship's bowsprit split into six writhing tentacles, and the wound where the figurehead had been now gaped in a gnashing beaked maw. The tentacles ripped up vast wads of the kelp and stuffed them into that snapping mouth, tearing open a path for the ship. Barely human shapes struggled on deck, hacking at the questing tendrils.

"Gods and devils, I think they might escape!" Miko said.

"Three points to port, Boxley! I want to get the hell away from that thing before it breaks free!" I cringed at the horrific roar from the maw of the bestial ship.

We bore off and set the massive headsail. It would draw on a beam reach, and nearly doubled our sail area. We shot forward into the mists, leaving the embattled *Crimson Hawk* struggling to escape our trap.

"I would have loved to get a closer look at that ship's transformation, but I daresay it wouldn't have been worth the risk," Shepherd said wistfully.

Miko and I exchanged a look and shook our heads. Without saying a word, I knew that she shared my thoughts; if I ever saw that monstrosity again, it would be too soon.

Chapter Thirty Four
The Eye of the Serpent

Love and loss test the human soul.
The Lessons of Quen Lau Ush

From the journal of Preel Longbright –
Never before have I wished I'd never witnessed a thing of beauty. The center of the Serpent's Eye was truly beautiful, but the pain of that memory is more than I can bear.

Lulled by the ship's motion, I woke gently and stretched, feeling rested and calm. I blinked, and found Hemp staring at me from across the cabin, his homely features fixed in a worried frown.

"What's wrong?"

"Oh, nothing, lady. Just worried for you." He shrugged. "You been sleepin' an awful lot, is all."

"I know." I felt stiff all over from so long in the narrow bunk, but Shepherd's magic had put my mind at ease for the first time in months. "Sorry. I just needed it, I guess." I levered myself up, and Hemp was there to steady my stance when I hit the canted deck. "How is everything? Where are we?"

"No sign of *Crimson Hawk* since that last tussle. Don't rightly know where we are. We tacked about three watches ago."

"Half a day?" I had slept too much. My stomach confirmed this with a growl. "Is there anything to eat?"

"Oh, sure! I'll be back in too shakes!" Given a purpose, Hemp dashed out of the cabin.

I relieved myself in the chamber pot and risked some careful stretches. We were heeled, of course, but not as severely as before. I recalled the past two days clearly, at least the hours I'd been awake, and wondered at my own state of mind once again. *Calm, orderly, sweet solace...*

Hemp had been more afraid than I'd been during the encounter with *Crimson Hawk*. We'd received no details from anyone, only that we'd escaped and Jhavika's ship had been entangled in a bed of kelp. My fear, hate, love, and dread for those I cared for had all been blunted; I could think about what might have happened objectively, without my conflicting emotions driving me mad.

One question rose to the fore: was Jhavika dead?

We'd never employed my talent to learn if the commands of the master of the scourge survived the master's death. Now, perhaps, we could know. Sitting on the edge of the bunk, I closed my eyes and concentrated on the possibility of Jhavika's death. Sorrow, blunted by Shepherd's magic, yes, but real. Deep down, I still loved my poor sister. The enchantment, it seemed, yet held.

Hemp knocked and entered with a bowl of goat stew, cheese, flatbread, and a cup of water. "Here you are, lady."

"Thank you." I ate with a will, my stomach gurgling happily. I thought of our progress and what little I knew about the Serpent's Eye. "Do you know how much longer to the center of the maelstrom?"

"Soon, so the word goes." Hemp shrugged again. "Can't come soon enough for me."

I nodded. Once the scourge was destroyed, we would both be free. The truth shone like a clear horizon beyond a stormy sky. *Soon...soon...*

A knock at the cabin door snapped my attention from my meal. I put the bowl aside and stood on the steeply inclined deck. Footing on this boisterous ship was tricky, but I was getting the hang of it.

"Yes?"

The door opened to reveal Shepherd. "Ah, you're awake. I hoped you would be. We'll be emerging from the mists into the center of the Eye soon. If you're feeling well enough, it's a sight worth seeing."

"I'm fine. I'd like to see it." Truthfully, any excuse to get out of this cabin would have been welcome. Then I hesitated a moment. "Is the captain on deck?" Despite my desire for fresh air, I feared seeing Kevril.

"He is. He agreed not to speak with you, if that's your wish." Shepherd put out a hand. "Don't be afraid, Preel. We've very nearly reached our goal. You'll be free of the enchantment soon."

Soon...the truth... Magic or no, his words soothed my fears.

"Thank you." I clasped the dragonlord's hand and followed.

At the companionway, Hemp draped a weather cloak across my shoulders. I climbed the steep steps, gripped the coaming firmly, and stepped onto the deck. We were beating to windward, spray lashing aft. The entire crew seemed to be on deck, leaning on the rail and gazing about. My bare feet found easy purchase on the dragon bone planks, my muscles, stiff with disuse, loosening and warming with the welcome exercise as I shifted to maintain my balance on the rolling deck. I heaved in a deep breath of the salty, fresh air; it tasted good. We were still sailing through the rainbow-hued mists, but the sky seemed lighter ahead than behind. Shepherd guided me back into the lee of the cuddy cabin, and I gripped a hand rail to keep steady.

A glance confirmed that Kevril stood aft of the helm, one hand on a stay. His gaze strayed toward me for a moment before his eyes fixed forward and his mouth set in a tight line. He was ignoring me...as I wished. I felt neither love nor hate, just a muted sadness. Curiously, I wasn't sure if feeling this dull ache instead of raging emotions was a triumph or a defeat. It made me feel somehow less human.

"There!" Shepherd pointed, and I directed my attention forward.

Streamers of raw magic raced across the wind, glinting and sparkling. The mists thinned ahead. Thinner...thinner...and finally gone.

We sailed into the eye of the maelstrom.

I caught my breath at the spectacle. The eye wall curved away from us to left and right, a rainbow of scintillating colors, multihued lightning crackling along the edge. The air was clear all the way to the opposite side of the eye wall, perhaps ten miles. Overhead blazed the brilliant blue sky of a new day. At the very center of the clearing, a shaft of polychromatic light shot up from a frothing sea. And everywhere, there were dragons.

They flew in the sky, swam in the sea, plunged and frolicked in the waters, and cavorted in the magical spire of light. They breathed in the misty vapors and bathed in the lightning, reveling in the untamed arcane energy. There were dragonkin of every hue and shape, scales of every color, wings and fins of every size and configuration. I'd never realized there were so many types. Thankfully, they ignored us.

Magical beasts, immune to the effects of the wild magic. I wondered what that magic felt like. I wondered if I, a magical creature, might feel the rapture the dragons were obviously experiencing if I touched the raw energy of the Eye"s center.

"Odea preserve us," Kevril muttered, barely loud enough for me to hear. "Helm, pass the center of the Eye just to port. We need to get close enough to throw this damnable thing in."

The scourge will be destroyed here, I realized through my awe. *I'll be free of it.* I clenched the rail hard, praying to any deity that would listen for deliverance. Hemp rested a hand on my shoulder, and I could feel the tension in him. We would both be freed.

Who will I be? I thought. *Who will I love and hate, and who will love and hate me?* I both welcomed and dreaded the opportunity to find out, but whatever this future held, it was beyond my ability to influence now.

"SHIP!" someone cried, and we all tore our eyes away from the spectacle.

"Where away?" Kevril bellowed, but one sweep of the horizon revealed a ship parting the mists to the north less than a mile away.

"Gods! Is that *Crimson Hawk*?" Miko asked.

"I think so," Kevril answered, raising his spyglass. "Or, at least, it used to be."

Used to be? His words didn't register.

"She's survived." My voice broke at the sight, though my tempered emotions prevented me from feeling anything beyond subdued relief. Jhavika had survived the perils of the Serpent's Eye. When Kevril destroyed the scourge, she, too, would be free of its curse. My sister would have to relinquish her power, but she could start life anew. I could help her. "Jhavika..."

"It's even worse than before," Miko said darkly.

Worse? I raised a hand to shade my eyes, squinting at the ship. I didn't understand what she was talking about, until I realized what I was seeing. Then, I stared in abject horror.

Crimson Hawk had been transformed into some kind of gruesome beast. Tentacles as long as yardarms writhed at the prow, encircling a huge, beaked, spiny mouth that gnashed and snapped. Most of the sails were in tatters, but some had been transformed into wings that beat the air, the spars flexing and bending to drive the ship forward. Great undulating fins thrashed the water along the sides of the ship, the bow throwing an impressive wave.

And on deck, monstrous figures moved.

"Shepherd, may I borrow your spyglass, please?" I clutched the dragonlord's arm hard enough to bruise.

"I don't think that's a good idea, Lady Preel." Hemp's hand tightened on my shoulder. "We should go below."

"No!" I felt no love, no hate, no dread, but I had to see. "I need to see her."

Shepherd merely nodded and handed over the instrument.

Hemp steadied me as I focused the glass, and my breath caught in my throat. The crew had been changed into all manner of bizarre creatures, some barely human at all, others grown into the very workings of the ship. They flailed and screamed, howling out their torment, bleeding and slavering. And behind the helm stood Jhavika Keshmir, my beloved sister and hated captor, mistress of the scourge.

Changed...

She stood on chitinous legs that had torn through her breeches at the knee, one hand a mass of long, clawed fingers, the other a wriggling tentacle tipped by the steel head of a boarding pike. The latter she flailed across the backs of two crewmen who had melded into the wheel of the ship, their hands welded to the wood, the tentacular spokes entwining their arms. Jhavika's mouth, a fanged caricature of the one I remembered, screeched curses, driving the ship on. She lashed at the very planks beneath her feet, dark green blood flowing from the wounds, across the deck, and out the scuppers.

Oh, my poor sister...

Despite Shepherd's blunting magic, my heart welled with emotion: pity for her torment, sorrow for her lost life. Though others had hurled the insult, she hadn't been a monster in my eyes, not really. I'd seen her joy when I taught her yamshi, felt honest pleasure in her embrace. The scourge had enslaved her. Her bane had driven her into the Serpent's Eye, to mutilation and madness. Now, Jhavika truly was a monster. I wondered what would become of her once we destroyed the scourge.

"They're closing," Miko said.

"Yes, but we'll beat them to the center." Kevril's voice bristled with determination. "Not by much, but we'll beat them."

"What about *after*?" Miko asked.

Every eye on the quarterdeck turned to the captain.

"After...we run with everything this ship can give us on her best point of sail and every stitch she can fly."

His answer seemed to satisfy everyone aboard but me. I dared not ask, *What of Jhavika?* I might not care for her after the scourge was destroyed. I might hate her. I might curse her name for enslaving me, for lying to me, for making me love her. Then again, I might lament the loss of a loved one. I wouldn't know until it happened.

I handed the spyglass back to Shepherd and girded my fears.

We weren't the only ones watching the ship approach. The dragons took notice of *Crimson Hawk*, too.

Several swooped near the monstrous ship, diving close enough that their wingtips brushed the flapping canvas. An enormous sea drake breached close alongside, its sinuous neck craning out of the water as it eyed the ship. Something lashed out from the foredeck, whip fast, to strike the drake. I didn't see what it was, but the sea drake responded with a snap of its wings and a flip of its twin tails, sounding deeply. Whatever had struck it must have stung, or at least startled it enough to override its curiosity.

The other dragons and drakes gave the mutated ship a wider berth after that, but continued to show cautious interest. Still Jhavika screamed, and the crew howled, and the ship forcibly thrashed its way across the sea. The gap between us closed.

I looked over my shoulder at the core of the Eye, the shaft of magical energy shooting up from the depths, the water bubbling and frothing around it. My curiosity rose up unbidden. I'd studied magic for years, yet had never read anything that described such a phenomenon.

"What's the source?" I asked Shepherd.

The dragonlord shrugged. "The ultimate source is unknown, but the seabed rises below like a volcano. Instead of magma or ash, it spews wild magic, a *font*, if you will. The mists are the result of that magic reacting with the seawater and all the natural tiny organisms in it. They're too small for us to see, but once so energized, they orbit the center of the Serpent's Eye as planets orbit a sun or as the moon orbits our own planet."

"You've seen this font?"

"No, but my predecessors have. One built a capsule to delve the depths. There are renderings in our library of their findings."

"The blood pearl." I nodded back toward the scourge coiled on Kevril's hip. "That's how they got the blood pearl, isn't it?"

"Indeed, it is." Shepherd sighed sadly. "Would that we had known..."

"Too bad you didn't have a truthsayer," Hemp commented.

Shepherd looked at him, then at me. "My thoughts exactly, Master Hemp."

Avarice... I saw it clearly in the dragonlord for the first time. The shepherds may have excised their human desires, needs, and even some emotions, but they still longed for one thing: knowledge. And like the seemingly limitless font of magic beneath us, I was a limitless font of answers to any questions they might pose. I wondered just how free I would be if I chose to stay with them. Then again, I was a truthsayer, a slave by definition. I imagined Shepard would be a more benevolent master than most.

"Lay us right alongside it!" Kevril commanded, snapping my attention back to the world around me.

We were closing on the center of the Eye, the spire of magic now too bright to look upon without squinting. I shaded my eyes and stepped clear of the cuddy cabin's shelter. Something deep within me, something beyond emotion, beyond hate or love, required that I witness this.

Behind us, the horror ship neared, barely a hundred yards away now, the screams of the poor souls aboard clear on the magic-infused air. *Crimson Hawk*'s hull, spars, and sails shimmered in the font's aura, the serpentine appendages glowing as they thrashed. A ropy strand of tissue shot out from the bow of the ship, the tip hooked and lined with suckers, but it fell short behind us.

Kevril had been right; we would reach the eye before *Crimson Hawk* reached us...barely.

"Time to end this nightmare!" The captain plucked the enchanted scourge from his hip and moved to the windward rail. We would pass within ten yards of the bubbling font, a biscuit toss.

"Don't miss!" My voice surprised me, and Kevril as well.

He looked at me for a moment, and a smile tugged at his mouth. "I won't."

He didn't.

The scourge left his hand and flew in a flat arc, the dragon-leather thongs snaking out as the haft tumbled end over end. The instant it left the ship, the enchanted cat-o'-nine-tails shimmered in the unbridled flow of wild magic. A luminous dust trailed in its wake, like smoke from a burning brand. The bane of thousands of lives struck the water only a foot from the font itself, the impact throwing concentric ripples of magical energy into the air and water.

Faster than I could blink, the scourge was gone, sinking into the well of the Eye.

Behind us, a horrific wail rose on the air, a cry of agony and anguish so dire that my blood ran cold. Jhavika—I knew her voice, felt her pain. I clapped my hands to my ears, but it didn't help. She sounded as if she was being torn limb from limb. A nebulous pressure built within me, throbbing in concert with her cries.

My dear sister... The calming cocoon of magic that enveloped me shattered, the dormant shards of my shattered emotions flying free to lacerate my soul. *Jhavika...* I couldn't let it happen.

Chapter Thirty Five
Scourge in Hand

Refusal to surrender is unhealthy.
The Lessons of Quen Lau Ush

From the journal of Jhavika Keshmir –
I am no longer the person I was. I am no longer Jhavika Keshmir. I am not even human. I am the scourge. We are one.

Sanity and reason flew away from me like leaves in a tornado as I watched my scourge arc through the air toward the spire of magical energy. Pain tore through me, a visceral agony, as if my intestines were being ripped out. The enchanted dragonhide struck the sea, tearing an inhuman cry from my inhuman throat.

My scourge...

I tried to move, to go after it, but found my claw-like feet melded with the deck. My pike hand thrashed, carving chitinous flesh. The agony was nothing—the flutter of a butterfly's wings against my skin. I *had* to free myself. I had to reach my scourge.

Bone cracked and blood flowed…my bone, my blood. I tore away and scrabbled to the rail, trailing gore behind me. It didn't matter. My scourge was sinking. I hauled myself up to the rail, gasping to breathe, to scream anew, my eyes fixed on the site where my scourge had hit the water. We would pass close by, close enough. I gripped a shroud and crawled up onto the rail, the bloody stumps of my ankles raking across the rough wood, shards of bone and torn chitin grinding. My throat burned like fire. I tasted blood. Nothing mattered but my scourge.

As we passed the spire of magic at the heart of the Serpent's Eye, I leapt. As I fell, I heard my name, high-pitched, a horrified scream. A voice I knew. *Preel...*

I plunged as if into a pyre of icy flames, the water cooling my skin even as magic burned along my every nerve, surged through every vein, boiling my eyes and searing my flesh. Even beneath the waves, the pillar of wild magic shone like a sun, too bright to look at. Its energy beat against me like a hot wind, tearing at me, changing me. It also tore at my scourge. I had to save it before we both perished.

There! Through the haze, I spotted the sinuous coil of dragon flesh sinking below me. I kicked hard, my severed stumps leaving trails of blood. I thrashed downward, still screaming. Out of air, I drew water into my lungs, water like fire. My chest tore open, and I expelled the useless frothy pink tissue. I drew another breath over my gills and kicked my newly forming flukes, driving myself deeper.

As I neared my scourge, I espied tendrils of fraying tissue streaming away from it. The blood pearl glowed, seeping red ichor into the magically charged sea. It was coming apart, dissolving, its pain, my pain.

I dove hard, reaching out to hook it with my serpentine pike. I pulled it in, and my clawed hand closed on the sweet haft.

Ecstasy, agony, fulfillment, despair, rage... A thousand sensations and emotions inundated me, engulfed me. I stared at the dissolving flesh of the scourge, at my own flesh enfolding it, the two weaving together as one. The pulsing blood pearl burned a new home in my arm, my blood surging through it, then down the braided dragon flesh to the very tips of the nine thongs. Its claws were now my claws; its flesh, my flesh; its magic, my magic.

We became one.

I laughed and drew magic-laden water deep into my chest, over my gills, and out the fluttering slits between my changing ribs. The scourge and I were a single being, and there was only one thing left in the world that I needed.

Kevril Longbright...

My flukes thrashed, propelling me forward. I would rip his heart from his chest and take his dragonship for my own. His crew would be my slaves, his truthsayer my companion, his dragonlord my court wizard. I would take them all, then the Blood Sea, then the world.

Chapter Thirty Six
'Til Death Do Us Part

The price of freedom is paid in blood.
The Lessons of Quen Lau Ush

From the diary of Kevril Longbright –
There was a time in my life when all I desired was freedom. Now, I've learned that there are more precious things. I've shackled myself, but my slavery is a willing one, and I wouldn't trade it for all the gold in the world.

I caught my breath as the misshapen Queen of Haven leapt from *Crimson Hawk* into the center of the maelstrom.

"Jhavika!"

Preel's agonized scream tore at me like claws. I whirled around to see her struggling in the restraining grasps of both Hemp and Shepherd. She thrashed and kicked, clearly panicked, but unable to break free.

"It's over!" I heaved a ragged breath. "Boxley! Bear off!"

"No!" Preel fought to free herself, twisting and clawing. "Go back! Jhavika! She'll *die*!"

"Yes, she will, and good *fucking* riddance!" I gripped a stay as we came around to the southwest. "Wix, rig the headsail! Preel!" I started toward her. Still she howled in rage, struggling to escape. "Preel! It's destroyed! The scourge is *gone*! It's over!"

"Nothing's over, you murdering bastard!" Spittle flew from her lips, and she continued to struggle. "She's still alive! We have to go *back*!"

I stopped cold. *Not over?* I actually checked my hip to make sure the scourge wasn't there. "Shepherd, I thought you *helped* her. The scourge is gone. What the hell's wrong?"

"My spell has failed, Captain. And the scourge, *apparently*, is not yet destroyed. Its enchantment still seems to be very much active." The dragonlord gripped Preel gently, but firmly. "It may take a few minutes for the spells that bind the components of the scourge together to fail completely."

"Hemp, take her below! We've got to get the hell away from *Crimson Hawk* before it decides it's hungry!" I looked back, but the monstrous ship had already veered away from the center of the Eye, not toward us, but to the north. I didn't know or care why, as long as it wasn't coming after us. "Bring her downwind, Boxley, steady on a course of two seven zero, and run the log. I need to—"

"*Captain!*" Miko's terror-stricken cry brought me around, but before I could ask what she wanted, I saw it.

Jhavika Keshmir scrabbled up over the taffrail onto the deck.

Preel screamed in horror, and I very nearly did the same, for the creature that rose before us bore little resemblance to the bright-eyed, beautiful woman I had known. Jhavika wasn't even remotely human anymore.

Only a portion of her face and her serpentine pike hand were the same. Her other arm had melded with the scourge. The ruddy blood pearl pulsed in her forearm. At the end of the limb, like too many grotesque fingers, writhed the nine thongs, alive, each now sporting a tiny dragon head with fanged jaws dripping venom. Jhavika's once beautiful hair crawled across her scalp like the flaccid tentacles of an anemone. Chitinous plates armored her torso, pierced by ribs distended and morphed into articulating legs like a lobster's. Bloody water oozed from gill-like slits in her sides. Her lower body curved backward, multilegged beneath a fluked tail. Worst of all, her lower jaw now split into a pair of horrible mandibles that clacked and gnashed hungrily.

"Captain Longbright!" The voice barely resembled Jhavika's, but there was no mistaking it. "Breathe your last. I have you!"

My hands sought the comforting hilts of cutlass and dagger, and, finally, I found my voice. "All hands! To arms! Shepherd, get Preel to safety! Shipmates! With *me*!"

The Jhavika creature scrabbled forward, and I met her halfway across the quarterdeck, Miko and two more stout crewmen at my side. My cutlass and dagger parried the first sweeping blow of her pike hand, but the force of it knocked me back a step. Gods, she was strong. Though my dagger raked aside the flailing heads of the scourge, the fangs cut burning tracks across my forearm. I flinched as the telltale sting of poison shot up my arm and prayed that my immunity to the scourge's poison held firm.

The pike hand struck at my face, and I missed a parry. The blade cut a furrow in my neck, knocking me back again, but Miko's katana flashed past my ear and sheared through the wrist. The fleshy member fell to the deck, squirming like a decapitated serpent.

Jhavika howled in rage and skittered back. "Preel! Hemp! Kill Kevril Longbright!"

A scream and a scuffle behind me, and I risked a glance. Both Preel and Hemp were struggling now, Preel still in Shepherd's grasp, and Hemp grappling with another crewman, trying to wrest a crossbow from his hands.

"Hold them!" I roared, whirling back to face Jhavika.

I paid for my lapse, the jaws of the scourge latching onto my arm. I slashed and bellowed obscenities, but my cutlass failed to sever the heads. Miko's komei blade might have fared better, but she was busy parrying and hacking at the writhing remnant of Jhavika's severed arm, green-black blood spraying her across the face.

Then Wix arrived.

"Die, you scaly fook!" He waded in, ignoring Jhavika's flailing attacks, daggers flashing. One swept the scourge aside, tearing the fanged heads free of my arm, and the other smashed into Jhavika's face, ripping away one mandible. The fangs of the scourge scraped across his hand, however, and Jhavika howled in triumph.

Spitting blood, she screamed, "Wix! Kill Kevril *now!*"

Wix whirled and charged me, his face contorted in horror.

"Shit!" I backed, parrying madly. I'd never been Wix's match and doubted I would last long, not with the magic of the scourge driving him to kill me. "Wix! Stand down!" Two more parries, the force of his blows numbing my arms.

"Fight me!" He raged. "Kill me! Do it!"

"No!" I ducked a punching strike too slow, and the spiked guard of his dagger caught my temple.

The force spun me around, blood blinding one eye, but I crouched and slashed low. My cutlass laid open both of his thighs just above the knee, not bone deep, but deep enough to stagger him. Wix roared and lunged. One dagger I caught on the guard of my own, but the other hooked my cutlass and tore it out of my grasp. I couldn't backpedal fast enough, and fell. Snatching my spare dagger from my boot as Wix landed on top of me, I crossed blades to keep the spiked guards of his daggers from my eyes.

His weight drove the breath from my lungs and pushed the inch-long bronze spikes downward. I heaved, but he outweighed me by half. "Wix! Stop!"

"Can't!" He gritted his teeth, clearly trying to fight the enchantment of the scourge, but unable to break free. "Kill me, sir! You've *got* me, just *do* it!"

Wix was right. I had him. One of my daggers had both of his pinned. I couldn't hold them at bay without the strength of both arms, but I could pull one dagger free and bury it in his heart before he killed me. The move played through my mind: easy, just twist, pull, strike...and kill one of my closest friends.

"NO!" I thrashed my legs and drove a knee into his groin.

His eyes rolled up for an instant, his strength waning, but he roared again and bore down. If I didn't do something soon, I was a dead man.

Desperately looking past him, I saw Miko fencing with Jhavika, her katana sweeping and darting masterfully. She'd scored several cuts, but couldn't get past the scourge without getting bitten. A crewman lay on the deck beneath Jhavika's pincer legs, fighting to keep them from piercing him.

Then, behind them all, I saw salvation arrive in the guise of a fourteen-year-old girl with a boarding axe.

Boxley swung outboard on a halyard, then back in, determination and terror writ large on her face. She released her grip on the line and lent all of her momentum to the blow. The axe's narrow head split Jhavika's skull like a melon. The monster collapsed to the deck, shuddering and twitching. Miko stepped up and brought her katana down across Jhavika's neck, and the cloven head rolled away.

I felt the fight leave Wix, and he rolled off. I dropped my daggers and eased him down. "You all right?"

"Fook, no!" He grimaced and coughed, curling into a fetal position. "You fight like a fookin' *girl*, sir."

"Well, since a *girl* just saved both of our lives, shut the *fuck* up!" He was bleeding badly, so I split the legs of his trousers and quickly bound the wounds. "Hold fast, we'll patch you up as soon as we can."

"I'm fine, sir." He gasped for breath. "But if you could find my testicles, I'd be obliged."

I coughed a laugh and looked around the deck. Blood and tears flowed with equal plentitude. Hemp knelt only feet away, a loaded crossbow in his hands and one of Shepherd's people lying beside him nursing a bleeding mouth. Boxley clutched Miko in a tearful embrace, both of them mired in Jhavika's vile blood. And Preel...

Preel lay in Shepherd's arms, heaving sobs, trembling, her face in her hands. I couldn't imagine what she was feeling, and didn't try. She would need time to recover, but she was in good hands. I longed to go to her, but it was too soon.

"It's *over*." I wiped the blood from my eye and staggered over to clap a hand on my midshipman's shoulder. "Damn fine timing, Boxley. Now, man the helm and bring us around. One more pass by the center, and we'll dump this fucking thing over the side." I didn't know if I meant the scourge or Jhavika's corpse, then realized they were one and the same. The dragon-head thongs of the scourge still twitched and gnashed their teeth.

"Aye, sir!" Boxley released her grip on Miko and saluted, her eyes streaming tears. She hurried to the wheel and started shouting shrill orders.

I clapped Miko on the shoulder. "*Damn*, she's gonna be one *hell* of an officer someday."

"She already is, sir." Miko sighed and wiped gore from her blade.

"Right you are."

We stared down at the twitching corpse as the dragonship came around with deft precision and settled on a close-hauled course straight at the spire of wild magic. *Crimson Hawk* still sailed north, closing in on the edge of the eye-wall, apparently disinterested in us now that its master was dead and her commands revoked. I glared down at the convulsing scourge and shuddered in revulsion.

"Tell me it's over, Miko."

"It will be soon, sir." She gripped her komei katana in both hands and brought it down hard, severing the scourge from the rest of the vile corpse. "Just one more thing to do."

"Yes, there is."

We sailed within ten feet of the font of wild magic this time. Miko and I heaved the oozing remnants of our nemesis overboard, first the scourge, then the dismembered corpse. The deck was still slick with gore, but I hesitated to dip a bucket into these enchanted waters to wash it away.

Finally, when it was done, I gave the command I'd been longing to give for days. "Take us home, Boxley."

"Aye, sir! Helm's alee! Set the headsail for a port-side broad reach! Mains athwartships! Lively now!"

The dragonship came around sweetly, and the huge headsail rose, booming like thunder as it filled. The two mainsails spread outboard, snapping full like the dragon wings they were. The flat hull surfed upon the swells, running before the wind. We were headed back to Shepherd's keep and a world only mildly immersed in magic. I'd had my fill of mists and dragons and abominations.

I looked to Preel, still sobbing in Shepherd's arms. The dragonlord met my eyes and shrugged noncommittally. Only time would tell if the woman I loved had survived.

Chapter Thirty Seven
The Only Question That Matters

Knowledge is power, but ignorance is bliss.
The Lessons of Quen Lau Ush

From the journal of Preel Longbright –
I should have known. So many memories. Lies and truths, feelings and actions, words that I would never live down. I am not who I was. I will never be. There is now only one question in my mind.

The morning after my sister was killed, Kevril visited me. He asked permission, as I knew he would. He'd always been considerate that way.

All my memories of him were clean and unadulterated now: the tenderness, the moments of bliss, staring into each other's souls, our bodies conjoined, one flesh. I loved him. I knew I did. I always had. I knew the lies for what they were, but still, memories cannot be altered by magic, or by the banishment of an enchantment either. There were still so many questions in my mind, so much I had to tease apart to truly understand myself.

I remembered hating Kevril and loving Jhavika. Even though I knew the scourge had forced me to feel these things, those feelings had been real to me. I no longer hated him. I no longer though of Jhavika as my sister. I knew they'd been lies, but I remembered believing both. I remembered all the vile things I'd said to Kevril, all the vitriol and accusations, spewing at him my pure unadulterated hatred. How could he ever care for me after that? *Had* he cared for me as I cared for him? How could I know?

Nevertheless, I agreed to see him. It was the least I could do.

The knock was tentative. I cleared my throat and said, "Come in."

He did, clean and patched, the gashes on his neck and over his eye stitched. I'd seen him worse. I longed to touch him, to kiss him, to hold him, but I couldn't. I dared not trust my emotions. Not yet.

"Thank you for agreeing to talk to me, Preel. I know you're still...having problems."

I nodded. "It's the least I could do, considering...everything." I sat on the deck with my back braced against the bulkhead. I wanted to ask him to sit next to me, but couldn't bear that yet, so I waved toward the single stool that stood at the tiny desk. "Please, sit down."

He did, his hands clenched in his lap. "How are you?"

What a question. I actually barked a coarse laugh and shook my head. "I don't know yet. I'm still...sorting things out."

"I'm sorry." Kevril shifted, looking to the door. "If you want me to leave..."

"No!" it came out too loud, too vehement, almost hysterical. "No, please. I want to try to explain, so you can understand."

"All right."

There was hope in his eyes. The sight of it made me shudder. So much had happened between us that I dared not hope.

"There are things I remember, things that I now know weren't true. Things that were tricks induced by the enchantment. I remember believing things, *feeling* things, and it's...hard to distinguish between a real feeling and the memory of a false feeling." I cleared my throat. "I'm sorry. I'm not making much sense."

"No, you are. It's all right, Preel. Please, I *want* to understand."

I looked into his eyes and saw confusion. Gods, I knew him so well, could read his emotions as clearly as I could read a book. But what was real and what was not? I couldn't know.

"I hated Jhavika for stealing me away from you." My throat constricted, and I had to clear it before continuing. I couldn't look at him. I looked at the scars on my wrists instead. "I tried... I tried to take my life, but I couldn't. The glass wouldn't break, and the eating utensils wouldn't pierce living flesh. I...tried."

"I'm sorry."

"*Don't!*" Again, hysteria honed the word like a razor. "*I'm* the one who should be sorry. I failed. I didn't think... I couldn't know..."

"Don't be sorry for surviving, love."

Love... I remembered how that word had stabbed me before and choked on my breath. I shook my head and coughed. "Please. Let me finish."

"I'm..." I knew what he was going to say, but he saved it. "I'm listening."

I nodded, reaching back for the facts, the bits I knew to be true. "I didn't think I was enchanted by the scourge. I had no wounds, and there was no reason for her to do it. It's not like my talent's *voluntary*, after all."

Kevril just nodded, attentive, caring. *Love? Maybe...*

"Thinking back, she must have done it when I was unconscious, either when I was drugged the night I was taken or after the first question she asked me. I don't know how, and it doesn't matter." I sniffed and tried to think calmly. "I didn't know for sure until weeks later, after I spoke to you. I still hated her, you see, so when she told me to love her like a sister, and I suddenly did, I knew. But by then it was too late."

"It's *never* too late." The vehemence in his voice startled me.

"Maybe." I shook my head, staring at my hands again. "I tried to provoke her to command me, at first, just to find out if I was enslaved. It didn't work. She was too smart. Later, when I knew, I remembered things she said in passing that were actually subtle commands. Believe me. Trust me. Relax. Enjoy yourself."

"And you did."

"Yes." I met his eyes again and knew that he understood; he had been there himself. But did he understand *everything*? I had to be sure. "What I'm having difficulty with now is teasing apart the things I know are true and the things that *might* be true, or might be subtle lies. Memories can't be altered. Similarly, memories of *feelings*, even though the feelings are induced by magic, can't be altered. Like when you told me about the party with Roque and Temuso, Jhavika commanding you to enjoy it."

"And I did, even though I knew I didn't want to."

"Yes, and you *still* remember enjoying it. Every bit of it. Whether it was induced by the scourge or not, those memories never fade."

"Yes."

"And I remember loving Jhavika like she was my sister. I know it's a lie, but I still remember."

"And you remember hating me for all the things Jhavika told you I'd done to you, like manipulating you, lying to you."

"Yes." I sniffed and stared at my hands. "I know it's not true, but...I still need to figure this out. In time..."

"Take all the time you need, Preel." Kevril stood then, and I was suddenly struck by the fatigue dragging at him. I wondered if he'd slept at all. "We'll go ashore when we reach Shepherd's keep, and you can sort it all out. Shepard told me that you asked him if you could stay on at the keep. I know you haven't made a decision yet, but know this: whatever you decide, I'll honor it. If you decide to stay, you'll be safe with Shepherd, and I know you'd be happy studying magic for the rest of your life."

"What about..." I couldn't finish the question, my throat once again closed. *What about Kivan and Bert, Quiff and Rauley, Tansy and Quibly? What about Scourge? What about us?*

Kevril knew; he didn't need my words. "We won't know about the others until we get back to Haven. I haven't figured out exactly how we're going to *do* that, yet, but we've got time. Shepherd has agreed to put us up in the keep for a while."

"Oh. All right." That, at least, would give me time to think this through. "Thank you, Kevril." I met his gaze once again, but I didn't get up. I didn't dare. Touching him would start something I didn't know if I wanted yet...or ever.

"You're welcome." He stepped to the door, put a hand on the latch, then stopped. He didn't look back at me when he said, "I love you, Preel. If you remember anything, please remember that."

"I'm trying." I could promise nothing more.

"I know." He left, and I could breathe again.

I stared at my hands, at the scars on my wrists, at the light abrasions where the enchanted manacles had rubbed my skin for days, but no more. Kevril had given me the key, trusting me enough not to hurt myself.

Trust...

Hemp returned, carrying food, as always. "Brung you a nibble! Hope yer not tired of goat cheese!"

I wasn't, and his ebullience was hard to fault. Hemp had been insufferably happy since the destruction of the scourge. I wished I was.

"Thank you, Hemp." I patted the deck beside me. "Sit with me?"

"Happy to!" He did, and we nibbled sharp goat cheese and crispy biscuits for a time in amiable silence. Finally, he broke it. "Since I didn't see the captain bleedin' anywhere new, I guess your conversation went okay."

I smiled at his weak attempt at humor. "Better than I expected, but not as good as I'd hoped." I didn't really know what I'd hoped for. There were still too many memories rattling around in my mind: mistrust, betrayal, manipulation. Lies, yes, but I'd believed them. What if they weren't lies? What if Jhavika had told me the truth about that one thing. She had known Kevril much longer than I, had known him intimately. *What if... What if...*

"You make a decision yet?" he asked.

My decision: stay or go, security or love, a life of quiet contemplation or danger?

"No, not yet." I rubbed the old scars on my wrists.

Hemp eyed me sidelong. "Mind if I tell you a story, Lady Preel?"

I returned his look. "A *true* story?"

"Oh, aye, true as the sun in the sky, I swear!" He made a sign with one hand that would invoke Odea's wrath if he lied.

"Well, as long as it doesn't involve your exploits with the working ladies of Haven, I'll listen."

"As a matter of fact, that *is* a part of it, but I'll skip over the juicy bits for you." He sighed and nibbled a slice of cheese. "It's about the night that Jhavika lashed me with the scourge. I can talk about it now, you see, and I thought if anybody needed to know exactly what a cruel and heartless soul that woman truly had, it would be you."

I didn't know if I wanted to hear it, but maybe he was right. Maybe I *needed* to. Maybe I still couldn't see the truth for myself.

"Perspective," I said quietly.

"Aye, that. My old pap only said one thing worth a damn his whole life, and that was you could judge a person by their *actions* only. Not by their promises or their words, but by what they *done*. You need to know what Jhavika done to me and the poor lass I was with that night."

I cleared my throat and nodded. "All right."

Hemp told his tale without faltering, though his voice sounded strained in places. Tears trickled down my cheeks by the end. Cold rage and deep shame for ever loving someone who could do that to another human being—not out of need, but on a whim—made me sick.

"So, you see, you got your own memories, my word, the captain's word, and the word of every member of his crew what she was, and what *he* is."

"The crew hates me, Hemp. Everyone but you, anyway."

He snorted in indignation. "Oh, horseshit! What makes you think that?"

"After all the things I said? They *should* hate me."

"Your pardon, Lady Preel, but you're *wrong*!" Hemp sat up and glared at me. "Every jack and jane aboard *Scourge* loved you like you was family. We *knew* it was the scourge talkin'. Hells and demons, you don't hate *me* for what *I* done, do you?"

"No, but—"

"No buts!" He poked me hard in the shoulder with a stiff finger. "They *love* you, Lady Preel. We *all* do! That alone ought to help you make your decision."

I nodded and wiped my eyes. "It ought to, but it can't tell me the truth."

Hemp looked at me with a furrowed brow. "What truth is that?"

"There's no way I can know if..." My words trailed off as a slow chill of realization settled upon me. *Truth...* I sat up as if struck by a bolt of lightning. "Odea's sweet tits, I *can!*"

Hemp looked shocked at my oath. "Pardon?"

"I *can* know the truth!" I gripped Hemp by his shirt and shook him. "I'm a gods-damned truthsayer!"

"I know that, Lady Preel, but... What are you tryin' to tell me?"

"I need you to ask me a question, Hemp. One that will invoke my talent. It's been plenty of time since the last one, and there's a question I need to know the answer to. It'll help me make my decision. Will you ask me?"

"Um...sure. I'm not sure if the captain would—"

"Oh, *stop* it!" If Hemp had one fault, it was his unwavering devotion to Kevril Longbright. "It's not *his* decision, it's *mine*! Will you ask me or not?"

"Yes. Just tell me what to ask."

"I have to use the chamber pot and climb into my bunk first." I stood, pulled the pot from its nook, and started working at the knot of my pantaloons. "Turn your back."

Hemp lurched up and whirled around so quick that he staggered. I peed, pulled up my pantaloons, replaced the pot, clambered into my gimbaled bunk—I'd gotten better at it—and assumed a comfortable posture.

"Ready!"

"All right." Hemp turned back around and stepped to the side of my swaying bunk. "What do you want me to ask?"

"I need you to ask me if Kevril Longbright loves me like I thought he did, or not."

"Lady Preel, you don't need your talent for that! I can tell you right now that he—"

"Hemp! No, you *can't!*" I glared at him. "You're so utterly devoted to Kevril you'd believe anything he said! I need to know the absolute truth!"

He reddened, but nodded. "Fine. I'll ask."

"*Thank* you." I settled back and nodded.

"Ready?"

"Yes."

Hemp asked, "Does Kevril Longbright love you the way you thought he did, or different?"

My talent seized me, arching my back and stiffening my joints, tearing the answer from my throat. It taxed me, a torrent, a wrenching gush like I'd never felt before.

The answer stabbed me to my very soul.

"No..."

Chapter Thirty Eight
Reunions and Farewells

Goodbye is the most painful word in any language.
The Lessons of Quen Lau Ush

From the diary of Kevril Longbright –
So strange that the day that brought me my greatest joy also
brought me my worst torment. My ship, my crew, and the
woman I love. I should have known better than to hope for
all three.

Emerging from the mists of the Serpent's Eye felt like being
reborn. Stars. Gods, how I'd missed them.

The dragonship sailed downwind like a runaway coach; we would
cover the distance back to Shepherd's keep in two days instead of
three. Never in my life did I think I'd welcome the sight of Valaka Isle,
but I couldn't wait. I watched the sky lighten, the stars vanishing one
by one, the sunrise obscured by the looming wall of mists behind us.
When eight bells came, I could just make out the highest peaks of
Valaka. Three or four hours, at most.

Time... We have time.

"My watch, Captain," Shepherd said, a warm hand on my shoulder.

"Thank you. Our dead reckoning was spot on this time. I'm happy to be free of the mists." I stretched and yawned. Sleep had been hard to come by, bunking with Wix, irritable as his legs slowly healed. If he apologized one more time for trying to kill me, I feared I would throttle him in his sleep. "Please send someone to wake me when we're close."

"I will." The dragonlord gave me one of those enigmatic smiles and nodded. "I thank you for your skilled command of our ship, Captain Longbright. It's been an...enlightening trip."

"I'll never be able to thank you enough, Shepherd. If you hadn't offered to help us..." I shuddered to think what would have happened.

"Well, the past is the past, and immutable. Only the future is still uncertain. We must look forward."

"Yes, we must." I nodded and went below.

After a thoroughly unappetizing breakfast—gods, I missed Bert—I stole into my cabin. Wix was snoring, and I managed to slip out of my boots and salty clothes without waking him. I boarded my bunk and stared at the overhead, the dark dragon bone planks fitted together so cunningly I couldn't even feel a seam with my fingertips. An amazing ship, and she had served us well, but I wouldn't miss her.

I missed *Scourge*.

Sleep came hard, but I managed to drift off. *Time. We have time...*

"Sir!" Boxley burst into the cabin without knocking, earning curses from both Wix and myself. "Sir! Sails sighted windward of Shepherd's Keep! Ship hove to! We think..." She choked on the words. "We think she might be *Scourge*!"

"*Scourge*?" My feet hit the deck and I was into my pants, boots, and jacket in record time. The entire crew was on deck, and Miko met me with a grin so broad I didn't even need the spyglass she offered me. "Is she?"

"Aye, sir. Gods know how, but she's *Scourge*."

"Well, bugger me sideways!" I took the glass and beheld my ship, my heart soaring in my chest.

We were still miles off, but she was hull up, smartly hove to, sails trimmed perfectly, pitching lightly in the seas about a mile from the leeward shore. As we neared, I could make out figures on her deck, but couldn't recognize anyone yet. A white flag broke out from the mizzen.

"Shepherd, can we heave to within hail?"

"Of course."

"Thank you!"

I watched *Scourge* as we approached, my spyglass riveted on her quarterdeck. Most of the ship's complement had turned out. I spotted Kivan and Rauley straight away, but not Quiff. Tansy had one arm in a sling. I didn't see Bert and many others. My heart ached. When we rounded their stern, Kivan raised a bandaged hand and waved. She looked a little stunned. The ship she'd sketched had come to life.

We came upwind and trimmed sails to keep the dragonship stationary. When we settled some forty yards abeam of *Scourge*, I cupped my hands and bellowed. "Ahoy, *Scourge*! Good to see you!"

Kivan raised a speaking trumpet. "Damned good to see *you*, sir! You destroyed the scourge?"

"Yes!" I wondered how she couldn't know, assuming that Jhavika's prize crew undoubtedly included her slaves. No matter; I asked the question I needed to know most. "How did you fare with *Crimson Hawk*?"

Kivan's face reddened. "Fifteen dead, twenty-five sorely wounded. Quiff died, sir. Quibly, Foist, Getry..." She named the others, each one a dagger in my heart. But she didn't say Bert's name.

"Bert?" I asked when she'd finished.

"She's fine, sir! We owe her our lives, along with this one!" Kivan smiled and clapped Spike on his skinny shoulder. "Spike convinced the prize crew that he and his mates had been pressed and wanted nothing to do with Captain Longbright. They offered to help manage the ship, and gods know they needed the help, shorthanded as they were. Bert poisoned their food, and Spike and his cutthroats managed the rest!"

"Bloody fine!" I exchanged a grin with Miko. "Good investment, those ragamuffins."

"Aye, sir."

"Will you be coming over, sir?" Kivan shouted. "We can ferry you over in a launch. The beach is too rough to land!"

Realization punched me in the gut. *Time. We have no time.*

"Stand by!" I turned to Shepherd. "Is there any way to ferry people from shore to the ship?"

The dragonlord frowned. "Not easily or safely, Captain. You could tell your crew to anchor on the leeward shore where they were before. You and the others could trek overland once Preel's made her decision. Your bosun, however, may have difficulty walking that distance."

Wix muttered an obscenity just loud enough for Shepherd to hear.

"We'll do that." I cupped my hands again. "Launch a longboat, Kivan! Wix and Miko will repair aboard. The rest of us will stay at the keep for a time, then join you overland. Anchor in the same spot on the leeward shore!"

"Aye, sir!" She waved and barked orders, then raised her trumpet again. "How long, sir?"

"I don't know." I thought about it and guessed. "A few days, at least. It all depends on—"

"I've made my decision, Kevril."

Preel's voice brought me around. She stood with Hemp in the lee of the portside cuddy cabin, sheltered from the spray. I hadn't seen her come on deck. Her eyes met mine for a moment, then she looked away, up at Shepherd's keep.

"And...?" I dared ask.

"I'm staying here."

Her voice trembled. I knew the decision hadn't come easily, but that didn't lessen the blow. I felt for a moment like my knees would fold. *Gone... She's lost to me.*

Miko gasped, Wix muttered a curse, and Boxley whirled to face Preel.

"Lady Preel! You—"

"Belay that!" I snapped, cutting Boxley off. My knees steadied. I'd promised to honor her decision. "Very well, Preel. Shepherd, we'll ferry over to *Scourge* and leave you in peace." I held out a hand to the dragonlord. "Take care of her."

"I'm honored that you trust me to do so, Captain Longbright." Shepherd gripped my hand warmly.

"I'm sorry, Kevril," Preel said then. "I think it's for the best."

"I'm sure that you do. Be well." I started to turn away, but Hemp stepped forward.

"Sir! I'd like to ask if I might accompany the lady. She needs a familiar face."

I stared at him, feeling doubly betrayed for a moment, then realized he was right. Hemp would take care of Preel. "Of course, Hemp. And thank you." I held out my hand to him. "You're dismissed."

"Thank you, sir." He shook my hand hard, his grip painfully tight. "I promise..."

"Carry on, Hemp." I released his hand and turned back to *Scourge*. "Change of plans! We're coming aboard, Kivan! Prepare to set sail!"

"Aye, sir!" She waved and grinned.

The launch splashed, and a crew of six rowers brought her over with Spike at the tiller. I saw my people aboard, then turned once more to look back, but Preel was gone.

Lost to me...

A dagger slipped between my ribs into my heart.

Enough! I'd had enough pain. I had my ship and crew to think of. There was something to be salvaged from this situation, I was sure. As Captain Tan had noted, Haven was going to be in utter turmoil for some time. If nothing else, Jhavika's former slaves on the Council might well shake my hand and entrust me with assembling a Haven navy. If that didn't pan out, we could always just go back to pirating; it was what I did best, after all.

I boarded the launch and took the tiller myself.

"Good to see you kickin', Captain," Spike said with a grin.

"Good to *be* kickin'." I shook his hand and ordered my rowers to bend their oars.

Back aboard *Scourge*, there were grim and tearful reunions. Kivan saluted smartly, standing stiffly, obviously still in pain from her injuries.

"I'm sorry we sent Jhavika after you, sir," she said, glancing past me. "I had to reprimand seaman Spike for breaking your trust and disobeying a direct order, but since he saved our lives *and* the ship in the end, I figured I'd leave punishment to you."

I cocked an eyebrow at Spike. "Disobeyed a direct order?"

"Aye, sir, I did. It was either that or stand and watch that maniacal bitch skin the lieutenant. I'll take my stripes and wear 'em proud, sir!"

"*Skin* her?" I turned back to Kivan. "Are you all right?"

"I will be, sir. Bert patched me up."

"Good." I looked back at Spike. "You're confined to quarters for the day, Spike. Thank you for saving my stubborn lieutenant's life." Since his quarters were forward with the rest of the off-watch, I'd just given him a day off work.

"My pleasure, sir!" He snapped a salute and hurried off.

"Sir?" Kivan touched my arm, her eyes searching the deck. "Lady Preel?"

The knife twisted. "She chose to stay with the dragonlord, and I promised to honor her decision. She'll be safe here, at least, and comfortable. Hemp's staying with her as well."

"I see." She cleared her throat. "Orders, sir?"

"Give us a little sea room, then hold our position. I want to watch them bring the dragonship ashore. The deck is yours." I climbed the steps to the quarterdeck and strode to the taffrail, running my hands over the familiar wood. It felt warm and alive, my ship, my home. *Two out of three, Kevril*, I told myself.

"Can't say I'm going to miss that dragonship," Miko said beside me. "Rough-riding bitch, and that heel! I feel like I'm standing on solid rock right now."

"True enough." I didn't feel much like talking, and Miko took the hint.

We stood in silence as Kivan maneuvered *Scourge* farther from shore and hove to again. A small crowd had descended the steps from the keep to the beach. Four of them pulled a stout line, and a buoy popped to the surface just beyond the surf line. I watched Shepherd con the dragonship in a tight arc until her bow came upwind, and a crewman forward snagged the buoy with a boathook. They tied the line off at the bow and slacked sheets.

Ashore, the dragonlord's crew cranked the windlass that pulled the dragonship's cradle ashore. The ship backed toward the rocky shore, the buoy obviously tied to the cradle's framework. The surf tossed waves over the dragonship's bow and pitched her violently a few times as the thick black chain clattered along the rock beach.

Slowly, the cradle rose underneath the ship. A few bumps, and the dragonship settled firmly in place to be hauled up high and dry.

"Nice move," Miko ventured.

"Yes, it was." I raised my spyglass and watched as the shore crew secured the ship to the cradle and raised a boarding ladder.

People descended the ladder one by one. I spotted Hemp, then Preel. She worked her way down easily, light footed and graceful. She had always been graceful, even in chains. On the beach, she looked to sea, and her eyes fixed upon us. The wind ruffled her short hair, her dark eyes unreadable, blank. Hemp stood at her side, speaking to her. She shook her head, her lips moving. I wondered briefly what she was saying, but it didn't matter. Preel had made her decision; it was probably for the best.

"Be safe, love." I lowered my spyglass and turned my back on the woman I loved. "Make sail! Bear off due south, Mister Kivan. Set a course for Haven. We've got work to do."

"Aye, sir!" She saluted smartly.

I went below, paused long enough in the galley to give my rotund cook a warm embrace that left her for once speechless, then went to my cabin.

My cabin...

Our cabin, once. Not any longer. I stared around as if lost, wondering what, if anything, I could do to forget Preel. Of course, there was nothing. Her soul was etched into my heart forever.

"At least you're safe, love." I went to my liquor cabinet and pulled down a bottle, not bothering to look at the label.

Chapter Thirty Nine
The Pirate's Heart

Some questions are best left unanswered.
The Lessons of Quen Lau Ush

From the journal of Preel Longbright –
I'm an idiot sometimes. I have it on good authority. The truth
isn't always the right answer.

After five days at sea aboard the dragonship, the stillness as the
vessel settled into its cradle felt strange to me. I felt clumsy, awkward,
constantly expecting the deck to pitch and heel. On deck, Hemp
steadied my arm as I crossed unsteadily to the ladder.

"Careful, now, Lady Preel," Hemp warned as I started to descend.
"You ain't got your land legs yet."

"I'm fine," I lied. I wasn't fine, and he knew it. My decision had
left me feeling dead inside. I'd abandoned the only man I'd ever loved.
Nothing could fix that.

Shepherd can fix it, I thought, working my way down rung by rung.
The dragonlord could transform me to stone, take away my anguish,
my wants, my sorrow. I could be at peace.

Hemp steadied me on the uneven footing of the beach, and I paused to get my balance. The air was heavy with sea mist, thick and salty. I drew a deep breath and savored it. Some distance to the east, a pillar of white sails marked *Scourge* where she lay hove to, all but stationary. They had stayed long enough to see us safely ashore.

Of course, they did. That was the kind of man their captain was: kind, caring, loving, considerate. And I had broken his heart. *But at least it'll go on beating.*

I watched the ship for a time, my beloved home for all of six months, the most joyous time of my life. Light glinted off of something on the deck, a flash of brilliance, a spyglass, perhaps. Was he watching me? Was he saying goodbye? I raggedly breathed in the sea air, then let it go.

The truth... How ironic that I am tormented by my own gift... The answer to the question I'd had Hemp ask still plagued me, but I had made my decision. *For the best...*

"You okay, lady?" Hemp asked.

I shook my head. "No." I would never be okay again, but it was for the best. It was my only chance to save him.

"I can't believe you're throwin' it all away," Hemp said.

"I didn't."

"You *did!*" he insisted.

"No, Hemp. I saved him. I saved him from *me!*"

The answer...so much more than I bargained for. I'd been expecting a simple yes or no; that was how I had worded my question. But Hemp had changed a single word and invoked my talent to a degree I'd never felt before. *Can one word make so much difference?* Of course, it could; who knew that better than me? Though Hemp had asked me a simple question, the answer had been anything but simple.

No...Kevril Longbright didn't love me as I thought he did. He loved me far more than that. He loved me more than his own life, more than his ship, his crew, the sea, and his very freedom.

Kevril was hopelessly, infinitely in love with me. And because I am a truthsayer, I would be his bane unto death. My god-cursed talent would attract every avaricious, greedy, maniacal lord, king, emperor, and cutthroat in Haven and beyond, until one of them finally murdered him to take me away, just like Jhavika had nearly done. He would love me at his own peril, stand between me and every danger, and rescue me when I fell prey to someone else's greed. And I knew that the right word was 'when', not 'if.' The word was out now. Jhavika's people knew what I was, and they were now free of her control, free to tell the world that Kevril had stolen away Jhavika's truthsayer. All of Haven would know, all the world.

"The only way I could save him was to break his heart."

"Horseshit!"

I looked at Hemp like he'd slapped me. From the look on his face, I thought he just might. "*What?*"

"I said that's a load of horseshit, Lady Preel." The muscles at his thin jaw bunched like knotted wood.

"It *isn't!* I'm a gods-damned *truthsayer*, Hemp. Here, I won't draw anyone's attention. I can live out my life without bringing all Nine Hells down on anyone." I pointed to *Scourge*, my voice rising in pitch and volume. "There, I'll only bring pain and blood and death. You *know* it's true! The only way I could save Kevril from me was to leave him!"

His face flushed. "We're fookin' *pirates*, Preel!" He took a step on the uneven rocks, looking like he might actually strike me in anger. Shepherd's people stared at us, obviously worried. "You think that's a *safe* profession? Do you not know the captain at *all?*"

I stood my ground. "I know him *perfectly!* I know he'll try to protect me from every threat until someone kills him trying to take me!"

"Yes, he will, but you didn't stop to think what he'll do *without* you!"

"Without me?" I barked a scornful laugh. "He'll *live!*"

"No, he *won't*, Lady Preel. He'll *die!*"

I rocked back on my heels, turning an ankle on a stone. "What?"

"I said, he'll die!" Hemp took a breath, obviously struggling for calm. "You think you know him, but you don't know him like I do. Without you, he's got no reason to live. He'll go back to piratin', start takin' chances, maybe even try to take over Haven. Or worse, just drink himself to death! Hells, after gettin' rid of Jhavika, he'll have his own fookin' *navy* if he wants it. He won't stop until someone stops him, and he'll take every soul aboard *Scourge* down with him!"

"He won't," I argued. "He wouldn't do that to them."

"Not intentionally, no, but he'll die inside and stop lovin' them. I've seen him push people away before. He thinks you don't love him, and it'll kill him."

"Kill him?" Doubt speared me like an icy lance. I looked to *Scourge*, wondering if Hemp was right. Canvas fell from the yards, blossoming like a great white flower. The ship turned off the wind, making way, and my heart sank. "It's too late."

"Too late?" Shepherd stepped into my view, that plain face set in a quizzical frown. "What do you imagine it's too late for?"

"To change my mind. He's gone." I waved a hand toward the ship now charging off toward the southwest cape.

"It's *never* too late to change, Preel." The vehemence in dragonlord's voice caught me off guard. "You are a truthsayer. Say what you *know* to be true."

"I *love* him!" The words tore from me as if my talent had been invoked, but the voice was my own. The icy spear of doubt melted.

Shepherd chuckled and nodded. "I thought so." Pulling the slim silver rod from a sleeve, the dragonlord raised it high and spoke one unintelligible word.

Light and sound erupted from the rod, soaring aloft to boom like thunder and flash like lightning, a deafening report. Sparks showered down from the explosion brighter than day.

"That'll get their attention, all right!" Hemp laughed and wiggled a finger in one ear.

"Here." Shepherd handed me a fine spyglass. "Look for yourself."

I did, focusing the instrument on *Scourge*'s quarterdeck. I saw Miko and Kivan pointing and gesticulating, then Boxley scrambling up the mizzen shrouds with a spyglass. She turned it to me, perched precariously with her legs wrapped in the ratlines, and waved.

I raised a hand and waved wildly back.

Boxley shouted down to the deck, and the ship veered upwind, coming around in a slow, careless tack. They were coming back.

I turned to Shepherd. "But I said... I said I'd stay."

"Oh, you'd be *miserable* company, Preel!" Shepherd laughed and raised the silver wand. Gently, the wand touched the tattoo inscribed upon my forehead. A bright light blinded me for a moment, then Shepard's inscrutable smile resolved before my eyes. "Go to him, truthsayer. The waves will buoy you up. You don't belong here. Go to the man you love and save him."

Save him...

I looked helplessly to Hemp.

"Go, damn it, or I'll throw you in the fookin' sea myself!"

I ran down the stony beach, heedless of turning an ankle. My feet touched the sea...and shimmered. The waves splashed up to wet me, but I didn't sink.

Magic... Thank Odea!

I dashed into the pounding surf, stumbling on the uneven footing, falling, splashing, doused by wave after wave, but never sinking below the surface. I spat and coughed seawater, scrambled on hands and knees through the breakers, wet to the skin, but determined. A curling breaker caught me full on, filling my weather cloak and knocking me flat. I scrambled up, shucked out of the heavy canvas, and struggled onward.

Beyond the curling waves, I found my feet and ran, stumbling, staggering, unsteady, but running full out. *Scourge* veered closer, sails drawing, dangerously close to the rocky shore. I heard their voices, calls, my name, cries to call up the captain.

I concentrated on keeping my balance and running on. Gasping for breath between breaking waves, coughing and spitting, I prayed that Shepherd's spell would last long enough to keep me from drowning. Realization that I didn't swim a stroke urged me to a greater pace, as did the thought of what might lie beneath the waves. How ironic if I was torn limb from limb by a hungry shark only yards from my goal.

By luck or providence, I wasn't.

Scourge rounded up into the wind only scant strides away, a cargo net hastily draped over the leeward side. Cheers and cries of encouragement rang out, bellows and epithets, laughter. Gods, what sweet music to hear the love in their voices.

I gripped the rough hemp of the cargo net and scrambled up. Eager hands helped me over the rail, steadying me on my feet as I coughed and heaved breath. Everyone spoke at once, pounding my back, offering help, a cloak, a cup of something that scalded my throat and lit a fire in my belly.

Chris A Jackson

"Quiet, you scallywags! Let her breathe!" Wix's bellow silenced the crew.

"Thank you all," I sputtered as they backed away. Past the grinning faces, the sterncastle door opened.

"Captain on deck!" Miko shouted from the quarterdeck.

The crew parted, an aisle opening before me. Kevril stood there in shirtsleeves and trousers, stocking footed, staring at me in shock.

"You..." His voice faltered, his face flushed scarlet.

"I'm sorry I ever doubted you."

"Doubted *me?*" He looked confused, his pulse pounding hard at his throat.

"I *love* you, Kevril Longbright!"

His face went pale, eyes wide with shock, and his knees folded.

I dashed forth and slammed into him before he hit the deck, bowling him over, clutching him to me, crushing the breath out of him. His arms encircled me, weakly, then stronger, then desperate. My mouth found his, lips, tongue, frantic to taste him. He tasted like salty whisky.

The cheers of the crew finally penetrated the pounding in my ears. Our lips parted, and I gasped breath. Our eyes locked, mine reflected in his, one soul to another.

"I'm so sorry," I managed between choking gasps, my vision blurred by tears. "I doubted you. I was wrong. I know that you love me. I just... I didn't... I was worried that..."

"Shhhh, love." Kevril released me and rose, then pulled me up, a feather in his arms. "It's all right."

"I *never* should have doubted you!" I grabbed his hair and pulled his face down for another lingering kiss, devouring his mouth, much to the amusement of the crew. "I'm sorry I broke your heart."

"It's all right, love. It's healed already." He smiled, and my own heart filled. "But if you doubted that I really loved you, how did you learn the truth?"

"Easy." I kissed him again, hard, demanding, then pushed back to gaze up at the man I loved. "I asked a truthsayer."

About the Author

Born and raised in Oregon, Chris meet his wife and soulmate, Anne, while attending graduate school in Texas. Since then they have been nigh inseparable: gaming together since 1985, sailing together since 1988, married since 1989, and writing together off and on throughout their relationship. Most astonishingly, they have not killed each other during the creation or editing of any of their stories…although it was close a few times. Since 2009, the couple has been sailing and writing full-time aboard their beloved sailboat, *Mr Mac*. They return to the US every summer for conventions, always happy to sign copies of their books and talk with fans.

Preview Chris' books and get updates on upcoming events at jaxbooks.com. Follow Chris and Anne's cruising adventures at www.sailmrmac.blogspot.com.

Novels by Chris A. Jackson

From Jaxbooks
A Soul for Tsing
Deathmask

Blood Sea Tales
The Pirate's Scourge
The Pirate's Truth
The Pirate's Bane

Weapon of Flesh Series
Weapon of Flesh
Weapon of Blood
Weapon of Vengeance
Weapon of Fear *
Weapon of Pain *
Weapon of Mercy *
(* with Anne L. McMillen-Jackson)

The Cornerstones Trilogy
(with Anne L. McMillen-Jackson)
Zellohar
Nekdukarr
Jundag

The Cheese Runners Trilogy
(novellas – also on Audible)
Cheese Runners
Cheese Rustlers
Cheese Lords

From Dragon Moon Press
The Scimitar Seas Novels
Scimitar Moon
Scimitar Sun
Scimitar's Heir
Scimitar War

From Paizo Publishing
Pirate's Honor
Pirate's Promise
Pirate's Prophecy

From Privateer Press
Blood & Iron (ebook novella)
Watery Graves

From Fantasy Flight Games
The Deep Gate (hardcover novella)

From Falstaff Books
The Dragons of Boston Trilogy
Dragon Dreams
Dragon's Nemesis (Spring 2020)
Dragon's Legacy (Spring 2021)

Check out these and more at
JAXBOOKS.COM
Want to get an email about my next book release?
Sign up at http://eepurl.com/xnrUL